WELCOME
TO
LEO'S

WELCOME TO LEO'S

with stories by
Rochelle Alers
Donna Hill
Brenda Jackson
Francis Ray

St. Martin's Paperbacks

WELCOME TO LEO'S

"Second Chance" copyright © 2000 by Rochelle Alers.
"Eye of the Beholder" copyright © 2000 by Donna Hill.
"Main Agenda" copyright © 2000 by Brenda Streater Jackson.
"Sweet Temptation" copyright © 2000 by Francis Ray.

Excerpt from *The Turning Point* copyright © 2000 by Francis Ray.

ISBN: 0-312-97588-0

Printed in the United States of America

St. Martin's Paperbacks edition/December 2000

St. Martin's Paperbacks are published by St. Martin's Press, 175 Fifth Avenue, New York, N.Y. 10010.

10 9 8 7 6 5 4 3 2 1

CONTENTS

WELCOME
TO
LEO'S

Second Chance

Rochelle Alers

This novella celebrates:

the three divas—
Brenda Jackson, Francis Ray, and Donna Hill, and
my editor, Glenda Howard—
thank you for believing in Leo's.

*The Lord has determined our path; how then can anyone
understand the direction his own life is taking?*
—PROVERBS 20:24

1

Leigh Walcott stood in the doorway to Lawson's Gourmet on Washington, D.C.'s Connecticut Avenue, waiting for the downpour of rain to subside long enough for her to make it to her car without getting soaked through to the skin. The early spring humidity was so oppressive that she had left her raincoat in the car.

As usual, she had purchased more than she could carry, but it had been a while since she had shopped exclusively for herself. Adjusting her oversize leather tote, she reached into its cavernous depths. It bulged with containers filled with pâté de foie gras, delicate crackers, petit fours, several bottles of her favorite wine, and a bouquet of cellophane-wrapped pale pink tulips. She withdrew a small, compact umbrella and pressed a button, and it opened smoothly with a soft, swooshing sound.

She had gotten up earlier that morning, berating herself for neglecting the most important person in her life—herself. It was the first time in months that the whirlwind activity of her business had slowed enough for her to claim a week to devote to her personal entertainment. As she was a professional event planner, her days, weeks, and months were filled with an ongoing, never-ending cycle of conventions, office parties, baby and bridal showers, weddings, bar and bat mitzvahs, family reunions, conferences, graduations, and retirement dinners. This was the first week in more than six months that she had nothing listed on her calendar, and she intended to take advantage of the coveted eight days.

She had forced herself to get out of bed, despite the fact that she was bone-tired and it was raining. However, it had been raining in D.C. for the past three days. Most people in Chocolate City complained about the absence of sunlight, dreary damp days and nights, but only under their breath. The winter had passed without a single flake of falling snow, with most days unseasonably warm and dry, prompting many meteorologists to predict a water shortage if the below-normal precipitation continued into the spring and summer.

Leigh had planned the week to include preparing her favorite dishes, viewing a few of the movie videos she had purchased—many months ago still in their original cellophane packaging—catching up on reading one or two of the many books lining the shelves of the built-in bookcases in the office of her spacious apartment, and listening to music from stacks of CDs.

Afterward, she would take a deep breath, exhale, then start up her hectic schedule all over again. Next Sunday she was expected to be on hand at the wedding of a senator's daughter. The young woman had elected to have a civil and religious ceremony. She was to be married by a Supreme Court justice, followed by an Episcopal mass at the Washington Parish Christ Church. The church's history boasted that it was the oldest ecclesiastical edifice in the District, and its congregation included many of Washington's present and past notable citizens, including presidents Jefferson, Madison, and John Quincy Adams.

The falling rain slackened and Leigh clutched her leather tote to her chest while balancing the umbrella with her right hand. She waited for traffic to slow down, then sprinted across the street. She felt the moisture seeping through the canvas covering of her deck shoes as she waded into a deep puddle. A car sped by, sending a shower of water off the roadway like a geyser. The swirling puddle splashed up, washing over her and pasting the fabric of her khakis to her legs and thighs.

Swearing softly under her breath, Leigh concentrated on reaching the opposite curb. A soft cry of surprise and fear escaped her parted lips when she misjudged the height of the sidewalk and her right foot slipped off the curb. Pain—sharp, burning, and blinding—gripped her ankle, radiating up her leg and not permitting her to keep her balance.

One moment she was standing, and within seconds she found herself seated on the curb, moaning in agony. Biting down on her lower lip, she blinked back tears. Her pulse raced uncontrollably as she struggled to maintain her composure.

"Are you all right, lady?"

She registered a soft male voice somewhere above her. Shifting her umbrella, she glanced up at the dark brown faces of a young man and woman. "I just twisted my ankle." The explanation was squeezed out between clenched teeth.

"Do you think you can stand up?" asked the young woman, her large, expressive eyes filled with genuine concern.

Leigh shook her head. Her umbrella rested beside her on the sidewalk, while the falling rain pasted her professionally coiffed, chemically relaxed silver-gray hair to her scalp.

"I don't think so." Even if she could stand up, she doubted whether she would be able to maintain her balance. Not with the intense throbbing pain.

The young man swept back his jacket, plucked a cellular phone off his waistband, and dialed three numbers. Meanwhile his female companion picked up Leigh's umbrella and held it over her head in an attempt to protect her from the falling rain.

She was in pain and thoroughly embarrassed. She was sitting on the curb of one of the busiest, trendiest streets in the capitol district, temporarily disabled. Two teenagers had come to her aid while other well-dressed D.C. professionals in designer couture rushed past her as if she were a piece of discarded debris floating along the curb and into the sewer.

She had lived in D.C. for the past ten of her fifty-three years of living, and never had she felt more detached than she did now. People talked about New Yorkers being cold, distant, but the same could be said for D.C. citizens. She had come to the realization that the only thing that elicited a spark of interest in the residents of the nation's capital was a political scandal.

A smile softened the young man's classically handsome

features as he hunkered down beside her. "The police are sending an ambulance to take you to the hospital."

Leigh's thickly lashed hazel eyes crinkled in a forced smile. "Thank you."

"No problem, lady. My sister and I will wait with you until they come."

Staring at her rapidly swelling ankle, Leigh experienced twin emotions of annoyance and embarrassment. She was annoyed because she should have been more careful and embarrassed because she was sitting on a street corner in the rain like so many homeless people she saw on the streets of the city, existing in their private world of anguish and hopelessness.

Her gaze swung back to the youth who had come to her rescue. "What's your name? Somehow I'd like to repay you for your kindness."

"My name is Kyle Jackson and my sister is Keisha. But you don't have to pay us. Our dad is a D.C. cop, and—"

His words were drowned out by the sound of a wailing siren. The vehicle eased up along the curb, the driver mindful of not splashing more water onto Leigh's already-soaked clothing.

The emergency medical technicians worked quickly, lifting her and her bulging tote onto a gurney, and within minutes she stared up at the ceiling of the ambulance speeding toward the municipal hospital.

Dr. Scott Alexander turned off the overhead lights in his spacious office, closed the door, and unconsciously emitted a sigh of relief. It was the first time in a very long time that he looked forward to relaxing. It had taken years, thirty-seven to be exact, for him to permit something other than medicine to become an integral part of his life.

Several years ago he had driven from his apartment in a Federal-style Georgetown row house to McLean, Virginia, to visit a friend whom he had not seen in more than twenty years. He had passed an abandoned farmhouse with a FOR SALE sign listing a realtor's telephone number. He'd stopped and copied down the number, and it wasn't until a week later that he called to inquire about the property. The agent set up an appointment to show him the house and surrounding acreage, and three months later he closed on a 1912 farmhouse and carriage house that sat on thirty acres amid overgrown weeds and a riot of wildflowers.

More than two years had elapsed since he had purchased the dilapidated property, but now the structure had been fully restored to its original grandeur, along with a total landscaping makeover.

Tomorrow when he awoke he would begin his day as Scott Alexander, not Dr. Alexander, chief of the Trauma Unit at the city's largest municipal hospital. He was scheduled to start an unprecedented month-long vacation, and he intended to use the time to begin the leisurely process of settling into his new home.

He made his way down the highly waxed hallway, nodding and smiling at the nurses and technicians as they wished him an enjoyable vacation.

"Dr. Alexander!" Turning, Scott stared at his secretary as she quickened her pace to reach him before he left the building. "I'm glad I caught you," she confessed. "Dr. Franklin just left a message. He wants you to call him at home anytime after nine. He says he has good news for you."

He nodded, smiling at the highly skilled, efficient middle-aged woman. "Thanks, Merilyn."

Merilyn Hawkins returned his smile. "Enjoy your vacation."

"I have every intention of doing just that." There was a hint of laughter in his deep, soothing voice.

"You go, Chief," Merilyn whispered under her breath.

She had worked for Scott Alexander for more than six years, and she could not remember the last time he had taken more than three consecutive days off for what he called vacation leave. Once he had submitted the vacation request for a month's leave, rumors were circulating around the city's largest municipal hospital that Dr. Scott Alexander had discovered something that held a greater appeal than medicine.

She surmised that perhaps he had become involved with a woman but dismissed that notion as soon as it entered her head. She had known Scott to date several women; however, none of them had even come close to getting the brilliant doctor to commit to a permanent relationship.

Scott walked through a set of double doors and made his way along a winding, narrow tunnel and stepped into an area and the bustling activity of the Emergency Room. Residents, nurses, and technicians were attending to a half-dozen children who were screaming for their parents.

"What happened?" he asked a nurse as she attempted to calm a little boy who wouldn't let her touch his injured arm.

The woman stared at him, vertical lines appearing between her clear blue eyes before realization dawned. She had not recognized Dr. Scott Alexander. His mixed-gray hair was concealed under a denim baseball cap that matched his long-sleeved shirt and jeans.

Her frown deepened. "Some idiot ignored the flashing red lights on a school bus and plowed into several kids who were crossing the street."

She reached for the child again and he let out a blood-curdling scream: "No! Don't touch it!"

Scott signaled a passing orderly. "Get him to Radiology." His order was issued in a soft, no-nonsense tone. The powerfully built man scooped up the protesting child and carried him out of the waiting room.

Scott's gaze swept around the space, lingering on the lone figure of a woman sitting in a corner, her right foot elevated on a chair with a plastic bag filled with ice taped to her grotesquely swollen ankle. He studied her profile, noting the rigid set to her delicate jaw. There was no doubt that she was in pain.

Turning, Scott walked over to the reception desk, an expression of annoyance tightening his handsome features. Two of the three workers were taking medical information from the parents of the injured students, while another practically reclined on her chair in front of a computer terminal, filing her nails.

"Miss Voss, may I have a moment of your time?"

The clerk sat up quickly, dropping the emery board when she recognized her boss's authoritative voice. She could not believe her bad luck. First she had cracked her acrylic nail, and now the chief of the department had caught her filing it. She was still on probation, and she doubted whether Dr. Alexander would forget the incident when he had to sign off on whether she would become a permanent employee.

"Yes, Doctor?"

"Has anyone taken care of the patient with the foot injury?"

The young woman glanced at the computer screen. "She was seen in triage and is now waiting to be x-rayed."

"How long has she been waiting?"

"Almost ninety minutes."

Scott shook his head. "That's thirty minutes too long."

Since becoming chief he had instituted a policy that no one should have to wait longer than an hour in the Emergency Room before being seen or treated. A triage team had been set up to evaluate each patient before referring them to the appropriate medical professional.

"Give me her chart," he demanded. He had not bothered to disguise the annoyance in his voice.

The clerk handed him a chart, and he scanned the computer-generated sheet. Fifty-three-year-old Leigh Walcott had twisted her right ankle. The physician's assistant had indicated that because Ms. Walcott could move her toes he concluded the ankle was not broken.

"Get me a lab coat, Miss Voss. And please try to take care of your nails on your own time."

The clerk shot up from her chair, embarrassment staining her pale cheeks. She considered herself lucky to escape with only a verbal reprimand. She had heard from veteran employees that Dr. Scott Alexander ran his department like a storm trooper. And she had also heard that he was a workaholic, controlling, but an extremely compassionate doctor. This was one time she hoped that he was in one of his compassionate moods.

*   *   *

"Ms. Walcott?"

Leigh opened her eyes, tilted her chin, and stared up into the large, dark penetrating gaze of a tall man with close-cropped coarse salt-and-pepper hair. She glanced quickly at the ID badge hanging from the pocket of his lab coat.

Her gaze widened as she studied his face—feature by feature. Dr. Scott Alexander was so breathtakingly male that she found it difficult to speak. His features were strong, each one carefully defined to make for an arresting face. His forehead was broad and high, nose bold with a straight bridge and slightly flaring nostrils, cheekbones pronounced, giving his face a rawboned appearance, and his mouth was firm—the thinner upper lip offset by the sensual fullness of the lower one. His eyes were large, dark, intelligent, and penetrating. However, it was his coloring and the texture of his skin that held her entranced. His complexion was flawless, nearly poreless, and called to mind a smooth whipped dark chocolate mousse. If it had not been for a neatly barbered mixed gray mustache, she would have doubted whether he'd claim any facial hair.

"Yes?" She had finally recovered her voice, and the breathless quality sounded foreign even to her own ears.

Scott sat down on an empty chair beside her. "I'm Dr. Alexander, and I'm going to treat your ankle. I've ordered a wheelchair for you so you can be taken to have your ankle x-rayed."

She emitted an audible sigh of relief and flashed a wry smile. "Thank you."

Returning her smile, he tilted his head at an angle. "How did you injure it?"

Heat suffused Leigh's face. Dr. Alexander's sensual smile made him even more attractive. Almost as attractive as the man who had captured her heart and refused to let her go. The tightness around his firm mouth had vanished with his smile, the frown creasing his forehead had disappeared, and the deep grooves in his lean cheeks appeared, drawing her attention to his strong chin.

"I feel like such a klutz. I misjudged the sidewalk."

Scott's smile broadened, the minute lines around his eyes crinkling attractively. "You're lucky you didn't fall on your face." *And it would have been a pity if you had injured your very beautiful face,* he added silently.

Lowering her lashes, she averted her gaze. It had been a long time, a very long time—thirty years to be exact—since she had found a man attractive. The first and only man in her life had been her late husband. She had married Leonard Walcott at twenty-one, given birth to their son at twenty-two, then lost both at twenty-three when a drunk driver claimed their lives in a head-on accident. She had spent three weeks in a New York City hospital after a plastic surgeon had reconstructed her face, but it had taken years before she was able to put her life back together.

"You're right, Dr. Alexander. I am very lucky."

His gaze moved from her thick, damp hair down to the smoothness of her golden brown face. She had given her age as fifty-three, and despite her silvered hair he found her skin as radiant as that of a woman in her early thirties. Her bone structure was exquisite—high, prominent cheekbones, a short rounded nose, delicate chin, full, pouting mouth, and minute mole on her left cheek. However, it was her eyes that had garnered his rapt attention. They were large, round, and filled with an intelligent gentleness; the color was mesmerizing; sweeping black lashes highlighted the brilliance of shimmering pinpoints of gold—a gold that was an exact match for her flawless complexion.

He did not know what had prompted him to treat Leigh Walcott as his patient, because since he had become an administrator he had not had the responsibility of being an attending physician. He also did not know why he had memorized the personal information she had given the admitting clerk. He knew Leigh's age and address, the name and address of next of kin, and her marital status. Glancing at her small, delicate hands with the bare fingers verified that she probably wasn't engaged.

His gaze returned to her entrancing profile, wondering

how long she had been widowed. He doubted whether it could have been too long, because he was certain that any woman who looked like Leigh Walcott would not remain single for any appreciable period of time.

An orderly pushed a wheelchair into the waiting area, stopping at the admitting desk. His expression of surprise was apparent when he steered the chair to Scott and Leigh.

"You ordered a chair, Dr. Alexander?"

Scott stood up, nodding. "Yes. Please help Ms. Walcott into the chair and I will take her up to Radiology."

In less than a minute Leigh found herself seated in a wheelchair, her leather tote on her lap, and Dr. Scott Alexander maneuvering the chair down a corridor and into an elevator.

She stared at the elevator doors as they closed, and the panic began. Years of pain, grief, and loss came rushing back as if it were the cold, wintry night thirty years before. Even though she closed her eyes, she still could see the wipers leaving icy streaks on the windshield; she remembered squinting against the bright, watery lights from oncoming traffic and could hear the *slip-slap* of tires on the snowy roadway. She remembered everything with painstaking clarity before the exploding sound of metal, plastic, and glass merged—then the pain and an enveloping, comforting blackness. A shadowed existence that lasted a week—a week wherein she hadn't known that three lives were lost within seconds: her young husband, their infant son, and the intoxicated driver whose out-of-control vehicle had crossed a median to collide head-on with hers.

Her fingers tightened on the arms of the chair as her chest rose and fell heavily. Tears leaked from under her lids, and she cried silently for the loss of her loved ones and a part of herself.

Scott saw her shoulders shaking. He reached out and placed a large comforting hand on her shoulder, his fingers tightening on the delicate bones under the damp pale blue button-down oxford blouse.

"It's all right, Leigh," he crooned in a deep, comforting tone. "I'm going to take care of you."

2

Leigh managed to bring her fragile emotions under control once the X-ray technician completed taking pictures of her ankle and foot. Dr. Alexander helped her back into the wheelchair, then took her to one of the examining rooms. She felt the heat from his large body and inhaled the sensual scent of his cologne when he helped her onto an examining table.

"I'm going to write you a prescription for something that will take the edge off your pain."

Her head came up and she met his direct stare. "I don't need a painkiller."

His dark gaze lingered on her face before shifting to the bruised, swollen mass of flesh concealing what should have been a slender ankle. "Are you sure?"

Leigh combed her fingers through her limp hair. "Yes. Very sure."

"If that's the case, then why were you crying?" he questioned with a significant lifting of his expressive eyebrows.

She clamped her jaw, turned away from him, and set her chin in a stubborn line. She needed Dr. Alexander to treat her ankle, not her mind. After all, she did not think his specialty was psychiatry.

"Ms. Walcott—"

Whatever he was going to say was preempted by the appearance of the radiologist, who had walked into the room and slipped the pictures of Leigh's foot under a lighted screen.

Scott moved over to the screen, studying the X-rays; he pushed his hands into the pockets of the lab coat and tilted his head. "No break and no fracture," he announced. Shifting, he smiled at her over his shoulder. "It appears to be a sprain."

Leigh sighed audibly, returning his smile with a bright one of her own. There was no way she could've dealt with a broken ankle—especially not with her running her own business. She needed to be mobile when dealing with caterers, musicians, and hotel and restaurant personnel.

Walking back to the table, he eased her down until she was reclining. "I want you to remember the word *R-I-C-E*. It is a four-pronged remedy whose initials stand for Rest, Ice, Compression, and Elevation."

"How much rest?"

His gaze fused with hers. "You should stay off your leg for a day or two. Put a plastic bag with crushed ice against your ankle at fifteen-minute intervals. Compression is wearing an elastic bandage, which I'm going to show you how to wrap. Last, but not least, put your leg up for the first twenty-four to forty-eight hours, applying ice during this period. After that, apply heat. It will reduce the pain and speed healing."

"When do you predict the swelling will disappear?"

"Probably in two to three days. A sprained ankle will usually heal itself within a few weeks. But if you find that you must be up on your feet, then wear a lace-up boot. It will help compress the area. A cane or crutch is also advisable to help you get around. If you need a letter for your employer verifying your disability I will have one of the secretaries complete one for you."

"Thank you for offering, but that won't be necessary. I work for myself."

"Do you spend a lot of time on your feet?"

"There are occasions when I spend hours at a time on my feet," she replied cryptically.

"I hope you'll be able to minimize your activity for at least the next three to four days."

Leigh looked up at the ceiling, nodding. She was fortunate because she had a week's respite. Now she would be forced to stay off her foot and relax.

"Should I follow up with my own doctor?"

"That shouldn't be necessary unless . . ." His words trailed off.

Her head came around and she stared at him staring down at her. "Unless what, Doctor?"

Scott could not believe he was at a loss for words. He regarded her for a moment, his mind floundering. What was happening to him? What was it about Leigh Walcott that had him off balance?

"Unless you have an orthopedist."

A tense silence enveloped the room as Leigh and Scott stared at each other, her gaze widening as he grew more uncomfortable with each passing second.

"I don't," she confirmed softly.

Swallowing, he composed himself. "If the swelling doesn't go away after three days, then call me and I'll refer you to one." He wrote down his pager number on a pad advertising a pharmaceutical company, tore off the page, and gave it to her.

"Thank you." Leigh folded the paper and slipped it into the pocket of her blouse.

He selected an elastic bandage from a supply in a drawer in the medical chest and removed the plastic covering. Pressing a level on the examining table, he raised the portion on which Leigh's feet rested.

"Wrapping your ankle will become a simple task once you get the hang of it," he stated, supporting the heel of her foot in one hand while he slowly and deftly wound the elastic bandage around her misshapen ankle.

Leigh nodded, staring intently at his large, well-groomed hands. A slight smile teased her soft mouth. "I can assure you that it won't look like that after my first attempt."

Scott glanced up, meeting her amused expression. "You'll do all right." His gaze shifted as he concentrated on securing the bandage with two metal fasteners. "What type of business enterprise do you have?"

"I'm an event planner."

Lowering her foot, he returned to the head of the table, curved an arm under her shoulders, and helped her into a sitting position. He felt the warmth of her soft body through the cotton fabric of her blouse. Lowering his head, he inhaled the haunting fragrance of sweet vanilla clinging to her skin and clothing. Not only did Leigh Walcott look good, but she also felt and smelled good. And it took only an instant for Dr. Scott Alexander to conclude that he had been spending too much time at the hospital and not enough with women, because his medical career had always been the top priority in his life.

Crossing his arms over his chest, he tilted his head. "You organize conferences and conventions?"

"Conventions, conferences, weddings, family reunions, and anything that resembles a celebratory gathering."

"How long you been in business for yourself?"

An expression of satisfaction shimmered in Leigh's eyes. The ongoing success of her business had become a source of great pride for her.

"It will be ten years this fall."

Scott arched an eyebrow as he looked at her beneath half-closed lids, his quick mind formulating a plan that would allow him to see Ms. Leigh Walcott again. What he had to uncover was just what it was that made her so attractive to him.

"Do you have a business card on you?" he questioned. "I'm thinking about hosting a little something for my mother's eightieth birthday."

"When is her birthday?"

"August twentieth."

Leigh calculated quickly. "That's only four months away."

He nodded. "I know it's not much time, but would you consider putting everything together?"

"I have to check my calendar."

"Shall I call you, or do you want to call me?" he asked with deceptive calmness. His pulse raced with anticipation while he successfully schooled his features to mirror a calmness he did not feel.

A sweep of thick black lashes shadowed Leigh's brilliant hazel eyes. "I will call you," she said in a low, soft, clear voice that seemed to come from a long way off.

Scott felt as if he had just won a personal victory. It was easier than he thought it would be. However, he had not lied to her about his mother. The last time he had met with his three sisters they had talked about giving their mother a birthday bash. His eldest sister had begun a listing of names of all Irene Alexander's friends and relatives. They had all agreed that it would not be a surprise. What they had not agreed upon was where to hold the event.

Leigh and Scott shared a smile as he assisted her off the examining table and into the wheelchair. He called for an aide to return her to the lower level, his gaze lingering on her until she disappeared into the elevator; then he tried to force his confused emotions into order.

He had come on to Leigh Walcott! Subtly, but the fact remained that he still had come on to her.

Leigh managed to make it up the flight of stairs to her apartment, leaning heavily on a crutch for support. She had stopped twice before she finally made it to the top. The pain in her right foot was excruciating, and she berated herself for not accepting Dr. Alexander's offer of a painkiller.

"R-I-C-E," she mumbled under her breath. Rest, Ice, Compression, and Elevation. Unlocking the door to her apartment, she pushed it open and dropped her leather tote on a wrought-iron bench in the entryway.

A soft groan escaped her parted lips as she limped into her spacious living/dining room. Easing down to a love seat, she reached over and picked up the telephone and called a friend. She left a message on her answering machine to use the extra set of keys to retrieve her car from the parking lot near the stores along Connecticut Avenue.

Getting out of her damp clothing was the next task, and she pushed off the love seat and made her way to her bedroom. Half an hour later, she lay in bed, her injured foot propped up on two pillows, sipping a cup of herbal tea. The two extra-strength over-the-counter pain relievers she had swallowed were working quickly. Her eyelids fluttered as she gave in to the drowsiness sweeping away the throbbing in her ankle.

When she woke up it was to streams of sunlight pouring into her bedroom. What she could not believe was that the pain in her foot was more severe than it had been the day before. She remembered Dr. Alexander's advice: *"Put your leg up for the first twenty-four to forty-eight hours, applying ice during this period."*

Easing her legs over the side of the bed, she reached for the crutch leaning against the wall next to an armchair with a matching ottoman. Securing the crutch under her armpit, she hobbled to the bathroom for her morning ablution before she began the task of icing her foot.

Scott lay on an oversized hammock strung between two massive columns of the screened-in back porch, listening to the soft sounds of cool jazz coming from the powerful speakers concealed within the ceiling. Dusk had fallen, blanketing the verdant manicured lawn with a mysterious gray-blue haze.

Closing his eyes and crossing his bare feet at the ankles, he gave in to the soothing, healing sensations coursing throughout his mind and body. He had spent the past two days touring the Virginia countryside. There were several occasions when he stopped to make purchases for his new home. The four-bedroom farmhouse claimed more space than he would need, but that had not stopped him from purchasing and renovating the property. And after two nights of sleeping under the farmhouse's roof he realized that at fifty-five he wanted a slower, calmer pace. He planned to keep his Georgetown apartment for another five years. Then he would resign his position at the hospital and set up a family practice in McLean.

The distinctive sound of the beeper attached to the waistband of his jeans garnered his attention, and he sat up. Pressing a button, he studied the lighted dial. He recognized the 202 D.C. area code but not the number. Swinging his feet over the hammock, he retreated into the house to return the page.

He dialed the number and waited for a break in the connection.

"Hello," came a softly modulated female voice.

A wide smile revealed his straight white teeth when he recognized the voice coming through the receiver. "Scott Alexander returning your page."

"This is Leigh Walcott."

"How are you?"

"Much better, thank you."

"How's the ankle?"

There was slight pause before her voice came through the receiver again. "It's still a little swollen."

"Are you staying off it?"

"I'm trying."

His smile faded with this disclosure. "I'm coming to see you tomorrow."

"That won't be necessary," she said quickly. "I just wanted to let you know that I'm free for August twentieth if you want me to handle your mother's birthday celebration."

His smile returned. "Pencil me in for the date. I know we don't have a lot of time to pull everything together, so I'd like for us to get together as soon as possible."

There was a slight pause before Leigh asked, "When do you want to meet?"

Scott decided to be direct, because he was too old to play games. "Tomorrow. We can discuss everything over dinner."

"Dr. Alexander—"

"Scott," he insisted.

"Scott," Leigh repeated.

"Yes, Leigh?"

"Can we postpone dinner until I'm able to put my foot in a shoe?"

"Putting on a shoe should not be a problem."

"Why?"

"Because I'll bring dinner to you. Look for me tomorrow evening around seven. Good night, Leigh."

"Wait . . . don't hang up!"

"Yes?"

"You don't have my address."

"Oh, yes, I do. Remember, I was your attending physician." Pressing a button, he ended the call. Within seconds his beeper went off again. Scott stared at the number, smiling. It was Leigh. This time he would not return her page. He wasn't going to give her the opportunity to cancel their date.

A triumphant smile lifted the corners of his mobile mouth. A date! It had been a long time since he had had a date. Much too long.

3

It had taken hours for Leigh's temper to cool after Scott Alexander had not answered her callback. She had spent most of the night cursing Dr. Scott Alexander for his pompous arrogance. Just who did he think he was anyway? Was he so used to giving orders at the hospital that he felt he could do the same with her? Well, the doctor was in for quite a surprise. She had always been her own person, and even more so since she had set up a thriving enterprise. What the pretentious Dr. Alexander had not known was that she did not entertain men in her home or conduct business meetings in her apartment.

Her frustration returned when she was forced to search her closet for a shoe that would accommodate her slightly swollen foot and ankle, and when the clock approached seven o'clock she was ready for the arrogant man. If Scott Alexander wanted to discuss business over dinner, then he would be forced to, but only on her terms.

*   *   *

Scott parked his automobile in front of a large Victorian-style house along a quiet residential street in Washington, D.C., at six-fifty-five. Arriving at Leigh's apartment at seven would give him time to confer with her as to what she wanted for dinner; then he would call in the order to one of his favorite D.C. restaurants. Waiting for the food delivery would give him and Leigh the opportunity to outline what he wanted for his mother's birthday gathering.

He turned off the car's engine and reached for his jacket on the passenger seat. Two minutes later he stood in the vestibule of the house, clutching an enormous bouquet of pale pink roses in one hand while ringing the bell labeled WALCOTT with the other.

"Yes?" came the now-familiar feminine voice through the intercom. A voice he had come to look forward to hearing, a voice that sounded as if she had come from a northern region of the country and a voice that was soft, feminine, and very professional.

He pressed the TALK button on the intercom. "Scott."

"Come on up."

The bell for releasing the lock on the door buzzed, and he pushed it open. The entryway to the structure was furnished with tables and lamps beckoning another period in history. He climbed the curving staircase, wondering how long it had taken Leigh to make it to the second level with her injured foot. A plush burgundy runner and matching stair risers cushioned his footsteps as he counted twenty stairs.

The door to Leigh's apartment was at the head of the stairs, and it opened as he raised his hand to ring the bell. A lump formed in his throat, not permitting him to swallow as he struggled to force air into his lungs.

Leigh Walcott stood before him, smiling sweetly. Her hair was a mass of tiny silver curls that fell over her forehead in seductive disarray. Straightened, the blunt-cut strands ended at her chin, but the soft, shiny curls added volume to her luxurious, shimmering hair.

She had exchanged her khaki slacks and blouse for a pair of black wool crepe slacks and a pleated-front white long-sleeved silk blouse. She had managed to push her injured foot into a pair of black ballet-type leather shoes. A light cover of makeup accentuated her luminous eyes and lush mouth.

Swallowing with a modicum of difficulty, Scott forced a smile and raised his hand with the flowers. "A get-well offering," he said hoarsely.

Leigh felt the heat flare in her face as she stared at the exquisite bouquet of roses with a profusion of baby's breath. The roses were the exact shade of the tulips that had not survived the harrowing day when she had spent more than two hours in the Emergency Room.

Her lashes shadowed her brilliant gaze. "Thank you, Scott. They're beautiful."

"You're quite welcome." He stood motionless, staring down at her bowed head, and it was the first time that he realized how petite she actually was. At six-one he towered over her by almost a foot. He doubted whether she was more than five-two or five-three.

"May I come in, Leigh?"

Her head came up quickly. "Of course. Please, come in."

She stepped aside, and he walked into a spacious entryway boasting an exquisite parquet floor. The space contained a side table with a Tiffany lamp, several small black-and-white photographs with images of smiling black children, and a wrought-iron bench. A tall clay container in a corner doubled as an umbrella stand.

Leigh closed the door and her eyes briefly. The emotions she felt when she first saw Dr. Scott Alexander were back. His casual attire was gone, and in its place was a pair of tailored taupe-colored slacks, a navy blue blazer, and a white silk shirt with a banded collar. He was also taller and broader than she had remembered. And whenever he stared at her with his hypnotic dark eyes she felt as if he could see inside her head and heart to the years of loneliness and denial. Could he really see that for thirty years of widowhood she had not allowed a man into her life or into her bed? The trauma of losing the man she had loved from childhood and the tiny child whom she had carried beneath her heart for nine months, then lost after another six, eased with time, but not completely.

Turning, she led the way to the living room, feeling the heat of his gaze on her back. "Please have a seat while I put these in water."

Scott did not sit but stood in the middle of the living room admiring the carefully chosen furnishings. Cream-colored walls provided the backdrop for a grouping of two facing love seats in front of a fireplace. The mantel was crowded with tiny white votive candles in crystal holders. The creamy upholstery created an illusion of openness and space, while a glittering crystal chandelier enhanced the space's friendly and receptive air. Decorative needlepoint pillows provided a colorful contrast, which was carried over to the cushions of six chairs flanking a mahogany table in an adjoining dining area. Potted green and flowering plants, lush ferns, and towering trees turned the apartment into a lush oasis.

By the time Leigh limped back to the living room carrying a crystal vase filled with the roses, he had opened the French doors and stepped out onto a veranda that provided a view of the city with the lighted dome of the Capitol in the background. The veranda ran the width along the rear of the apartment, and he knew that if he turned to his right and walked several feet he would be able to stand outside Leigh Walcott's bedroom. A wrought-iron table with seating for two garnered his attention, and he knew instinctively that Leigh spent many hours on her veranda, eating, dining, and whiling away the hours as she enjoyed the backdrop of the city from her elevated position.

Leigh placed the vase on the table surrounded by the love seats, then walked over to the open French doors. Her gaze lingered on the width of Scott's broad shoulders as he rested his hands on the railing.

"I'm ready to go out now."

Scott turned at the sound of her voice. "I thought I informed you that we would be eating in?"

Folding her hands on her narrow hips, Leigh shook her

head, the curls moving as if they had taken on a life of their own. "You did not inform me, Dr. Alexander. You issued a mandate. What you did not do was wait for me to tell you that I never entertain in my home when I have to discuss *business.*"

He looked down at her slippered feet. "Will you be able to get around on your ankle?"

She affected a haughty look. "I don't see why I should have a problem. After all, my attending physician will be with me."

Pushing away from the railing, Scott swore under his breath. Leigh had turned the tables on him. He wanted to see her again, but alone. He did not want any distractions that would interfere with his search to uncover why he was drawn to her.

One thing he knew it was not, and that was sex. He had always been very discreet when it came to his sexual encounters. What had once been a vigorous sex drive in his youth had tapered off with age; however, at fifty-five he still had no need for a performance-enhancing drug that would assist him to initiate or complete the act.

He moved over to Leigh and reached for her hand. "Come sit down and let me look at your ankle."

Leigh shivered despite the warmth of the night and her apartment and permitted Scott to lead her back into the living room. She floated down to the love seat and closed her eyes when he sat down next to her. He was close, too close for her to relax completely.

She did open her eyes when he raised her foot to his thigh, removed her shoe, and unwound the length of elastic bandage from her ankle. Her gaze was fixed on his lowered head. His salt-and-pepper gray hair was cut close to his scalp, and its coarseness verified that Scott Alexander would enter old age with all or most of his hair.

Scott concealed a smile when he noted the deep rose-pink color on her professionally groomed toes. Most of the swelling had left her toes and instep. However, the puffiness around her ankle was still apparent.

"It looks pretty good," he stated, offering her a smile. "You're healing quickly."

"I'll know it's healed completely once I'm able to put on a pair of three-inch heels and go out dancing."

Leigh chided herself as soon as the statement was out of her mouth. What was she talking about? She hadn't danced in years, and sharing a dance or two at her clients' soirees did not count.

Scott went completely still, his gaze fused with hers. "Will you allow me the honor of taking you dancing? Strictly personal," he added quickly.

"Don't you dance with your wife?"

He shifted his eyebrows at her query. "No."

"And why not?"

"Because I don't have a wife, that's why."

It was her turn to raise her eyebrows. "That's a pity, because you seem like a very nice man. And because you are I would have assumed that you had a wife."

A smile tugged at the corners of his mouth. "Why, thank you, Leigh. However, you didn't answer my question. Will you go dancing with me?"

She returned his bold stare, unable to look away when she felt a curious swooping tug at her innards. The idea of dancing with Scott excited her. She had deliberately shut out any and every man who had expressed an interest in her for thirty years, but there was something about the man holding her foot within his strong grasp that made her forget her pledge not to open her heart because she feared loving and losing again.

"I'll let you know," she said in a breathless whisper.

"When?"

"When you discharge me as your patient."

Throwing back his head, Scott let out a roar of laughter. And if anyone at the hospital had heard him they would have thought that he had lost his mind. Most of the hospital staff saw him smile, but the smiles were always reserved for patients, while few had ever heard him laugh aloud. The running joke was that he was married to the hospital and as a jealous mistress medicine would not tolerate a woman in his life.

He rewrapped the bandage, his smile in place. "If that's the case, then I will be certain to make regular house calls to check your progress."

"I thought doctors stopped making house calls years ago."

He glanced over his shoulder at her. "Not this doctor." He replaced her shoe, which went on easily. "If we're going to eat out, then I'd like to suggest a place."

Scott stood up, extending his hand. She placed her smaller hand in his, and he pulled her effortlessly to her feet, the top of her head coming up to his shoulder.

"Where?"

"Leo's."

A bright smile wrinkled her nose and crinkled her eyes, charming him with the expression. Her smile was like a ray of sunshine—bright and warm. He had suggested her favorite D.C. restaurant.

Scott closed the doors to the veranda while Leigh went to retrieve the jacket to her pantsuit and her handbag. He waited for her at the door. She limped over and locked it behind them.

Then without warning, he leaned down and scooped her up into his arms. She caught his neck to keep her balance.

"What do you think you're doing?" The heat from his chest seared her body.

"Carrying you down the stairs, Sunshine. I haven't eaten since eight o'clock this morning, so I don't want to have to wait another hour for you to make it down to the street."

Her mouth gaped, closed, then opened again. "It doesn't take me that long to maneuver the stairs, thank you." She managed to look and sound thoroughly insulted.

He lifted her higher, her lips only inches from his mustached mouth. "Indulge me, Leigh. Please let me play superhero tonight."

Lowering her lashes in a demure gesture, she pursed her lips and nodded. "OK, Super Doc."

He laughed again and pressed his mouth to her curling hair. "Thank you, Sunshine."

Leigh felt the warmth and strength of Scott's right arm around her waist as soon as he assisted her through a set of massive mahogany doors affixed with gleaming brass fixtures at Leo's. Golden recessed ceiling lights sparkled against floor-to-ceiling stained-glass windows, turning them into rubies, sapphires, citrines, emeralds, and diamonds.

The soft sounds of hushed conversations, taped music, sensual laughter, and ringing of glasses and silverware filled Leo's with the warmth and quiet animation that made it one of the most popular supper clubs in Washington, D.C.

The club had become a popular dining and meeting place for many of D.C.'s citizens. The menu boasted continental and southern cuisine that appealed to politicians, college professors, judges, civil servants, law enforcement officers, college students, attorneys, members of the clergy, secretaries, and the many visiting foreign dignitaries.

She and Scott were met in the spacious waiting area by one of the four owners. A polite smile curved Noah Hardcastle's sensual mouth when he recognized the attractive middle-aged couple.

"Good evening. Welcome to Leo's."

Scott returned the smile, removing his arm from Leigh's waist and offering his right hand. "Thanks, Noah."

Noah took the proffered hand. "It's been a while, Doc."

Scott nodded. "That it has." Turning his attention to Leigh, his gaze lingered on her perfect profile. "I'd like to introduce Miss Leigh Walcott."

She flashed a friendly smile. "Hello again, Noah."

Moving closer, the restaurateur gathered Leigh to his chest and dropped a kiss at the corner of her smiling mouth. "Hello back to you, beautiful."

Scott stood, completely stunned by the scene unfolding before his startled gaze. He did not know why, but he never would have thought that Leigh frequented Leo's enough to know the owner personally. And seeing Noah Hardcastle hold and kiss her with what was a comfortable familiarity elicited a rush of jealousy. Scott did not know anything about Leigh Walcott except the information she had given when she was admitted to the hospital's Emergency Room, yet he was experiencing the foreign emotion of jealousy and resentment—resentment because another man was interacting with Leigh in the manner he had wanted to.

He wanted to take her in his arms and taste her lush mouth. He wanted to hold her close enough to have her body's heat merge with his, and he wanted to inhale the haunting sensuality of a fragrance claiming vanilla, iris, and Oriental spices as its properties.

Pulling back, Leigh stared up into the eyes of the tall, handsome man cradling her in a loose embrace. "I'll be checking with you sometime next week for the Royce party."

"Tyrell told me earlier this morning that he had finalized the menu you discussed with him."

"Tell him I'll call him tomorrow."

Noah released her. "Enough shoptalk." He nodded to Scott. "Let me get the hostess to show you to your table."

Scott's arm circled Leigh's waist once again, and she unconsciously moved closer to him, her hip brushing intimately against his muscular thigh. Her left arm curved around his waist inside his jacket as she placed most of her weight on her left leg.

A young woman, wearing the standard restaurant uniform of a white blouse with a mandarin collar paired to a black skirt, approached them, a practiced professional smile in place. "Follow me please and I'll show you to your table."

Even though it wasn't quite seven-thirty, Leo's was nearly filled to capacity. They opened six nights a week for after work and dinner and Sunday mornings for their celebrated brunch offerings. The supper club featured live music on Fridays, Saturdays, and Sundays, while taped soft jazz selections were offered all other nights. One Wednesday evening each month was set aside for Amateur/Open Mike Night to showcase new and upcoming talent.

The hostess directed them to a round rosewood table with

seating for two in a corner that permitted them a view of a raised stage for a band, the large bar, and an adjacent area with an elaborately designed parquet floor area for dancing. The table, like all of the others in the rosewood and stained-glass decorated space, claimed a small Tiffany lamp and a colored oil candle.

Scott seated Leigh before he sat down opposite her, thanking the hostess as she placed two menus on the table. He stared across the small space at his dining partner, admiring the soft golden shadows falling across her face from the flickering candlelight. His gaze slid downward to the slowly beating pulse in her smooth throat before returning to linger on her composed features.

Leigh met his bold stare, her delicate eyebrows lifting slightly. "Is there something wrong with my face?" Her tone was soft, even.

Scott blinked once. "Not that I can see. Why do you ask?"

"You're staring at me."

His expression was impassive. "I like staring at you."

As casually as she could manage, she asked, "Why?"

Leaning back against the comfortably cushioned chair, Scott flashed a half-smile. "I'm surprised you would ask me that, Leigh. You have to know that you're an incredibly beautiful woman."

Lowering her lashes, she stared down at the menu in front of her. "I know nothing of the sort."

Reaching across the table, Scott covered one of her hands with his, tightening his hold when she tried extracting her fingers from his strong grip. "Well, I'm telling you that you are."

She clamped her jaw tightly rather than scream at him that he didn't know what he was talking about. That the face he saw was not the face she had been born with.

"I think you'd better take a look at your menu," she said instead. "Didn't you tell me that you hadn't eaten all day?"

Scott released her hand and turned his attention to the menu. He didn't need to look at it to know what he wanted to order because his need to know more about Leigh Walcott had surpassed his craving for food.

He managed to give her a surreptitious glance at the same time a waiter approached their table. The young man was dressed entirely in black—shirt with a mandarin collar and slacks.

"My name is Bobby, and I'll be your server this evening." He placed a wine listing on the table, flashing a friendly smile. "The sommelier will be here in a few minutes to take your beverage order. I'll give you some time to look over the menu; then I will be back."

What Scott had to remind himself was that Leigh had offered to organize his mother's birthday party, which was four months away. And he knew he would be given the opportunity to see her at various stages before the event. He had time, but more important than time was the fact that he was an extremely patient man.

Leigh surveyed the menu while Scott studied the wine list, both pretending interest in the printed selections while refusing to acknowledge what was so apparent—a silent, sensual attraction binding them together.

4

Leigh waited until she had taken several sips of a quality-vintage pale blush wine to withdraw a small spiral notebook and pen from her handbag.

Peering through her lashes at Scott, she offered him a smile. "You're scheduled for Saturday, August twentieth, for your mother's eightieth birthday. What's your mother's name?"

"Irene Alexander."

"Her health?"

"It's very good considering her age. Why do you ask?" he questioned.

Raising her chin, Leigh gave him a direct stare. "She's

the guest of honor, and when I contract with the caterer I must make certain to order the appropriate foods. If she's a diabetic or has food allergies, then the caterer must be informed of any dietary restrictions."

Scott took a sip from his own wineglass, nodding his approval. There was no doubt Leigh was a professional. "What else do you need to know?"

"How many people do you intend to invite? What time of the day do you plan to host the event? Where? Do you have any food preferences? And what price range have you considered? I also need names and addresses of the invitees so that I can mail out the invitations. I want to know if the party is going to be a surprise or Mrs. Alexander will be aware of the arrangements. The age range of the guests will also be a factor, along with if you'll want flowers, balloons, and other decorations.

"You must let me know who will be hosting the party, because the names will be printed on the invitations. I will include with each invitation a response card with a self-addressed stamped envelope. I've established a practice of having the response cards returned to me at my company's post office box because, unfortunately, many people don't bother to respond one way or the other. This usually puts the hosts in an awkward position. I will follow up with the telephone calls. I believe if they're rude enough not to respond, then I will take the responsibility of putting them on the spot. If they decline, then that will give you the opportunity to invite someone who will be more appreciative and considerate. And it's perfectly appropriate for guests to receive an invitation up to two weeks before the response date."

Scott leaned back, whistling softly. "You are one serious party planner, Leigh Walcott."

She watched him with smug delight. "I've never had a complaint."

"I can see why. I'm going to need your services for another event."

Leigh's surprise was apparent when her delicate jaw dropped slightly. Within a span of days an unintentional encounter with Dr. Scott Alexander had her planning not one but two events for him.

"How much time are you giving me for this one?"

Grimacing, he shrugged broad shoulders under his jacket. "Just about three weeks."

Schooling her features not to reveal her rising apprehension, she said, "Tell me about it."

Scott disclosed that Dr. Mark Franklin was leaving Capitol Medical Center to accept a position in New York to teach corneal surgery. "He came to us four years ago as a surgical resident and quickly distinguished himself as a medical genius. It was only a matter of time before one of the larger private teaching institutions recruited him."

Flipping a page on her pad, Leigh wrote down the name of Mark Franklin, and over the next two hours she and Scott discussed the plans for his colleague's going-away party while sharing a crab salad in endive leaves, a lobster, potato and green bean salad with a pesto vinaigrette, and entrées of a rack of spring lamb marinated in garlic, allspice, cumin, and thyme and roast chicken with a mushroom-pancetta stuffing, and side dishes of stuffed eggplant and Moroccan vegetables.

She stopped between forkfuls to make notations in her notebook. "I recommend that you hold your colleague's party here at Leo's. I'll check with Noah to see if I can reserve the smaller private room. The advantages are that you intend to invite fewer than thirty people, it's centrally located, and the food is excellent."

Scott touched his napkin to the corners of his mouth, his gaze lingering on Leigh's bowed head as she continued to make notations on her pad. He had considered himself fortunate enough to spend two hours with her, yet he still hadn't uncovered what it was about the event planner that made him want to know her better.

Her delicate beauty was obvious, despite her refusal to acknowledge it. What he had discovered was that she was controlled—very, very controlled. She was also extremely professional. Not once had she allowed their conversation to veer to anything that could be construed as personal in nature.

"I will go along with your recommendation to have Mark's party here," he stated firmly.

"If the room is available," she reminded him.

"And if it isn't?"

"Then I'll see if I can call in a few favors to get in at Kinkead's or Georgia Brown's. Let's not rule out Leo's until I talk to Noah."

Leaning forward, Scott lowered his voice. "How long have you known Noah Hardcastle?"

"I met him when he, his brothers, and his cousin opened the restaurant."

"The two of you appeared to be quite friendly."

Replacing the top on her pen, Leigh dropped it in her handbag along with the small notebook. She was hard pressed not to laugh. She did not want to believe that Scott's ego was bruised because Noah had kissed her.

"That's because we are. We happen to be very good friends." It was her turn to touch the corner of her napkin to her lips. "If it's all right with you, I'd like to leave so that I can elevate my foot."

Scott glanced over his shoulder, looking for their waiter. He caught the young man's attention, signaling with a barely perceptible wave of his hand. Turning back to Leigh, he reached under the tablecloth, caught her right leg, and raised it until her foot rested on his knee.

"What do you think you're doing?" she hissed, clearly startled by the gesture.

"Elevating your foot, Ms. Walcott."

"That's not necessary, Dr. Alexander."

"Yes, it is. I don't want you to do anything to prolong the healing process, because I'm truly looking forward to taking you dancing."

Heat and color flooded her face, and she berated herself for mentioning dancing. She had found Dr. Scott Alexander attractive—very, very attractive—and as long as they maintained a professional association she was safe; however, what he did was remind her of how long she had been without a man in her life. And what she refused to acknowledge was that she had managed to repress her sexual urges for thirty years, but even that was shattered completely when she picked up the telephone and dialed his pager number. Within seconds of hearing his soft, drawling voice a shiver of awareness had swept over her, leaving her shaking with a rush of long-forgotten desire.

Their waiter returned to the table. "Are you ready to order dessert?"

Leigh shook her head and Scott also declined, requesting their check. The young man totaled their bill, placed it in a small leather binder, and left it on the table.

Scott glanced at the total and withdrew a credit card case from the breast pocket of his jacket. He settled the bill and five minutes later they stood in the restaurant's parking lot waiting for his car to be brought around.

Leigh sighed inaudibly as she settled herself on the soft saddle tan leather seat of the late-model Mercedes-Benz sedan. Closing her eyes, she felt the heat of Scott's tall body when he sat down beside her. Suddenly all of her senses were heightened in the darkened space. The sensual fragrance of his cologne and the luxury car's richly appointed leather interior merged, calling to mind a single word—*male*.

The man sitting beside her was so unequivocally male that she found herself pressing her thighs together to stop their trembling. All she wanted to do was go home, lock her door, and climb into bed to sleep and forget that she had denied herself companionship for three decades because she was paralyzed by the fear of loving and losing. She wasn't willing to take the risk—not again.

They arrived at her house and she suffered Scott's closeness for the second time when he picked her up and carried her up the staircase to the upper level. She unlocked her door, then thanked him for dinner, promising she would call him the following day to confirm the location for Mark Franklin's party.

He stood motionless, staring down at her as an unreadable

expression settled into his even features. "I'll be waiting for the call."

He turned and made his way down the staircase, stopping before he moved off the last stair. He turned to find her in the doorway watching him. A slow, mysterious smile curved his mouth under his mustache as she raised her right hand and waved to him.

"Good night, Scott," she whispered under her breath.

"Good night, Leigh."

Her hands were trembling when she stepped back and closed the door. He had heard her. And he had to know that she liked him—liked him a lot.

Scott drove back to McLean, chiding himself as soon as he walked through the door of the enormous farmhouse. He should have spent the night in his Georgetown apartment, because then he would not have to be reminded of how solitary his life was once he left the hospital. Over the years his apartment had become an oasis, a safe haven, filled with books and memorabilia of his hobbies and his childhood, while many of the rooms in the farmhouse were still empty— as empty as his existence was without his medical career.

He climbed the steps to the second story, reliving the two coveted hours he had shared with Leigh Walcott. A violent shudder racked his large frame with a sexual awareness.

He had lied to himself. He wanted to see Leigh again, but he also wanted to share more than just time with her. His vow not to become involved with a woman had been shattered completely when he walked into the Emergency Room and saw a tiny woman sitting by herself.

What he had not known at the time was that he had connected with her. Her solitude had merged with his.

5

Leigh sat in the office at Leo's with two of the quartet of owners. She stared at the dates on her leather-bound calendar spread out on the table.

"I need the smaller room for May twelfth. I'm expecting a party of twenty-six."

Noah Hardcastle stroked his luxurious coal black mustache with his right forefinger as he visually surveyed his own calendar. "It's open."

She flashed a relieved smile. She did not think she would be able to reserve the room for the Franklin gathering on such short notice. The moment Noah had opened the restaurant's calendar for the month of May she had noticed that very few times and dates were not reserved for a social function in either of their two private rooms.

"Wonderful. Put me down under 'Dr. Mark Franklin.' "

"What's the occasion, Leigh?" Tyrell Hardcastle questioned.

She smiled at Noah's younger brother, who was Leo's master chef. The resemblance between all the brothers was remarkable, but even more so between Tyrell and his identical twin, Tyrone. Ty and Roni, as they were known by family and close friends, claimed golden brown skin, sandy brown hair, large, slanting clear brown eyes, high cheekbones with a distinctive mole on the left cheekbone, and a strong cleft chin. All of the Hardcastle men had inherited the chin of their retired army career officer father, Leo Hardcastle. Leigh suspected that most D.C. sisters frequented Leo's because all of the tall, well-built, and extremely attractive Hardcastle men were very eligible bachelors.

"A promotion and relocation."

Tyrell nodded, jotting down notes on his calendar. "What time do you want to begin?"

"Six." She ticked off all of the items she had discussed

with Scott. "I want a cocktail hour beginning at six. The doctor is a zealous sports fan, and because he's moving to New York City I'd like a theme reflecting the state's colors of orange and royal blue. I plan to pick up sports paraphernalia of the Yankees, Mets, Knicks, Giants, Jets, Rangers, and Islanders. I'll also take care of the flowers and balloons."

"How about music?" Noah queried.

"Just a piano player." The gathering was too small and intimate for a band or taped music.

"Sit-down or buffet?" Noah continued.

"Buffet. But I'd like you to set up the room using smaller tables."

Tyrell shifted his sweeping light brown eyebrows. "How small?"

"Seating for two. The hospital will be giving the doctor a party in their employee cafeteria the week before, and I'd like to offset that with a smaller, more intimate gathering."

"Nice contrast," Noah stated, making notations on his calendar. "I'll set up fifteen tables for two. You've decided on a theme, music, and room setup. All that's left is the food." His dark gaze shifted from Leigh's face to his brother's, and it was the first time he noticed she and Tyrell shared similar facial characteristics: coloring, eye color, and a mole on their left cheekbone.

"Let's hear it, Leigh," Tyrell urged, his pen poised over a page he had labeled: "Walcott/Franklin/May 12/6:00p/26–30 guests."

She had come up with the menu for the Franklin party. Scott had given her the responsibility of putting the menu together. He had mentioned that Mark loved caviar, champagne, and crab cakes.

"I want smoked salmon, curried scallop, and cucumber canapés. Coriander lime shrimp, cold shrimp with vegetable spring rolls. Please include your fabulous miniature spinach pies, Worcestershire mushroom rolls, and the ubiquitous Buffalo wings. The guest of honor's favorites are deviled crab cakes and caviar."

Tyrell scribbled in a shorthand only he could decipher. "What about dinner?"

"Butterflied lamb with braised garlic and thyme, roast turkey and chicken, fillet of beef with paprika, coriander, and cumin, and baked red snapper. I want lots of vegetable dishes—steamed spinach in garlic and olive oil, glazed carrots with grapes and walnuts, asparagus or green beans with ginger, and accompanying green salads."

"What about desserts?"

"Any of your miniature pastries and tarts will do."

Tyrell pushed back his chair and walked over to a computer. Five minutes later he printed out a single sheet and handed it to Leigh. She perused the page, nodding her approval. The small private party would be costly, but she was certain it would be a rousing success. When she had asked Scott about monetary limits he had said there wouldn't be any.

Opening her handbag, she withdrew her checkbook and wrote out a check for 25 percent of the total, which included gratuities for the servers, bartender, and pianist.

She flashed a satisfied smile. "Messrs. Hardcastle, it is always a pleasure to do business with you." She had set up everything she needed for Mark Franklin's party, as well as finalized the menu for a dinner for a couple who were celebrating their fiftieth wedding anniversary in another two weeks.

The brothers stood up, towering above her by more than a foot. Noah circled the table and pulled back her chair. "It's *our* pleasure, Leigh. Whether you realize it or not, you've increased our clientele appreciably after every party you booked with us."

"Noah's right," Tyrell added. "We were talking about making you a partner."

"It wouldn't work," she said.

"Why not?" the brothers chorused.

"Because I'm not a Hardcastle."

"Who's not a Hardcastle?" questioned a low, sultry female voice. Tall, reed-thin, and incredibly beautiful Ayanna Hardcastle strolled into the office, the smell of Chinese food wafting from the plastic bag she cradled to her chest. As a certified public accountant she was responsible for the supper club's finances.

Ayanna smiled at Leigh. "You could become a Hardcastle if you stopped playing hard to get with Noah, my older and very mature first cousin."

"Mind your business, Ayanna," Noah warned softly.

Tyrell shot his first cousin an angry glare. "How many times have I told you about bringing outside food into the restaurant?"

Ayanna affected a moue. "I wouldn't bring in Chinese food if you added a few dishes to the menu."

Leigh gathered her materials before she witnessed what was certain to become a good-natured Hardcastle family feud. Senior partner Noah Hardcastle was the eldest and most level-headed of the quartet, and at thirty-seven the divorced restaurateur wasn't looking to remarry, even though his brothers and cousin tried setting him up with every single woman who expressed an interest in him. But what most women did not know was that Noah was totally committed to the overall day-to-day operation of Leo's. Even if Leigh had not been sixteen years his senior, what the Hardcastle twins and cousin had not known was that she, too, had no desire to remarry.

Scott removed the stethoscope from his ears and wrote down his mother's blood pressure in a small diary. His accusing dark eyes met her equally dark ones. "It's higher than it was last week."

"That's because Marion made fried fish and I had a couple of pieces," Irene Alexander retorted. "You act as if I'd killed somebody."

He replaced the sphygmomanometer and stethoscope in a small black leather case, his mouth tightening in frustration. "High blood pressure is a killer, Mother."

Irene swatted at his hand. "Don't take that tone with me, Dr. Scott Alexander." She knew her son was angry with her because he had addressed her as "Mother."

Giving her a long, penetrating look, Scott forced a smile. "I'm sorry, Mama."

She patted his arm. "And I'm sorry that I'm not following my diet."

Leaning over, he kissed her baby-soft, paper-thin cheek. "It's only slightly elevated."

What he didn't say was that he was going to read his oldest sister the riot act for serving their mother fried foods. Marion Evans had finally convinced their elderly widowed mother to sell her house and move in with her and her husband after their youngest daughter moved away to attend college in the Midwest.

"It will be better when you come next time."

"I'm sure it will." He winked at her. "I have to see Marion about a few things; then I'll be right back."

Pride shone in Irene Alexander's eyes. She loved her three daughters, but her only son had become her pride and joy. Not only was he the image of her late husband, but as Scott grew older even their obsessions had become similar. With George Alexander it had been teaching; medicine for Scott. However, George had taken time to marry and father four children, while Scott had not married or fathered one child.

Turning her head, she stared at her reflection in a mirror on the back of the door in her bedroom. A slight smile curved her firm mouth. She looked much younger than eighty. At least that was what she was told by most of the widowed gentlemen down at the senior center.

Scott had spent over an hour with his sister, going over the names and addresses of the people they intended to invite to their mother's birthday celebration, when his pager went off. Recognizing Leigh's number, he withdrew a cellular phone from the breast pocket of his shirt and punched in her number.

His face lit up with unabashed pleasure when he heard her voice. "Good afternoon, Leigh."

"Good afternoon, Scott," came her soft response. "Dr. Franklin's party is confirmed for May twelfth."

"Excellent. I'm at my sister's house, and we've just completed compiling the names and addresses for the invitations."

"Good. I'm going to need them as soon as possible."

"I'll meet you later and give them to you. We've decided to hold the event at my place in Virginia." Marion Evans raised her eyebrows at her brother in a questioning expression.

"Where in Virginia?" Leigh questioned.

"McLean."

"Where are the majority of your guests coming from?"

"D.C. and Maryland."

"That's not too far. I'll have to see it before I make arrangements with a caterer."

Scott glanced at his watch. "I'm in Reston right now. I should be leaving here within the hour. I'll pick you up at three-thirty."

"OK."

"Good-bye."

There was a slight pause before she said softly, "I'll see you later, Scott."

He ended the call and returned the palm-size phone to his shirt pocket. "Where were we?"

Marion tucked several strands of liberally streaked gray and black hair behind her right ear. She resembled her brother more than her two younger sisters.

"When did *we* decide to hold Mama's birthday party at your house?"

Ignoring her sarcasm, he gave her a level stare. "When *I* decided to underwrite the entire cost of the affair. It's the least I could do for you, Gladys, and Nicole."

"Are you feeling guilty because you've never had to write a check for college tuition or to the orthodontist?"

His expression sobered and he glanced away. "No, Marion. It's not guilt, but there are times when I wondered how my life would have been if I had married or had children."

"It's not too late, Scott."

"I refuse to father children at fifty-five."

She placed her hand over his. "I wasn't talking about you having children. You know my friend Sandra still asks about you."

"She's not my type, Marion."

"Who is your type?"

"Definitely not Sandra Davis. I want to remind you to watch Mama's diet," he said, changing the topic. "No more fried foods."

"But she insists, Scott."

"Don't listen to her."

"The woman lives under my roof, not yours. You try ignoring Irene Brooks Alexander."

"If her blood pressure goes up the next time I take it, then she's coming home with me for a couple of weeks."

Marion gave her brother a long, lingering look, then said, "All right. I'll monitor her diet. Stop scowling and give me a kiss."

Scott kissed his sister, hugging her before he took his leave, promising to return within a week. He returned to look in on his mother, warning her again about her diet.

Scott rang Leigh's doorbell, identified himself, then waited for the door lock to disengage. He had not realized how much he had looked forward to seeing Leigh Walcott again until he made his way up the staircase to find her waiting for him. Her smile was radiant.

"Hello again, Scott."

"Hello, Sunshine."

Leaning down, he pressed a kiss to her forehead while inhaling the fragrance of her soft, curling hair.

"I'm ready." Her voice had dropped an octave. A sensual smile curved her lush mouth as she closed the door and locked it behind her.

Scott hadn't missed the mysterious glow in her brilliant eyes. Offering his arm, he led her slowly down the staircase and out to the street and his car. He opened the door, helped her in, then rounded the automobile and took his seat behind the wheel. A foreign emotion of utter fulfillment welled up in his chest. His sister had asked him who was his type, and he could now answer honestly that Leigh Walcott was his type.

He had not begun to recognize his own needs until he met her. He had never been able to offer a woman all of himself before. Now he was ready to open himself up to receive what little Leigh was willing to relinquish. And he would willingly accept friendship—if that was all she was offering.

6

Leigh found herself talking incessantly during the drive to McLean. She did not know whether it was because she was anxious or she just had a lot to tell Scott. He was silent, nodding in agreement as she delineated the details of his colleague's party.

Once they entered the town limits for McLean, he slowed the car and smiled at her. "You've been very busy."

She shared his smile. "Very busy for someone who's on vacation."

"You're on vacation, too?"

"Just for the week. This is the first week in months that I haven't had anything scheduled."

Scott maneuvered onto the local road that led to his property. "When's your next event?"

"Sunday."

He calculated quickly. Three days. If somehow he could see her every day for the next three days then he would consider himself an extremely lucky man.

"I'm free for the next three and a half weeks," he informed her.

"Lucky you."

"I'm lucky if I take all of it."

A slight frown creased her smooth forehead. "Why shouldn't you?"

"I usually cut my vacations short and go back to work

before my scheduled time to return. I've accrued so many days that the human resources department has threatened that I'm going to lose them if I don't take vacation leave."

Turning her head, she stared out the passenger-side window. "You know what people say about folks who can't stay away from their jobs?"

"Yeah, I know," he drawled. " 'Get a life.' "

"Do you have one outside the hospital, Scott?"

He steered the Mercedes sedan into the driveway in front of an attached carriage house, put the car in park, and turned off the engine. Unbuckling his seat belt, he turned and stared at Leigh's averted profile.

"No, I don't," he admitted after a long silence.

Shifting, she turned and stared back at him. "Why not?"

Closing his eyes, he shrugged a broad shoulder. "I don't know," he stated in a hoarse tone.

Leigh did not know how, but she felt his emptiness, his uncertainty. It was what she had felt when she woke up in the hospital to discover she had lost her husband and infant son. She had felt as if something had cut her heart out, leaving her hollow, unfeeling, and without hope.

Reaching up, her right hand grazed his smooth-shaven jaw. "Was it painful losing her?"

Scott opened his eyes, his fingers curling around her delicate wrist, holding her captive. Moving closer, he felt the moist warmth of her breath whisper over his lips.

"It wasn't a her, Leigh, because I've never been able to love a woman."

Her gaze widened with his confession. "But why?"

"Because I've allowed medicine to become an obsessive, jealous mistress. From the first time my father bought me a microscope I was hooked. I ate, slept, walked, and talked anything that resembled science. It wasn't until my second year in college that I decided I wanted to be a doctor. The first day I entered medical school I was addicted."

"But . . . but didn't you see women?"

"Only when it was convenient."

Her gaze widened. "Oh, I see." And she did see. He probably sought out a woman when he needed a physical release.

"I've never used a woman, Leigh." Unknowingly he had read her mind. "At least not the way you think."

"What am I thinking, Scott?"

"That I've used women for sex."

"Well, haven't you?"

His lids lowered over his penetrating eyes, concealing his innermost feelings from her. "No. Whenever I shared a woman's bed it was always mutual."

She nodded at the same time a smile softened her mouth. "I respect your honesty."

"What about you, Leigh?"

"What about me?"

"Are you willing to be honest with me?" He brought her hand to his lips, pressing his mouth to her inner wrist.

It was her turn to shutter her gaze as her breath quickened. The brush of the hair over his upper lip on her sensitive flesh elicited a delicate trembling she was helpless to control. She was certain he felt her pulse fluttering against his lips.

"What do you want to know?"

"How old were you when you were widowed?"

Squeezing her eyes tightly, Leigh leaned forward, her forehead resting on Scott's hard shoulder. He lifted her effortlessly over the gearshift until she sat on his thigh.

"Twenty-three," she whispered, registering his slight intake of breath. "We were returning home after sharing Christmas dinner with my mother and stepfather when a drunk driver lost control of his car and crossed the median. He hit my car head-on, killing himself, my husband, and our six-month-old son instantly. I woke up a week later in a hospital with the news that I had lost my family."

"I'm sorry, Leigh. I'm so sorry," Scott whispered over and over.

She snuggled closer to his comforting warmth. "I left the hospital after three weeks with a face I did not recognize as my own. A team of plastic surgeons had to reconstruct my jaw, chin, and give me a new nose. So, this face is not the one I was born with."

Now he understood her reaction when he'd called her beautiful. "Even though I find you incredibly beautiful, it's not the outward beauty that's most important."

"It's the only thing that's visible."

"No, it's not, Leigh. I see a woman who's artistic and also quite talented. You're hardworking, independent, dependable, and ambitious. The doctors may have changed your face, but they could not change your smile. I love your smile, Sunshine. It's warm, mesmerizing, and it lights up your entire face."

Pulling back, she smiled up at him. "You see a lot, Dr. Alexander."

He arched his eyebrows. "What do you see, Ms. Walcott?"

Her smile slipped away. "I see a man, a very brilliant doctor who has distinguished himself as chief of the Trauma Unit in the nation's capital's busiest municipal hospital. But I also see a man who is pursuing me with the craftiness of a fox."

He nodded. "Go on."

"But what you don't realize is that I've been my own person too long to let myself be taken in by your charm."

"You think I'm trying to charm you?"

"Yes." The single word was emphatic.

Scott shook his head slowly. "It has nothing to do with charm or craftiness. I like you—any- and everything I've seen about you. It's just that simple."

"You liking me is not going to prove anything."

"Let me be the judge of that," he insisted.

"I can't promise you anything."

"Did I ask you to?" His fingers splayed over her delicate jaw as he lowered his head. "Why don't you let everything unfold naturally?"

Leigh wasn't given the opportunity to come back at him when he brushed his mouth over hers. He tasted her mouth in soft sampling kisses, testing her response. When he felt her press closer, he increased the pressure on her mouth until her lips parted, allowing him full access to the passion she'd buried along with her late husband. He teased her mouth, pulling back whenever he felt her retreat. He began at one corner, placing light kisses around her moist, parted lips until she swallowed back a groan.

Leigh felt as if her mouth were on fire. The slow, drugging touch of Scott's kisses left her mouth throbbing with heat and delicious sensations she had not thought possible. He devoured her mouth, then pulled back until his lips' touch became a mere whisper. Never had she been kissed like this.

Closing her eyes, she melted into the strength of the man holding her to his heart. She felt everything that was Scott Alexander, the unyielding strength in his upper body, the power in his arms and hands, the hypnotic scent of his cologne merging with the natural scent of his masculine flesh, and the surging, probing hardness under her bottom. His heat swept to her, bringing with it a heaviness in her breasts that spread downward to the secret, hidden place at the junction of her thighs.

Her eyes opened and she stiffened. Scott had aroused her in the same manner that she had aroused him. "No," she moaned against his marauding mouth. "Please stop."

Scott heard her plea through a haze of passion that threatened to devour the whole of him. And he would welcome it just to experience what it would be like to lie with Leigh Walcott.

Burying his face between her scented neck and shoulder, he groaned softly. "I'm sorry, Leigh. I can't believe that I've waited to get to fifty-five to make out in a car like a randy teenage boy."

Lowering her head, she laughed softly. "It would not have been possible if your fifty-three-year-old companion wasn't so amenable."

He raised his head and stared at her flushed face. "You're not angry with me?"

She wagged her head slowly. "No."

His features softened in a sensuous smile. "Good." The warmth of his smile echoed in his voice. Pulling away, he winked at her. "Don't move. I'll help you out."

Leigh sat half-on, half-off the driver's seat when Scott pushed open the door and stepped out. He extended a hand and pulled her gently out of the car and to her feet. There was a mysterious gleam in his eyes as his gaze swept over a powder blue cotton/silk blend twinset worn over a pair of khakis. She had replaced her ballet slippers with soft navy-blue leather tie-up shoes whose tops covered her ankles.

She covered her eyes with a hand to shield them from the bright sun and glanced around her. She could not believe the quiet magnificence of the farmhouse and the surrounding verdant landscape unfolding before it like a plush green carpet.

"It's perfect," she whispered softly. Scott moved behind her, his chest molded to her back, and curved an arm around her waist. Shivering slightly, she welcomed his warmth and strength. "How long have you lived here?"

"Four days," he said close to her ear.

Glancing back over her shoulder, she frowned slightly. "You just moved here?"

"I bought the property a couple of years ago. It's taken that long to renovate it to its original specifications."

"Where did you live before?"

"I still have an apartment in Georgetown. I plan to use this as a permanent residence once I retire."

She gave him a skeptical look. "Aren't you too young to retire?"

"Technically I can retire at fifty-five with an excellent benefit package. However, I'm going to wait another five years. What I want to do is set up a family practice."

"Here?"

"No. I'm thinking of something closer to town. I've always wanted to be a small-town country doctor." Dropping his arm, he grasped her hand. "Come into the house and I'll show you around."

She followed him up several steps to the structure with massive columns supporting a wraparound porch. He opened the front door, and the panorama unfolding before her gaze rendered her speechless. It claimed refinished wood floors, a curving staircase, towering ceilings, elaborate moldings, and a first level with floor-to-ceiling mullioned windows. French doors, fireplaces, and walls of terra-cotta red, sunflower yellow, sky blue, and emerald green set the stage for a residence with living, dining, and entertaining elegance.

Of all of the rooms in the house, it was the kitchen, with a massive cast-iron stove taking up an entire wall, that held her completely enthralled. The three remaining walls were lined with new red bricks.

"What a wonderful place to prepare a Thanksgiving or Christmas dinner," she mused aloud.

Crossing his arms over his chest, Scott tilted his head, staring at her enraptured expression. "Will it do for your caterer?"

Shifting, she smiled at him. "It will more than do. I'm going to love putting your mother's birthday celebration together here."

"Do you want to hold it indoors?"

"I prefer out-of-doors. But that will depend upon the weather." Excitement had fired her golden eyes.

"I still haven't completed decorating some of the rooms, so if you plan to hold it indoors, then let me know what you'll need."

"Don't rush," she reassured him. "It's better to entertain with less than more. I've seen disastrous results when guests spilled a drink or food on antique pieces or family heirlooms."

He realized Leigh was right. He had purchased furnishings for his bedroom, living room, and kitchen. The table, chairs, breakfront, and buffet server for the dining room were on order, and he expected delivery by the middle of July. He had furnished one guest bedroom, leaving the other two empty. It had taken two years to make the house habitable, and he realized it would probably take another two before he completed decorating the entire structure.

Scott glanced down at his watch. It was nearly five o'clock. "What do you say we discuss everything over dinner?"

"OK." Leigh was quick to agree. She'd only eaten half a grapefruit and a bowl of oatmeal earlier that morning.

"Why don't you sit on the porch and put your foot up while I throw a little something together?" he suggested.

"Do you need help?"

He gave her a gentle smile. "You can help me the next time."

She arched her eyebrows but did not say anything. It was apparent he expected a next time. Making her way slowly out of the house to the front porch, she sat down on a cushioned chaise and stared out at a swath of green surrounding the meticulously restored early-twentieth-century farmhouse.

Scott had confessed that he liked her, and she had been too much of a coward to reveal her own feelings. She did like Scott Alexander—liked him a little too much.

What was there not to like? He was handsome, brilliant, compassionate, generous, and hardworking. But he also knew exactly where his life was going. He had planned to retire from the hospital and set up a family practice, while she wasn't certain whether she wanted to live in Washington, D.C., for the rest of her life. And there were times when she thought about giving up her business to return to working at a hotel as a banquet manager.

After losing Leonard and Justin, she had spent three years in therapy, trying to make sense of her existence. She had questioned why she had survived while they'd died. There were many times when she blamed herself because she had been the one driving. Leonard had drunk several glasses of wine with dinner, and because she was still breast-feeding she had not consumed anything alcoholic. Therefore, she had become the designated driver and the only survivor.

It took many more years before she convinced herself that she had done nothing wrong, that it was the other driver's fault. She had become such an emotional wreck that she permitted her parents to talk her into giving up her apartment to live with them. Even though she had been a wife and mother, she found herself a child for the second time in her life. Her older brother tried matching her up with a few of his single friends, but she rejected the men as soon as they were introduced. Then it became her sister's turn. What Robert Mason and Anna Mason-Reynolds refused to acknowledge was that their sister's fear of loving and losing overrode their best intentions to see her married again.

She returned to college at thirty and earned a degree in hotel and restaurant management. She spent the next ten years working in four-star New York City restaurants and hotels. The experience served her well once she decided to set up her own business. Then she relocated to Washington, D.C., to work as a banquet manager for a prestigious hotel chain. Her professional manner caught the attention of many of the guests who attended the social events at the hotel, and several asked her whether she would coordinate private parties for them.

She was reluctant to accept their proposals but rethought her options after she planned a dinner party for a foreign diplomat and his wife. One client quickly multiplied into more than half a dozen until she tendered her resignation and concentrated on establishing her own business. Now, after ten years, Walcott Planners, Inc., had become a successful, thriving enterprise.

She had become a success in all areas of her life except the private component. Men were attracted to her—the face she was given—but she had become an expert in keeping them at a distance. Every man except for Scott Alexander. And the doctor pursued and continued to pursue her with the same energy he afforded his profession—with an unyielding, controlling passion.

Closing her eyes, she smiled a soft, gentle smile. Maybe—just perhaps—she would lower her guard just once. Low enough to let herself succumb to the renewal of desire that had kept her from a restful night's sleep since she had met Scott Alexander.

7

Leigh hadn't realized she had drifted off to sleep until she felt someone shaking her gently. She recognized the soft, drawling southern cadence before she opened her eyes.

"Wake up, sleepyhead."

Her heavily lashed lids fluttered as she tried focusing on the face only inches from her own. "Scott?" She was still disoriented.

"It's time to eat, Sunshine."

A lazy smile parted her lips. "I'm sorry I fell asleep."

"Don't be. You probably were exhausted." Bending down, he gathered her up from the chair as if she were a small child. Her arms curved around his neck, and she laid her head on his shoulder. "How's the ankle?"

"Better," she slurred.

"I'll look at it later."

"Thanks." Her voice was still heavy with sleep.

Scott carried her into the house and through a narrow hallway that led to the back porch. The sun was setting and shadows had blanketed the surrounding landscape in mesmerizing shades of gold, green, and gray. He had taken his breakfast on the screened-in porch earlier that morning, watching pinpoints of light crisscross the sky. It was then that he decided he would put in an illuminated water garden filled with fish and lilies. He also planned to extend the garden to include hedges, fields of wildflowers, and herbs and put in hundreds of night-blooming flowers and fragrant white blossoms for a moonlight garden.

He had thought that buying the farmhouse and the surrounding property was the best decision he had made in years because it allowed him an alternative to spending all of his free time at the hospital, but that was before he met Leigh Walcott. Now, she was the best thing to touch his life—even better than medicine.

* * *

Leigh shared a leisurely dinner with Scott with lighted candles and softly playing smooth jazz as the backdrop for what had become a relaxed and laugh-filled interlude. She outlined what she had planned for his mother's birthday party. Seeing the excitement in his dark eyes at her suggestions filled her with the confidence that whispered to her that she would not and could not give up her business to return to working for a hotel chain. The menu and entertainment would be varied, keeping in mind that children would also be attending the celebration of a woman who had recently become a great-grandmother for the fourth time.

They dispensed with business when the conversation veered to their families. She revealed that she was the middle child in a family where her parents were divorced the year she turned ten. Her mother had remarried three years later. Her older brother, Robert Mason, was a practicing defense attorney for the New York City Bronx County Court, while her younger sister, Anna Mason-Reynolds, taught African-American history at a New York college. Leigh's brother and sister each claimed two children, making her an aunt to three nephews and one niece.

Scott disclosed that he was one of four children, and the only boy, born to George and Irene Alexander. George had been an educator all his life. He began teaching in a one-room schoolhouse in what had been segregated Washington, D.C., before he returned to Howard University and enrolled in their law school to earn his law degree. He eventually taught constitutional law at his alma mater for more than twenty-seven years before he passed away at the age of seventy-eight.

There was a comfortable silence, with only the sound of music coming from the concealed stereo speakers, before Scott's voice floated up in the solitude of the warm spring air.

"Why didn't you remarry and have more children, Leigh?"

She went completely still, her gaze fixed on the flickering

candles on a nearby table. He was asking her a question so many had voiced in the past. In fact, it was a question her mother continued to ask her.

"I haven't . . ." she began, searching for the right words. "I haven't found the right man."

Placing an elbow on the table, Scott rested his chin on his fist. "What would constitute the right man?"

"I don't know," she replied honestly. "There was a time when I told myself that he would have to have all of the formulaic qualities: be attractive, educated, solvent, in good health, moral, and sensitive. All of the things people put in the personals when they're looking for a companion or a significant other."

"And now?"

"Now it doesn't matter. I'm fifty-three, and definitely not planning on having another child."

"I'm certain there are a lot men who are—"

"Don't say it, Scott," she interrupted angrily. "Please don't," she continued, her voice softening. She placed her napkin beside her plate. "I think it's time I left. I want to begin printing up the invitations tonight."

Scott nodded, forcing a smile. He rose to his feet, circled the table, and pulled back her chair. He was disappointed that she wanted to return home, but he had to consider himself fortunate enough to have spent as much time as he had with her.

"Come inside with me. I want to take a look at your ankle."

Leigh leaned heavily against Scott's side as she made her way slowly up the staircase to her apartment. She could not remember when she had enjoyed the company of a man as she had his. In fact, the only man's company she had ever enjoyed was her late husband's—and that had been more than thirty years ago.

She put her key in the lock and pushed open the door. Turning, she smiled up at Scott. "Thank you for a wonderful day."

He nodded, smiling. "Thank you for your company." He took a step, his hands slipping up her arms and bringing her closer. "Have you made plans for Friday night?"

"No, I haven't. Why?"

"I'd like to take you to Leo's for dinner. There will be a band performing on Friday that is a favorite of mine."

He was asking her out, and she wanted to refuse but didn't. "I'd like that very much."

Scott lowered his head. "And I like you very much."

Leigh's mind told her to resist Scott Alexander, but her body refused to listen as she pressed her breasts to his chest at the same time her arms curved around his waist. She melted into his embrace, committing his scent to memory, the comforting crush of his solid strength. Despite the fact that he was a middle-aged man his body had not gone soft. His belly was still flat, and there was no evidence of excess flesh around his waist. He wore his clothes well and appeared to be in peak condition.

And in that instant she wondered what he would look like without his clothes. A tremor of arousal shook her as she swallowed back a moan.

Scott's hands moved up and cradled her face between his palms. He stared down at her, his gaze moving slowly over the delicate bones that made up her exquisite face. She had closed her eyes, and a thick fringe of lashes lay on her high cheekbones. He stared at her moist parted lips seconds before his mouth covered hers hungrily. He moved his mouth over hers, devouring its softness. Kissing her mouth was not enough. What he wanted to do was kiss her—everywhere. There was not an inch of her sweet flesh that he did not want to taste. The blood roared in his head and pooled in his groin as he felt his control slipping away.

Leigh was on fire—everywhere. Scott's kiss was an inferno, setting her aflame and making her blood boil in her veins. She had to stop—make him stop—or she would invite him into her apartment and into her bed.

It took Herculean strength for her to push him away. "Good night, Scott." She did not even recognize her own voice as she turned, stepped into the entryway, and closed the door behind her.

"I'll pick you up at eight," he said through the barrier separating them.

She leaned against the door, unable to see the rising passion in Scott's face as he pressed his forehead to the door while at the same time he struggled to bring his volatile emotions under control. As she placed a hand on the solid surface, her fingers curled into a fist while she breathed in and out through her open mouth. She lost track of time as she stood in the same spot waiting for her respiration to return to a normal rate and for the soft pulsing between her thighs to subside. And when it finally did, she limped slowly to her bedroom and lay across her bed, fully clothed, to relive the feelings Scott Alexander had aroused in her just being who he was.

Leigh woke up early Friday morning, completed her morning ablution, then headed for her office. She had designed the invitations for Mark Franklin's party on her computer the day before. She had hand-printed the names Scott had given her on pale green envelopes with dark green ink for Dr. Franklin's guests in the Chancery italic hand calligraphy. If she had had enough time she would have hand-lettered the entire invitation.

Hand-lettering Scott's mother's invitations and envelopes would take her several weeks to complete. He and his sister had compiled a listing of more than sixty names.

She opened the doors to a tall, narrow oak cabinet with shelves filled with vellum and parchment paper in an assortment of colors ranging from blues and grays to the palest ivory. Matching envelopes in varying sizes were stacked in bins of pullout drawers.

She selected a pale ivory shade with matching response cards and envelopes. Sitting down at a drafting table, she turned on a lamp, adjusted the angle, and opened a wooden box containing her pens, nibs, and ink. It was late morning when she stopped briefly to eat brunch, then returned to the task of trying to complete as many invitations as she could before she readied herself for her dinner engagement with Scott.

The sky had darkened with angry rain clouds when Leigh stepped into her bathtub filled with warm scented bubbles. She had sat at the drafting table so long that her lower back muscles were aching. But her persistence had paid off. She had completed a dozen invitations and response cards. The task was long, tedious, and expensive, but Irene Alexander's guests would probably keep the invitations as souvenirs long after they stopped talking about her eightieth birthday gala.

Raising her right foot, Leigh stared at her ankle. Most of the swelling had disappeared, even though she still could not move quickly or put too much pressure on the foot. She had sat on the floor in front of her closet trying on shoes that would be appropriate for the dress she had selected. It was a black long-sleeved sheath in a stretch knit that ended just at her knees. When she had tried it on she whispered a prayer of thanks that it still fit her. She was a perfect size 6. The garment usually called for a high-heel shoe, but she had chosen a black patent-leather pair with low stack heels.

Glancing at the clock on the counter, she picked up a bath sponge and began washing her body. She allowed herself extra time to moisturize her body with her favorite body cream and perfume. And when Scott rang her doorbell at exactly eight o'clock, she had removed the pins from her doobie hairdo, styling the shiny silver strands until they framed the delicate bones of her face, and had artfully applied a cover of makeup to highlight her best features.

She pressed the button for the intercom. "Yes?"

"Scott," came a firm male voice through the small, round speaker.

Pressing another button on the wall, she disengaged the lock on the downstairs door. She left her apartment door open and retreated to her office to retrieve the invitations for Dr. Franklin's party. She had wrapped them in clear cellophane and secured the bundle with a dark green satin ribbon.

Scott left his wet umbrella outside the door, then wiped his damp feet on the mat before he stepped into the entry. His eyes widened in appreciation with Leigh's approach. It was the first time he had seen the outline of her body. The clinging fabric revealed every curve, every dip, of her petite frame. His gaze dropped to her shapely legs encased in sheer black hose. She was perfect. A perfect little package of unabashed feminine sensuality!

Even her hair was different. It was parted off-center and feathered to frame her face. He did not know which he liked better—the curls or the slick sophisticated style that curved around the nape of her neck and under her chin.

Leigh felt her pulse racing when she surveyed Scott in an expertly tailored pin-striped charcoal gray suit. There was no doubt that it had been made to fit his wide shoulders, long legs, and slim waist. A patterned tie in geometric shapes of gray, black, and white lay against the background of a stark white shirt with French cuffs. His cuff links were oval mosaics of onyx and mother-of-pearl ringed in yellow gold.

Her vermilion-colored mouth curved upward in a smile. "You look very nice, Dr. Alexander."

He bowed from the waist. "Thank you, Ms. Walcott. And may I say you're looking exceptionally beautiful tonight?"

She blushed to the roots of her hair. "Thank you." She handed him the colorful package. "Your invitations for Mark Franklin's party."

He took the bundle, staring at the hand-printed names. "Calligraphy?"

Picking up her cashmere shawl from the table, she draped it over one arm. "You're paying top dollar, so you should expect the best."

Curving an arm around her tiny waist, he kissed the top of her head. "You're an incredible woman, Leigh Walcott."

"You'll change your tune when you get my bill next week."

He shook his head. "I don't think so, Sunshine. You are worth every penny and more."

Scott waited for Leigh to lock up her apartment; then he

picked up his umbrella and escorted her down the stairs, holding it over her head as he helped her into his car.

The rain came down in torrents, making driving hazardous. Scott had switched on the fastest speed of the wipers and slowed down to less than ten miles an hour. What should have been a ten-minute trip to Leo's took twice as long. He maneuvered in front of the restaurant and waited for the valet to escort Leigh into the waiting area. Scott then gave his keys to the young man carrying an oversize umbrella and sprinted the few feet to the entrance.

Noah Hardcastle was in the waiting area, greeting his patrons. He recognized Leigh and walked over to kiss her cheek.

"What brings you out tonight?"

"I'm with Scott Alexander."

Noah's dark gaze swept around the room, lingering on Dr. Scott Alexander. It was the second time within a week that Leigh had come to Leo's with the doctor.

"Good luck," Noah whispered close to her ear. He had seen Scott Alexander bring women into his family-owned restaurant in the past, but never the same woman twice. It was apparent that the brilliant doctor was quite taken with the pretty widowed party planner.

Noah had to admit to himself that if Scott was pursuing Leigh, then he had excellent taste in women. There had been a time when Noah had been interested in her, but she had deftly sidestepped any and all of his offers for a non-professional liaison, claiming she was too old for him. He managed to salvage what was left of his tattered male pride and thanked her for her honesty. One thing he was grateful for was that she hadn't said he was too young for her. He would turn thirty-eight his next birthday, and two years after that he would be middle-aged. Twenty was young, not forty.

Scott moved into the crowded area and again felt a rush of jealousy when he saw Leigh with Noah Hardcastle. He forced a polite smile while curving his left arm around Leigh's waist. "Good evening. I have a reservation for eight-thirty."

Noah returned the smile. "Good evening." He glanced at the printout of the day's reservations taped to the podium separating the waiting area from the dining room floor. "Your table is ready." He signaled the hostess to show them to their table.

Leigh felt the bite of Scott's fingers tightening along her rib cage. "Scott! You're holding me too tight." Her voice was a hoarse whisper.

He loosened his grip and let out his breath in an audible sigh. "I'm sorry, darling."

She noted the direction of his gaze and then the twitching muscle in his lean jaw. Her gaze shifted from Scott to Noah Hardcastle, then back to Scott. Moving closer, she placed her right hand over his jacket lapel.

She waited until they were shown to their table and she was seated opposite him to say, "There's nothing going on between us. Never has or will."

The stiffness left Scott's body. He stared at her, smiling. And with her admission he felt an indefinable sensation of quiet assurance settle into his being. He'd tried denying his emotions, but they had persisted until he had to acknowledge that he was falling in love with Leigh Walcott. He hadn't known her a week, yet he wanted to spend all of his time with her.

8

Scott had secured his favorite table, and he and Leigh were permitted an unobstructed view of the stage where a sextet played backup for a talented female vocalist.

A spotlight highlighted the singer's dark, smooth face and curvaceous body encased in white satin. Her singing repertoire included Lena Horne, Sarah Vaughan, and an incredibly soundalike Billie Holiday.

Leigh watched Scott's face as he nodded his head, keeping in tempo with the music. The band, comprised of a bassist, saxophonist, percussionist, trumpeter, guitarist, and keyboard player, was excellent. They segued into more popular upbeat smooth jazz selections that she'd heard the afternoon she spent with Scott in McLean.

The vocalist ended a number amid a vigorous round of polite applause; she paused to take a sip of water, then returned to the microphone. "I want to thank all of you for coming out to Leo's on such an incredibly wet night. But I suppose good food and music can make one do crazy things." There was another smattering of applause. "I'd like to try out a few new numbers tonight. Me and the band had the incredible pleasure of touring with another band who we feel is awesome. They surprised us when they played a few of our more popular selections, and we'd like to do the same here tonight. Hiroshima, wherever you are tonight—these are for you."

There was a suffocating hush as the keyboard player's synthesizer simulated the distinctive sound of Japanese strings with "Ripples in Our Waterfall." The percussionist and bassist backed the singer up with the chorus, and soon every head in Leo's bobbed in rhythm to the seductive song.

When they segued into a more upbeat "I Love How You Love Me" Leigh felt the heat of Scott's penetrating gaze on her face. She was pulled into the force field of his dark, burning eyes, and she didn't know how she could, but she felt what he was feeling. Closing her eyes, she shook her head. *It couldn't be happening,* she thought. She didn't want to feel anything for him—especially not love. She wanted to like him, but she could not afford to feel anything deeper than that.

She picked up her goblet and took a sip of cool water to bathe her constricted throat. She had made it through thirty years without a man in her life, while within the span of one week one man had scaled the walls she had erected to keep out all men who had expressed an interest in her.

Dr. Scott Alexander had made her aware of herself—as a female. She now experienced a renewal of desire—something she had denied for many, many years. And now, sitting across a small table in Leo's, listening to the sensual words of love flowing from a woman's mouth had her identifying with the chanteuse. If she permitted Scott into her life would she also echo, "I love how you love me"? If she slept with him, would he want more?

Could she afford to take the chance? After all, he was fifty-five and had never married, and she doubted whether he'd want to give up his bachelor status now. Reaching across the table, she placed her hand over his. They shared a smile—a secret smile reserved for lovers.

Scott watched the flickering light from the oil candle throw shadows over Leigh's golden brown face. His gaze lingered on the shape of her sensual mouth, a mouth he had sampled, a mouth he could never get enough of. His gaze moved downward to the soft swell of breasts under the revealing black dress, and he felt a stirring of desire. He was only two years older than Leigh, but there were times when he felt she was much younger than fifty-three, and he knew it had nothing to do with life experience. His life had been uneventful compared to hers, but what he suspected was that she was sexually inexperienced. He doubted whether she had had more than two lovers in her life.

The band ended their number and took a break while everyone, including restaurant staff, applauded and whistled in appreciation.

"They're fabulous," Leigh remarked, her eyes shining with excitement.

Scott nodded. "I saw them once when I was out on the West Coast, and I couldn't believe my eyes when Tyrone booked them for Leo's."

"Did I hear someone mention my name?"

Scott and Leigh glanced up to find Tyrone Hardcastle standing beside their table. He was the image of his identical twin brother, except that he wore his hair in twists that fell to his shoulders. Juilliard-educated Tyrone was responsible for the supper club's musical program.

Scott released Leigh's hand, stood up, and offered his right hand to Tyrone. "It's been a while, Roni."

"I've been doing a little traveling. I love Leo's, but I have to keep my fingers on the pulse of the music industry." He smiled down at Leigh. "Hello, beautiful. How are you?"

"I'm wonderful, thank you. I've missed you."

Tyrone placed his hands over his chest. "Don't play with my heart, Leigh. It can't take another rejection from you."

"Player," she whispered good-naturedly.

Leaning down, Tyrone kissed her cheek. "Stay well." He straightened. "I'm going to let you two enjoy your dinner, because as you know, we always want you to come back to Leo's."

Scott patted the younger man on the shoulder, then retook his seat. He gave Leigh a teasing grin. "The Hardcastle men really have a *thing* for you."

"Jealous, *darling?*"

His grin faded and he stared at her until she dropped her gaze. "Yes, I am. Quite jealous."

She looked at him again, her lips curving into a beguiling smile. "Good."

His eyebrows shot up. "Good?" She nodded slowly. Vertical lines appeared between his eyes. "I'm not into playing head games, Leigh."

She recognized his veiled warning. "Then that makes two of us."

"Point taken, Sunshine."

Both had acknowledged that their interest in each other went beyond a working relationship. Where it was going neither would be willing to predict. However, they were mature and patient enough to let it unfold naturally.

Leigh could not remember when she had enjoyed a more relaxing evening. The chefs at Leo's had outdone their usual culinary mastery with a succulent offering of black-eyed pea soup with smoked turkey, pan-seared tuna prepared in a coconut curry sauce, a grilled vegetable medley, and an endless assortment of desserts served in sauces and custards.

She placed her hand over her wineglass when Scott lifted the bottle to refill it. "No more, please."

He put down the bottle. "Do you want any more dessert?"

"Where would I put it?"

Scott tilted his head. "I believe you have a little room just behind your ear," he teased.

"I don't think so. Even that space is filled." She had had her fill of music, wine, and food. "I'm ready to leave whenever you are," she stated, successfully smothering a yawn.

Reaching into the breast pocket of his jacket, Scott withdrew his credit card case. "Do you have anything planned for tomorrow?"

"No. Why?" Tomorrow would be her last free Saturday for several months.

His head came up and he gave her a direct stare. "I'd like you to spend the night with me in McLean. We'll sleep in late; then I'll prepare brunch. After that I'll give you a tour of the property. I want to show you where I want to put in a water garden."

Leigh shook her head, her hair swaying gently with the gesture. "No, Scott. I can't."

"You'll have your own bedroom," he said quickly, hoping to allay her suspicions that he wanted to seduce her.

"I have to work on your mother's invitations."

"One day, Leigh. I'm only asking for one day."

She heard his plea, unaware of what it took for a man as proud as Scott Alexander to beg a woman for her companionship. She wanted to say yes, but as it was things were moving too quickly.

"I'm sorry, Scott. Perhaps another time."

He hid his disappointment well as he settled the bill, leaving a more than generous tip for the waiter. The rain had slackened considerably by the time the valet brought Scott's car around to the front of Leo's. He assisted Leigh into the Mercedes, humming to himself as he slipped behind the wheel. He hadn't realized he was humming "I Love How You Love Me" until he escorted her up the staircase to her apartment.

"I'll call you," she said softly.

Scott forced a smile. "Thank you for a lovely evening." Bending down, he kissed her cheek.

Leigh stood in the doorway, watching him descend the stairs. She waved at him, whispering good night, but this time he did not turn around or acknowledge her. She did not know why, but she felt as if they had silently said good-bye for the last time.

Closing the door, she locked it, then sat down on the bench, her hands folded on her lap. She sat for a long time, trying to comprehend who she was and why Scott Alexander had come into her life. Why had she permitted him in when she had kept every other man out?

The questions nagged at her until she finally rose to her feet and made her way to her bedroom. However, sleep was not the balm she sought, because she tossed restlessly, her mind filled with erotic dreams that left her trembling and moaning in frustration. The rain had stopped and the sky had brightened with the promise of a new day when she finally succumbed to the exhaustion where the image of Scott faded enough to offer several precious hours of peace.

Leigh called Scott several times over the next two weeks, but not to commit to coming to McLean to spend the night at his house. Their conversations were cordial when they discussed the upcoming party at Leo's for Mark Franklin or the update for his mother's birthday celebration. It was only when Leigh attempted to end the call that she felt his silent energy through the wire. She knew he was waiting and willing—willing for her to come to him. But she couldn't—not yet.

Leigh walked into the office at Leo's at three o'clock the afternoon of Dr. Mark Franklin's party and was surprised to find that Scott had arrived only minutes before. Rising slowly to his feet, he stared at her as if she were a complete stranger.

It had been two weeks since they had seen each other, and each noticed changes in the other that hadn't been apparent the last time they were together.

She saw the gauntness in his face that indicated that he had lost weight, and he noticed that she wore a pair of shoes with a medium heel—not quite three inches. Not high enough for them to go out dancing.

Leigh offered him a sensual smile, her heart pounding wildly against her ribs. "Hello, Scott."

He inclined his head. "Leigh."

Noah looked at the older couple, then stood up. "I'll be right back." Neither glanced at him when he walked out of the office, closing the door behind him.

She ran her tongue over her lower lip, drawing Scott's gaze to the motion. "The flowers and balloons will be delivered at four," she began in a hushed tone. "Did you see the sports memorabilia? I hope—"

"Stop it, Leigh," Scott interrupted softly. "You don't have to rattle on about what you've told me before."

She felt heat flare in her face. "You don't have to be rude, Dr. Alexander."

He took a half-dozen steps and stood inches from her. He had almost forgotten how lovely she was, forgotten how good she smelled. A smile eased the hardness in his jaw. "I'm sorry," he whispered. "Forgive me."

Closing her eyes, Leigh shook her head. "There's nothing to forgive, Scott."

Opening her eyes, she took in everything about the man who haunted not only her nights but also her days. And seeing him again reminded her that she could not ignore the truth any longer. It had only taken three weeks, but she had fallen in love with Scott Alexander. Not the doctor who had taken care of her injured ankle, but the man who reminded her that she was a woman—a very lonely woman who still desired a man.

His dark gaze moved leisurely over her face, taking in the coiffed hair framing her face, the white silk blouse under a tailored black suit, and the sheer black hose and plain leather pumps.

Pushing his hands into the pockets of his suit trousers, he angled his head. "How's the ankle?"

She glanced down at her feet. "I'm able to wear a three-inch heel."

A slight smile touched his mouth. "Does that mean you're ready to go dancing?"

Tilting her chin, she offered him a sensual smile. "Am I still your patient, Dr. Alexander?"

"Didn't I formally discharge you?"

"No."

His smile matched hers. "Then I'll be certain to do that."

"When?"

"Whenever it's convenient for me to examine you. You'll have to let me know when you're available."

Panic rioted in her when she realized she wanted to see Scott again, and not as his patient nor him as her client. "I'm available tonight," she stated in a firm voice that masked her apprehension.

Scott crossed his arms over the front of his crisp white shirt. "At what time?"

"After the party," she replied quickly before she lost her nerve. "I'll meet you in McLean." Turning on her heels, she walked out of the office.

Scott was still standing in the same spot, an expression of complete surprise freezing his features, when Noah returned to the office.

9

Scott managed to make it through the evening's festivities without making a complete fool of himself. Leigh's offer to come to McLean had shocked him. He had not seen her for two weeks; then she had consented not only to seeing him again but also to spending the night under his roof.

His astonishment continued with the elegance of the farewell party she had put together for his young protégé. Mark Franklin had graduated at the top of his class at Meharry Medical College, selecting ophthalmologic surgery as a specialty. Mark had sought him out after he felt the chief of ophthalmology had placed undue pressure on him during a surgical procedure.

Scott shared his own experiences of being the only African-American doctor at a veterans' hospital in the Midwest with Mark and encouraged the brilliant surgeon not to let anything or anyone set his limits. After their first meeting they had established a habit of meeting once a week for dinner, where Scott had unknowingly become his mentor.

The setting in the private room at Leo's was intimate and elegant. Small baskets of flowers served as the centerpieces for each table along with colored oil candles. The pianist Tyrone Hardcastle had hired for the evening claimed a repertoire of selections from familiar classical compositions to popular contemporary tunes. The highlight of the evening was the large wicker baskets filled with memorabilia representing every major New York sports team. Mark made a tearful speech, thanking everyone in attendance for their unwavering support during his tenure at the hospital. The bookish-looking surgeon summed up his speech by thanking Dr. Scott Alexander for their weekly chats. All eyes were fixed on the chief of the Trauma Unit when Mark stated that Scott had become not only his mentor but also someone who had counseled him like a father. All knew that Mark had lost his father to complications of diabetes, which had resulted in the older Franklin losing his sight and both legs first.

Scott had sat at a table with his personal secretary, his expression impassive. Thirty-four-year-old Dr. Mark Franklin had reminded him that he was old enough to be his father, and although it never bothered him that he had not fathered a child, Mark had subtly reminded him that he had become a father—a surrogate father. His own gaze was trained on Leigh as she stood in a corner, observing everything. He was fifty-five and she fifty-three and both were too old to think about having children, and he knew if he had met her ten years before the thought could have been a definite possibility.

They would never share a child, but they could share their lives. And as soon as the notion entered his head he knew that he loved Leigh Walcott enough to offer sharing everything he had with her.

He loved her enough to propose marriage.

"I've gone and lost my mind," Leigh whispered under her breath when she turned onto the local road leading to Scott's home. She could not explain what had possessed her when she told Scott that she would spend the night with him.

She had tried rationalizing that it was because she missed him, that she was lonely. All of the excuses she had come up with were shattered completely once she realized that she had fallen in love with him. And it was not the same love she had had for Leonard but a gentle, comfortable love that was relaxed, uncomplicated. Unlike her much younger late husband, Scott had established himself in his career and had made concrete plans for the rest of his life. She knew that if she and Scott established a permanent relationship they would never debate whether there would be enough money to make a major purchase or what would be the best methods for child rearing. At age fifty-three and fifty-five their only concerns would be their health as they grew older, their aging parents, and the distribution of their resources when updating their wills.

Everything should have been quite simple, yet for Leigh it wasn't. What she could not do was let go of the fear that if she loved Scott too much she would also lose him. It had happened with Leonard and Justin, and she knew there was no way she would make it back this time if she lost Scott.

Minute lights were positioned along the curving path leading to the farmhouse, like the lights along an airport's runway. A golden glow spilled from the many mullioned windows on the house's lower level. It was after eleven and it was apparent that Scott was up waiting for her.

She slowed and parked her car behind his Mercedes, then shut off the engine. Gathering her handbag and an overnight tapestry bag off the passenger seat, she opened the door and stepped out into the cool nighttime air.

The sky was a dark blue and littered with a profusion of

twinkling stars and a distinctive full moon. Staring up at the large yellow sphere, she smiled and shook her head. That explained why she felt so strange. Full moon—bizarre behavior.

Leigh placed her foot on the first stair of the porch and froze. Scott stood above her, fingers splayed at his waist. He had changed out of the suit he had worn to the party at Leo's and into a pair of jeans he had paired with a stark white T-shirt. Her gaze moved slowly down his well-toned body, lingering on his bare feet. A passing breeze caught the scent of soap and aftershave as he walked down the steps. The lanterns flanking the front door lit up the wraparound porch but failed to illuminate his dark face.

She wanted to see his expression and ascertain whether he was pleased that she had come as promised. She wanted validation that he needed her as much as she needed him.

Leaning down, Scott took her overnight bag from her loose grip. His free arm curved around her waist, tightening as he moved closer. "Thank you for coming."

Tilting her chin, she tried seeing his expression. "Are you pleased that I came?"

His warm, mint-scented breath feathered over her face when he lowered his head. "There are no words to describe what I'm feeling at this very moment."

Resting her head against his muscled shoulder, Leigh drank in the comfort of his nearness. The solidness of his body, the fragrance of his aftershave mingling with his body's natural masculine scent, and the strength of his arm around her waist were what she had missed and had been missing for three decades. She missed sharing her life with a man.

"Let's go in, Sunshine," he crooned close to her ear.

Leigh followed him into the house, again marveling at the uniquely chosen furnishings that reflected a long-ago period in America's history. The world was poised for a new century, while he had elected to go back in time when he'd purchased and decorated a farmhouse with articles reminiscent of a different era.

Scott placed her overnighter on a drop-leaf table near the curving staircase, then returned to the door and locked it. The sound of the tumblers falling into place seemed unnaturally loud in the swollen silence. Turning, he stared at Leigh. She stood in the middle of the living room staring back at him.

She had also changed her suit, and in its place was a black cotton pullover and slim black skirt that ended at her knees. His eyes crinkled in a knowing smile when he noticed she wore a pair of patent-leather sling-strapped heels. The golden light from a floor lamp highlighted the curvy perfection of her bare legs.

Her smile, slow in coming, matched his. Raising her arms, she said, "Where's the music, Scott?"

Closing the distance between them, he took her into his arms and spun her around in an intricate dance step. He stared down into her brilliant light brown eyes, his gaze making silent love to her face.

"Do you want to dance here or on the back porch?"

"The back porch," she whispered when he tightened his grip on her waist.

They made their way through the hallway that led to the back of the house and stepped out into a space awash with the glow of flickering candles. The soft sound of music flowed from the speakers hidden within the ceiling of the screened-in space.

Scott stopped to slip his bare feet into a pair of leather loafers, then reached for Leigh again. Molding her slender body to his, he marveled at how well she fit in his embrace with the additional three inches her shoes afforded her.

One moment they were dancing; then without warning their mouths were joined in a hungry kiss. His kiss was urgent, exploratory, while hers was soft, gentle. His fire spread to her, and Leigh could not stop the moans coming from her parted lips. Each time her tongue met Scott's she felt as if a streak of lightning had struck, shattering her into minute pieces. She floated in and out of a drugging passion when his hands slipped down her spine and cradled her hips, pulling her closer where she felt the outline of his rising ardor pushing against her middle.

Scott groaned as if in pain, her name slipping out in a fevered whisper. His hands moved up and cradled her face, and he slowly and methodically kissed every inch of her silken skin, his tongue tracing a path down the side of her neck to the rapidly beating pulse in her throat.

"Please," she sobbed against his hot mouth.

"Please what, darling?"

She was on fire. Her breasts had swelled against the lace of her bra, and a rush of wetness bathed the secret place between her thighs. It had been a long time, too long, since she had been aroused to the passion Scott had sparked in her. She wanted more than his touch or kiss. She wanted all of him—his weight bearing down on her, his hardness filling her where she did not know where he began and she ended. She wanted to feel his heat, taste his flesh, and experience a sweet ecstasy that she had forgotten existed for her.

Her tongue swept over the hair on his upper lip, and he gasped sharply. "What is it you want, baby?"

Burying her face against his shoulder, she closed her eyes. "Don't make me beg you, Scott."

"I want you, Leigh," he mumbled in her hair. "I want you so much."

A violent shudder shook her body. "Then take me."

Scott released her, extinguished the candles, and pushed a button on a wall, shutting off the stereo unit. Then he swept her up into his arms and returned to the house, taking the stairs two at a time.

Leigh only caught a glimpse of a king-size iron bed with a crocheted antique covering before Scott placed her on his bed and turned off the bedside lamp. He lay down beside her, threading his fingers through hers.

"How long has it been for you?"

Closing her eyes, she bit down hard on her lower lip, then said, "I've only slept with one man."

It was Scott's turn to close his eyes. There had only been one man and that man had been her husband. Thirty years—

she had waited thirty years for him. And knowing she was willing to share her body with him made her even more special, precious.

Opening his eyes, he turned to face her. Silvered light from the moon cut a swath across the bed, highlighting her face. His breath caught in his chest when he saw the serenity in her expression. There would be no shadows across her heart this night.

"I'll go slow," he whispered. "I want you to stop me if I hurt you."

Leigh nodded, then gave herself up to the mastery of the man whom she loved enough to share her body with.

There was only the sound of their breathing as clothes were shed and flesh exposed in the silvered light. Scott's fingers feathered over her body, leaving her trembling from his touch. She wanted him to take her and end her erotic torment, but he didn't. He touched and kissed her in places that made her rise off the mattress. His sensual lovemaking swept away thirty years of loneliness and guilt.

Scott forced himself to go slow in his attempt to awaken the sleeping passion Leigh had locked away from any man who had approached her for more than half her life, and as he aroused her his own ardor grew stronger until he feared losing control. He pulled away from her, pausing to protect her, then slowly eased his hardness into her long-celibate body. She gasped aloud at the invasion and he stopped, waiting until he felt her relax before continuing.

Fingers of fire rippled under Leigh's skin as she welcomed the rush of sexual desire she hadn't felt in years, and she opened her thighs and mouth to receive the passion Scott so willingly offered her.

His hands roamed over her breasts and down her thighs before returning to her breasts. Everything seemed to happen in slow motion as their bodies moved in exquisite harmony with each other. Waves of ecstasy throbbed through her, and she gasped in sweet agony when the involuntary ripples began. And in the seconds before she touched heaven she felt Scott's hardness expand, the sound of his breathing quicken, and the scent of their bodies merge until they were each one with the other.

The screams she sought to restrain exploded from the back of her throat and she was left crying and trembling from the aftermath of an explosive rapture that transported her to a place where she had never been before.

Scott experienced his own turbulent release as Leigh breathed the last of her passion into his mouth. His heart pounded painfully in his chest while he struggled for his next breath. He called her name over and over, collapsing on her smaller frame and unable to believe the lust Leigh had elicited in him. He had slept with women whose names he had forgotten, but never had any of them touched the very core of his being. It took him a while to realize that he had never given them all of himself because he hadn't been in love with them. It was different with Leigh, because not only did he love her, but he was in love with her.

Leigh pushed against his shoulder and he loathed withdrawing from her scented body. But he knew he was crushing her and somehow found the strength to roll over. Gathering her close, Scott held her until she fell asleep. A satisfied smile curved his mouth before it became a full grin. He was the one—the one to offer Leigh Walcott a second chance for love. Waiting until he heard her soft breathing deepen, he left the bed and retreated to his bathroom to shower.

10

Leigh woke up the next morning to bright sunlight and an empty space beside her. Turning over on her back, she gasped when she felt the soreness between her thighs. She ached—all over. But it was a delicious ache. A gentle smile tilted the corners of her full mouth when she recalled what she had shared with Scott.

Closing her eyes, she recalled the feel of his hands and

mouth on her body, her face burning in remembrance. He had branded her body and her mind with his lusty passion. She reveled in the memory of what they had shared until she glanced at a clock on the bedside table. It was after eight—two hours beyond her usual rising time. She could only spend the morning with Scott, because she had to return to D.C. for an engagement party later that evening.

Swinging her legs gingerly over the bed, she made her way to the bathroom and found her overnight bag on a low table near a round sunken bathtub. She filled the tub with a handful of her favorite bath salts, then brushed her teeth. Half an hour later she walked into the bedroom to find Scott sitting on an armchair, waiting for her.

His penetrating gaze took in her freshly scrubbed face and her hair brushed off her face and secured with an elastic band. She appeared fragile, almost ethereal. Rising to his feet, he extended his arms.

"Good morning, beautiful."

Leigh walked into his embrace, burying her nose against his laundered shirt. "Good morning, darling."

Pulling back, he stared at her, wondering if she was aware of the captivating picture she presented. He loved her smile. He loved everything that made Leigh Walcott who she was.

"Breakfast is ready."

Leigh nodded. "I'm going to have to leave around noon. I have an engagement party tonight."

"Where?"

"In D.C."

Scott hid his disappointment well when he forced a smile.

"We can still see each other tomorrow morning," Leigh continued. "Why don't you meet me at my place around eleven? I'll treat you to Sunday brunch at Leo's."

Brushing his mouth over hers, Scott whispered, "You've got yourself a deal, Sunshine."

Leigh lay between Scott's outstretched legs, his chest supporting her back. She moaned softly as he massaged the tight muscles in her shoulders and upper back. She shifted slightly and the warm oil-slick water lapped over her breasts.

Closing her eyes, she gave in to the magic of her lover's fingers kneading away the tension that had begun earlier that evening at a raucous sweet sixteen party. She had barely waged a successful battle with more than two dozen adolescents, some of whom had devised a few of the most ingenious schemes she had ever encountered to sneak alcoholic beverages into the private party.

Scott pressed his mouth to the side of her neck and inhaled the sweet, clean fragrance of her upswept hair. "You're working too hard, Leigh. If you continue at this pace you're going to burn out."

"I'm fine, Scott."

"You're not fine and you know it. Two days ago you were nearly flat on your back from a tension headache, and now you're so stressed you can hardly move your neck."

She moaned softly, then said, "I have to work."

"You don't have to work," he argued softly.

Moving with some difficulty, she peered at him over her shoulder. "I still have a few years before I'm eligible for retirement and Social Security benefits."

"I wasn't talking about you collecting Social Security."

"What are you talking about?"

Curving an arm around her waist, he lifted her effortlessly until she straddled his thighs. He stared at her, a lethal calmness in the depths of his dark gaze.

"Marry me, Leigh. I'll take care of you."

She went completely still, momentarily speechless. "You're kidding me, aren't you?" she asked once she recovered her voice.

"No, I am not."

She registered his impassive expression and the cutting edge in the four words. She emitted a nervous laugh and a frown formed between Scott's eyes. He had to be kidding, because after sleeping with him for only three months she doubted whether their relationship had progressed to the stage where they could consider something more permanent.

"No, Scott."

"No what, Leigh?"

"I can't marry you."

"And why not?"

"Because . . . because it's not like that."

His hands tightened around her waist. "Like what?"

"It's not going to work. I enjoy your company, Scott. But not enough to marry you and give up what I've had to sacrifice in order to make my business successful," she lied smoothly.

She'd lied to him and she continued to lie to herself. She did not want to love him, even though she did. She saw him once or twice each week, even though she wanted to see him every day. And the nights when they were apart she lay in bed, her mind filled with frightful memories that reminded her she had lost Leonard and Justin because she had loved them too much. She'd loved Leonard Walcott from grade school, and years later when he had asked her to marry him and have his children she had not hesitated. She had it all, then lost it all.

Marrying Scott Alexander was not an option.

He recoiled as if she had slapped him. "You enjoy my company, Leigh. Is that all I am to you—company?"

She ran her tongue over her lower lip, drawing his gaze to the spot. "No," she replied, shaking her head slowly. "You're more than company."

His hands moved from her waist to cradle her face. "What am I?" She stared at him, unblinking. "I love you, Leigh. I've never said that to another woman."

She closed her eyes, shutting out his intense expression. "You love the passion I offer you."

"Look at me, Leigh. Open your eyes," he ordered harshly. She complied, her gaze narrowing. "You're wrong, darling," he continued in a softer tone. "It has nothing to do with sex."

"I didn't say sex. I said passion."

His temper exploded. "Dammit, Leigh! Don't play word games with me."

Her temper rose to match his. "Take your hands off me.

I think I should leave before I say something I'll find myself regretting."

"Let's talk about this."

"There's nothing to talk about. I won't marry you. Now, please let me go."

He dropped his hands and she stood up, water dripping from her tight petite body. Scott sat in the tub, watching as she stepped out and reached for a towel to cover her nakedness. He sat in the same spot, staring out into nothingness; ten minutes later he heard the sound of a car's engine fading in the distance.

He had lost her because he had proposed spending the rest of their lives together. He loved her and she had thrown his love back in his face.

How could she offer up so much of herself while shrugging it off as simply enjoying his company? If he wanted company, then he could easily pay a stranger to occupy his time.

His temper cooled and the water in the bathtub cooled. The heat and the passion he had shared with Leigh Walcott had grown icy with her rejection. The first and only woman he had confessed to loving, the first and only woman whom he had offered to share his life and name with had spurned him without a pretense of *Let me think about it.*

He had waited fifty-five years to become a fool!

Leigh managed to communicate with Scott about his mother's birthday celebration like the professional she had been trained to be. She called him to finalize last-minute details, leaving messages on his answering machine at his apartment in Georgetown during the week or at his McLean farmhouse on the weekends. He returned her calls promptly and there was nothing in his voice to indicate they had once shared a physical liaison.

Her decision to use the chefs at Leo's to cater the food for Irene Alexander's party had gleaned a thumbs-up approval from Scott, and the week before the scheduled gala found Leigh communicating with Tyrell or Noah for a daily update.

She sat across a small table in the rear of the supper club, talking to Noah. "I think I'm going to need that extra server, just to be on the safe side."

He nodded, smiling. "Good move, Leigh." His smile faded when he noticed her clenching her teeth as she ticked off a listing of typed items. "How's the doc?"

Her head came up quickly and she stared at him as if he were a stranger. "What are you talking about?"

"Dr. Scott Alexander, Ms. Walcott."

She schooled her expression not to reveal the anxiety she had felt when Noah mentioned Scott's name. "What about him?"

"What's up with the two of you?"

"Nothing, Noah. I'm trying to finalize everything for his mother's birthday party, which should be in full swing in another twenty-four hours."

Stroking his thick silky black mustache with his forefinger, Noah tilted his head and stared at her. "I'm not talking about his mother's party and you know it. I got a call from Scott a couple of weeks ago to cancel his standing Friday night dinner reservation. I must admit that I got used to seeing the two of you come in on Friday nights and Sundays for brunch."

"Mind your business, Noah."

Ignoring her softly spoken warning, he reached across the table and held her hands captive. He tightened his grip when she tried pulling away. "I like you, Leigh. A lot. And because I do I'm concerned about you. Life threw you a nasty curve when you lost your husband and son, but when I saw you with Scott Alexander I knew you had been given a second chance. Anyone with a pair of eyes could see that you guys have something special—special enough to last you the rest of your lives."

Her gaze narrowed as she became wary. "Did Scott ask you to talk to me?"

Noah let go of her hands, leaning against the cushioned

back of his chair. "Why would you say that?"

Glancing over his head, Leigh pursed her lips. "He's jealous of you."

"What!" The single word exploded from the restaurateur.

Leigh told him about Scott's reaction whenever he saw them together, watching an expression of disbelief fill Noah's dark brown eyes.

"The man is jealous because he's in love with you."

"I know that," she replied smugly.

"Then what's the problem, Leigh? Aren't you in love with him?"

"Yes. I love him."

"And?"

Leigh glanced away, sighing heavily. "He wants me to marry him."

Noah's brooding handsome face split with a wide grin. "Congratulations." His smile faded quickly when he noted the pain Leigh was unable to conceal. "You turned him down." She nodded slowly. "Why?"

A rush of tears filled her eyes and she successfully blinked them back before they fell. "I'm afraid of losing him, Noah."

"You've lost him, Leigh. The moment you rejected his proposal you lost him."

"He's still alive."

"I'm not talking about death. That's the final loss."

"I can't, Noah."

He reached for her hands again, holding them gently in a loose grip. "Yes, you can, Leigh. I've seen the way you look at Scott and I have to admit that I was jealous because there was a time when I wanted you to look at me like that."

"You're too young for me."

"There! You've finally said it."

"Well, I am too old for you."

"No, you're not, Leigh. You're not too old for me and you're perfect for Scott Alexander. Give the brother a chance to love you totally. Promise me you'll give him a chance."

She gave him a lingering look. "What do you get out of this?"

"The satisfaction of adding you and Scott to the increasing list of patrons who met and fell in love at Leo's. And because you're so special to the Hardcastles, I'm offering an engagement party—gratis—for your family and close friends."

"Noah Philip Hardcastle, you're trying to bribe me."

Rising slightly, he leaned across the table and pressed a light kiss to her lips. "No, I'm not, beautiful. I just want you to be happy. It's time you put your past behind you."

Her smile was dazzling as she stared at the attractive cleft in his strong chin. "I believe you're right, Noah. I love you, friend."

"Love you, too, friend."

The weather on the day of Irene Alexander's eightieth birthday celebration was perfect. The sun was hot, the humidity bearable, and a warm summer breeze set the stage for a festive outdoor celebration at Dr. Scott Alexander's farmhouse in McLean, Virginia.

Leigh maneuvered into the driveway and parked behind Scott's car at eight-fifty-five. He stood on the porch awaiting her arrival. He was casually dressed in a pair of jeans, running shoes, and a faded Howard University T-shirt.

There was nothing in his expression to indicate that he was pleased to see her, and Leigh had affected a professional demeanor by the time she stepped out of the car to meet him.

She stared up at Scott staring down at her. "The tent man called me and said he'll be here at nine."

Crossing his arms over his chest, Scott wagged his head. "It's been three weeks since we've seen each other and you can't even offer a 'Good morning, Scott.' I'll even take a formal, 'Good morning, Dr. Alexander.' "

Leigh felt as if her emotions were under attack. "Good morning, Scott. Is that better?"

He glared at her. "No, it's not. We need to talk."

"What about?"

"Us."

"Not now. Not today."

"When?"

Her heart was pounding so loudly she was certain Scott could hear it. "Friday."

He shifted an eyebrow. "Where?"

"Leo's."

His stoic expression never changed. "I'll pick you up."

"Don't bother. I'll meet you there."

There was a long, swollen silence before a sensual smile softened Scott's mouth under his neatly barbered mustache. He took a step, bringing him within inches of her, and lost himself in her brilliant golden gaze, the haunting fragrance of her velvety skin, and the sensual magnetism that made him lust for her like an addict craving a drug.

"OK, Sunshine."

It was after midnight when Leigh finally collapsed on her bed from sheer exhaustion. She could not remember when she had felt so depleted. The guests for Scott's mother's birthday celebration began arriving at noon, and a steady stream continued throughout the afternoon. There was a never-ending supply of food, liquid refreshments, and music. Two large tents were set up to provide comfort for the more than sixty people who had come to honor the Alexander matriarch.

Scott had introduced Leigh to Irene Alexander, and when the older woman greeted her warmly she wondered if Scott had revealed their past relationship to his mother. She liked his family—they were warm, unpretentious, and fun-loving—however, it was nearly ten-thirty when the last of them piled into their cars and drove away. She had remained behind until eleven to make certain everything was picked up and packed away before she returned to her own home in D.C.

Her back and legs ached from being on her feet for more than twelve hours. She needed Scott. She needed him to love her, comfort her, and soothe away her aches and pains.

A hot rush of tears filled her eyes when she realized how much she missed him. Seeing him again after a three-week absence was a shock to her senses when she realized how much she loved him.

She was going to take Noah Hardcastle's advice and give Scott a chance, while permitting herself a second chance.

Noah stared at her, his gaze betraying his approval. "You look marvelous, Leigh."

A rush of attractive color darkened her sculpted cheekbones. "Thank you."

She had spent the morning and part of the afternoon at her favorite day spa, where she had had a complete beauty makeover. She had elected to have her hair washed with a special shampoo that made it gleam like polished silver. Her stylist had curled and pinned it up off her neck, adding several inches to her diminutive frame.

It had taken her less than five minutes to select a dress for her dinner date with Scott. It was a sleeveless black silk crepe with a revealing rounded neckline that exposed the tops of her small, firm breasts. Sheer black hose and a pair of high-heel pumps pulled her winning outfit together.

Noah winked at her. "He's waiting for you."

She had decided to be fashionably late. Scott had waited fifty-five years for her, and she knew instinctively that another fifteen minutes would hardly matter.

Winding her way through the crowd standing along the magnificent rosewood bar, she walked over to the table she had come to think of as hers and Scott's on Friday nights and late Sunday mornings.

He didn't see her at first, but when she stood beside him his head jerked up. The look in his dark, penetrating eyes was one she would remember all of her life. First there was surprise, then unabashed love. A look of love that stopped her heart for several seconds.

Pushing back his chair, Scott rose slowly to his feet. He swallowed several times, then said, "Hello, Leigh."

She flashed a sexy smile. "Hello, Scott. Aren't you going to invite me to sit down?"

"Of course." He pulled out her chair and seated her. "I've ordered a drink while I was waiting. Would you like something before we order?"

"I'll take a club soda."

He sat down, staring at the soft red color outlining her lush mouth. "That's odd, because I also ordered a club soda."

Placing her small evening purse on her lap, Leigh shifted her waxed eyebrows. "Perhaps we're both operating on the same wavelength tonight."

"I hope you're right," he mumbled under his breath.

He gave the waiter her beverage order, then turned his attention back to the woman sitting opposite him. He couldn't believe she could improve on perfection, but she had. Her face was dewy soft, her brilliant eyes shining like polished amber, and her dress clung to every curve of her tight body. His gaze lingered on the swell of golden breasts rising above the revealing neckline, and he concluded that Leigh Walcott was a woman who would grow more beautiful with age.

"What do you want to talk about, Scott?"

Her soft query pulled him back to why they were sitting across from each other at Leo's. "I love you, Leigh," he began with preamble.

"I know that." Her voice was low, soft.

"And my love has nothing to do with *passion*. You make me whole, Leigh. I never realized what was missing in my life until you came along."

Closing her eyes, she sucked in a lungful of air. "I love you, Scott." She opened her eyes to find him staring at her, his mouth gaping in shock. "And because I love you I'm afraid of losing you the way I lost my first husband and my son. I've grieved for more than half my life. I don't want to have to go through that again."

"What makes you think you'd lose me before I lost you? What if we marry and I lose you? Do you think you have a monopoly on grieving? And if you get up and walk out of this restaurant without committing to a future with me, then I'm going to grieve, Leigh. And because I love you so much I know I will grieve for the rest of my life."

Her lids fluttered wildly. "You can't!"

"Can't what?"

"You can't do that."

"Why not, Leigh? Why not?"

"Because I won't be responsible for that kind of pain."

He waited a pulse beat, then said, "Take away the pain, darling. Free me from the grieving that started the day you walked away from me."

Her eyes filled with tears when she realized what she had done to him, to herself. "Yes." The single word was a ragged sob.

"What?"

"I will marry you, Scott Alexander, whenever and wherever you want."

Scott shot to his feet, fists clenched, shouting, "Yes!"

All of the patrons in the dining area stared at the tall, well-dressed man as if he had taken leave of his senses.

"Noah! Noah Hardcastle, I need you."

Leigh covered her face with both hands, thoroughly embarrassed by Scott's outburst. "Sit down and be quiet," she hissed through her fingers.

"Noah! Tyrell! Tyrone! Ayanna! I need one of the Hardcastles."

Ayanna and Tyrone approached the table, consternation clearly etched on their faces. Their concern deepened when they recognized Dr. Scott Alexander bellowing for them.

Ayanna placed a hand on the sleeve of his suit jacket. "Is there something wrong, Dr. Alexander?"

He gave her a dazzling grin. "There's nothing wrong that a round of champagne won't fix."

Tyrone shook his head. "Say what?"

"Champagne toasts for everyone."

Ayanna glanced down at the mysterious smile curving Leigh Walcott's lips. "What's the occasion?"

Leigh rose to her feet and curved an arm through Scott's. Smiling up at him, she blew him a kiss. "We're going to be married."

"Hot damn," Tyrone sputtered, reaching for and pumping Scott's hand vigorously. He turned to his cousin. "Tell Malik to bring up a couple of cases of the good stuff. I think we're going to raise the roof a bit at Leo's tonight."

Tyrone headed for the stage area while Ayanna made her way over to the bar. Leigh ignored all of the curious stares when she turned into Scott's embrace. The man holding her to his heart had given her a second chance to love, and for that she would be eternally grateful.

Tyrone mounted the stage and picked up a microphone. A ring of white light shone on his shoulder-length twists when the spotlight was trained on him. "Ladies and gentlemen, I would like to make an announcement. D.C.'s own Dr. Scott Alexander and Leigh Walcott have just informed me that they are to be married." He pointed to the couple locked in a passionate embrace, eliciting a thunderous round of applause from everyone in the supper club.

"They would like everyone to share their joy with a champagne toast." A waitress handed him a glass of pale bubbling wine. "Doc and Leigh, all the best for a long and happy life together."

Turning in Scott's embrace, Leigh leaned back against his chest, smiling as the band launched into the popular Kool and the Gang hit "Celebration."

Her gaze swept around the room, stopping to linger on Noah Hardcastle. He nodded and she lowered her lashes in acknowledgment.

Someone thrust a glass at her and she turned to stare up at Scott. She touched her glass to his, took a sip, then rose on tiptoe to seal her pledge.

She had listened to Noah; for that she would always be grateful. She was grateful for life, because she had been given and had accepted a second chance to love.

Eye of the Beholder

Donna Hill

1

It was Saturday. The last Saturday in July, to be exact. The dawning of her thirty-first birthday. No big deal under ordinary circumstances. After all, she'd spent the past thirty of them in relative quiet, maybe some cake and ice cream when she was a young girl growing up in Mississippi, but that was generally the highlight.

Since she'd moved to D.C. a bit more than ten years ago, she'd forgone the cake and ice cream and usually stopped by the church, praising the Lord for giving her another year, excitement or not.

Jae stretched her compact body beneath the pristine white cotton sheet and allowed her eyes to adjust to the already-hot beam of morning sun. However, she thought, pursing her full lips into a pout, her sister-friend Tara Mitchell had vowed on a stack of Bibles—which Jae immediately stated was blasphemous—that there was no way she was going to allow her dear friend to spend her thirty-first birthday sitting in a pew.

"Jae Crawford," she'd said, "you're gonna have your holier-than-thou self cushioned right up inside of *Leo's* if it kills me, and even if it kills you!"

Jae tossed out all sorts of excuses at the outrageous ultimatum. But Tara had been relentless, badgering, bullying, and sometimes sweet-talking her into submission over the past three weeks. It had gotten so bad that Jae stopped answering her phone. But then Tara resorted to leaving a string of messages on her answering machine and had even stooped to sending a telegram.

Jae wasn't quite sure if she'd finally caved in from pure exhaustion to make Tara shut up, or maybe, just maybe, the enticing idea of being in an upscale supper club like Leo's—

in the heart of D.C.—surrounded by people she'd never run across as an English professor at Georgetown University had finally eased under her skin.

She'd prayed on it. Lord knows she did. And now here she was, mere hours away from walking into a den of sin and degradation.

Jae turned to her side and switched on her clock radio that was always set on her favorite gospel station. The rich, soul-stirring sounds of Shirley Caesar poured into the sparsely furnished but orderly room.

"Well," she sighed, letting the music fill her and ease her worried soul. "It's just this one night, this one time." She'd be there in body but not in spirit, she vowed. She'd do this for her friend because she knew it would make Tara happy, and Lord knows Tara had always been there for her. And then, come Sunday morning, she'd go to church, sing her heart out with the gospel choir, and pray for forgiveness.

Tara fought to keep the appalled look off her face when Jae answered the door. The straight brown dress that wasn't even fashionably long, just long, with the high collar, plain white buttons, and fake pearls would have been perfect for a ma-trons' ball, but not for a trendy spot like Leo's.

The brown blended in with Jae's complexion, making her look like one brown blob with some white tossed in for fla-vor.

Tara wanted to holler when she took in Jae's makeup-less face, severe bun, and low-heeled brown shoes. But instead she put on her best smile and effusively greeted her friend who should have been held without bail by the fashion po-lice.

"Hey, girl, happy birthday," she singsonged.

"Hi. Come on in. I'm almost ready."

Thank goodness, Tara thought, *maybe she isn't actually dressed yet.* Tara stepped in and closed the door behind her. She crossed her recently manicured fingers behind her back and sashayed inside, hips swinging, barely contained within the clingy black miniskirt.

Tara went straight to Jae's bedroom and directly to her closet. Maybe there was something in there that was in the vicinity of stylish.

"Need a sweater or something?" Jae asked, appearing like a spoonful of brown gravy in the doorway. "You're probably going to need one to cover up those bare arms."

"Uh, no. Just checking out your wardrobe." She should have insisted they go clothes shopping, Tara thought miserably. "You, uh, wearing what you have on?"

Jae adjusted the doily-like collar. "Yes. Why?"

Tara widened her eyes and forced a smile. "Just wondering. Uh, don't you think you'll be, uh, too warm?"

"I'm sure I won't be." She crossed the room and picked up her pocketbook—you couldn't call it a purse—and draped the thick straps over her arm. "We aren't planning to stay long, are we?"

"I was hoping we could at least stay long enough for a drink and to get some dinner." Tara grabbed her hips in that stare-you-down style of hers. "Damn, girl, it's your birthday! Loosen up for a hot minute. It might do you some good. And is that the only thing you have to put on?"

Jae's expression fluttered for a moment as if the nerves beneath her skin had lost control. "Y-y-you know this isn't something I w-w-wanted to do," she stammered like she was going to cry. "But I knew how much it meant to you." She pressed her lips together, then sputtered again. "And, yes, this is the only thing I have to wear." With that she turned on her low-heeled pumps and stomped out of the room.

Tara could have smacked herself for being so callous. Jae had never been to a nightclub in the thirty years of her overly sheltered life. She was nervous and edgy. Tara would have to remember to be patient, take her time, and ease her friend through the evening. She smiled a bit. It was almost like losing your virginity. You wanted to, but you were still terrified of the unknown. And if the guy didn't treat you right it made for a bad experience. But if he did . . . Her smile widened. You were bound to come back for more.

With that analogy in mind Tara sauntered out to the front of the apartment where Jae was seated on the couch looking like a woman about to walk the plank.

Yeah, this was going to take some serious *foreplay*.

2

Tara drove around the block of the club three times before she found a parking space—nothing unusual for a weekend. Leo's was always packed on Friday and Saturday nights, and even Sunday afternoons there was a line waiting to get in for their famous down-home brunches.

"The joint is jumping tonight," Tara said enthusiastically, her toes already tapping. "Look at all these cars."

"Is this the only place in town?" Jae asked, amazed at the line of cars parked on both sides of the street.

Tara chuckled. "Honey, let me tell you something. The brothers and sisters that hang out at Leo's are D.C.'s cream of the crop. Politicians, entrepreneurs, actors, models, you name it. No telling who you might see," she added, cutting off the engine of her Infinity.

"Hmm." Jae peered out of the window and saw a stylishly dressed couple heading for the entrance to the club. Self-consciously she adjusted the pearls at her throat and smoothed the mud brown dress. Maybe she could have worn something a little brighter, she mused, a bit more revealing. Truth was, she didn't have anything revealing. But what was done, was done, and the sooner the evening was over the better.

"Ready?" Tara chirped.

Jae flinched like a shot had been fired. She pasted on a smile. "Ready."

Tara had been right, Jae thought in utter astonishment. The place was jumpin'. Some sort of every kind of somebody was in here. She didn't know if she was more fascinated with the montage of people or the stunning decor.

The incredible stained-glass windows were something right out of the cathedrals of Rome, juxtaposed against the patterned parquet floors, rosewood tables, Tiffany-shaded lamps, and an intimidating rosewood bar with its brass railing that matched the fixtures on the double mahogany doors.

She'd heard about Leo's—maybe *overheard* was a better description. Plenty of the faculty members had mentioned the great music, excellent food, and upscale crowd. Though her interest had been moderately piqued, she'd never pursued it. It didn't sound like the kind of place she wanted to be seen in. But what if one of her colleagues saw her? What would she do? What could she possibly say? she wondered, her heart suddenly thundering with dread. If it hadn't been for Tara badgering her, she wouldn't be in this predicament. She tried to duck behind one of the pillars while they waited. She peeked out at the customers: laughing, talking, dancing, hugging. Everyone seemed like they were having a really good time. She unclutched her purse from the death grip at her chest and slowly lowered it. If someone saw her, so be it. She swallowed hard. "Lord help me," she murmured; she was going to try to enjoy herself.

Leo's was so busy, Jae and Tara had to wait twenty minutes for the table Tara had reserved a week in advance. Making themselves comfortable at the bar, Tara ordered a frozen raspberry daiquiri and Jae ordered a ginger ale with a twist.

"I am so sorry, girl," Tara apologized. "I thought a reservation would get us a quick table. This is the busiest I've ever seen the place."

"It's OK," Jae said, always gracious. "I'm fine right here." She took a handful of peanuts from the bowl and emptied them onto her paper napkin, then popped one into her mouth.

"So . . . what do you think so far?"

"I guess it's OK. Not as noisy and smoky as I thought it was going to be."

Soft jazz played from some hidden place in the background.

"They have live bands on the weekend," Tara offered. "That should be a real treat." She took a long sip of her drink and popped her fingers to the beat. "What's really great is Open Mike Night, once a month on Wednesday." At Jae's frowning expression she explained, "Amateur Night, like at the Apollo Theater in New York. Except they don't boo people off the stage at Leo's."

Tara looked around, her eyes widened. "Really?"

"Yep. It's a howl. But sometimes you get some fabulous folks that turn the place out."

At that point the waitress, decked in the *de rigueur* black skirt and white blouse with a mandarin collar, came to escort them to their table.

"I'm Carolyn, your waitress for this evening, and on behalf of Leo's I'm truly sorry for the wait, ladies. As you can see we're really busy tonight," she said, reconfirming the obvious. "Mr. Hardcastle would like to offer you both a drink and appetizers on the house for your inconvenience." She handed them each a menu. "I'll be right back to take your orders."

Tara's brows rose and stayed there as she watched the waitress move around the circular tables. She turned to Jae. "Did you hear that?"

"Is that customary?"

"Not that I know of. But I'm impressed. Hmm. I wonder *which* Mr. Hardcastle it was. There are three of them, you know. All related some way or the other. And a sister or a cousin or something, too. I've never met any of them."

Tara arched her chin to see above the heads in the room and her gaze landed on a tall, sleek *GQ* brother. Her heart did a stutter step, then settled. He was looking right at her. If she didn't know better she'd swear she was having a hot flash. And he was coming her way.

Noah stopped at Jae and Tara's table. "I hope you ladies will accept my apologies." He was talking to both of them, but his eyes were glued to Tara. "Compliments of the house is the least I can do for your wait."

Tara slowly licked her lips. "It's definitely a way to catch a customer's attention and have them come back for more."

"That's the goal," Noah responded, his voice a sultry baritone. "To keep them coming back." He stuck out his hand. "Noah Hardcastle, part-owner of Leo's. I can assure you if I were on duty tonight, this would have never happened. We have a new part-time manager in-training."

Tara slipped her hand in his and thought she would faint from the heat of it. "Tara Mitchell. And this is my friend Jae Crawford. We're celebrating her birthday tonight."

"You've come to the right place. The band tonight is sensational. Happy birthday, Jae. I hope you enjoy yourself."

"Thank you," Jae mumbled.

Noah bent his six-two frame a bit closer to Tara. "I don't usually do this, Tara, but can I steal you away from your friend for a moment—just long enough for us to dance this one number?"

Tara couldn't believe her luck and prayed that her knees wouldn't buckle when she stood up. She turned to Jae. She knew what she was about to do was cruel and unusual punishment for her unsophisticated friend. But Jae was just going to have to forgive her this one time, 'cause Noah Hardcastle was Fine! With a capital *F*. "I'll be right back, OK?"

Jae nodded in reluctant agreement, but she looked terrified.

"Thanks, sweetie." Tara extended her hand to Noah, who helped her from her seat, and they walked out onto the dance floor.

Jae wished she could just crawl in a hole. What was she supposed to do now? How could Tara leave her like that? And for some man she didn't even know. Was that what places like this did to people, stripped them of their good sense? Her eyes darted around like someone looking out for enemy fire. She clutched her glass with both hands and brought it to her mouth.

"Good evening. I hope I'm not interrupting you."

The deep, rich voice came from behind Jae's left shoulder.

She turned and looked up into the most perfect male face she'd ever seen, sun-dappled brown, full lips, eyes that were almost exotic, and close-cut wavy hair that only Mother Nature could endow. She gulped down her ginger ale.

"Good evening." She turned away and stared into the glass.

"I noticed you when you came in."

She glanced up suspiciously, then looked away. "You mean you noticed my friend Tara, don't you?"

"No. I mean you. Mind if I sit down?"

Her head snapped up. Her mouth opened, then closed. Was she being "picked up"? Her pulse started to race.

"My, uh, friend will be back in a minute, I'm sure," she stammered, stalling for time. *Where was Tara?*

"Then maybe it'll be all right if I keep you company until she returns." He grinned and the sweetest set of dimples etched themselves into his cheeks.

"Just . . . until she gets back." She pulled her purse a bit more secure against her stomach.

"Clyde Burrell," he said, slowly sitting down, his long, lean body moving with easy fluidity. "First time here?"

"Yes."

He smiled again. "I figured as much. I'm sure I would remember if I'd seen you before."

Jae jutted her chin. "This isn't the type of place I usually come to."

Clyde angled his head, fascinated by the changing hue of her brown eyes and the silky smoothness of her dark brown skin. He'd always been partial to dark women, and even beneath the drabness of her clothing there was a sparkle about her, an innocence that caught his eye the instant he saw her. For some bizarre reason he had an urge to protect her, especially when he saw her suddenly alone with that deer-caught-in-the-headlights look. She seemed so out of place, his heart went out to her.

"What do you enjoy doing on a Friday night?"

She lowered her gaze. "I generally go to rehearsal."

"For . . . ?" he prompted.

"Choir rehearsal. I sing in a gospel choir."

Clyde braced his forearms on the table and linked his fingers together. "I bet you can sing, too."

Was he teasing her? She decided not to respond.

"What's your name?"

"Why?"

Clyde arched back. "So I know what to call you."

"I don't think you'll have to be calling me anything. My friend will be back any minute and . . . and I don't just give my name out to anyone. I know all about you slicksters. Fast-talking women into who knows what," she added indignantly, edged on more from anxiety than from contempt of this man. Actually, she wanted to talk to him but didn't have a clue as to what to say and couldn't fathom why he was talking to her in the first place. Maybe he felt sorry for her. It was obvious she was out of her league. Wait until she got Tara alone. She was going to give her a piece of her mind.

"What makes you think I'm anything like a—what did you call me?—a slickster?" He tried to keep the laughter out of his voice. He'd been called a lot of things in his time, but that was an original.

"Well . . . because."

"Because what?" he challenged, liking the slight twang in her voice.

"Because why else would you be here?"

"Maybe because the food is good, the music is good, and I get to meet *nice* people like you," he said emphasizing the word *nice*.

Jae suddenly felt terrible, being so rude to someone she didn't even know. It was so unlike her. But this whole evening was so unlike her. "I'm sorry," she mumbled. "It's just that . . ."

"What?" He leaned closer and she found herself swimming in his gaze.

She swallowed. "It's just that this . . . isn't the sort of thing I do. I'm not used to . . . to all this. And the people . . ." She looked around helplessly. "Nightclubs, clubs in general, to me, are places that people come to get drunk, pick up women, rub all over each other in the dark." That's what her preacher father had always told her, and she believed him, had no reason not to. She looked around at the entwined couples, the heads bent close together in secret conversation, the dimness that hid them.

"That bad, huh?" Clyde teased.

The waitress returned, saving Jae from saying any more. "Are you ready for your appetizer?" she asked.

"Can I suggest something?" Clyde asked, his near-black eyes twinkling in the candlelight.

Jae nodded.

"The Buffalo wings are to die for." He grinned.

Jae looked up at the waitress. "That sounds fine."

"And another ginger ale with a twist of lemon," Clyde added, and Jae smiled for the first time since she walked into Leo's.

"Now will you tell me your name?" he asked once the waitress left.

"Jae. Jae Crawford."

Clyde nodded. "Nice. Different and nice. Just like you."

Her heart thumped.

"See, that wasn't so hard." He paused, watching her expression soften. "So tell me, Jae Crawford, what do you do, when you're not coming to places like this?"

She hesitated a moment, then looked directly at him. "I'm an English professor at Georgetown University," she said with a note of pride.

"I'm impressed. English wasn't my strong suit, but I didn't do too bad. Where are you from originally?"

"Mississippi."

"I thought I detected an accent in there. I like that, too."

She ducked her head and sipped her soda. "What do you do?" she asked, slowly getting the hang of this small-talk thing.

He thought about telling her of his real profession, but prudence won out. His better judgment told him a woman like Jae Crawford wouldn't take too kindly to his often wild way of life, and for whatever reason, what she thought of him mattered. "I'm an . . . accountant."

Jae perked up. "Really. My brother is an accountant. That's hard work. Very respectable profession."

"Uh, yeah, it is," he said, wanting to change the subject. "How long have you been singing in the choir?"

Her entire expression lit up. "For as long as I can remember. I love singing."

"You should come down to Open Mike on Wednesdays."

She shook her head vigorously. "I couldn't do that."

"Why not?"

"I—I just couldn't. I only sing in church."

He leaned closer. "If I invited you to come back next Wednesday night, would you at least come?"

She blinked rapidly. What was he asking her? "Uh, I, why?"

"So you could see what it was like. I think you'd really enjoy it."

"Oh, I don't—"

"At least think about it. It would be fun."

"You come here often?" she asked suspiciously.

Clyde cleared his throat. "Every now and then. There are some really nice people here. I think you'd be surprised if you gave them a chance."

Tara said that all the right people came to Leo's, and now that she'd finally come, it really wasn't so bad. And now Clyde. He seemed nice enough, and he was an accountant. How bad could he be?

The appetizers arrived and Tara had yet to return.

"Dig in," Clyde said with a grin, watching her as her eyes danced across the succulent wings. "You're going to love them. I'm tellin' you."

Jae reached for a wing and delicately brought it to her mouth. She took a tiny bite, and the sticky sweet taste mixed with just the right amount of hot pepper and seasoning glided across her tongue and danced a little number before sliding down her throat and making her tummy beg for more.

"Hmm," she hummed, taking a bigger bite this time. "You

were right," she said between bites, and dipped into the bowl for more.

Clyde chuckled in delight. "Try it with the blue cheese." He took a wing, swiped it in the creamy white dressing, took a bite, and chewed like he was in heaven. A tiny white dot hung at the corner of his mouth.

"You, uh have . . . something . . ." Jae pointed toward his mouth.

His tongue flicked out and tested the corners. "Better?"

She grinned and shook her head. "Missed."

He tried again, then looked at her wide-eyed.

"Nope." She picked up her napkin and reached toward him, then stopped, realizing what she was doing. She didn't know this man. What must he be thinking?

Clyde gently clasped her hand, his gaze holding hers, and brought the napkin to his mouth.

With her heart racing and her body suddenly on fire she dabbed at the spot and snatched her hand away as if she expected it to be snared in a bear trap. She reached for her glass, realized how much her hand was shaking, and changed her mind.

"Thanks," he said softly. "Nothing worse than going around all night wearing blue cheese dressing as an accessory. Especially when you're trying to impress someone."

Her eyes snapped up. She swallowed hard. "I suppose. You certainly have enough to choose from," she said quietly, avoiding his stare.

"I wasn't talking about anyone. I was talking about you. I'd like to get to know you better, Jae."

She couldn't be hearing right. This time the glass made its way to her lips. She took several swallows before speaking. "Why?"

Clyde grinned. "If nothing else, you're direct. I like that." Then he shrugged. "Because you're nothing like any of these women in here, Jae Crawford, English professor. Nothing like anyone I've ever met. I knew that the minute I saw you."

She didn't have a clue as to what to say. Casting aside

the subtle offers from her colleague Clarke Wells, the chairman of her department, was one thing. This was something entirely different.

Clyde spied Noah and Tara returning to the table and didn't want Noah blowing his cover. "You think about it, OK? I'd really like to see you on Wednesday." He rose. "I've got to go. It was great meeting you, Jae." He took her hand and kissed her palm. "Maybe I'll see you before you leave."

Before she could respond he was maneuvering through the crowd. He stopped when he reached Noah and Tara and whispered something in Noah's ear, to which he nodded.

"Seems like all I've been doing tonight is apologizing," Noah said, helping Tara into her seat. "I must apologize for keeping your friend away for so long. Please forgive me."

"No problem," Jae replied, her mind still on Clyde Burrell.

"I'll see you later," Noah said to Tara.

"Looking forward to it."

"Enjoy yourselves, ladies." With that he turned and walked away.

"Whew!" Tara blew out. "I am in heaven, girl. Do you hear me? Noah Hardcastle. Your sister-friend has just hit pay dirt." She slapped her palm on the table. "The brother has it going on," she rambled. "Fine, funny, smart, and sexy as all hell." She turned to Jae and covered her mouth, knowing how Jae felt about cusswords and the mention of sex. "Oops, sorry."

"No problem," Jae said dreamily.

Tara frowned. "Are you all right?"

"Yep." She looked at her friend's quizzical expression. "I'm really glad I came."

Tara's brows rose. "You are? Oh, Jae, I'm so glad. After we got here I just knew I'd made a mistake and I shouldn't have forced you to come if you didn't want to."

"I met someone," she said in a whisper.

"You?"

Jae nodded. "His name is Clyde Burrell."

"Where is he? What does he look like?"

"He walked up to you and Noah as you were coming back to the table."

Tara nearly choked. "Him?" she asked incredulously, recalling the handsome man she'd briefly glimpsed and thought would definitely be someone she'd talk to if she wasn't with Noah.

"Him," Jae confirmed.

Tara raised her glass in a toast. "Happy birthday, girl!"

Jae clinked her glass against Tara's. "Let the choir say, 'Amen.'"

3

For the next few days Jae moved through her routine with a secret smile on her face and a glow in her eyes. Sure, she'd only met him that one time and they'd only talked for a short while, but she couldn't stop thinking about Clyde, thinking about how nice he was, such a gentleman and so handsome. And he seemed interested in her.

A part of her was certain he was only being nice, but another part of her, that untapped part, wanted—needed—to believe that maybe he did like her, at least a little bit. Just a little bit.

Several of her colleagues at the university commented on her obvious change in demeanor. But she didn't respond. She was still sorting it all out herself.

Finding an empty seat at the table in the teachers' lounge, Jae pulled out her peanut-butter-and-jelly sandwich, mused, and munched.

She'd had few and short-lived relationships with men. Growing up in the Delta with a preacher for a father—the only child and a girl—didn't lend itself to allowing her to become worldly.

"Save yourself for your husband," her mother would warn.

"Fornication is a sin against God," her father would faithfully remind her.

"A man will tell you all kinds of sweet things to get what he wants, Jae," her mother often said. "Don't be fooled. Keep your skirts down and your legs closed."

"But how will I know when the right man comes along, Mama?"

A soft look came into her mother's eyes when she looked at her daughter.

"You'll know, sweetheart. It's a feeling that can't be compared to anything else."

"Like what, Mama?" she asked eagerly, wanting to discover the sweet mystery of love.

Her mother folded her hands atop the wooden kitchen table. It wobbled for a moment, then settled.

"When you see him, you feel warm inside like you done just had a cup of tea. Your heart beats a little faster when you think 'bout him, and you always feel like smilin' even when there ain't nothin' to smile 'bout." Her lashes lowered, shielding her eyes, "And one day you'll wake up and realize you don't ever want to be with anyone else." She gazed at her daughter. "That's how you'll know."

Jae wanted to feel those feelings, experience the joy she saw shared between her parents. But it had always eluded her—that magic.

Tara always insisted that Jae needed to open up, experience the world, give herself more options than church and work. "All those folks already know you, girl," Tara would say. "Whatever impressions or decisions they have made about you been made already. It's over time you venture out to greener pastures."

Tara was right, Jae reluctantly concluded. She did need to broaden her horizons. However, she was still hard-pressed to believe that a decent, God-fearing man could be found in the smoke-filled, alcohol-laced atmosphere of a nightclub, even one as nice as Leo's.

But it sure would be nice if Clyde Burrell was the exception.

"You look like you discovered the fountain of youth," Clarke Wells commented as he took an empty seat beside Jae. "Whatever it is that has you looking happy from the inside out looks good on you." He put his paper plate loaded with apple pie on the table.

Clarke Wells was the chairman of the English Department. He'd asked her out on several occasions during her time at Georgetown. He seemed nice enough and was obviously intelligent and not bad to look at, and his colleagues held him in high regard. On the surface, and on her checklist of attributes for possible life-mates, Clarke Wells was right up there at the top. Yet each and every time he'd ask her to join him for a cup of coffee or maybe a movie, Jae remembered her mama's words: "When you see him, you feel warm inside." She didn't feel that way about Clarke and didn't think she ever would.

Jae glanced up at Clarke and saw the sincerity in his eyes, mixed with the quiet sadness of acceptance.

"Thanks." She smiled, then took a bite of her sandwich. "How is everything?"

"Personally or professionally?" he asked, the shadow of a smile gently curving his wide mouth.

"Why don't we stick to professionally?" Jae responded, adjusting the collar of her white blouse.

He cut into his slice of apple pie. "The department is doing well overall, considering that it's always difficult to get teachers during the summer. The evaluations from the English students have been positive."

"You should be pleased."

"I am," he said without much conviction. He lowered his voice. "I would be more pleased if you'd finally agree to dinner." Hope hung in the air.

Jae stared at her sandwich, then at the carton of juice on the table. She waited for that warm feeling. It never came. "Clarke, I really can't . . . shouldn't."

He blew out air through his pursed lips, then pushed up from the table. "Maybe one of these days you'll change your

mind. I'm really not a bad guy once you get to know me."
He picked up the paper plate and walked away.

"You should have gotten the man's number before you let
him slip away," Tara was saying over the hum of her blow-
dryer. She held the phone to her ear with her shoulder.

"I couldn't do that," Jae muttered.

"You could; you just didn't. You liked him, didn't you?"

"I suppose."

"You did. Don't lie. I saw that look on your face and you
haven't stopped talking about him."

Jae smirked and was glad Tara was on the other end of
the phone. "I have no idea what you're talking about."

"Yeah, right. You know what you need to do?"

"What?"

"Let me take you shopping and treat you to the hair sa-
lon."

"My clothes and my hair are just fine the way they are."

Tara's entire face knotted up. It was a good thing she
loved Jae like a sister. "Girl, it's a new day. You got a fine
man interested in you. It's time for a change. You are going
to take him up on his invitation to come back on Wednesday,
aren't you?"

"Hmm." She grinned. "I've been thinking about it. Not
sure."

"Don't think; just do it," Tara said, getting excited. "Noah
called," she singsonged.

"And . . .?"

"We're going out on Sunday. It's his night off. I can't
wait."

Jae wished she could be more like Tara, just jump right
in a situation with both feet, be more aggressive and out-
going. Tara never lacked for a man in her life. She always
had a date for Friday night, or any other night she chose.
Most people couldn't figure out how she and Tara became
and remained friends. If there were any two people who were
unalike, it was Jae and Tara. But from the first time they met
in a college math class they clicked. Jae always believed that

the attraction was the fact that they were so different. They each gave what the other needed. Jae offered Tara stability and cool rationality, while Tara provided excitement and a glimpse into the world in which Jae never ventured.

"I think I will go to Leo's next week," Jae said suddenly, surprising herself with the declaration.

Tara shut off the blow-dryer, eyes wide. "Now you're talking," she said, grinning from ear to ear.

Jae tugged on her bottom lip with her teeth as she listened to Tara rattle on about what a great time they were going to have. But Jae wasn't really paying attention. All she could think about was the possibility of seeing Clyde Burrell again.

Her heart beat a bit faster and she wondered if it was truly one of the signs her mother had told her about. For the first time in her life she wanted to find out. She hoped that Clyde meant what he said.

4

Clyde sat in the back office of Leo's. As the entertainment manager for the club, it was his responsibility to line up the bands, solo performers, and poets and confirm the acts for Open Mike Nights.

He went over the itinerary for the program that night, but his mind kept drifting back to the woman he'd met on Friday—Jae.

He put down his pen and leaned back in the leather chair, fingers linked behind his head. There was nothing about Jae Crawford that remotely resembled anything that he was accustomed to in a woman. He was used to the model types, the kind of women who turned heads in a three-sixty when they entered a room. They were generally light on conversation and heavy on stunning looks and sensuality. Which had been fine with him until lately.

He supposed his rude awakening came when he woke up next to the most incredible-looking woman he'd seen in ages and for the life of him couldn't remember her name, nor did he want to.

It gave him some serious food for thought, and as a result he'd sworn off women for the past two months and was really trying to examine himself and where his life was going.

And then there she was, Jae Crawford, an oasis in the midst of the desert. There was no pretense about her, no false anything—hair or body parts—from what he could tell. And although she came across as shy and painfully naive, almost old-world, there was an honesty about her that was incredibly refreshing.

He wondered if she'd come back tonight. He hoped she would. When he'd seen Noah coming toward their table all Clyde could think about was getting away before she found out what he really did for a living. And then she was gone before he had the opportunity to get her number.

Of course he could've found out from Noah, since Noah hadn't stopped talking about Tara since that night and the two women were friends. But Clyde had a sense that his getting Jae's number from anyone other than herself wasn't something she'd appreciate.

So, all he could do was wait and hope. But what kept prickling his conscience was his little white lie. How long could he pull it off before she found out the truth? Maybe just long enough for her to get to know him—then he'd tell her. Hey, he wasn't even sure what he was doing all this thinking and worrying for. He'd probably never see her again, anyway.

"Come on, girl, my treat," Tara whined and begged. "At least get something bright and sleeveless. This magenta linen dress looks great on you."

Jae assessed herself in the three-way mirror of the boutique in the Galleria Mall. Tara had practically twisted her arm to get her in there, and they'd nearly gotten into a shouting match over Jae's choice of outfits: a navy blue suit, a

metal-gray dress, and yet another brown outfit that made
Tara wince and run outside to smoke a cigarette.

After the dust finally settled, the sales clerk brought out
the dress that Jae was wearing.

"It's simple but stylish," the young woman was saying.
"And the color is perfect for you."

Jae didn't say it out loud, but she was stunned by her
appearance. She looked at least five years younger, and the
simple straight cut of the sheath brushed her hips, giving
them a gentle outline. The modest V-neck was cut low
enough to be alluring without giving away too much.

As she turned this way and that she was amazed at the
definition of her arms and the round curve of her behind.
Her daily exercise regime actually did more than get her
adrenaline flowing in the morning.

Jae spun toward a hopeful Tara. "I'll take it," she said, a
shy smile on her mouth. Her sable brown eyes sparkled.

Tara held her palms up to the heavens. "Hallelujah!"

Jae was adamant about no makeup but caved in on a cute
pair of strappy sandals. Packages in hand, Jae and Tara returned to Jae's apartment to get ready for their night out.
Tara had her change of clothes with her. She wasn't taking
any chances that Jae may have a moment of weakness and
put on something from her closet. If she did, they might just
have to throw down.

Jae had no idea so many people were out on the town on
a Wednesday night—the middle of the week. Hump day, as
Tara often called it. "Half way through the week," she'd say.
"Almost over the hump." Well, there were sure a bunch of
folks trying to get to the other side tonight.

Just as on the previous Friday, they had to wait for a table.
Jae was so nervous she could feel the perspiration trickling
down her back even under the blast of the air-conditioning.

"Suppose he doesn't show up," Jae lamented, scanning
the club above the rim of her glass.

Tara patted her arm and tapped her foot to the beat of
Whitney Houston's latest hit. "Just chill, Jae. Even if he

doesn't show up, you look so good it will be his loss when someone else snatches you up."

Jae screwed up her nose. She didn't want to think about the possibility that Clyde wouldn't be there. And she certainly didn't want to imagine some other man "snatching" her up.

Noah's smooth, crooning voice wrapped around them in welcome: "Good evening, ladies."

Tara pivoted like a prima ballerina on the bar stool. A smile bloomed across her red lips.

"Noah," she said on a breath of what sounded like a promise.

He leaned down and kissed her cheek. "You look wonderful," he whispered in her ear. He turned to Jae and stuck out his hand. "Noah Hardcastle."

Tara giggled.

"I know," Jae said quietly. "We met last week."

He frowned for an instant; then recognition lit his eyes. "Jae! I . . . didn't recognize you."

Tara winked at her from beyond Noah's shoulder and mouthed, *I told you.*

Jae took a nervous sip from her glass of ginger ale. "Is that a good thing?"

Noah blinked several times, momentarily caught off guard. "Absolutely." He pulled in a breath, then addressed Tara. "I'll see about getting you two a table right away. Consider yourselves my guests for tonight."

"Thanks, Noah," Tara said.

"Be right back." He cut through the crowd of people lined up at the entrance and whispered to the hostess who had the clipboard of names. Jae watched her nod her head, then come in their direction.

"If you give me a few minutes I'll get you two settled. OK?"

"Thanks," they chorused.

"I still haven't seen him," Jae said in a pseudo-whisper.

"He'll be here. It's still early. Besides, it will be worth

the wait when he sees you. If his reaction is anywhere near Noah's you got it made, girl."

Jae smoothed her hair. She'd gotten rid of her customary bun, added water and some sheen, and her natural shoulder-length tresses twisted into a halo of spiral curls. It was easy for her to understand why Noah didn't recognize her. She hardly recognized herself.

"Your table is ready, ladies," the hostess said, returning to them. "Follow me."

Not only did they get a table ahead of all those people on line; they got one right in front of the stage.

"It pays to know folks," Tara giggled, settling down in her seat.

Jae tried to look around without being obvious, which was extremely difficult considering they were seated up front.

Sighing, she resigned herself to the fact that Clyde had a change of heart, and maybe she should as well.

"She's here?" Clyde asked, a mixture of excitement and anxiety rolling through his stomach.

"Yeah. And I almost didn't recognize her. I'm telling you, man, the woman looks good."

Clyde smiled, remembering the quiet woman with the soft eyes that had plagued his thoughts for the past week. Hmm, Noah saying she looked good? What did that mean? He knew Noah's tastes bordered on the exotic, which was why they'd gotten along so well and often double-dated. His description certainly didn't sound like the woman Clyde remembered.

"Did you tell her yet?" Noah asked, putting the bar receipts in the safe.

"Naw." Clyde adjusted his tie, his collar suddenly tight.

"Well, you can't have her thinking you're an accountant." He chuckled.

Clyde took his jacket from the coatrack and put it on. "If she had any idea I was the entertainment manager for Leo's, she'd be off like a shot."

"Why?"

"Believe me, brother, Jae is nothing like the kind of

women we're used to. She's real conservative and has old-fashioned ideas about nightclubs and entertainers in general."

Noah shook his head. "So when she finds out—and I'm sure she will—what then?"

"By then we'll know each other better. She'll see I'm cool and everything will be fine."

Noah glanced at his buddy from the corner of his eye. "You're asking for trouble, bro. Her and Tara are friends. She's bound to ask me about you, and I'm not trying to get caught up in your mess. If she's all that put off by what you do, why are you bothering with her in the first place?"

Clyde thought about Noah's question. He'd asked himself the very same thing over the past few days. And the answer was simple—he really didn't know. There was just something about Jae Crawford that struck a chord in him, and he wanted to find out what it was.

"Just do me a favor—don't say anything. At least for the time being. I'll work it out." He headed for the door, stopped, and turned. "Promise?"

Reluctantly Noah nodded, watching his friend walk head-long into disaster. "For now," Noah mumbled.

Clyde stepped out into the club, scanning the patrons. Another full house. Ayanna, Noah's cousin and the real accountant for the club, would be pleased. He checked his watch. Open Mike would start in about forty minutes. He wanted to get some time in with Jae before dealing with the performers. Noah mentioned they had a center stage table. He headed for the front of the club and stopped dead in his tracks.

The eyes and smile he'd know anywhere. He remembered those. It was everything else that went with it that didn't look in the least bit familiar.

Who was fooling whom?

5

Jae's heart started to race. She wasn't sure if it was the thrill of finally seeing him again or the stunned expression on his face. She swallowed as Clyde started walking toward her.

He couldn't have been more than six tables away when he was stopped en route by four different women who practically draped themselves around him like scarves each time he ran into one.

Jae turned away. She didn't want to see any more. She knew she shouldn't have come. She felt like a fool with this stupid dress and this stupid twisty hair. This wasn't her and Leo's wasn't where she should be.

"Excuse me a minute," she mumbled to Tara, who was engrossed in watching the couples on the dance floor.

Tara's head snapped around. "Whatsup?"

"Going to the ladies' room."

"OK," she said, popping her fingers to the beat. "Hey, isn't that him?" she asked, spotting Clyde in close conversation with a shapely brown bombshell. Tara's eyes narrowed.

"Don't know, don't care." Jae grabbed her purse and hurried off.

Tara jumped up and took off after her. She was sure Jae was thinking all sorts of tabloid things about the man; maybe she would, too, in Jae's shoes. But the reality was it could be nothing other than the man being good-looking and popular—with the ladies. Well, she still had a few good tricks up her sleeve. She'd teach them to Jae whether she wanted to learn them or not.

She weaved around the tables, up-close bodies, and smack into the hard chest of Noah.

"Whoa." She wobbled back a step and Noah caught her around the waist.

"Hey, hey, what's the hurry? Don't tell me you and your friend didn't get the table I set up for you."

Tara blinked, regaining her composure, and when she looked up into Noah's come-hither eyes she nearly forgot her mission. "Oh, yeah, we got the table. Thanks." She peeked around his broad body. "I was going after Jae."

"Something wrong?"

She looked up at him, started to tell him, but held her tongue. This was between sisters. Noah was a doll and all, but she didn't know him that well. "Just women stuff. I think she has my lipstick in her purse," she lied, smooth as satin.

"Your lips look good just the way they are," he murmured in a way that made the inside of her thighs twitch.

"You certainly know what to say and when," she said coyly.

"Only speaking the truth." He lightly tapped her lips with his. "See you later?"

"Definitely."

Noah patted her shoulder and walked over to attend to the other guests.

When Tara pushed open the door of the ladies' room, Jae was seated on the short floral-patterned sofa, staring at her entwined fingers.

"Jae, honey," she said softly and eased down next to her. She slid an arm around Jae's tight shoulders. "What's wrong, girl? Whatever it is, we can fix it."

Jae briefly glanced up, her eyes glistening. She shook her head and mumbled, "Nothing."

"Nothing! You look like you're about to bawl—about nothing? Come on. What is it? You saw him with those chicks, right?"

Jae nodded.

"So what? You don't know what the deal is. Maybe he knows them—from work or something." That explanation sounded lame even to her, considering how they were all up in his face. But she stuck with it for Jae's sake.

"They look like accountants to you?" she demanded with a snap to her voice Tara couldn't remember hearing before.

"So what you gonna do, hide in the bathroom behind some females and a man you barely know? Not on my watch, my sistah." She stood, then pulled Jae up by her hand. "Go fix your face. We're going back out there and we're going to have a damned good time. And when he does show up, and he will, just act like nothing ever happened."

"How's he going to invite me down here and then hug up with all those different women? I knew I shouldn't have come."

"Jae—"

"You don't understand, Tara," she said, her voice shaky and soft. "This was hard for me. There hasn't been anyone . . . who interested me . . . or who acted like they were interested in me back for a long time." She sniffed. "I know it's silly to be all upset, but I really thought . . . it might be something . . . you know."

Tara felt almost as bad as Jae did. She knew how shy and how very conservative her friend was and that she didn't give her heart away easily. Now the first time she took a chance she got her fragile feelings trampled on.

"Listen, Jae, we have two choices: either we can pack up our marbles and go home, or we can step out there like the queens we are and pay the brother no never mind. If he's about anything he'll come around and he'll probably have an explanation. You have to decide whether or not you want to hear it."

Jae thought about it for a moment. Tara was right. And she probably was overreacting. It was true, she didn't know Clyde or what he was really about. She'd allowed her fantasies to get the best of her. She drew in a breath and looked at herself in the mirror. A slender vision in magenta with a halo of cottony soft hair stared back at her. Tara didn't get her the dress for nothing, she concluded.

"Let's go," she said with attitude, raising her chin a notch. "It's his loss."

Tara blinked back her disbelief and linked her arm through Jae's. "Now you're talking. So listen, when you get back out there, this is what you do . . ."

6

Clyde finally shook off the hangers-on who believed that he alone held the key to their success. It seemed that every singer and musician with a stalled career believed Clyde could work miracles for them. Over the years, working in the entertainment business, some of his closest associates were record and movie producers, band leaders looking for new talent, and club owners seeking that shining star for their establishments.

He liked what he did—maybe *loved* was a better word—and he was good at his job. He'd developed a reputation for having a good eye, a great ear, and integrity. His skill for spotting star potential was almost legendary in the business. Clyde made certain that anyone who stepped up on the stage of Leo's was treated fairly and with respect. Part of his job was not only booking the regular acts but also screening the performers for Open Mike, to determine not so much the level of talent but the quality of the act to ensure that what they brought to the stage would not be offensive to Leo's upscale crowd. That alone was probably the most difficult part of what he did, because more often than not the "would-bes" wanted a private session or to talk with him "alone" about their careers—like that last group of women. At times it was amusing, but not tonight. Not when the latest assault had been conducted in front of Jae, who knew nothing about his real life—the type of life she had no love for.

He glanced at his watch again. He needed to get backstage and check on the lineup. He peered over heads, trying to spot Jae and her friend. *Must be in the ladies' room.* If that was the case, no telling how long they would take. Or maybe Jae had left. His heart sank at that dismal thought.

He was just about to make his move backstage when a flash of hot pink caught his attention. *Jae.* A surge of relief flooded through him and he started to signal her when a well-dressed, thirty- or early-forty-something man stepped up to her, clasped her shoulders, and kissed her possessively on the cheek. That wasn't so bad. What was worse was that she seemed genuinely happy to see him as she introduced him to her honcho, Tara, and the three of them went to their table. *She came to meet someone else?* His ego went into a nose-dive.

"What brought you out here, Jae? I never thought I'd see you in Leo's," Clarke said, helping first her, then Tara into their seats.

"I'd heard so many people talk about their talent night, I thought I'd see for myself," she responded. "And Tara finally convinced me."

"What about you?" Tara asked. "Come here often?"

"No. Don't get out much. Just thought I'd treat myself. Was tired of staying at home." He looked pointedly at Jae. "You look . . . incredible," he said with a touch of awe in his voice.

"Thank you."

"Can I get you ladies anything?"

"Nothing for me," Jae said quickly.

"I'm fine, too."

Clarke signaled for the waitress. "Well, I'm starved."

The waitress arrived with a menu, which Clarke quickly perused and handed back. "I'll have the sirloin steak medium well, baked potato, and a side salad."

The waitress jotted it all down. "And what will you be drinking tonight?"

"Ginger ale with a twist of lemon."

Jae's gaze flashed in surprise at Clarke a moment, then settled. *Hmm.*

The band segued into a slow number, a lesser-known Billy Strayhorn ballad, and Clarke turned to Jae. "Would you like to dance?"

She started to say no but remembered Tara's words of wisdom on their way out of the ladies' room. *"Let him see you having a good time. If he can do it, so can you."*

Jae pulled in a breath. "Sure."

Clarke stood, helped her out of her seat and onto the parquet dance floor. Tara sat back with a smug smile on her face. This couldn't have worked out better if she'd planned it.

"I'm . . . really not that good," Jae said as Clarke eased her into his embrace.

"You don't have to be," he said quietly. "Just relax and follow me. OK?"

She nodded against his chest and inhaled the spicy scent of his cologne, tentatively adjusted herself to the long, hard lines of his body. Slowly she forced herself to unwind, close her eyes, and let Clarke guide her to the music. His feet seemed to move so effortlessly to the rhythm, shifting and gliding, without any thought. She clung to him and let the music and his body take her away. This was nothing like the organ, piano, and tambourines that she was used to. But it was just as nice, had its own special quality. And she liked it, really liked it. When was the last time she was held this way, experiencing the pleasure of a man's attention? ·

"I never thought I'd ever get this close to you, Jae," Clarke whispered. "Something I've dreamed about for a long time."

Jae stiffened, stumbled, and stepped back. She looked up at him, and the warmth that flowed from his eyes and the gentle smile on his face touched her in a way she didn't expect. It was sudden, taking her by surprise, and she wasn't sure what to make of it. She looked at Clarke, really looked at him. There was a kindness to him, a sincerity. He was a good-looking man, with strong African features: a smooth birch brown complexion, a firm chin, sharp cheekbones, full lips, and a broad nose. Put all together he made a handsome picture, and the sprinkling of gray in his hair gave him a distinct, elegant appeal. She swallowed.

"I . . . don't know what to say," Jae finally responded.

"Don't say anything. Just dance with me. Even if this is the only time." He gently pulled her back against him and swayed to the music.

*   *   *

Clyde leaned against one of the pillars and watched the intimate exchange. Inexplicably he felt cheated, angry. He knew he possessed no claims on this woman. He didn't even know her . . . but damn it, he wanted to. Wanted the chance. More than he imagined. But it was obvious that whoever that man was, he was important to her. Clyde spun away and headed backstage.

There were five acts scheduled for Open Mike and each one was better than the last. The uppity audience let down their hair and stomped and shouted, whooped and hollered their approval after each performance.

Clarke stayed with them all night, and Noah made intermittent pit stops to the table to check on Tara and check out Clarke for Clyde.

"You need to be up there, Jae," Tara insisted. "You'd put them all to shame. I'm telling you, girl!" she shouted over the applause. She turned to Clarke, feeling some admiration for the wonderful way he was treating her friend. He seemed to anticipate her every need, handing her things, refilling her drink, attentive to whatever she said. And he engaged Tara in a conversation as well, asking about her job as a buyer, her interests, and even her favorite movies. *Yeah, he was a nice man.*

"You should hear this chile sing. Make Mahalia weep." Tara laughed.

Jae shook her head. "Tara, please . . . you're embarrassing me."

"You sing?" Clarke asked, his dark brown eyes sparkling with delight.

"Only in church."

"Which church?"

"Bethel Baptist on Piedmont NW," she said quietly.

"Really? I'd love to hear you."

"The doors to the church are always open."

"Maybe I'll surprise you one Sunday." He grinned.

Jae reached for a buttered roll. "You go to church, Clarke?"

He lowered his gaze. "I have to admit, not as often as I should."

"Never too late, you know."

Clarke nodded, assessing Jae Crawford in an entirely new light. He shot his cuffs and checked his watch. "Well, ladies, I don't know about you two, but I have a full day tomorrow, and as quiet as it's kept, I'm not as young as I look," he teased. "I still need my eight hours." He looked at Jae, leaned closer, and lowered his voice. "It was really . . . really wonderful spending time with you tonight, Jae. Maybe you'll think about us doing it for real next time." He stood and extended his hand to Tara. "Great meeting you, Tara. Hope we can do this again sometime."

"Yeah, me, too," she said sincerely.

"Good night. Get home safely." He turned and walked out.

"You never told me Clarke was so nice and good-looking, too. The way you made him sound, I thought he was a nutty professor type."

Jae giggled. "I don't think I realized it myself," she confessed. "Thanks for not letting me feel sorry for myself."

"Girl, I couldn't let you go out like that. We're a team, remember?"

"Yeah, we are, aren't we?"

"Sorry things didn't work out with Clyde."

Jae shrugged. "Guess it wasn't meant to be."

"Yeah, guess so. You ready?"

Jae yawned. "Yes. I have an early class tomorrow."

They both rose and headed for the exit.

"Oh, wait just one minute, Jae. I want to find Noah and say good night."

"Sure. I'll be right out front." She stepped out into the muggy night air and gazed up at the hazy sky. *Another hot one tomorrow,* she thought absently.

"Jae . . ."

Her heart hammered. Slowly she turned around to stare into the eyes of Clyde. She swallowed. "Hi."

Clyde slid his hands into his pockets. "I thought we would

get a chance to spend some time together tonight."

She didn't respond.

"Looked like you were pretty busy."

"Really. So did you," she tossed back.

He rocked his jaw back and forth. "Good friend of yours?" he probed.

"Why?"

"Listen, I'm sorry about tonight, Jae. I meant every word of what I said the last time we saw each other. You've been on my mind ever since. I want to get to know you. Can I make it up to you . . . somehow?"

"Like what?"

"You tell me. What can I do? Dinner, a movie? You name it and it's yours."

She looked at him for a long moment. "Dinner. Saturday night."

He grinned like a kid, dimples flashing. "You got it."

Tara stepped up with Noah's arm around her waist. "Well, hello," she said, giving Clyde the up-and-down once-over.

"Hi. Good to see you again."

Tara turned to Noah and kissed him gently on the lips. "See you tomorrow," she whispered.

"Six o'clock. Your place."

"I'll be waiting." She turned to Jae. "Ready?"

Jae nodded and began to walk off. Clyde grabbed her hand.

"Can I have your number so I can call you, finalize our plans?"

Jae flashed a look at Tara, then turned to Clyde. He pulled out a business card and pen from the breast pocket of his suit. Jae gave him her phone number.

"I'll call you."

"Famous last words," Tara mumbled sarcastically.

"Tomorrow," Clyde affirmed, cutting Tara a sharp look.

"Good night," Jae said to both men as she and Tara sauntered slowly off to Tara's car.

"Well, Ms. Thing," Tara teased from behind the wheel of

her car. "When it rains it pours. You go 'head with your suddenly diva self."

Jae laughed in spite of herself. That may all be true about her new cute self, but what was she going to do now?

7

Jae didn't know how to behave, which way to look, when she ran into Clarke the following day.

"I see you made it in today," Clarke commented as he waylaid her in the corridor.

"We left shortly after you, actually." She held her briefcase against her chest.

"I had a really nice time." He stared at her a moment, taking in her navy blue below-the-knee skirt and prim white blouse. Her hair was once again pulled back into her routine bun at the back of her neck. Maybe what he saw last evening was her nighttime outfit. This attire was probably more appropriate for the work environment, because to tell the truth, if he had to look at Jae the way she looked last night, he'd never get any work done.

"Have you thought any more about my offer?"

She ducked her head. "To be honest, I really didn't . . . but I will."

"I hope so. I know I can show you a nice time. And I think we get along really well, Jae."

She smiled. "Yeah, I think we did, too."

"Well," he said on a breath, "I'd better let you get back to class. Have a good day."

"You, too." She hurried off down the hall, with the thought of Clyde's early-morning phone call on her mind.

Her phone had rung at seven that morning, and she couldn't imagine who would call her at such an hour.

"Hello?"

"Good morning. This is Clyde."

"Clyde? Is . . . something wrong? She checked the bedside clock. "It's seven in the morning."

"I know. I apologize for calling so early, but I wanted to catch you before you left for work."

Jae sat up in the bed, rubbed sleep from her eyes. "Yes?" she said tentatively, her pulse beginning to pick up a beat.

"I was hoping that maybe I could pick you up . . . later or something and we could have dinner together. Talk. You know."

Certainly she'd hoped he'd call, but she never expected it to come so soon. "Uh, tonight I—"

"Please say, yes, Jae. I want to make up for last night." Why was he pushing so hard? Why did he even care? he wondered again, realizing how ridiculous he sounded, how desperate.

"Well . . . I . . . Is seven o'clock good for you?"

"Any time you say. Can I pick you up at home or would you like to meet me?"

A real date. "Uh, you can pick me up at my apartment."

Clyde released an audible sigh of relief. "Great. What's the address?"

She gave him the address and cross-streets.

"So . . . I'll see you tonight . . . at seven. I'm looking forward to this evening. Have a great day, Jae."

"Yes, uh, you, too."

Thrilled, dazed, and totally amazed, she hung up the phone, grinning from ear to ear. A date. A real date. Her first one in longer than she could count, Jae mused as she halfway listened to one of her students extol the virtues of the new wave of black commercial fiction authors. There had been a few intermittent outings with one man from church, she recalled, her thoughts drifting again. But nothing of note ever happened—that spark never ignited. True, Clarke had been quite clear about his intentions, but until last night a relationship with him wasn't in the cards. However, it was Clyde who had stirred her, made her daydream of the possibilities. She wasn't quite sure what it was about the man that attracted her. He was certainly great to look at; he spoke with intelligence and was decidedly charming. But so was Clarke.

She sighed as the student ran down a laundry list of whom he considered noteworthy black writers. All she could attribute her attraction to was that warm, sparkling feeling, and she hoped that it turned out to be all that she'd been told it would.

"I'm going to need to take the night off," Clyde was saying as he and Noah sat in the office of the club.

Noah looked up from the shift schedule he was working on. "Tonight? Pretty short notice. Everything cool?"

"Yeah, yeah. Everything's all right." He crossed the room to the mini-refrigerator, pulled open the door, and took out a can of Sprite. He popped the top, taking a long swallow as if trying to fortify himself.

Noah watched, smirked, then went back to what he was doing. He'd known Clyde long enough to sense when he had something on his mind. Noah also knew that Clyde needed some space in order to tell it. And he would. Clyde wasn't as complicated as some people made him out to be. Basically, Clyde Burrell was a hardworking man who tried to treat people decently. Even the women with whom he'd been involved in short flings had nothing but good things to say about Clyde. Noah guessed what they liked was his honesty. He didn't pull punches and told it like it was. Except this time.

Noah frowned. What Clyde was doing with this woman Jae was totally out of character for him. For a million bucks he couldn't figure out why Clyde felt compelled to lie to Jae. True, it was a little lie, but those can lead to big repercussions.

"Can I talk to you, man?"

Like clockwork, Noah inwardly chuckled. He put down his pen and slipped off his designer reading glasses. "Sure. Whatsup?" He leaned back in the chair.

Clyde paced back and forth in front of Noah's desk. "You ever just do something on impulse?" he asked suddenly.

Noah shrugged. "Sure, I guess. Why?"

"Ever have it backfire on you?"

"Where's all this going?"

Clyde blew out a breath, stopped prowling the floor, and braced his palms on Noah's desk. "I'm taking Jae out tonight."

Noah's brows rose in surprise. "She accepted—after last night?"

"Didn't sound like she wanted to at first. I wouldn't have blamed her."

"Yeah, me neither."

Clyde cut him a look, then resumed his inventory of the floor. "Anyway, she agreed. And so we're going to dinner."

Noah slowly nodded his head, easily keeping up with the snail-like telling of this tale without any effort.

Clyde plopped down in an empty chair in the corner of the room, reminding Noah of the old school days when you were sent to sit in the corner for misbehavior. Irony?

"This woman scares me," Clyde confessed, the astonishment evident in his voice. "Scares the hell outta me." He shook his head, bewildered by his state of mind.

Scared? Clyde? Does not compute, Noah thought. He folded his hands in front of him and waited. Clyde had his attention now. *This ought to be good.*

"I mean she's nothing like any of the other women I've dated." He looked at Noah for confirmation. "Nothing. She's very conventional, pretty naive, good to look at but not a superstar. She's shy, and I swear, if I didn't know better I'd bet money she's never been in bed with a man. So what's the fascination, you ask? She is. Simple. Can't explain it, man. First time I saw her I felt something. Like a light went on."

Noah looked at his friend in amazement. In the ten years he'd known Clyde, he'd never heard him talk about a woman the way he was talking about Jae—and he barely knew the woman. Noah shook his head. He was speechless.

Clyde got up and resumed his trek across the hardwood floor. "So what do you think?"

"Think?" Noah echoed.

"Yeah."

"About what?" he volleyed, stalling for time.

"About what I just said."

Noah's brows rose and fell, rose and fell again. He rubbed his chin like a magic lamp, then blew out a long breath. "Let me put it this way, brotha. You need to come clean with this woman. If you even think you can really get into her, you need to be honest. This isn't like you. If anything, you've always been too upfront." He blinked, then frowned. "And please explain to me how she scares you. Looks pretty harmless to me."

"Believe me, looks deceive. I don't know, man, when she finally started talking and telling me how she had a real problem with the fast life, and all the people in it, I suddenly didn't want to be in that category."

"So you'd rather be in the liar category?"

"Naw, it's not that. It's just . . . she's the first woman I'd met in ages that didn't want something from me."

"Think that's the real deal? That she wasn't interested and that's what's pulling you?"

"I don't know. Maybe. But when I saw her with that guy last night and you telling me they seemed to be having a really good time together . . . I knew I didn't want to blow it. So . . . I called her and I'll see her tonight. See how it goes."

"And you're going to tell her, right?"

Clyde glanced away. "I will when the time is right."

"So explain to me what you're going to tell her about, uh, your new line of work as an accountant. You hate numbers more than I do."

"I'll think of something." Suddenly his expression brightened. "Hey, I could ask Ayanna for some tips. She's a whiz with numbers."

Noah's cousin Ayanna was the club's bookkeeper, and Noah looked upon her more as a younger sister than a cousin.

"That's out, brotha. Don't even think about involving her in your mess."

"Yeah, yeah, you're right. Sorry," he mumbled. "Moment of desperation."

A brief silence hung between them.

Clyde switched topics. "So what's happening with Tara? You two seem to be hitting it off."

"Tara's great. A lot of fun, smart, sexy. I like her. But, hey, we'll see what happens. I'm not trying to rush into anything else."

Clyde nodded in understanding. "Listen . . . I know what I'm doing isn't cool, but I'll work it out."

Noah held up his hands, palms facing Clyde. "Hey, brotha, it's your show, I'm just a curious audience member waiting to see the last act." He stood. "I gotta run some errands." He walked past Clyde, patted his shoulder. "Talk to you later." He continued toward the door, stopped, then turned. "Good luck tonight, man. I mean that."

"Thanks." *I'm gonna need it.*

8

"Get outta town!" Tara screeched into the phone. She picked up an exquisite set of gold costume jewelry and held it up for inspection. She'd just closed a deal hovering near the one-hundred-and-fifty-thousand-dollar vicinity. Her commission check was going to have her humming all the way to the bank, one of the many perks of being an international buyer for the very upscale jewelry boutique. Jae's news was icing on the cake. "Called you first thing this morning, huh? Told you. All you had to do was play it cool. He'd come around. Worked better than I thought." She laughed. "You see Clarke today?" She returned the jewelry to the case it was shipped in.

"Yes. It was a bit unnerving. I mean, after dancing with him last night, then seeing him in the hallway and trying to act like nothing happened."

"Nothing did happen . . . did it?" Tara asked coyly. "I

mean, I know you've always said you had no interest in Clarke, but last night . . . well, it looked to me like the two of you got along just fine."

Jae was thoughtful for a moment. She did enjoy herself with Clarke. At first she'd convinced herself to go along with the program because she'd been disappointed about Clyde and seeing him with those women—women so unlike herself. But as the evening wore on, she'd realized what great company Clarke was. Still, she wanted to feel "that thing," and unfortunately, as nice as Clarke was, she didn't feel it— at least she didn't think she did.

"Yes, we did get along," Jae finally admitted. "But. . . ."

"Yeah, I know. You don't have to tell me. I understand perfectly. 'Nuff said. So, you're going on a date with Mr. Clyde," she teased.

Jae suddenly felt a warm tingle as if she'd stuck her big toe in a tub of sudsy water. "I'm so nervous."

"Listen, he's just a man. You're a wonderful, intelligent woman. Just relax and be yourself. Let him see what a catch you are."

Jae smiled. If there was one thing she could always depend on, it was Tara's support. Sure, she was at times loud and raucous, even a bit risqué when the mood hit her. But she was a decent woman and a true friend. Now, if she could only get her to go to church more often.

Jae had changed her clothes a total of five times in the last hour. Panic was beginning to take over. If Clyde was any type of gentleman he'd be on time, which meant in twenty minutes.

She stared at herself in the full-length mirror that hung on the back of her closet door. Staring back at her was a rather ordinary-looking woman, nothing stunning about her, nothing to take your breath away like those women who were all over Clyde the other night. She had a well-toned body, a decent amount of hair, and a pleasant-enough face. But nothing about her said, "Wow!"

She heaved a sigh. Why did he really want to be bothered with her? she worried.

"Beauty is in the eye of the beholder," she heard her mother whisper as plain as if she stood beside her.

"Maybe," she said halfheartedly. Giving herself one last look in the mirror, she marched over to the bed and snatched up her powder blue cotton shift with the tiny yellow sunflower design. "And what you see is what you get," she said with conviction.

Jae's doorbell rang at precisely seven o'clock. Her heart banged in her chest. She took one last look in the mirror and smoothed her French roll in place. With a deep breath of resolve she marched to the door and pulled it open. Her stomach did a slow somersault, then settled as her body flushed with a caressing heat.

"Hi, Jae." A languid smile moved like a slow drag across his mouth.

"Hi." She swallowed. "You want to come in for a minute?"

"Sure."

She stepped aside and the totally male scent of him drifted past her nose, escalated her pulse.

Clyde quickly took in his surroundings: simple, tasteful, no grandeur. *Just like Jae,* he mused. He turned and she was standing in the archway of the living room and his insides suddenly shifted. She looked almost angelic standing there—expectant, unsure . . . inviting. He had the overwhelming urge to kiss her—right then—experience what he knew would be the sweet innocence of her mouth. But instinctively he knew she wasn't ready for that. With Jae he would have to take his time, tap into the hidden quality inside himself that he rarely used—patience.

"I hope you like Mexican food." He slid his hands into his pants pockets.

"I love it," she said on a soft puff of air.

To Clyde's ears it sounded like so much more, and without warning the thought leaped into his head: *One day I want you to say that about me.* The idea jarred him, stirred him out of his almost hypnotic reverie. He pushed out a breath.

"Ready?"

She nodded. "Let me get my purse and we can go."

El Toro, the restaurant, was located in the heart of Georgetown, a pleasant twenty-minute drive from Jae's apartment.

On the trip over, Clyde let the sounds of soft jazz play as a delicate backdrop to the light but informative conversation. Through gentle probing he'd discovered Jae loved to swim, but only in pools with her head above the water, and she hated the spray from the shower to hit her in the face—which he thought was totally bizarre and utterly charming. She enjoyed cooking down-home food and was allergic to cats.

"I'm not allergic to them, but cats give me the willies," Clyde confessed with a slight shiver. "They seem so sneaky."

Jae laughed. "You don't seem to be the kind of man who is scared easily—especially by a cat."

He angled his head in her direction and grinned. "Things aren't always as they seem, Jae Crawford—and neither are people."

His gaze held hers for a moment and she knew just how true that statement was.

All through dinner Clyde told hilarious tales of growing up as an identical twin, and the array of pranks he and his brother, Cliff, played on unsuspecting victims.

"Our parents got so fed up with our getting suspended from school for one stunt or the other that we had a home tutor for the last six months of seventh grade." He chuckled at the memory.

"You two sound like you were a handful. Your poor parents."

"We gave them hell, that's for sure."

"Where's your brother now? Does he live in D.C. as well?"

Clyde's eyes grew dim; his gaze drifted away. He reached

for his margarita and took a long swallow. "He was killed in a car crash five years ago."

Her breath caught. "Oh, Clyde, I'm so sorry." Instinctively she reached for his hand. "That must have been devastating for you."

He swallowed. "It's gotten better. But some days are harder than others. Especially birthdays."

Her heart ached for him. "The Lord doesn't give you more than you can bear, Clyde." She paused a moment, thoughtful about what she was about to say, not wanting to sound preachy. "Do you pray?"

He twisted his lips. "To be truthful, only when things go wrong."

"It helps, you know."

He shrugged slightly. "Maybe. Hasn't helped so far."

"Maybe you're asking for the wrong things."

He looked at her curiously, the candlelight on the table casting soft shadows across her face, illuminating her eyes. "How can you ask for the wrong things? I thought the deal was 'ask and you shall receive.' "

"It's not that simple," she responded gently. "Sometimes the things we think we want aren't really the things we need."

"How do you know the difference?"

"We don't. But He does."

Clyde made a disparaging noise in his throat and took another drink. How many nights had he lain awake after his brother's untimely death and asked, begged, to have him back, for God to change things, to at least take the pain away? No answers, no change. And the guilt wouldn't go away, either. He was supposed to have gone with Cliff that night. But he'd begged off, deciding to hang out with the woman of the moment. Cliff was disappointed. It was a pre-birthday celebration, but Clyde insisted that they tie one on on their birthday night as they always did. But "always" never came. If only he'd been with Cliff. He would have told him not to take that turn so fast, not to have that last drink. He would have—but he wasn't there. Wasn't there. There was no answer to the questions that plagued him. No salve for the guilt he felt—the guilt he'd never shared with anyone.

Jae watched the montage of emotions dance across Clyde's face, darken his eyes, tighten his lips. Beneath the facade of an outwardly together man was someone in pain.

"What if I could prove you wrong?" she asked.

His eyes flickered, then focused on her. "Prove what wrong?"

"That there are answers."

He tipped his head to the side. "How?"

"Come to my church this Sunday."

He lowered his head and shook it slowly. "Church. Hmph. Roof might cave in if I show up."

Jae grinned. "I'll take the chance if you will."

"You singin'?"

She smiled and nodded.

He thought about it a moment. "And if I do show up . . ." He leaned forward. "Will you go out with me again?"

"You drive a hard bargain, Mr. Burrell."

"I'm going to take that as a 'yes.' " He reached for her hand, raised it to his lips, and placed a tender kiss there.

A shiver raced through her and she knew in that instant that it would be hard to say no to much of anything that Clyde Burrell asked of her.

9

It was about noon. The club was closed, but the comforting sounds of staff moving about preparing for the after-work crowd filled the air: soft laughter, the opening and closing of doors, water running, china and silver making their distinctive resonance. This was one of Clyde's favorite times of the day. A time for him to clear his head and think about the evening. He'd booked a great band, and they were in the throes of a rehearsal jam session. The crowd tonight was going to love them. They were a local band, and this was just the opportunity they needed to get some real exposure. He absently tapped his foot to the beat while sipping a glass of Coke, and his thoughts drifted to Jae and the wonderful evening they'd spent together. He had surprised himself by revealing that still unhealed part of him. What surprised him more was that Jae didn't seem to think less of him, think of him as weak for nearly breaking down in front of her. She was so unlike any of the other women he dated, whose main concern was themselves and what they wanted. Jae was nothing like that. Her concern had been him. Had he spoken aloud his pain to some of his former "associates," he was certain that their response would have been to retell some tale of their own, make the conversation about them, not understanding the depth of his pain. Jae didn't do that. Instead, she tried to find a way to offer him some solace. And it touched him in a way that nothing had in quite some time.

"So how'd it go last night?" Noah asked Clyde as he slid onto a bar stool next to him.

Clyde turned toward his buddy. "Great." His broad smile confirmed his words.

"Really. Glad to hear it worked out. So, you really like this woman, huh? Not just someone to get next to for a minute?"

Slowly Clyde nodded. "Yeah, I really like her. More than I first thought. She's . . . special. That's the only way to put it."

Noah placed his forearms on the bar counter and a faraway look came into his eyes. "I think I finally know what you mean, man."

Clyde glanced at him from the corner of his eye. "Meaning . . ."

"That's how I'm starting to feel about Tara."

"You?"

"Yeah, me." He chuckled. "Can you believe it? At first I was just attracted to her because of how she looked; you know the drill. But since we've been talking and spending time together I see what a great woman she is. She's for real, you know."

Clyde nodded in agreement. "I know exactly what you mean. Never thought I'd see it happen to us, man."

"Who you tellin'? I knew I was going to be the professional bachelor."

"Think we're finally growing up?" Clyde teased.

"Better late than never."

They were both quiet for a moment, thoughtful.

"You tell her yet, man?"

Clyde shook his head. "Naw."

"Don't blow this over some bull. If she's all that you say she is, she'll understand."

Clyde turned questioning eyes on his friend. "What if she doesn't?"

Noah quirked his lips, then shrugged. "A relationship built on deceit is doomed to fail, man. Simple."

"Yeah, I know. I don't want to blow this. It just feels right." He paused. "I told her about Cliff."

Noah's eyes widened for a moment. He knew how close Clyde was to his brother and the guilt he felt over his loss. He'd seen the change in Clyde after Cliff died. He became wild, running from one relationship to the next, not staying long enough to care. Noah knew it was a way of protecting himself from becoming attached and possibly hurt. Yet it was something he never talked about. But Noah knew. He always knew. Yeah, this woman had gotten hold of Clyde's heart.

"I promised her I'd come to her church," he said quietly. "Imagine me in church." He laughed lightly, took a sip of his drink.

"Ain't such a bad thing, you know."

Clyde shrugged. " S'pose not. I'm just not expecting anything, you know. But it would make her happy. Plus I'll get a chance to hear her sing. Tara swears she can blow."

"Hey, you don't have anything to lose." Noah patted him on the shoulder and stood up. "Talk to you later."

"Hey, Noah."

"Yeah?"

"Does, uh, Tara know you and I are friends?"

"Subject hasn't come up . . . yet. But I'm telling you, brotha, when it does I'm not gonna lie for you. I'm going check on baby bro Ty and see what he's whipping up for the main course tonight."

Clyde raised his chin in acknowledgment and Noah headed for the kitchen. Clyde drummed his fingers on the hardwood counter. It was true the lie couldn't go on forever. But maybe just a little while longer. Just until he and Jae were tight. Then he'd tell her. He really would.

Jae and Tara met for lunch, something they often did when Tara was in town and not jaunting about the globe looking for a great deal. Her buying trips generally took her out of the States for a cumulative total of three months per year, in search of the perfect stone, delicately woven gold, and auctions of one-of-a-kind pieces. When she was in town, her time was pretty much her own, barring any mandatory meeting. Her schedule was much more flexible than Jae's with her designated one hour for lunch, but they made the most of it.

"I know you don't have a whole lot of time," Tara was saying, "but you know how I feel about college cafeteria food. Cafeteria food in general." She screwed up her nose.

"We could go to that outdoor café that you like. They have great salads and they're fast."

"Sounds good."

They started walking, taking in the sights and sounds of a summer afternoon in the nation's capital.

"So are you going to leave me in suspense until I bust, or are you going to tell me about your date with Clyde?"

They stood in front of the door of the café and were quickly escorted to a table outside, beneath the green-and-white-striped awning.

"Can we at least sit down first?" Jae teased, feeling light and incredibly happy. She purposely took her time scouring the menu, even though she knew what she wanted. Then she pondered what she was going to drink, knowing the only thing she did drink was ginger ale.

"You're about getting on my last nerve," Tara said from between tight lips.

Jae busted out laughing. "You should see your face."

"You did it. Now tell me what happened. And don't leave anything out. I want to live vicariously for a minute." She grinned mischievously.

Jae explained in her precise professorial manner everything that had happened, from her frantic search for something to wear to her inviting Clyde to church.

"And he agreed?" Tara asked incredulously.

"Yep."

Tara took a healthy bite of her salad. "Good for you, girl," she mumbled over a mouthful of spinach. "What does Clyde do again?"

"He's an accountant."

"Yeah, right. With a firm or what?"

Jae frowned for a moment. "I don't really know. We haven't talked about work much."

Tara pointed her fork in Jae's direction. "First thing a woman needs to know about a man is that he's stable, has someplace to go every day, and doesn't live with his mama."

Jae chuckled. "I'm sure all those things are in place. Clyde is a steady kind of guy. Has his program together."

"As long as you're sure." She took another forkful of salad. "I'd still find out where he works and how long he's been there. That's just basic information, girl. When you don't have it, it's almost like a man only giving you his beeper number and not the one at home."

Jae pursed her lips. If Clyde opened himself up about his brother, something she was certain pained him deeply, she was sure he would be willing to tell her anything else, especially something as mundane as where he worked. *It just hasn't come up, is all*, she convinced herself. But all the way back to the university, Tara's comment kept repeating in her head: *"That's just basic information, girl."* Yeah, it was, wasn't it?

*   *   *

Between preparing for finals for her class and her report for the department and Clyde's clandestine schedule at the club, the next time they had the opportunity to get together was two weeks later to attend a concert in Rock Creek Park. Chaka Khan, who hadn't given a live performance in years, was the featured artist, and the park was packed to bursting.

Clyde held tightly to her hand, and they wove their way around the bodies, blankets, and coolers. Finally they found a lone patch of grass and claimed it.

"Not as close as I would like, but it beats watching it from the street," Clyde said with a chuckle as he spread out the blanket he'd taken from the trunk of his car.

"I've never seen her live. I've heard some of her music," Jae said, beginning to unpack the basket of snacks she'd prepared.

"Then you're in for a real treat."

It was a perfect summer night. Not too hot, the sun just beginning to dip below the horizon, with a light breeze rustling through the trees. *Perfect,* Jae thought. Just as the past few weeks with Clyde had been.

Since the night they'd gone to dinner, although they didn't see each other as much as she would have liked, they talked every day. Clyde had gotten into the habit of calling her first thing in the morning and the last thing at night. She looked forward to his calls, to their long chats when they talked about their childhood, their hopes, friends, family fables, and each other.

Yet each and every time Jae mentioned anything about his job or asked questions about how his day had gone, he became evasive, saying his job was a boring list of numbers and forms, nothing worth taking up their precious time discussing. So she'd let it go, not wanting to rock the boat and stir up the gentle wave of discovery they were riding. But in the back of her mind she kept hearing Tara's warning.

The concert was a hand-clapping, stomping, whooping and hollering event. After Jae got over the frenzy of the crowd, she found herself joining in the revelry. She was so engrossed with the music, the beauty of the night, the excitement of the crowd that she didn't notice at first that Clyde's arms surrounded her, his body pressed to the back of hers, swaying to the music. She could feel the hair on the back of her neck flutter with the soft puffs of his breath, feel the vibrations along her spine as he hummed along to some of his favorite tunes. She found herself relaxing against him, not wanting to pull away, but get closer. Suddenly she didn't hear the music anymore, didn't see the montage of colors that blanketed the green splotches of earth. All she could feel was the strength of Clyde's arms; hear, the low timbre of his voice. It was just the two of them, beneath the shadow of the willow tree illuminated by the light of the quarter moon. And the warmth started in her center and shot straight to her head.

"I had a great time tonight, Jae," Clyde said softly as they stood in her doorway.

"So did I."

He stepped closer, his gaze holding her in place. Her heartbeat ran wild. His hand slipped behind her head and eased her closer. She could feel the warmth of his breath brush tantalizingly across her lips. And then she felt them, soft, tender, moist.

An almost inaudible groan hummed deep in his throat, and he pressed closer, his free arm wrapping around her waist.

The changes in her body were swift and precise, beginning with the juncture between her thighs, scurrying up to her stomach, through her chest, raising her nipples to hardened peaks. She trembled when his tongue grazed her lips.

It took all of his willpower not to go further, to take her right there and then, in her doorway. The sensation was so overwhelming it left him weak with its intensity. This was what he feared, the powerlessness, the feeling of losing control, of giving his emotions up and surrendering them to another. But he couldn't help himself. He wanted Jae. Wanted her all to himself. Now. But prudence intervened, and reluctantly and with great difficulty he pulled back and rested his head against hers, then brushed the expanse of her neck with a tender kiss.

"Good night, Jae," he said in a strained whisper. He pulled farther back and looked at her, saw the glow that seemed to radiate around her. And at that moment she was the most beautiful woman he'd even seen. It came from within, wafted around her like a halo. A beauty that would never fade. He swallowed hard, realizing just how deeply he was falling for her. "Is your offer to go to church still open?"

She smiled softly. "Always."

"What time?"

"Service starts at eleven."

"I'll be there." He touched his lips to hers. "Sleep well, angel. I'll see you tomorrow." He turned and hurried away before he was unable to leave at all.

In a daze, Jae closed the door, turned, leaned her back against it, and closed her eyes. Her entire body vibrated. This was what she'd waited for, knew she would one day find. And she had. "Let the choir say, 'Amen,' " she murmured.

10

He rode around the block of the church at least a half-dozen times. He watched the people in all their finery strut and stroll. But he couldn't seem to simply put the car in park, get out, and go inside.

The last time he'd set foot in a church was his brother's funeral. He'd never had a reason to go back since. All it held for him was painful memories. Thank God his parents had not been alive to witness it all. Their pain would have been too much for him to bear.

"The Lord doesn't give you more than you can bear, Clyde." He took a breath and squeezed into a parking space, yet he still had the overwhelming urge to pull out and go home, explain to Jae later, make something up. He sat there for a few minutes more, the waves of memories washing over

him. But he'd offered; he'd promised. He'd do it for Jae. A promise was a promise.

Clyde got out of his Lexus and moved toward the open doors of Bethel Baptist Church just as the choir began its opening song, "Peace Be Still," the hymn Reverend James Cleveland made famous so many years ago. He felt so out of place. He'd rather be back at the club, in the environment where he felt most at home. As the choir eased into the rocking harmony of the song, the choir director waved his arms to heighten, then reduce the volume of the swirl of voices that supported the lead singer, a frail girl who could not have been more than sixteen. She reared back her head and sang the lyrics to the hymn with such conviction that the entire building seem to shake from its foundation to the ceiling.

After the girl finished her solo, the pastor stood slowly and walked majestically to the pulpit dressed in a long, flowing white robe, with a black cross emblazoned over his heart. He was a strong, sturdy, short man, with long black hair over his ears and a closely trimmed mustache. For several seconds he waited for the commotion following the song to subside before he opened the large Bible before him.

Clyde settled back and watched Jae and the others in the choir take their seats behind the minister.

"Today, we'll do something different rather than give a long sermon about the Glory of God and the mission," the minister spoke in the rich baritone voice so often heard in Southern Baptist churches. He paused for dramatic effect, letting the echo of his words float into the rafters of the great room, then settle down gently onto the heads and hearts of the faithful.

Standing on the edge of the stage, he held up his arms, the gathered material of the robe forming great wings while he stared up as if hearing the muted whispers of the Almighty. Clyde smiled momentarily; he understood the power of theater in the church and the sublime ability of the pastors to play to that special moment. Still, he glanced back at the large doors leading to the street, wondering what Jae would say if he left the service.

Clyde sighed, feeling extremely restless, shifting his feet under the pew. Suddenly his heart stopped as the choir stood again and Jae took center stage before the mike. One choir member adjusted it to Jae's height, smiled at her, and rejoined the others lined up in a wall of white robes. Clyde didn't know what to expect, but any doubt about her talent immediately vaporized when her smooth, silky voice caressed the lyrics to "Amazing Grace." He was bowled over by the maturity in her singing, her expressive phrasing, her ability to twist and bend notes like the best jazz singer. She sang with such assurance and confidence, with such warmth and control, that it seemed she knew there was nothing she couldn't do with her voice.

Jae stood erect and beautiful, poised and smiling. She held nothing back and the congregation sensed this gift of hers to them and responded in kind with a reverent silence. Clyde got the feeling that she had done this to them many times before, weaved this spell that held them speechless while she reworked the song in her own highly personal style. Even the minister was nodding his head in time to her vocals. She had them all in the palm of her hand, totally under her control. Imagine the power of Aretha melded to the agility of Sarah. Or the honesty of Carmen wedded to the force of Mahalia. It was all there in Jae's eagerness to reach out and touch her audience, the Faithful. He could only imagine what she would do with the excitable crowd at the club, the die-hard fans who traveled from club to club hoping to hear something new. They'd go crazy if she sang like this there. Now he had no regrets that he had come. He'd heard that song countless times but never sung like this. A smile played across her face as she acknowledged that the people sitting before her understood what she was doing to the song and how she was acknowledging God's gift to her.

When Jae completed the song, the people shouted and cheered like they were at a rock concert. Clyde joined them in their love for her. He didn't have to hear any more. The woman was not only beautiful, but she also could sing her heart out. While the service continued with more sermons,

Bible reading, and songs, he sat there plotting and planning how he could get her to perform at the club. What he would say, what he would offer her.

"So what did you think?" Jae said to him as they later walked out toward the church parking lot. "Did you like it?"

"Yes, I'd say you had a little talent," he teased. "You can sing a little bit."

That pleased her and she nudged him in the side, laughing. "No, really, what did you think?"

"Jae, you're terrific," he said. "I had no idea you could sing like that."

"Are you glad you came?" She was watching his face with an intensity that made him forget the uneasiness he had felt when he first entered the church.

"You bet I am. And I'm sure that everybody else that came today is as well. Do you sing like that every Sunday?"

"Yes, but today I only did the one song. I usually do two or three. Mr. Johnson the choir director, wanted to give Aleta a chance to sing. She's the thin girl who sang before me."

He laughed. "And she wasn't bad, either. Probably more record producers should spend some time in church and the business wouldn't be so full of these non-singers that they have to overproduce and overdub to make sound decent. Man, this was well worth the trip."

"But . . . . besides the singing did *you* get anything out of the service?"

He was thoughtful for a moment, knew what it was she was really asking him. "Yes, I have to admit that I did. I know I was reluctant at first. To tell you the truth, I sat outside and thought about going back home. But," he breathed deeply, "I feel better, good inside, you know?"

She smiled broadly and took his arm. "Yes, I know."

They walked arm in arm toward his car. "We still have a deal, you know."

She cocked her head to the side.

"Don't act like you don't know what I'm talking about. You said if I came to church you would sing at Open Mike

Night. And after hearing you today, there's no way I'm going to let you back out. No way."

"But, Clyde—"

"No buts—"

"What I was going to say is that . . . I've never sung outside of church, Clyde, the protection of the choir." She gazed down at her shoes, then up at him. "To tell you the truth . . . I'm kinda scared."

"Baby, what you have you should share, not just inside these walls but everywhere folks will take a minute to listen." He grinned broadly, his eyes shining with sincerity.

She stared at him a moment, thinking about all of her childhood conversations with her parents and her pastors about using her gift to praise God. And how those trashy secular songs that had the kids shaking and grinding were simply sinful. No matter how much she'd tried to tell them about some of the beautiful songs that weren't choir tunes, they didn't want to hear it. Finally she had resigned herself to singing gospel, going along, listening to her parents and to the church. But . . . deep inside there lived that "other" voice, that "other" self that wanted to get out, that hummed Billie Holiday tunes, scatted like Ella, and turned up the notches like Sarah—in the shower. Her heart raced. Maybe it was time.

Jae took a deep breath of resolve. "Are you sure?" she asked. The possibility of performing at the club filled her veins with an infusion of excitement.

"Never been more sure of anything in my life."

She stopped short. He turned, looked curiously at her.

"I'll do it." Her heart raced.

He pulled her to him and kissed her full on the mouth and didn't give a damn who was watching.

"You won't regret it, baby; I promise." But even as he said the words, he wondered how he was going to keep his real life in the background as she stepped forward.

11

"I agreed, but now I'm scared to death," Jae confessed to Tara that next night over the phone lines. She sat in her sweats on the edge of her bed, legs crossed, rocking her right foot back and forth.

"Girl, if I had a voice like yours I'd be singing all the time. You'll be fine. When are you planning to do it?"

"I guess the next Open Mike Night," she said, feeling a bit giddy. "But what do I do, just show up?"

"Hmm. Good question. I'll ask Noah and see what the procedure is and let you know."

Jae sighed heavily. "OK. Thanks. How are things going with you and Noah these days?"

"Can't complain, girl. The man is a dream."

"You deserve someone nice, who treats you good."

"So do you."

"I think I've found him, Tara. I really think I have."

Across town, another kind of confession was under way and the hatching of a desperate plan.

"And just how do you intend to pull this one off?" Noah wanted to know.

"That's why I'm talking to you, man. Give me some ideas."

"Give you some ideas! I told you weeks ago to tell the woman the truth." He sat down heavily on his living room couch and glared at Clyde. "You're the entertainment director. All acts come through you. Right or wrong?"

"Don't quiz me, man."

"Right or wrong?"

"Right! OK, I messed up." He got up from the love seat, went to Noah's bar, and fixed himself a shot of scotch on the rocks.

"I still don't see what the big deal is. If she digs you, just explain the real deal to her and the reasons why you lied to her in the first place. Simple."

"To you," he grumbled and tossed the drink down in one swallow without wincing. "You don't know the kind of woman she is. Very conservative, old-world almost. God-fearing and all."

Noah leaned back on the couch and stretched his arm along the top. "If you have a better suggestion, I'm listening. What, you think she's gonna strike you down with lightning or something?" He chuckled.

Clyde twisted his lips, knowing that Noah was going to hit the ceiling when the words tumbled out of his mouth. But . . . "I was hoping you would hook her up for me. Take care of things. Just for this one night, Noah, I swear, and I'll tell her. I will. After she sings. She's nervous enough as it is. If I tell her now she'll back out. And this woman has talent. Real talent. You know the kind of folks that come to Leo's. Record scouts are always hanging out there. She has a real shot and I don't want her to blow it because of me."

Noah cut him a nasty look, inhaled deeply, and blew out a long breath. He pointed an accusing finger at Clyde. "This is the last time. I don't want to get involved in your little schemes. Understand? You straighten this out."

"I will. I will."

Just then the phone rang.

"Hello?"

"Hi, honey. It's me."

"Hey, babe." A smile of delight drifted across his mouth, and Clyde saw Noah's entire body relax. *It was Tara.*

"Listen, you remember my friend Jae?"

Noah's lashes flickered and he glanced at Clyde. "Yeah. Why? What's up?"

"She's been seeing this guy Clyde and he finally convinced her to sing at the club. I was wondering what the process was. What does she need to do?"

"Oh, uh." He swallowed. "Just, uh, tell her to give me a call. I'll set everything up."

"Really? Great. I'll tell her." She paused a moment. "Are you OK? You sound funny."

He cleared his throat. "No. I'm fine. Just chilling, watching the game."

"Oh, OK. Anyway, will I see you tomorrow?"

"Absolutely."

"Call me before you turn in."

"Promise."

"Bye, sweetie."

"Bye." Slowly he hung up the phone. Now Clyde had him lying, too. What next?

Open Mike Night finally arrived. Noah kept his part of the bargain, finalizing all of the arrangements for Jae to appear as part of the evening's lineup. He reluctantly made sure that Clyde's name never came up in any of his discussions with the singer, but he worried about what would happen if Jae found out that he was now a co-conspirator in Clyde's scam to get the woman to perform. And there would be hell to pay if Tara discovered what he was doing. He didn't want to jeopardize their relationship over some foolishness Clyde was concocting. Why couldn't the man just deal aboveboard with Jae? Then none of this would be necessary.

When Jae took to the stage, backed by a trio of bass, piano, and drums, Clyde lurked in the shadows, making himself invisible, staying out of sight. But within earshot. She sang a brief melody of Lady Day tunes, "My Man," followed by "I Cover the Waterfront" and "What a Little Moonlight Can Do." Noah was stunned by how well she interpreted the old jazz standards, giving them more body and juice than he expected from a church singer. She rocked the house, leaving the crowd yelling for more.

As she walked from the stage among the cheering patrons, feeling totally exhilarated, she spied Clyde being cornered by a wildly gesturing white man. She moved steadily through the rows of tables in their direction, unnoticed by the two men who were deeply involved in their conversation.

"Clyde, how long have I known you?" the well-dressed

white man was saying. "So you've been holding out on me. Why didn't you tell me about this singer? With pipes like she has, my record label would be willing to give her damn near anything she'd ask for."

"I haven't been holding out on you," Clyde replied. "I just discovered her myself."

"Is she with anybody? Does she have a contract with any label right now?"

"No, she's brand-spanking new to the scene. Come on, Mort, I'm not trying to brush you off, but let me talk to you about her next week sometime. We'll get together for lunch or drinks or something. OK?"

"Clyde, I hate when you get evasive on me. What are you running here? You almost run this joint. Hey, if you don't like somebody, they don't perform here. Simple." He pointed an unlit cigar in the air for emphasis. "So don't play the innocent with me. If you've hooked her up with somebody else, tell me. Don't lead me on."

Jae walked up and both men turned to face her. Mort, who was an executive with Raven Records, started his hard sell on her within seconds, but Clyde cut him off with a wave of his hand. Abruptly he moved between Jae and the man, grabbed her by the elbow, and ushered her toward the back-stage area where no one was allowed except the performers and staff.

"What was that all about, Clyde?" she asked. "Who was that man?"

"Nobody, Jae. Let's talk about it later. All right?"

Clyde pivoted and headed back for the dressing room, with Jae following, not content with his answers. She had other things to ask him. Before he could get to the refuge of the room, a large black woman intercepted him, literally placing herself between him and the door. A tall, nerdy teenager stood with her, watching everything with a bemused expression.

"Now, Mr. Clyde, you promised me that you'd let my Edgar go on tonight and you broke your promise," the woman said, shaking her head for emphasis. "You broke your word. At the last minute, this woman sings in his place. That ain't right. You know that ain't right."

Clyde smiled graciously and asked for her patience. "Can we talk about this later? I'm busy right now."

The teenager, dressed in hip-hop clothes, tapped him on the arm. "Mr. Clyde, everybody knows you the starmaker. You sign somebody up here for Open Mike Night and they get discovered and blow up overnight. Next thing you know, they living large. You the man. Everybody know that."

"Excuse me," Clyde said, noticing that Jae was standing there, witnessing this sideshow. "Can't you see that I'm very busy?"

"But you promised me, gave me your word," the boy's mother insisted, with menace in her words. "As this club's entertainment director, you can do anything you want. My boy can be the next D'Angelo or Puff Daddy; all you got to do is to give him a break. Let him sing and you'll know what I'm talking about. Just let him sing."

"Please, ma'am, can we talk about this later? I beg you. I'm very busy."

"This is the very reason why we can't get anywhere as a people, because of folks like you," the woman snarled and walked away. "A black man's words don't mean a damn thing anymore. Folks'll lie to you in a heartbeat and with a straight face, too."

Jae watched the woman push her way through the crowd, grumbling under her breath, with one hand dragging her lanky son behind her. No sooner had the woman and her son disappeared into the folds of the crowd than a stunning, fresh-off-the-cover-of-*Essence*-magazine-looking woman stepped up to Clyde and planted a full, open-mouth kiss right on his lips.

"Clyde, baby," she crooned, stroking his cheek with a long pearly pink nail. "I thought tonight was my night. You promised me. You still gonna get me in the lineup, right?"

Clyde gulped and tried to step out of the vise of her perfume. "Vanessa." His eyes darted to Jae's, a mixture of outrage, hurt, and disbelief hovering there. Clyde placed his hand squarely on Vanessa's bare shoulders. "Not tonight, Vanessa. I'm sorry. We'll work something out for next time. Call the office." He extricated himself and finally made his escape, almost running into the dressing room, totally drained and shaken.

Jae walked in behind him and stood quietly as he plopped into one of the chairs facing a vanity mirror. His face seemed to sag right before her eyes. He knew he was busted. The truth was out. There was no lie he could tell that would get him out of this mess.

"Why did you lie to me, Clyde?" Jae's voice was flat, cold, and almost lifeless. "Why didn't you tell me who you really were?"

"Because I was afraid I'd lose you. I didn't know what you might do if you knew the truth. So I didn't tell you."

"But I trusted you. One of the reasons I sang tonight was because of you. You convinced me that what I'd kept buried inside all these years was right; it was possible. Why didn't you tell the truth and let me decide what I'd do?" Her eyes filled, but she'd be damned if she'd let him see her cry. "You ruined everything. You ruined the night for me."

Clyde, for once, lost his power to speak. What could he possibly say that would allow her to trust him about anything? How could he tell her how much he really felt for her when everything he said would be seen as a lie?

"Why don't you answer me, Clyde?" she insisted, her voice rising. "Why don't you say something for yourself?"

"Because I don't know what I could possibly say that would make everything better at this point. I'd just dig myself deeper into a hole."

"Why don't you tell me some lies?" she snapped at him. "You seem to be really good at that."

He lowered his head in shame and regret. "I'm sorry, Jae. I really am."

She glared at him with intense burning eyes. "You played me for a fool, Clyde. Strung me along. What else have you been lying about?" With that, she stormed out of the room and slammed the door.

He sat there, looking at himself in the mirror, a big scowl on his idiot face, and lit a cigarette with trembling hands. What an ass he'd been!

12

Jae rushed past Tara on her way out, tears streaming down her face, ruining the perfectly wonderful makeup job Tara had spent hours creating. She felt devastated by what she had discovered.

"Jae!" Tara jumped up from her seat and ran after her. "Jae!" she yelled as she ran on high heels down the street. "Wait."

Finally Jae slowed down and leaned against the side of a building. Her chest heaved up and down as she tried to catch her breath.

"Honey, what's wrong? What happened?" Tara braced Jae's shuddering shoulders.

"He . . . he lied to me."

Tara frowned. "Who lied?"

"Clyde."

Between short gasps, Jae explained as best she could what Clyde had done, how he'd made a fool of her. She couldn't find the appropriate words to describe how deeply his betrayal of her had hurt.

"Why would he do something like that? Why would he want me to believe he was something he wasn't?"

"I don't know, honey. Maybe he . . . Damn, I don't know." But Tara's mind was racing. Noah had to be aware of what was going on. Clyde worked for him. He'd known all along. He was just as guilty as that liar Clyde Burrell. Noah Hardcastle had a lot of explaining to do.

After taking a hurt and disillusioned Jae home, Tara returned to the club and went on the hunt for Noah. She would get to the bottom of this.

"I told you this was going to happen, man," Noah said as he and Clyde stood in a huddle near the kitchen. "And you have me right in the mix."

All Clyde could do was look sheepish. He was wrong. Noah was right, had been from the beginning. "Listen, man, I'm sorry. I'll square things with Tara."

"You better. 'Cause here she comes now."

They both turned toward the fiery-looking woman, and Clyde knew from the expression on her face that he had better come up with something good. There had to be some way he could turn this around. Make things right.

Tara stood in front of them, hands on hips. She cocked her head to the side, looked from one to the other. Both men stood there with uneasy looks.

"How could you do that to her?" she lashed out at Clyde. "And you"—she pointed a finger at Noah—"are just as bad! You helped him pull this off."

Clyde stepped forward. "It wasn't his fault, Tara," he said in a quiet voice, attempting to calm her down. "He did it for me. Because I asked him to."

"Jae Crawford is one of the sweetest, most decent people I know. You have no idea what you've done."

Clyde held up his hands. "Just let me explain. Think whatever you want about me, but just let me try to tell you why."

Tara folded her arms and glared at him, shot a nasty look in Noah's direction, then turned back to Clyde. "I'm listening and it better be damned good."

Clyde started from the day he met Jae, the reason that he had gone to her table to meet her and the impressions that she had of club life, entertainers, and everyone associated with them. He added the bit about their arrangement and his visit to church.

"I know it was a stupid thing to do, to lie about something as simple as what I did for a living, but I just wanted her to give me a chance before she made up her mind about me, lumped me in with everyone else." He shook his head. "And once it was out there, it got harder and harder to take it back. But you've got to believe me. I care about Jae, *really* care about her. I don't want to lose her."

Tara softened her stance somewhat. "Think it's too late for that, my brother. If there's one thing I know about Jae it's that she has real strong convictions about honesty and how people treat each other. She'll put all her trust in a person until they prove her wrong. And if you do, she'll cut you off." She took a breath. "But she has a forgiving heart."

Clyde felt his first burst of hope.

"You need to talk to her. Maybe if you're lucky she'll listen."

"I'll make her listen." He made a move to leave, then stopped. "Thanks, Tara." He darted off before he could hear any response. He wasn't sure what he was going to say to Jae when he got to her house. *Maybe the truth for starters*, he chastised himself, and he tore away from the curb.

Clyde pulled up in front of Jae's house and glanced up at the window. The house was dark. What should he do? Suppose she wouldn't let him in. Suppose she shut him out. Refused to talk to him. He reached for his cell phone and punched in her number. The phone rang four times and the answering machine kicked in.

Jae lay in her bed, staring up at the ceiling, listening to Clyde begging her to pick up the phone, to listen to him. His words meant nothing now. He was a liar. She started to pick it up, decided not to. She didn't want to talk to him, not now, not ever.

Clyde talked until the machine beeped, indicating that he'd exhausted his time. He tossed the cell phone onto the passenger seat and reluctantly pulled off.

Jae watched from behind the curtain of her window as the Lexus and Clyde disappeared from view. She was glad that he didn't force her to face him. She had no idea what she might say. It was better this way, with him leaving.

For the next few days like clockwork, Clyde called Jae at home, asking her over and again to accept his apology, give him another chance. But she wouldn't relent. She didn't want to take the chance that somewhere down the line something bigger, something worse, might occur between them. She didn't want that. Once a liar, always a liar. Yet no matter how hard she tried, how much she attempted to keep Clyde out of her mind and her heart, he remained there beating stronger every day.

"What happened to all the sunshine that used to glow around you?" Clarke asked as he met Jae in the corridor. "You don't look too happy these days. Anything I can help with?"

"I'm fine," Jae replied without much conviction.

"Well, you don't look fine and you don't sound fine."

She tucked a wayward strand of hair back into her bun, avoiding his inquiring gaze as tears suddenly loomed in her eyes.

"Come in my office, Jae," he said gently, ushering her inside.

Once behind closed doors, Jae finally gave in to all the emotion she'd been feeling during the past week, and for some reason she couldn't fathom, she spilled the story out to Clarke.

For several moments after she'd finished, Clarke remained quiet. He'd known and cared about Jae since she'd come to work at the University. He'd tried to win her over and thought he'd had a chance that night at Leo's. But right up to now, nothing. What he *wanted* to do was play on her vulnerability, become more than just a comforting friend. He couldn't do that. Not to Jae, even as much as he wanted her.

"Listen, Jae, I know the importance you put on honesty and integrity. I see it every day in the way you live your life, the way you deal with your students and the staff. It's admirable. More people should be like you." He paused. "Unfortunately, we're not. We have faults; we lie, cheat, and screw up. What we do hope for, however, is a second chance, an opportunity to make it right. That's all Clyde is asking for. And if you didn't care about him as you're trying very poorly to pretend that you don't, you wouldn't be sitting here in my office crying over him." He took a breath. "You know I care about you, Jae. I've never made a secret of that. But you care about that man, maybe more than care. That's plain enough to me, a man who doesn't want to see it."

She looked up at him, shocked by his honesty.

"Give him a chance. Give yourself a chance. Even the worst sinner is allowed forgiveness."

She gave him a crooked smile, wiped at her eyes, and sniffed back her tears. "Thank you, Clarke . . . for being honest. And for being man enough not to take advantage of the situation. I really appreciate that."

"That's what friends are for, Jae," he said softly, realizing that whatever chance he may have had was quietly slipping away. But it would be all right and so would he.

She stood, leaned down and tenderly kissed his cheek, turned, and walked out, closing the door softly behind her.

"What I need is a plan," Jae said to Tara, who sat opposite her at the kitchen table.

Tara's eyes widened. "You? A plan?" She wiggled her finger in her ear. "I know I'm not hearing right."

"Don't be funny. Be helpful. I want to knock him out. Make him see what he's been missing," Jae said with a brand-new attitude. "I want to blow his mind."

Tara laughed out loud. "I don't know what hit you, honey, but I'm loving it. Why the big three-sixty?"

Jae sat back and folded her arms. "I've been doing a lot of thinking, a lot of soul-searching. As long as I'm a good person inside and treat people decently, that's what counts. The Man up above knows what's in my heart. I've always wanted to sing, sing whatever I wanted, but I'd been so brainwashed into believing it was wrong, sinful. That the show business life was one of degradation and only the lowest of the low were a part of it. It's all about what you are as a person. There are all kinds of temptations out there, and running from them and pretending they're not there won't make them go away. Just have to deal with them. And I plan to deal with mine. Truth is"—she grinned wickedly and briefly shut her eyes as she relieved the moment—"there was nothing to compare to how I felt when I got up on that stage. It was incredible. Something I've only dreamed about." She looked at Tara. "I want my chance, Tara. Are you gonna help me?"

Tara leaned across the table and so did Jae. Tara's mouth curved up in a grin. "Now, here's the plan . . ."

13

"I worked everything out with Noah. He owed me big-time. This was his payback. Now, Clyde has no idea you're going to be here tonight. So, the operative word is *cool*. Remember, *c-o-o-l*. 'Cause the brother needs to sweat just a minute longer."

Jae giggled nervously. "I hate playing cruel jokes on people, but in this case . . ."

"Trust me, you'll be forgiven. Ready?"

Jae nodded, tightened the belt on her trench coat, and stepped out of the car, the sound of her heels clicking against the concrete striking a distinctive no-nonsense beat.

"She still won't talk to me," Clyde lamented, his legs stretched out in front of him, slouching in the leather office chair. "Did you speak to Tara?"

"Hey, I was busy trying to patch up my own stuff with her. But yeah, I talked to her, tried to find out what's happening with Jae. Tara says she doesn't want to have anything to do with you." Noah lied smoothly but immediately felt awful when he saw the crestfallen look on his friend's face. But the truth was, he deserved it. Maybe this would teach him a lesson for the future.

Clyde slapped his hands down on the arms of the chair. "I don't know what else to do, man. I've tried everything. I . . . I love her."

Noah snapped to attention. "Have you told her?"

Clyde shook his head. "I figured she wouldn't believe that, either. I'm miserable without her."

"Hey, man, give it some time. It's only been a few weeks. She'll come around."

"Yeah, right," he said gloomily.

"Come on. Cheer up. We have a house full of people and we need to put on our best faces."

Clyde stood, put on a pasty false grin, and followed Noah out of the office and into the club.

"Have you seen him?" Jae whispered, looking nervously around the packed club.

"Not yet. Just relax."

The waitress came to their table and took their orders for appetizers, a rum and Coke, and a ginger ale with a twist.

"There he is," Jae hissed from between her teeth, spotting Noah and Clyde crossing the dimly lit floor on the other side.

"Ready?"

Jae tugged in a breath, slid the trench coat off, and let it hang on the back of the chair. The off-the-shoulder teal mini-dress in a body-hugging Lycra clung to Jae's every curve, leaving little to the imagination. Her naturally wavy hair hung loose, full and radiant around her perfectly made up face. "Let's go."

The two women rose and sauntered over to the bar. Every eye of every unattached male followed their progress. Quicker than they could wink, a good-looking man of about forty eased up alongside Jae.

"Good evening. Can I buy that drink for you?"

Jae turned slowly in his direction. "Thanks, but no."

"If you change your mind, I'm sitting at that table over there." He pointed to a table in the center of the room.

"I'll remember that," Jae said as smoothly as if she always turned down drinks from handsome strangers.

"Hey, you're pretty good at this," Tara teased when the man was out of earshot.

"I'm shaking all over and this dress makes me feel like I'm naked."

"Remember, cool."

*   *   *

The spotlight hit the center stage and Noah stepped up to the mike. "Welcome to Leo's. As always on Open Mike Night, we've set up some hot performers for you that I know you're going to love. Tonight we're going to do something a little different. We don't usually have encores, but this young woman was so baad when she was here last we had to have her back. Please put your hands together for the fabulous Ms. Jae Crawford."

Clyde jumped up from his seat like a shot from a cannon. "Jae!"

Jae's short, sultry walk to the stage was accompanied by whistles and whoops from the men and pleasant applause from the women. It was obvious by the smile on her face that this was a moment she truly enjoyed. She stepped up to the mike and the lights dimmed, creating a halo around her.

Clyde could hardly believe his eyes. *His Jae*, with a dress halfway up her hips, legs that went on forever, and a waist that women spent their lives trying to attain. *Jae*. She was exquisite, stunning, breathtaking, and when she belted out her version of Billie Holiday's "My Man" he knew he was hooked, lined, and sunk. And the way the men carried on, he wanted to run up on the stage, wrap his jacket around her, and lock her away forever.

When she hit that closing note with all the pain and conviction of a woman who loved her man no matter what, the crowd went wild. She milked that last note for all it was worth. With the grace of a seasoned performer, she took her bow and made her exit.

Tara was waiting for her at the door, applauding wildly, with tears in her eyes.

"Girl, you were too fierce," she said, handing Jae her coat.

"Did you see him?"

"Oh, yeah, I saw him all right. Looked like his eyes were going to pop out of his head. Come on. I'll give him five minutes and he'll be outside right behind you."

"What if he isn't?"

"Believe me, honey, he will be."

*   *   *

Clyde pushed past the patrons, dashed around pillars and harried waiters, and strong-armed through the glass-and-brass doors. His eyes darted up and down the block, and then he spotted her walking casually down the street with Tara.

"Jae!"

"Told ya," Tara whispered. "Go for it, girl."

Tara kept walking. Jae stopped and turned toward the sound of Clyde's voice, and as always whenever she saw him, that warm sensation flowed through her veins. He hurried toward her, arms outstretched, not wanting to risk the chance that she would turn and leave him standing there.

Her heart was beating so hard and fast, she could barely breathe. But she kept repeating over and over, *"Cool, cool, cool."* And then he was right in front of her, so close she could feel the heat from his body, inhale the rich scent of him that sent her pulse racing.

"Jae," he said on a breath. "Please, just give me one minute to explain."

She'd heard it all already from Tara but wanted to hear it from him. She folded her arms and waited.

"First, I just want to tell you how sorry I am that I lied to you," he stammered. "It was stupid and I misjudged you. I hurt you, nearly screwed up Noah's relationship with Tara, and lost you in the process. But, Jae, I want you back. I want another chance. I love you, Jae, from the bottom of my heart. I've never been so miserable in my life as I've been these past weeks. You've got to believe me." His eyes pleaded with her to understand, to accept, to forgive.

She knew Tara had insisted that she play hard to get, give him a rough time of it, make him pay just a little longer. Draw out his pain like twisting a piece of jagged glass stuck in tender skin. But she couldn't. All she wanted to do right at that moment was tell him how much she loved him, too. And she did.

Clyde stepped up closer, cutting off all space between them. "Say it again," he asked in a husky voice. His finger stroked her cheek.

"I love you, Clyde Burrell."

He took her in his arms and brought his mouth to hers, taking everything that he'd missed, retracing his steps, making all things between them familiar again. He didn't care who was looking, and neither did she.

SIX MONTHS LATER

Tara sat in the dressing room of Leo's looking at her radiant friend in the mirror as she slipped into her ears a pair of pearls, an engagement present from Clyde. Tara adjusted Jae's veil.

"Who would have thought that Jae Crawford would walk down the aisle of a supper club on her wedding day?"

Jae grinned. "What could be more appropriate?" she asked, turning around in the swivel chair. "This is where we met, fell in love, fell out, and this is where we'll seal our future—for the second time today." She giggled. "The church this morning was to make my parents happy. This is for me!"

"I hear you, sister. You have your vows ready?"

"Yep. I promise to love him forever, keep my skirts to my knees, and he'll come to church at least one Sunday a month."

Tara laughed and shook her head. "You two are definitely made for each other."

Ayanna stuck her head in the door. "We're ready when you are," she chirped.

"Tell them to hit it," Jae said as she stood and straightened her white satin gown.

Moments later they heard the strains of the live band playing the wedding march.

"They're playing my song," Jae said, heading for the door.

Tara picked up Jae's train and they walked out.

*   *   *

The instant Clyde saw Jae appear—in a completely different dress from the one she had worn that morning, an exquisite gown that fit her like a glove, arching above her knees, then fanning out behind her into a six-foot train—saw the radiant look in her eyes and the inviting smile on her lips, he knew, without a doubt, that life with Jae Crawford-Burrell was going to be full of surprises.

Just the beginning. . . .

Main Agenda

=

Brenda Jackson

We can make our plans, but the final outcome is in God's hands.
—PROVERBS 16:1 (THE LIVING BIBLE)

1

Lincoln Corbain sat at the bar of Leo's sizing up the crowd of people there. Since moving to D.C. over a month ago, he had discovered the upscale establishment was one with a very impressive clientele that ranged from politicians, musicians, and foreign dignitaries to college professors, bankers, and, like him, attorneys.

Compared to many of the supper clubs he had patronized in other major cities, this one had a certain homey warmth with its round rosewood tables that held small Tiffany-style lamps and colored oil candles. But at the same time it maintained a high degree of classiness with its double mahogany doors with brass fixtures, narrow floor-to-ceiling stained-glass windows, and intricately patterned parquet floor area specially designed for dancing. Even the bar stool he was sitting on was tall and padded with a contoured back that provided comfort to one's body while it coaxed you to relax and get in the groove.

Most of the people here tonight were, as he was fast becoming, regulars who usually rounded out certain evenings by dropping by to enjoy the good food, live entertainment, and an atmosphere that allowed you to unwind with someone or, if you preferred, by yourself, the latter of which he had decided to do tonight.

"So are you all settled in now?" the bartender named Flint asked Linc as he took away Linc's empty glass and placed another mixed drink in front of him. During the day Flint St. Johns worked as an agent for the IRS. He claimed the reason he moonlighted as a bartender one or two nights a week was because the extra money was too good to pass up and he enjoyed meeting people. He was also a close friend of Noah Hardcastle, one of the owners. Noah shared that ownership position with his younger identical twin brothers, Tyrell and Tyrone, and Ayanna Hardcastle, their female cousin.

Since the night Linc had first visited Leo's he'd decided that another thing he liked about this place was the open friendliness of the four owners. They usually made themselves visible each night and occasionally mingled with their customers.

"Yeah, I'm pretty much settled in," Linc replied, lifting the glass to his lips to take a sip of his drink. Whatever comment he intended to add was forgotten when he noticed the couple who walked in. He frowned, thinking that even in the dim lighting the woman looked familiar. His gaze sharpened as it flowed over her entire body from head to toe. When the memory hit him of where he knew her from, he drew in a deep breath seconds before his entire body went completely still.

Raven.

Linc forced himself to draw in another deep breath as he recalled exactly how long it had been since he had seen her. It had been well over four years since they had met during the week of the Black Colleges Weekend in Daytona Beach. At twenty-seven he had been in his last year of law school at Southern University, and at twenty-two she had been a senior at Florida A and M University majoring in journalism. And with the memory of their meeting came the memories of the red-hot nights of passion they'd shared within days after they had met.

He suddenly had poignant flashbacks of her body under his, wet and wild as she moaned out his name over and over again. Blood rushed to Linc's midsection when he remembered how she had felt in his arms and the immense pleasure he had gotten from having her there. And he had made doubly sure each time they made love that every intimate part of her body had felt cherished. He had been her first lover, an issue she had refused to talk about after he had realized that surprising fact.

Linc averted his gaze from her to the man by her side. Was he her husband, lover, friend, or associate? He released a deep sigh, realizing he didn't have a right to know the man's relationship to Raven, nor did he have a right to feel the heated jealousy that suddenly ripped through his gut.

His gaze returned to her. He liked the way she wore her hair now, chin-length and cut into a trendy and sassy style. The last time he had seen her she'd been sporting braids, a head full of them. They had met on the beach during a weekend when college students were known to have a wild and rip-roaring good time. They had both decided that after years of enduring countless nights of burning the midnight oil studying for exams, and with graduation only a few months away, they deserved to have fun and experience a week of momentary madness.

And they had.

At the end of that week, they had had no excuses or regrets for what they'd shared. Their time together had been too special for either. Nor had they made any promises to keep in touch. They had both walked away accepting that week for exactly what it was—a spring break fling.

But that hadn't stopped him from thinking about her often since then or realizing that any woman he had been intimate with since Raven had failed miserably in comparison. Nor had it stopped him from traveling to Tallahassee, Florida, the weekend after his graduation to look her up, only to discover she had left town already.

Linc sighed as his gaze continued to take in all of her. She was more beautiful than he remembered, and there was a certain degree of sophistication about her. It was probably the outfit she was wearing, he decided. The light blue dress flattered her body, as the silky material clung to her curves and showed off her gorgeous long legs. Her attire during their week together in Daytona Beach had ranged from skimpy tops and shorts and alluring bikini swimwear to nothing at all.

He had preferred her in nothing at all and had seen her body completely nude most of the time. During those times there had not been anything sophisticated about her. She became a sensuous and passionate diva whenever their bodies mated.

"Drink too strong?"

Linc glanced up at Flint and saw the man looking at him quizzically. "No, the drink's fine." When he glanced back in the direction of where the couple had been standing seconds ago, he saw a hostess leading them to a table on the other side of the room. Linc's irritation grew and he frowned into his drink before taking another sip.

"You sure the drink's OK?"

Linc lifted his head and noticed the look of concentration on Flint's face. "Yeah, I thought I may have recognized someone," he said, once again glancing across the room.

Following the direction of Linc's gaze, Flint studied the couple that was being escorted to a table. "Which one do you think you know? Raven or the man she's with?"

Linc lifted a surprised brow. "You know Raven?"

Flint lifted a brow of his own. "Maybe," he answered smoothly as a hint of a smile played at the corners of his mouth. "Do *you* know her?"

Linc stared at the bartender narrowly. He felt like he was being cross-examined and didn't relish the feel of that one bit. He couldn't help but wonder what Flint's relationship was to Raven as well, since the man had suddenly gone from friendly and talkative to tight-lipped inquisitive—a real IRS man.

Linc shrugged. He would never divulge to anyone the extent of his past relationship with Raven. What they had shared that week in Daytona was private and personal. "I met Raven while in Florida one year during college spring break," he finally said, hoping that bit of information would appease Flint's curiosity, because that was all the information he was giving out. "How do you know her?"

Flint went about dusting off the counter, and for a minute Linc thought he would not respond to his question. Finally Flint answered, "Raven is a friend of the Hardcastle twins."

Linc nodded. After a few silent moments he asked, "What about the man she's with?"

"I don't recall ever seeing him in here before."

"I wonder if they're an item," Linc said, glancing up at Flint, wondering if the man knew more than he was actually saying.

Flint stared at him a moment before leaning over the bar and saying, "If you really want to know that, why don't you just walk over there and ask her?"

Linc couldn't help noticing the challenge that flickered in Flint's dark eyes. He returned his stare. "I won't go that far, but I don't see anything wrong with saying hello to an old friend, do you?"

The smile at the corners of Flint's lips widened. "Not if that's what you want to do."

"What the hell, why not? Like I said, there's nothing wrong with saying hello to an old friend," Linc said as he slid off the stool. What he and Raven had shared four years ago was in the past but not forgotten . . . at least not on his part. He doubted that he would ever forget their time together. It had been too passionate, too mind-blowing, and too unforgettable.

As he crossed the room toward the couple, who did not notice him approaching, he knew it was not his intent to put Raven on the spot. Nor was it his intent to place her in an uncomfortable situation with the man she may be currently involved with, but there was no way he could leave the club without saying something to her.

And if the man she was with had a problem with it that was just too bad.

"This is a nice place, Raven. Is there any particular reason you brought me here?"

Raven Anderson looked up from studying her menu to meet John Augustan's gaze and couldn't help but smile. His eyes penetrated her as if they could see into her very soul and read her inner thoughts. And she knew they probably could. He hadn't built his publishing company into the huge success that it was by not being able to read people. After working for him for nearly a year, there was no doubt in her mind that he read her loud and clear. But to save time, she decided to cut to the chase.

"I have this wonderful idea for a story that I want to do for the magazine about the revived popularity of supper clubs."

John Augustan lifted a dark brow, looked down at the menu he held in his hand for a minute, then back up at her. Raven knew that in that brief moment he had pondered her idea. The question of the hour was whether or not he was interested enough to go for it. *The Black Pearl* was an informative magazine that dealt with real issues as well as entertainment news. A little less than two years old, the magazine had garnered a worldwide readership, and John was very selective about the articles that went into it. That was one of the reasons Raven enjoyed working as a reporter for his magazine. It had real class.

She was fully aware that John knew her time with his company was limited. She was a woman on the move, namely, to the top of her profession. But she was realistic enough to know that, in her chosen career, in order to get where she wanted to go, she needed to know all facets of journalism. Her constant goal was to be the best at whatever form of reporting she was involved with. Journalism was her life and she was good at it. Her dream was to one day become a Pulitzer Prize winner. Her mother had had that same dream before she'd let a man rob her of it. Raven was determined not to make the same mistake. Nothing would ever deter her from the one thing she wanted most in life.

John closed his menu. Raven could tell from the look in his eyes that he was interested. "Supper clubs like this one?"

"Yes. I think Leo's would be the perfect place to spotlight. It's the epitome of what a supper club is."

Raven stopped talking when the waiter came to take their order. It was only after the man left that she continued. "For a moment let your mind focus on at least one healthy meal a day, along with a dose of community, and what you'll come up with is Leo's."

"A dose of community?"

Raven smiled. "Yes. A place where several friends or acquaintances meet to share a meal periodically at a very classy night spot."

"Sounds like a nightclub," John said, taking a sip of the drink he had ordered.

"No, it's something totally different. Even the clientele is different. It's more diverse. A nightclub would appeal to a lot younger age group. Supper clubs normally draw people between the ages of twenty-five and seventy. They're more of a social and dining club for professionals who want to mingle with other professionals."

Raven glanced around before adding, "Elaborate decor, high standards, extremely good food, and live music. It's a place where new friendships are established and important business contacts are made."

"You're also painting a picture of a very intimate atmosphere where romantic relationships can be formed," John casually added, smiling.

"Yes, for some I suppose," Raven said quietly. In truth, there was nothing casual about what John had added. He of all people knew she didn't have a social life that included romance. He also knew that she preferred it that way. Serious involvements had a way of distracting people from their main agenda in life.

It was no secret to those who knew the three Anderson sisters, Falcon, Robin, and Raven, that they shared more than the names of birds. They were also of the same mind that making it to the top of their chosen professions was everything and something like love and romance was way down low on the totem pole. John had found that out the hard way when he had fallen in love with Falcon Anderson last year.

Although the subject of her oldest sister was something Raven and John always avoided, she couldn't help wondering if he still felt the same way he did when he'd asked Falcon to marry him and move with him to D.C. Falcon had turned him down, choosing her career as a stockbroker in New York over a lifetime with him. Raven had understood her sister's decision. Although John was an extremely handsome man at thirty-five and would be a great catch for any woman, their mother had drummed into her three daughters' heads very early in life not to let any man come before their obtaining their dreams. Their father had convinced Willow Bellamy that she hadn't needed to pursue her dream of becoming a news reporter, so she had dropped out of college and had gotten married instead. Then a couple of years later, he had convinced her that it wasn't important for her to work outside the home because he would always be there to take care of all her needs. But that was before he'd run off with his secretary, leaving his wife, and three daughters all under the age of five, fending for themselves.

"Well, John, what do you think of the idea?" Raven asked, not wanting to think about the hard times her mother and sisters had endured after her father's abandonment.

"Let me think about it. I'm sure you have a proposal ready for me to take a look at."

"Yes," she said, smiling. "It will be on your desk first thing in the morning. I just wanted to bring you here tonight so you can get a feel of the place."

"I'm impressed. How will the owners handle you doing an article on their establishment?"

Raven's face lit up. "They don't have a problem with it. I know two of the owners, Tyrone and Tyrell Hardcastle, personally. They're identical twins. Tyrell dated Robin some years back when the two of them attended the Culinary Institute of America."

"Who's Leo?"

"Their father, who's a retired army captain. They named the place after him."

John nodded. "And you're sure they don't have a problem with you hanging around and using this place as the basis of your research?"

"No, in fact, I've already cleared it with them. They know I will do a good job with the article. They also know that I—"

Raven stopped talking when she noticed John's gaze shifting from her to an object over her shoulder. She was just about to turn around in her seat to see what had captured his attention when she heard the sound of the rich and painfully sexy voice.

"Hello, Raven."

Raven drew in a quick breath. There was no need for her to turn around. It had been over four years, but she would know *that* voice anywhere. She still heard it from time to time even while she slept. Memories of that voice whispering seductive, inviting, and passionate words in her ears while his body stroked hers into a feverish pitch consumed her and made her feel all hot inside.

She forced herself to blink when Linc moved into her line of vision and stood next to their table. Her mouth opened to form a word of greeting, but nothing came out. She was too shocked seeing him after all these years when wanting to see him again had once been an ache she couldn't soothe. What they had shared that week had been too special to walk away from, but they had done so anyway.

"Linc," she finally found her voice to say, in a whispered breath. "What are you doing here?"

Raven watched his lips curve into a sensuous smile and felt robbed of her breath yet again. His smile had been the reason she had wanted to get to know him up close and personal when they had first met. If there was such a thing as actually drooling over a man, then she'd drooled profusely the moment Lincoln Corbain had smiled at her that day on the beach in Daytona. He was such a good-looking man with his towering height well over six feet, broad and muscular shoulders, medium-brown skin, and clean-shaven head. She had never considered a shaven head on a man sexy until she met Linc.

"I moved here last month to take a job with Brown, Gilmore, and Summers as one of their attorneys. And you?" Linc asked.

"I moved here a year ago and began working for Augustan Publishers."

John Augustan took that time to clear his throat, reminding Raven of his presence.

"I'm sorry, John; I'm just so surprised to see Linc. We haven't seen each other in over four years."

John's lips curved into a smile. "I understand."

Raven glanced quickly at John, thinking that perhaps somehow he really did understand. "John, I'd like you to meet Lincoln Corbain. Linc, this is John Augustan, my boss and good friend."

John stood and offered Linc his hand. "It's nice to meet you. Would you like to join us?"

"No, I was about to leave. I just wanted to come by and say hello to Raven. We haven't seen each other since college."

John nodded, smiling, as he sat back down. "The two of you attended the same college?"

"No," Linc replied, shifting his gaze from John's face back to Raven's. Heat touched her body just as though his gaze had touched her intimately. "We met during spring break one year in Daytona Beach." He flashed Raven another smile. "And for some stupid reason, over the years we didn't stay in touch."

Raven released a low sigh. The reason they had decided not to stay in touch had not been a stupid one. They both had had future goals in life that did not include a serious relationship with anyone. His dream had been to one day enter politics. It seemed the both of them were still hacking away at fulfilling their dreams.

"It was good seeing you again, Linc." She reached out and offered her hand to him.

Linc was silent for a moment, thoughtful as he took her hand and held it a little longer than necessary before letting it go. His gaze roamed over her face before settling on her mouth.

Raven couldn't help but remember the steamy, passionate kisses they'd shared and wondered if he was remembering those kisses as well. The contact of his hand when it had held hers, and her heart racing were causing extreme sensual heat to settle in the lower part of her body. There had been this hot, blazing chemistry between them from the very first. It was the kind of chemistry that had continuously burned between them that week they had been together. Even after four years he could still effortlessly ignite her flame.

"It was good seeing you again, too, Raven," Linc finally said. Nodding to John, he turned and walked away.

Raven didn't know whether she felt relief or disappointment that he had done so.

2

"Raven? Are you OK?"

Raven nodded, refusing to look at John for fear he would know that she was not OK. She had almost forgotten to breathe when Linc looked at her that one last time before walking off. She momentarily closed her eyes and drew in a deep breath.

She reopened them, thinking, *Incredible. Lincoln Corbain is still simply incredible. It should be against the law for any man to have this much of an effect on a woman.*

"You sure you're OK?"

John's question reminded Raven of his presence. "Yes, I'm fine," she replied. Her words were strained, unconvincing.

"Do you want to tell me about him?"

Raven looked up. John was smiling. "Come on. You can tell me. There was a time you and I were close to becoming a family."

Raven couldn't help but return John's smile. She knew he was trying to get her to loosen up some. He'd evidently realized that seeing Linc had her all tied in knots.

"Linc could have become to me what you became to Falcon," Raven said bluntly.

Surprise widened John's eyes at her comment. He leaned back in his chair as his eyes met hers intently. "Which was?"

Raven's gaze was steady as she returned his stare. "The

first man who made her think seriously about putting her heart before her career."

John was quiet for a while, almost too quiet. Then he asked, "And to you, Falcon, and Robin that's a bad thing, isn't it?"

Although Raven knew he was trying to make light of the question, his voice was tinged with anger, hurt, and pain. He stared at her, sipped his drink, waiting on her response. She knew he had loved Falcon deeply and probably still did. She also knew that Falcon had fallen in love with him and still loved him, although she had turned down his marriage proposal.

"Yes, it's a bad thing for us, and you know why we feel that way," she said, finally answering him. "I'm sure Falcon explained everything when she said no to your proposal."

John shook his head, not wanting to relive the memory of the night his heart had gotten ripped apart. Falcon, as well as her two sisters, staunchly believed that falling in love meant becoming dependent on that person. They believed getting serious with someone meant losing your identity and tossing aside your dreams. And nothing he had said could convince Falcon otherwise. Their mother had instilled it deep within their brains to always pursue their dreams and never become dependent on a man.

"I know you don't understand, John," Raven said, knowing the two of them had gone from being employer and employee to friends. "You don't know how hard it was on Mama and on us. You don't know the things we girls went without while growing up and the numerous jobs that Mama worked to make ends meet. And all because she'd become dependent on a man and believed that he would take care of her. Mama tossed aside her dreams for my father and then he left her high and dry."

"Every man isn't like your old man, Raven."

"No," she said. "But I have no desire to fish out the ones that are and toss them back. When I do become involved in a serious relationship it will be only after I've fulfilled every dream I've ever had or ever thought about having. No man is going to rob me of my dreams."

John took a deep breath and sighed. "And you think I would have done that to Falcon?"

Raven stared at him for a long time before replying. "It really doesn't matter what I think, John. Evidently Falcon felt that you could have."

He shook his head. "The three of your minds work alike. You know what they say about birds of a feather flocking together."

An inkling of a smile played at the corners of Raven's lips, but she didn't comment on his teasing her about the sisters' names.

"So what about Lincoln Corbain, Raven?"

Raven stared into John's eyes. "What about him?"

"Do you see him as a threat to your dreams?"

Raven nodded. "He could be if I allow him to be."

"But you won't?"

"No, I won't. You know what my goals are, John. I don't have time for a serious involvement at this stage in my life."

John smiled. "Then I'd have to say the man you just introduced me to may be your biggest challenge. He seems to be the type of guy who goes after what he wants with all intentions of getting it. And from the looks of things here tonight, he definitely wants you."

As soon as she got home Raven undressed and went into the bathroom to take her shower. Moments later she turned off the shower and toweled dry. Reentering her bedroom, she began smoothing lotion over every part of her body, loving the scent of it as it was absorbed into her skin. After that was done, she slipped into her nightgown. As she placed the bottle of lotion back on her dresser, her gaze was drawn to the framed photographs sitting there.

The first one was a picture of her mother that had been taken a year before her death. Willow Anderson had worked two jobs to send her three daughters to college and had died of cancer a couple of months after Raven, the youngest, had completed her studies. Her mother's struggles and determination to provide for her daughters without her ex-husband's help had earned her her daughters' undying love, inspiration, and respect. Willow had never asked David Anderson for anything; whether that decision had stemmed from pride or embarrassment Raven never knew. The only thing she did know was that her and her sisters' dreams had become her mom's main agenda. She had been determined to see to it that her daughters reached whatever level of success they aimed for. She never wanted them to find themselves in the position she had found herself in because of love.

Raven's gaze moved to the next picture. It was one of her and her sisters taken together last Christmas with Santa. Raven smiled. Of course it had been Robin who had insisted on sitting on Santa's lap. Raven shook her head at the memory. Robin and Falcon were more than just sisters to her. They were also her very best friends. Falcon was the oldest by two years and Robin next oldest by one. While growing up they had been one another's playmates and confidantes. In a way they still were. Although they now lived in different cities, they made it a point to get together at least three or four times a year.

Deciding to read before going to bed, Raven walked over to the bookcase and pulled out a mystery novel. Going into her living room, she got comfortable by stretching out on her sofa. Then it happened. Memories she had tried holding at bay suddenly raced through her mind. She thought about the Florida sun, the Atlantic Ocean, the sands of Daytona Beach, and the ultra-fine body of Linc Corbain in a pair of sexy swimming trunks while he played volleyball with some of his frat brothers. After the game was over he had walked over to her, introduced himself, and invited her to take a stroll with him along the boardwalk.

They had spent the next two days getting to know each other. He had told her that he was from Memphis, Tennessee, and came from a family of attorneys. His parents as well as his siblings were practicing lawyers. She in turn had shared with him that her single mom in South Carolina had raised her and her two sisters.

After those first two days that she and Linc had spent

together, she had spent the rest of the week with him in his room at the Adam's Mark Hotel. She had given him her virginity and he had given her a week of treasured memories.

Since the last time she had seen him, Linc's features had matured and were even more handsome. He had looked so good tonight dressed in a pair of casual slacks and a sports jacket. She hadn't noticed a ring on his finger, which probably meant he was still single.

She scowled to herself, disgusted that her thoughts would even go there. It should not have mattered to her if he was single or married.

But it *did* matter and she was not in the mood to try to convince herself otherwise. From the moment she had first laid eyes on Linc four years ago, everything about him had mattered. But she had been realistic enough to know that although their time together had been special, that week had meant the same thing for them that it had meant to the other thousands of students who had escaped to Daytona Beach. They were there to enjoy their break from school and to have a good time. No one had come to Daytona looking for any serious entanglements or lasting involvements. Nothing about that week was to be taken seriously. Her mind had understood that, although at times her heart had tried not to. It was only after she'd returned to school and gotten refocused that she remembered that no matter what, the career she wanted would always come first in her life.

She dated occasionally, but she had not yet met a man whom she allowed herself to get serious about. When a man became too demanding of her time, she'd had no qualms about cutting him loose and asking him to move on.

Leaning back against the sofa, she closed her eyes as she remembered other things about Linc tonight. His lips were fuller. Her gaze had been glued to them all the while he had been talking. Those lips had taught her how to kiss—really kiss. She still recalled every earth-shattering moment of their first kiss even now.

She had also noticed that his shoulders beneath his jacket seemed wider, stronger. She remembered holding tight onto those shoulders while he carried her piggyback across a stretch of beach to keep sand from getting into her sandals. Then there was the memory of the feel of her hands clutching those shoulders while he'd been on top of her, making love to her; sensuously stroking his body inside her, taking her over the edge of mindless passion and fulfillment; imprinting himself in her mind and a part of her heart forever. During that week she had spent with Linc, she had experienced the wonders she'd only heard were possible.

For months following their time together, her body had throbbed endlessly for his, craving the pleasures he had given her, remembering the sensations of sharing herself with him. To combat those feelings she had thrown herself full force into her first job after college as a reporter for a newspaper in Boston. But still, it had taken her a while to get over the hunger of his touch.

Raven reopened her eyes, no longer wanting to dwell on those thoughts. She didn't want her body to long for his touch like that again. And there was no way she could get involved with Linc again without the possibility of that happening. A hot and heavy involvement with him would be too easy to get into and would be hard as nails to get out of.

He would become to her like John had become to Falcon. A man she wanted but could not have; a man she could fall in love with; a man who could make her rethink her position on not putting her heart before her career. He was not one she could easily cut loose and ask to move on.

And those were things she could never risk happening.

Linc walked out onto the balcony off his bedroom and breathed a deep frustrated breath. His jaw tightened as the memory of Raven and John Augustan consumed his mind.

She had introduced him as her boss and her friend. They seemed comfortable with each other, and Linc couldn't help wondering if perhaps something was going on between them, although the man didn't seem the least bit territorial.

Why are you trippin', man? an inner voice asked Linc.

*You don't have any claims on her. It's been over four years
and you didn't have any claims on her even back then, so
chill. She can mess around with anyone she wants to. After
all, she's not yours.*

Linc shook his head, refusing to accept what his mind
was telling him. She was his. She was his in a way he had
never considered before. During that week in Daytona he had
made her his in the most elemental way, and in every sense.
Somehow more than their bodies had gotten connected. He'd
known it then but had walked away, not realizing its signif-
icance until he'd seen her again tonight.

From the moment he and Raven had met, he had known
there was something different about her. When she had
walked around on the beach, she seemed unaware that most
of the guys she passed by stared at her with open mouths.
She'd been the first woman he had met that week in Daytona
who had not been totally absorbed in the knowledge of her
appeal and allurement. That noticeable quality had stood her
apart from all the other sistahs on the beach that day. It was
obvious that she had felt confident about herself and hadn't
felt the need to prove anything to anyone by putting herself
on display or by doing anything to draw deliberate attention
to herself. That was what he had admired most about her and
what had caught his interest. There had been something so
open, unselfish, and unpretentious about her. She had em-
braced life to the fullest, and that week, while around her,
so had he.

Walking back inside his apartment, Linc paced the floor
a few times before making a couple of decisions. One, he
was determined to find out exactly what the real deal was
between Raven and Augustan. And two, no matter what that
situation was, he intended to make his interest known. He
had long ago accepted that that week in Daytona had meant
a lot to him.

After seeing her again, there was no doubt in his mind
that something was still there between them, something un-
finished. The Lincoln Corbain she had seen tonight was more

matured in his thinking, a lot surer about the things he wanted, and after recently turning thirty-one, he was wiser. And he had no intentions of letting Raven Anderson walk out of his life a second time.

3

"It's nice to know upfront that I'm being used," Raven said, smiling at her good friend Erica Sanders.

The waiter had just shown them to their table at Leo's. The soft lighting and the upbeat sound of reggae music playing in the background helped set the atmosphere of what was expected tonight. One Wednesday a month was Amateur/ Open Mike Night, to showcase new and upcoming talent. Raven and Erica had arrived early to get a good table near the stage. It was also the night that one of the owners in particular, Tyrone Hardcastle, usually put in an appearance, since he was responsible for anything having to do with music and entertainment at the supper club. It was no secret that Tyrone was Erica's current love interest.

"Serves you right," Erica said in a huff as she opened her menu. "You should have told me that you knew the Hardcastle twins personally. Instead, I had to find out just how well you knew them this morning at the staff meeting when John mentioned the article you'll be doing about this place and the inside connections you had."

Raven gave Erica a smile before saying, "You fall in and out of love at least once a month. How was I to know that your infatuation with Tyrone would last a little longer than the others?"

"I'd like you to know that this is the real thing," Erica said, grinning, as she leaned forward.

"Yeah, that's what you said last month about Paul Weston," Raven pointed out with a small, faint laugh.

Erica smiled when she glared at Raven for reminding her of that fact. "Let's forget about Paul, shall we?"

Raven shook her head as she looked at her own menu. She and Erica had become good friends after Erica had begun working for Augustan Publishers the same day that she had. Erica was such a likable person and the two of them had hit it off immediately. The thing Raven liked most about her, besides her heart of gold, was that she was a fun person to be around. The thing she disliked most was Erica's constant badgering of Raven for her non-existent social life.

Like her, Erica was twenty-six years old and not seriously involved with anyone. However, unlike her, Erica dated on a pretty regular basis. Raven much preferred spending her nights at home alone curled up in bed with a good book.

"So, when are you going to start writing the article?"

"In a few days," Raven answered, glancing up only briefly from her close study of the menu. "So I guess I'll be seeing a lot of this place for a while."

"I hope it won't be obvious what you're doing here. Some people may not appreciate being spied on while they're here enjoying themselves."

Raven lifted her head to look at Erica again, this time thoughtfully. "I won't be spying on them, but I can see how some people might think so. I guess I'll have to make it seem like I'm just one of the customers."

"That's not a bad idea. What you need is a man to bring along."

Raven shook her head, grinning. "I don't have a man to bring along."

"You could if you wanted one."

Raven studied Erica for a few moments as she tried to decide whether or not to respond to her comment. What the heck, she thought, she might as well let Erica give her habitual spiel about having a good man versus having a good job. She reached for her glass of wine and took a sip before casually saying, "I don't want one."

"Oh, yeah, I forgot. You think a good job is more important than a good man."

Raven inhaled sharply, deeply. "I've never said that I thought a good job was more important than a good man.

What I have said, on several occasions I might add, is that I'm a firm believer that a woman should not sacrifice her dreams just to be with a man. I have all intentions of one day settling down, getting married, and having a family. But only after I've fulfilled *all* my dreams."

Erica stroked her lip with her finger thoughtfully. "Hey, I'd love to fulfill all my dreams, too, especially the ones I have at night," she said, smiling wickedly. "All of them involve a man. Some good man. As far as I'm concerned, anything else can come later. I came to this city looking for a good job, and if things don't work out for me at Augustan Publishers I'll leave, looking for another good job. But a good man, Raven, a real good man, isn't easy to come by. I've been looking for a good man for years and they are getting snapped up fast. So I still say, give me a good man over a good job any day."

Raven knew Erica just didn't understand. The only people who fully understood her reasons for feeling the way she did were her sisters. "We're different, Erica, with different ideas about things. Our agendas and priorities are different. I like my life just fine and I'm sure you're happy with yours. How's that article you're doing on Smokey Robinson coming along?"

"Don't you ever get lonely?"

Raven exhaled a long breath. So much for trying to change the subject. "I'm too busy to get lonely."

"What you need is more of a social life and a good man in it. When was the last time you had some honest-to-goodness fun with a man? When was the last time you spent some time with a man and truly enjoyed doing so?"

Raven was grateful when the waiter appeared. She was spared from answering Erica's questions, although she knew what her response would have been. The last time she had had fun with a man and totally enjoyed it had been the time she had spent with Linc during spring break.

After the waiter had taken Raven's order he turned his attention to Erica. "And what would you like tonight?" he asked.

Erica smiled as she considered his question, for all of two seconds. "I'd just love to have Tyrone Hardcastle given to me on a silver platter."

Benjamin Goodman plucked the cherry from his daiquiri and popped it into his mouth before turning surprised raised brows to Linc. "You mean you actually saw Raven? Your Raven? Here?"

Linc leaned back against his stool at the bar. "Yes, I ran into her here one night last week." He knew that although Ben had never met Raven he had heard enough about her from him. He and Ben had attended college together at Morehouse and then had attended law school at Southern University in Louisiana. Neither of them had ever ventured to Daytona during a spring break; however, since it was their final year of law school and they had a reason to celebrate, they'd decided to do so. They were going to share a hotel room, but because of a family emergency Ben had not gone to Daytona Beach with Linc after all. Things had worked out just fine, since he met Raven that week and she had been the one who ended up sharing the hotel room with him most of the time.

After law school Ben had accepted a job with the state attorney's office in Atlanta and Linc had returned home to work in his family's law practice. Two years ago Ben had moved to D.C. as a federal prosecutor, and since then he had often encouraged Linc to join him there. It was only after things had died down from the scandal involving his father that Linc made the decision to leave Tennessee for the nation's capital.

"So, how did she look, man?" Ben wanted to know.

Linc took a deep breath, thinking of the words he could use to describe how Raven had looked the night he had seen her. Beautiful? Yes, she was that with her perfect oval face of sable brown, her lips, full and rounded over even teeth, her straight nose, and her square chin. Yes, she did look beautiful. But still there had been more. She had looked enchanting, exquisite, and totally feminine.

"Well?" Ben asked impatiently, leaning closer.

Linc moved his shoulders in a shrug. "She looked exactly like the person I fell hard for four years ago, even better. She looked older, more mature, and more sophisticated."

Ben nodded before taking another sip of his drink. Linc knew he really didn't have to explain things to his friend. Ben knew the same thing now that he had concluded four years ago: Raven Anderson must have been one hell of a woman to make such an impact on Lincoln Corbain.

"Did seeing her again bring back memories?"

Linc thought about Ben's question. "Yeah, man, seeing her again brought back memories." He had never been one to kiss and tell, so Ben didn't know everything that had happened between him and Raven that week, although Linc was sure Ben had pretty much reached his own conclusions. After Linc had returned to school after spring break it had been apparent to everyone who knew him, especially Ben, that something monumental had happened to Linc in Daytona.

"Did you get a chance to talk to her?"

Linc looked down in his drink as if studying it. "She was with someone."

A slow smile came to Ben's lips. "So she was with someone. That didn't stop you from making your presence known, did it?"

Linc's dark head came up. He met Ben's gaze and couldn't help grinning. "No, it didn't."

Ben raised his drink in a toast. "Spoken like a true, fearless Alpha man." He then glanced around the room. "Looks like the show is starting. Come on. Let's find a vacant table someplace before it gets too crowded in here."

The two men got up from the bar and headed toward the area where the night's activities were about to get under way.

For this month, Open Mike Night was being held once a week instead of once a month. Raven's eyes had been glued to the raised stage as she enjoyed the first act, a Billie Holiday reincarnation, when something—an instinct, an uncanny force, a powerful soul connection—pulled at her. She swept her gaze from the performer onstage to across the room.

She saw Linc at the same exact moment that he saw her.

Raven felt her heart speed up, her palms go warm, and her breath catch deep in her throat. He was with someone, another man, and upon seeing her he touched the man's shoulder, whispered something to him, and then the two of them began walking her way.

All the sights and sounds around Raven faded into oblivion as her mind and gaze held the two tall men moving in her direction. Both men were good-looking, but her eyes were focused on the one dressed in gray slacks and a nice dark-colored knit suit. Everything about him was potent and sexy. She was in awe that her attraction for him was as strong as it had been the first time she had laid eyes on him four years ago and as powerful as it had been last week when she'd seen him in this very same place. Nothing about the magnetism she felt toward him had changed.

Four years ago on the day they had met, she had not understood why her inner thighs clenched when he smiled at her or why her breath got caught in her throat when she took the hand he offered when he introduced himself to her. Then later that night, when they had shared their first kiss, she had not understood the intensity of it. It had been a kiss that had transcended into a language that was only communicated and understood by the two of them. It had been a kiss that deciphered their thoughts, feelings, and emotions into a gigantic ball of fire. That fire had translated itself into particular tongue movements as their mouths mated. Uncanny as it seemed, it was as if each knew and understood what the other was thinking whenever they kissed. A soul connection. Even now she could remember the delicious taste of him, the feel of the interior of his mouth, warm, sleek, moist. She had felt his expertise, had been the recipient of his artistry, and had benefited from his skill in knowing how to pleasure a woman.

She would forever be grateful to him for his unlimited patience and for being an expert teacher and a considerate lover. He had introduced her to her very own body, a body she'd had all her life but a body she'd been unaware could feel such things and could do such things. It was a body that had certain erogenous points and a body that could drive a man to distraction.

If there were such a thing as two individuals having kindred spirits, then she and Linc would definitely qualify. She had left Daytona Beach believing it had been destined for them to meet, just as much as she believed it had been destined for them to go their separate ways in the end with no regrets.

That was the main reason she believed seeing him again now was an unkind turn of events, one she would have to deal with. Carefully. Cautiously.

"Who on earth are you staring at?"

Erica's question cut into Raven's thoughts. Curious, Erica glanced over her shoulder and saw the two good-looking brothers weaving around tables as they moved in their direction. "Do you know them?" she asked Raven in whispered awe.

With her gaze still holding Linc's, Raven inhaled a slow breath and answered, "I know the one with the clean-shaven head."

"Wow! He's good-looking. Both of them are. Who is he?"

My first and only lover. The man who gave me a week of blazing passion four years ago. The man who could get next to me if I were to let my guard down. Instead she answered, "Lincoln Corbain. We met over spring break four years ago during my last year of college."

Erica, Raven knew, wanted to ask more questions. She wanted more details, but time wouldn't allow it. Linc and his friend were now only a few feet away. But if Raven knew Erica, the subject of Lincoln Corbain was far from over.

"Good evening."

His voice, as Raven had known it would, had an underlying sensuality that captivated, then soothed. He smiled and automatically her thighs clenched, her heart rate increased, and her breath caught. She was barely able to respond to his greeting. "Hi, Linc. Seems you like this place."

His smile widened easily and when it did a warming sensation moved from the center of Raven's clenched thighs upward to her stomach. "Seems you do as well," was his smooth reply.

Erica cleared her throat, reminding Raven that she and Linc were not the only persons present. "Linc Corbain, I'd like you to meet Erica Sanders, a good friend of mine."

Linc broke eye contact with Raven and shifted his dark gaze to Erica. He extended his hand to her. "Nice meeting you, Erica."

Erica returned Linc's smile as she accepted his handshake, all the while holding him in her ever-observant gaze. "Likewise, Linc."

Glancing at the man by his side, Linc said, "And this is my friend Ben Goodman. Ben, this is Raven Anderson and Erica Sanders."

Ben stepped closer, giving both Raven and Erica warm handshakes. "I'm honored to meet two such beautiful ladies."

"Would the two of you like to join us?" Erica asked quickly, not really surprising Raven with the invitation.

"We wouldn't want to intrude," Linc was saying.

"You won't be," Erica replied.

Linc's gaze moved to Raven. "Raven?" he asked, seeking her consent also.

"Yes, please join us."

With those words Linc took the chair next to her and Ben took the seat next to Erica. Raven knew all the reasons she should not want Linc and his friend sitting at their table. One was the very obvious sexual vibes radiating between her and Linc. You would have to be a dead person not to have picked up on it. There was no doubt in her mind that both Erica and Ben had noticed it. Then again, she thought glancing at Erica and Ben, maybe they had not picked up on it. It seemed the only thing capturing Erica's and Ben's attention was each other. Raven smiled inwardly. Evidently Erica's love interest for the month, Tyrone Hardcastle, had gotten kicked to the curve.

The waiter came over and took the new drink orders.

When that was out of the way Raven knew she could always count on Erica to get the conversation going.

"Before the two of you arrived, Raven and I were having an interesting conversation about the availability of good men. Are either of you married?"

4

"Ben and Erica seem to be hitting it off," Linc said after taking a sip of his drink, then setting it down.

Raven glanced across the room at the couple who had moved away from their table and were now seated together at the bar. They were leaning close with their heads together, laughing and talking like they were two old friends and not two people who had been introduced to each other less than an hour ago. But then, Raven thought, that's how things had been for her and Linc when they first met. They had quickly and easily connected. Their conversations had been comfortable and relaxed, not at all tense and strained like the one they were sharing now.

"Yes, it seems they are," was Raven's stilted response. She shifted in her seat under Linc's quiet, intense gaze, wondering how she could effectively bring the evening to an end before he could bring up anything about the time they had spent together in Daytona. She didn't think she'd be able to handle it if he did. For the first time in her life she was unsure as to how to pull herself out of a situation with a man that she was determined would not progress anywhere.

She cleared her throat. "So you aren't married?"

"No."

"Ever been?" Raven could have bit off her tongue for wanting to know.

"No. What about you?"

"Umm, no, I'm still single." *And I don't even have a lover. The last time I experienced deep-hot passion was in your arms*, she thought as her thighs instinctively tightened in response to the sudden jolt of heat that vibrated between them. She swallowed as his eyes held hers for a moment before moving down to her neck. She wondered if he could see the rapid throb of her pulse in her throat. His gaze then drifted back to her eyes.

"So how do you like publishing books?" he asked her quietly.

She was so held by his magnificent dark eyes that it took her a moment to realize he'd asked her a question. Tiny lines of a frown drew over her forehead. "I'm sorry; what did you ask?"

He smiled as he repeated his question. "I asked how you like publishing books."

"What makes you think I publish books?" she asked, bemused.

Linc's brows lifted and his gaze lingered before he replied, "The other night when I saw you here you were having dinner with your boss from Augustan Publishers. I understand they are a huge book-publishing company."

Raven nodded, understanding how he could have been misled. "Augustan not only publishes books; they also publish a monthly magazine called *The Black Pearl.* I'm one of their reporters."

She watched as the smile on Linc's face suddenly vanished. He leveled her a cold look. The transformation happened so quickly she hadn't had time to prepare herself for it.

"So, you're one of those people who think it's fun going around snooping into people's lives and printing things that are untrue."

Raven's spine stiffened abruptly with Linc's cutting remark and the unwarranted attack on her profession. An angry look flashed in her eyes. "I am not that kind of a reporter, Linc. I happen to enjoy the work I do, and the company I write for is not some sleazy two-bit publisher. Augustan Publishers has never been malicious to anyone, and as a reporter employed by them neither have I. And I don't appreciate you insinuating otherwise."

"Raven," Linc began, not knowing what he could say in

the way of an apology, and knowing he owed her one as well as an explanation. But how could he explain to her that a magazine reporter had nearly destroyed his family last year?

Raven had no intention of putting up with anyone taking potshots at her profession. Although she had to admit the behavior of some journalists gave a bad rap to the others in the industry, she would not tolerate anyone questioning her integrity. She stood. "Since it's apparent that you're offended by what I do for a living, I think it would be best if you and I parted company."

"No, please stay. I apologize for what I said earlier, Raven. I didn't mean to say it."

His words of apology were incredibly soft and filled with regret. But at the moment they weren't good enough for her. "Then why did you?"

Linc's solemn gaze lifted to hers and his gut clenched at the look in her eyes. His words had hurt her. "Please sit back down and I'll explain."

Raven hesitated a moment before returning to her seat. Her eyes, Linc noticed, were flashing fire. Even angry with him he thought she looked beautiful. The dark, fiery look in her eyes reminded him of another time her eyes were filled with dark fire. At that time, instead of conveying her anger it had conveyed her smoldering need while they made love.

"I'm listening."

Linc leaned back in his chair. "I am sorry for what I said earlier, Raven. It's just when you said you were a magazine reporter it caught me off guard."

Raven lifted a brow. "Why would it catch you off guard? You knew I was a journalism major in college."

"Yes, but as a journalism major you could very well have become a book editor."

Raven's eyes narrowed. "What do you have against magazine reporters?"

Linc inclined his head to look at her. "A magazine reporter nearly destroyed my family last year."

Raven was startled by his words, but looking at the grimness in his face she knew they were true. She also knew from the time they had spent together that week how close he was to his family. She leaned closer, struggling to deal with what he'd just said. "How?"

Linc stared at her, not really surprised by the care and concern he heard in her voice. "My father decided to run for public office as a judge. His opponent had a friend who knew someone who owned a publishing company. They decided to run a series of articles in a particular magazine accusing my father of various deeds ranging from spousal abuse to racketeering. All of them were untrue, but it wore all of us down denying every single charge."

A regretful sigh escaped Raven's lips. As a journalist she knew there was nothing anyone could have done to legally stop the slander. "Your father lost the election?"

"No, their plan backfired and he won. But the stress of dealing with such a negative campaign had gotten to be too much for him. He had a heart attack on election night mere moments before he was declared the winner."

A deep lump formed in Raven's throat. "Did he—"

"No, he survived and is doing fine now and is one of the best judges Memphis has ever had."

Raven nodded. She was glad. "And how is the rest of your family doing after dealing with all of that?"

"We survived. Some better than others."

Raven studied him, wondering if he was talking generally or specifically. She took a deep breath before asking her next question. During their week together in Daytona Beach, he had shared with her his dream to one day enter politics. "And you, Linc? How did you come out?"

"Bitter," he said, his tone level. The look in his eyes was filled with disappointment. "What happened made me rethink my future goals. I don't want to have anything to do with politics. Ever."

The disheartened sound in his voice made the lump in Raven's throat deepen. No wonder he had reacted the way he had when she told him that she was a magazine reporter. "I'm sorry, Linc. I'm truly sorry."

Linc captured the gaze that was looking up into his. He

wanted to reach out and smooth the sadness from beneath her eyes. Sadness that was there because of him. "It wasn't your fault, and I had no right to come down on you the way I did earlier just because you're a reporter, too."

"Thanks for sharing that with me. Now I understand." In a way she understood far more than she really wanted to. His dream of one day becoming a congressman from his home state of Tennessee had been destroyed by the actions of someone in her profession.

Neither of them said anything for a while; then Raven glanced at her watch. "It's getting late. I think Erica has forgotten we have to work tomorrow," she added with a tired sigh.

"Did the two of you come together?"

"Yes."

"I'll be glad to take you home if she's not ready to leave yet."

A flutter of nerves rose and twisted in the pit of Raven's stomach with Linc's offer. And at the same time, a caution warning nudged her. The last thing she needed was to share Linc's company any longer than she had to. "That's OK; I can call a cab."

"I can't let you do that. Besides, I'm ready to leave myself, but I don't think Ben is. It seems as far as he and Erica are concerned, the night's still young. I'll be glad to take you home, Raven."

Raven looked straight into Linc's eyes. Again she wanted to refuse his offer, but she was beginning to feel tired. Usually she would be in bed by now. She had never stayed at Leo's this late during a weeknight. She took a deep sigh. There was nothing wrong with Linc taking her home, she convinced herself. It would be up to her to make sure that's all he did. "Are you sure you don't mind?"

"I'm positive."

Raven hesitated briefly before finally getting to her feet. "Thanks. I guess we should let Erica and Ben know that we're leaving."

5

A sliver of moonlight that came through the car's window gave Raven an illuminated view of Linc's profile as he pulled his BMW out of Leo's parking lot.

Even a side view of him had its merits, she thought, liking the way his shirt stretched tight across his broad chest. Both of his hands were on the steering wheel and unlike her gaze, which kept drifting in his direction, his vision remained glued to the road in front of him as he expertly maneuvered the vehicle around the curves heading toward her home, following the directions she'd given him.

Although soft jazzy music was coming from his CD player, a timeless silence hung in the car's interior between them. The windows were lowered midway to take advantage of the October night's cool breeze, and a gust of air that came through pushed Raven's hair into her eyes. She reached up and pushed it back out of the way.

Linc had taken his eyes off the road when he brought the car to a stop at a traffic light. He saw Raven's hair flutter against her face and watched as she pushed it aside. Even with windblown hair he thought she looked perfect.

"When did you decide to stop wearing braids?" he inquired softly.

Startled by the sound of his voice, Raven looked over at him and saw that he was staring at her with eyes that were compelling and seductive. Taking a deep breath before answering, she said, "Right after college. I had a new job and wanted a new look to go along with it."

Linc nodded as he moved the car forward again when the traffic light turned green. "I like the change, although I think you looked good before, too."

"Thank you, Linc," she said, trying not to sound as pleased as she actually felt at his compliment.

His body leaned slightly forward, and without taking his

eyes off the road he slipped out the CD that was playing and put in another, one by Kenny G. Then he settled back in the seat while the stirring sultry sound of the man and his saxophone flowed around them. Linc placed his hand back on the steering wheel.

His hands, Raven thought, definitely still knew how to operate. She suddenly felt heated when her mind remembered how those hands, big, strong, yet gentle, had operated on her.

"How's your family?" he asked her, interrupting Raven's thoughts and sparing her any further self-inflicted torture from memories. "I recall you mentioning that your mother lives in South Carolina and your two sisters live in New York."

Raven leaned back against the seat. "Mama died a couple of months after I graduated from college."

"I'm sorry to hear that," Linc said, giving her a quick sorrowful look before returning his gaze back to the road.

"Thanks. That was a very difficult time for me and my sisters. We were very close to our mother. Her death was unexpected; at least it was for the three of us. She'd been diagnosed with a rare form of colon cancer the year before and didn't tell anyone."

Raven remembered the hurt and pain she and her sisters had felt upon finding out that their mother had gone through that year alone while encouraging them to pursue their dreams. It had all made sense as to why her mother had encouraged her to go to Daytona Beach and enjoy her spring break instead of coming home like she usually did. Willow Anderson hadn't wanted her around to get suspicious of anything.

"My sisters are doing fine," she said after a few brief moments. "Robin, the one who's a master chef, has been in Paris for six months studying at a renowned cuisine academy there. Falcon, the one who is a stockbroker, still lives in New York, doing what she does best with stocks and bonds."

"Do you see them often?"

Raven smiled. "Not nearly as often as the three of us

would like, since we're extremely close. But we're also extremely dedicated to our professions and know that with that dedication come sacrifices. Robin will be turning twenty-eight in two weeks and is returning to the States so the three of us can celebrate at my place. We always spend our birthdays together."

When Linc stopped at another traffic light, he glanced over at her. "Are husbands invited?"

"There aren't any husbands. Falcon and Robin are still single," she said, thinking how John had almost swept Falcon off her feet and had come awfully close to changing that single status. "And with no marriage plans in their futures," she added. "At least not until they fulfill their lifelong dreams."

"Which are?"

Raven didn't hesitate answering. "Robin wants to open a culinary school in New York, and Falcon wants to own her own brokerage firm one day."

Linc slowed the car down to turn the corner to the street where her apartment complex was located. He took another quick glance in her direction. "What about you, Raven? What are your plans for the future? What are your dreams?"

Raven thought carefully about the answers to Linc's questions. Not that she had to ponder what they were. Her mind was very clear and straight as to what her future plans and dreams were. She wanted to take her time and respond in such a way as to make certain that Linc would be clear and straight.

"My plans for the future are to continue doing what I've been doing for the past few years, and that is staying focused on my main agenda and working my way up to the top of my profession. More than anything I'd like to write that special exposé that could earn me a shot at the Pulitzer Prize. In the meantime, I'm learning all I can to be ready to start my own publishing company in a few years."

Linc pulled into the driveway of the Eagle's Nest Apartments and brought his car to a stop in front of her apartment building. He turned off the car's ignition and shifted around in his seat to look at her, capturing her with his eyes. "And what role does John Augustan play in all of this?"

Raven gave him a confused look. "John's my boss."

Linc nodded. "You also mentioned when you introduced the two of us that he was a good friend of yours."

Raven dipped her head, trying to remember everything about that night when she'd seen Linc in Leo's that first time. The only thing she remembered with absolute clarity was how good he looked. Any side conversations she'd had were totally unclear in her mind. "Yes, he's a good friend of mine."

"How good a friend is he?"

Raven raised her head and looked at Linc, surprised at the tone of his question. His gaze pinned her in place, forcing her to understand exactly what he was asking. Her stomach muscles quivered at the intensity of his gaze as he waited for her answer. She could lie and tell him that she and John were intimately involved and effectively put an end to any ideas he might have of renewing any sort of relationship between them. But then a part of her knew that lying to him would be the coward's way out. She had to believe in her ability to handle every aspect of her life, even someone she didn't particularly want in it at the moment, like Linc. He would be a threat not only to her peace of mind but also to all her future goals and plans. She had to be strong enough to keep her priorities straight around him, and she believed that she could be. She'd been shown too early in life what could happen if she didn't.

She met his gaze head-on when she finally answered him. "John's a very good friend. He's a very close friend."

Raven studied Linc's features to see what impact her words had on him. She watched as his eyes narrowed and his jaw tightened. A part of her body inwardly reacted to the thought that her involvement with another man bothered him.

"But," she continued, "he's an even closer friend to my sister Falcon. At least he was before she turned down his marriage proposal."

Linc frowned. It took him a few moments to catch on to

what Raven was telling him. "He asked your sister to marry him?"

"Yes. John loves Falcon very much, and I know she loves him just as much."

Linc's frown deepened. "Then why did she turn down his marriage proposal?"

"Bad timing. She has dreams yet to fulfill."

He lifted a brow, certain he had not heard her correctly. "Are you telling me that your sister loves John Augustan, but she turned down his marriage proposal because he asked her to marry him before she could fulfill her dreams?"

"Yes."

"Is this the sister who wants to one day own her own brokerage firm?"

"Yes."

The right side of Linc's mouth curled up into a half-smile. "Any reason she can't have both, the man and her dreams?"

"Yes. No woman should get seriously involved with anyone until she's fulfilled all her professional dreams. The most important thing that a woman can do is have a career and take care of herself and not have to be dependent on a man."

Linc stared at Raven. He could only assume those words were coming from the lips of a true-blue woman's libber. "And you actually believe that?"

"Yes."

"And your sisters? They believe that as well?"

"Of course."

Linc chuckled and shook his head. "Whatever happened to the idea of finding a balance and having both a personal and a professional life? What's wrong with pursuing them both?"

"You can't have both because there is no such thing as a balance. Someone is always expected to compromise and usually it's the woman. We're the ones who're asked to put our careers on hold, to follow our man from pillar to post or wherever his career may take him. We have the responsibility of raising the children and are expected to turn a house into a home for our family. Instead of being our own individual, we become our husband's other half. And if the man decides to up and leave one day, we're the ones who are left with nothing—no future, no career, no dreams. He will have stripped us of all of that."

Linc looked at Raven as lines of confusion showed up on his forehead. "Is there a particular person you know firsthand that this happened to?"

He saw her expression and knew his question had taken her by surprise. He watched as she drew in a sharp breath before slowly nodding. Looking away from him, at an object outside the car window, she answered, "Yes."

"Who?"

She looked back at him. "My mother. My father left her with three kids all under the age of five without ever looking back. She had given up her future, her career, and her dreams for him and he walked away and left her with nothing."

Linc studied Raven for a while and watched how the pain of her father's abandonment shone clearly in her eyes. "No, he left your mother with something. In fact, I believe that he left her with the most precious gifts he could ever have given to her, Raven. He left her with you and your two sisters. And I refuse to believe that at any time in your mother's life she would have preferred having a future, any dreams, or a career without the three of you being a part of it."

Without saying anything else he got out of the car and walked around the vehicle to open the door for her.

6

A long moment of silence stretched out between Linc and Raven as he walked her to her door. He hoped her silence meant she was thinking about what he had said. He knew it would not be easy to change her views or how she felt, but if he could give her some food for thought, that would be enough for now.

The problem he saw with Raven Anderson was that the

woman was too independent for her own good. There was nothing wrong with wanting to be successful, but the key was being successful on your own terms, without having to make unnecessary sacrifices.

"Thanks for bringing me home, Linc."

Raven's soft voice broke the quietness and invaded his thoughts. His gaze was drawn to hers, then slowly dropped dead-center to her lips, as he remembered the heated bliss he'd found there more than once. Thinking about those hot and heavy kisses sent a ripple of pleasure up his spine. Pure unadulterated male pleasure. He cleared a suddenly tight throat and said, "Anytime."

His gaze must have lingered on her lips much too long for comfort, he thought as he watched her unconsciously moisten them with a nervous sweep of her tongue. His gut clenched and his body experienced an acute craving to feast hungrily on her mouth.

"It's late. I better go in," she said, reaching into her purse to retrieve her door key.

When she pulled out the key he caught her hand in his. "I'll open the door for you," he offered, feeling tingles of desire inch through his veins from touching her.

Raven stared at him for a long, thoughtful minute. She knew his intent. He wanted to kiss her good night, and it wouldn't be the type of kiss that could be given on a doorstep amid possible prying eyes. This kiss would deserve privacy. There was kissing and then there was kissing . . . Lincoln Corbain's style. He had his own special technique. Linc didn't just kiss; he made love to your mouth while he was doing so.

"Do you think that's a good idea?" she asked on a long, deep indrawn breath, wondering why she'd asked such a question. Did she really expect him to answer no?

He smiled and nodded. "I think it's the best idea I've had all night," he said in a husky whisper, easing the key from her hand.

The warmth of his smile flooded Raven's whole being, and she couldn't deny him what he wanted, because deep

down it was what she wanted, too. As much as she wanted
to deny it, she couldn't.

She watched as he slipped her key into the lock and with
a twist of his wrist opened the door. Taking a deep breath
to calm her racing heart, she walked inside her apartment on
none-too-steady feet. Linc followed her in, closing the door
behind him.

Her hand automatically reached up to a nearby light
switch, but he captured her hand in his. "Leave it off for
now. There's enough light in here for what we need," he
whispered, gently pulling her to him.

Despite Raven's best efforts to drum up any sort of resistance to him, her body automatically leaned toward him and
felt his arms tighten around her waist, drawing her even
closer.

The first touch of his lips on hers sent the pit of her stomach into a wild swirl and set her body aflame. His mouth
covered hers hungrily, sending shivers racing from the top
of her head to the tips of her painted toes. She would have
fallen to her knees with the devouring impact of the sexual
hunger she felt if he hadn't tightened his hold on her. His
mouth moved deeply over hers, tasting her, feeding on her,
drawing her out.

And then he went in for the kill.

His hand around her waist slid to her behind, cupping it
and urging her body closer to the hard fit of him at the same
time that he inserted his tongue into her mouth, reacquainting
it with this special brand of intimacy they'd shared four years
ago. Instinctively she captured his tongue with hers, at first
shocked at the degree of her own hunger and the magnitude
of her smoldering desire. She heard herself purring, then
moaning as she melted like butter in his arms. Their tongues
mated hotly, profusely, greedily.

And then it happened, that unexplainable, uncanny, but
special form of communication they were able to share
whenever their mouths mated with such intensity. He was
the one sending all the silent messages and she was reading
them loud and clear. It didn't matter what roadblocks she

tried putting in his path or what goals she intended to reach or dreams she wanted to fulfill, he intended on being a part of her life from this night on.

"No," she said, suddenly breaking off the kiss and trying to push him away. She could not let him or any man have this type of control over her. She didn't want to be dependent on any man, not even for this.

"Yes," Linc whispered huskily, knowing she'd deciphered his thoughts. His hold on her tightened, refusing to let her push him away from her. He reached up and traced his finger up her cheek and along the curve of her cheekbone. His gaze was intent, purposeful, challenging. "I'm not going anyplace, so get used to seeing me."

She looked up at him, her dark brown eyes rebellious but still filled with desire. She spread her palms on his chest, seeking distance. "I don't have time for this."

"Then I suggest you make time by adding me to your agenda," he said, trailing a feathery touch of his finger down the curve of her neck.

"I have plans, goals, dreams. I'm too busy to get involved with anyone," she implored in a shaky voice.

"I'm not just anyone, Raven," he said softly, stroking her swollen lips with his finger. "I'm the man you became a part of four years ago. The first man to make love to you. We bonded, we connected, and we—"

"Screwed each other silly during a week of fun and games, Linc. That's all it was, nothing more."

Her crude description of what they'd shared didn't faze Linc. He knew she was lying to herself. He could see the mixture of longing and fear in her eyes. She was actually afraid of him, not physically but emotionally. "It was more. You know it as well as I do."

"It was lust," she said in a quivery and unconvincing voice.

"Call it whatever you like for now, but I can guarantee that you'll come to know the right word for it later." He recaptured her mouth in a smooth sweep, intending to block all thoughts from her mind. He wanted her full attention and

deep concentration. He would have time to prove to her that
that week had been more than just fun and games for him
. . . and for her.

He made this kiss even more hot and heavy than the one
before. He refused to let her forget what they had once
shared, and he refused to let her make it into something
sleazy and meaningless.

His tongue became dominant and he made love to her
mouth in a slow, sensual mating. He felt her tremble in his
arms. He felt the heat of her center through the silky material
of her dress as it came in contact with his hardness pressing
against her.

When he finally broke off the kiss she clung to his shoulders for support, her breathing unsteady. He pulled her to
him. "I have dreams, too, Raven," he whispered in her ear
as if there could be others around listening. His voice was
husky with emotion. "Occasionally at night when I close my
eyes I remember seeing you as I saw you that last night we
spent together. You on my bed, stretched out, your body
trembling while waiting for me. The look in your eyes told
me you weren't ready for our week to end any more than I
was. But we had agreed that that week would be all we'd
ever have. Neither of us was interested in continuing things
with a long-distance romance. We both had plans and dreams
that didn't include a commitment to each other. We knew
and accepted that then."

He breathed deeply as his gaze continued to hold hers and
his arms tightened even more around her. "That night, when
we made love it was more special than any of the other times
before, and do you know why, Raven?"

Raven was transfixed by the blazing intensity of his eyes.
"No," she said quietly.

"Because that night we connected in a way we'd never
done before. I never knew that two people could get that
close, that united, and could join so deeply."

Raven closed her eyes remembering. His foreplay that
night had been torturous and had pitched her body into a
frenzy of need, not only to be satisfied but also to become a

part of him. He had pulled every single emotion that she possessed from her that night. At one point she'd even been tempted to rip his condom off to feel the very essence of him inside her body. She had wanted it all. She had wanted to share every part of him, even a part that could have put her at risk of becoming an unwed mother. But luckily for them both, she'd retained her sanity and held back.

"Fate has brought us back together," he continued, lacing his fingers through hers. "I regretted letting you walk out of my life. So don't think I'm going to let you do it a second time."

He lowered his head and placed a soft kiss on her lips before releasing her. His mouth curved into a warm smile. "Get a good night's sleep and while you're doing so think about what we once shared and will be sharing again."

Without giving her time to say anything, he opened the door and walked out, gently closing it behind him.

An angry Raven sat pounding away at the keyboard on her computer. She was furious with anybody, everybody, but especially with herself.

Stupid! Stupid! Stupid! How could she have let Linc take control of things like she had last night? She had been putty in his hands and, more specifically, under his lips. The man could have told her that the U.S. capital was being moved to Hawaii and she would have believed him as long as he'd kept his mouth cemented to hers. His kissing abilities had gotten even better, not that they'd needed improving, mind you.

Sighing in disgust, she glanced toward the window on the other side of her desk. In the distance she could see the Lincoln Memorial. Today the name "Lincoln" did not sit well with her. At the moment, it was definitely not one of her favorites. She frowned. At least the Lincoln that the memorial was named for had been honest. There was nothing honest about the Lincoln who had taken her home last night. He had played dirty. He'd known she would not be able to resist his kiss, and the man had laid it on thick and heavy.

Raven exhaled and forced herself to return to the document she had just entered into her computer, the opening for the article on Leo's that she was writing for the magazine. She glanced down at the club's itinerary that Tyrone Hardcastle had dropped by her office earlier that morning. Leo's was open six days a week from Tuesday through Sunday for after work and dinner. They were open Sundays for brunch. There was live music on Fridays, Saturdays, and Sundays. All other nights you were entertained with taped soft jazz except for once a month on Wednesday nights, which were set aside to showcase new and upcoming talent.

Raven returned her thoughts back to the document she'd been working on, trying to collect her thoughts on the talent that had been showcased last night. She had been impressed and her attention had been completely captured . . . until she had spotted Linc. Scowling, she started pounding on her keyboard again as she tried to erase the memory of everything that had happened last night.

Raven looked up when she heard the knock on her office door. "Yes?"

A smiling Erica breezed in. "Good morning. Did you get home OK last night?"

Raven frowned as she stared at her friend—the deserter. "Like you care," she said, displaying her wretched mood.

Erica's eyebrows lifted. "Of course I care, but Ben and I thought you and Linc needed time alone to reminisce about old times."

"Well, you and Ben thought wrong." Raven narrowed her eyes. "And speaking of you and Ben, the two of you were awfully chummy last night."

"Oh, yes," Erica replied, her smile widening. "He's a nice guy. I really enjoyed his company." She then came and sat in the chair across from Raven's desk. "What about you, Raven? Did you enjoy Linc's company?"

"Not particularly." Raven would have loved to tell Erica that she had detested Linc's company because things had moved too fast between them last night to suit her. But she decided the less she talked about it the better off she'd be.

"So did he spend the night?"

"Of course not!" Raven snapped angrily.

Grinning, Erica was not put off by Raven's sharp tone. "Mmm, I was hoping that he had."

"Why?"

Erica leaned forward. "Because you, Raven Anderson, need a man in your life to get your mind off work for a while. You are a sistah who definitely needs a brother. A hot-blooded brother at that."

"No, I do not."

Erica smiled. "Trust me, yes, you do, and as your friend I need to tell you these things, since those two sisters of yours won't. They're just as mixed-up and confused as you are. Especially the one John's in love with. I can't imagine any woman in her right mind not wanting to marry him."

Raven didn't want to hear any more. "Don't you have work to do?"

With a small chuckle Erica shook her head and said, "Not at the moment. You don't know how excited I was to discover that you and Linc have a history."

"So what of it?"

"You know what they say—history has a way of repeating itself."

Raven arched her eyebrow and narrowed her gaze. "History can also come back to haunt you. It's my belief that what's in the past should stay in the past."

"Not if it looks anything like Lincoln Corbain."

Before Raven could give a scorching retort there was another knock on her door. "Come in."

Megan, her secretary, opened the door and walked in carrying a beautifully wrapped box. "This was just delivered for you, Raven." She placed the box on Raven's desk and walked back out before a surprised Raven had a chance to thank her.

Raven gazed at the box for a second before picking it up, wondering which one of her sisters had sent it. She began opening it, ignoring Erica's curious gaze. Raven pulled out the white card that had been placed inside the box and began reading it:

Another thing that I occasionally dream about is the memory of our walks on the beach. I hope this package helps you remember those special times, too.

Linc

Stunned, Raven stared at the card and reread it.

"Well, who's it from?" Erica asked without exhibiting the least bit of shame at being nosey.

Raven lifted her head and looked at Erica. Seeing no reason not to tell her, she said, "It's from Linc."

Placing the card on her desk, Raven removed the tissue paper stuffed inside the box. Tucked under it all was a beautiful glass case containing several beautiful seashells.

A breathless astonished sigh escaped Raven's lips as she stared at the gift Linc had sent her. She closed her eyes for a moment, remembering the sound of the ocean as they strolled along the seashore holding hands while looking for seashells.

"Raven, you OK?"

Raven slowly reopened her eyes to see Erica staring at her. She looked back down at the item she held in her hands. "It's beautiful, isn't it?"

Erica smiled as she stood up. "Yes, simply beautiful. Umm, I'd even say expensive. That glass looks like real crystal. Not only does Linc Corbain look good, but the brother has good taste. I think I'll leave you alone to think about whatever else he has that's good." She then walked out of the office, closing the door behind her.

Raven leaned back in her chair as she stared down at the package that had been delivered to her. She pursed her lips as she considered her predicament. Lincoln Corbain was pulling out all the stops to get next to her. He was using the one thing she couldn't fight, and that was the memory of their time together in Daytona Beach.

The man was definitely playing dirty.

7

Raven sat alone with a glass of wine in her hand as she studied the sights and sounds around her. Soft conversations flowed through the club and mixed in with the smooth sound of jazz music. Her gaze roamed the room, lingering and committing to memory those things she would need to make the article she was writing informative and interesting.

She had selected the right place to use as the basis of her story. Leo's, like so many other supper clubs that were now springing up in different cities around the country, had found its niche. She admired the Hardcastles for operating such an upscale establishment that was both formal and friendly. Supper clubs, which had once been local traditions, had quickly gotten replaced by franchise restaurants, mostly the bar-and-grill types. But those franchises did not provide the novel entertainment, delicious food, and coziness that supper clubs had. Restaurant entrepreneurs in their zealous haste to become dining giants had lost sight of those things that were tried-and-true favorites. The Hardcastles had not lost sight of them, which was probably the reason people kept coming back.

"Would you like to order dinner now?"

Raven lifted her head to look up at the waiter who had appeared by her side. "No, not yet, but I'd love to have some more wine."

The older man nodded as he went about refilling her glass. After he left, she took a sip and began thinking about someone she had promised herself that she would not think about. Linc.

Today he had sent her another gift, a small potted palm tree. The plant was gorgeous, and she'd found the perfect place in her house for it. The card that had accompanied the plant had said:

Remember the palm trees swaying in the Florida breeze and our picnic under them as we watched the sun dip below the Atlantic Ocean.

Linc

Raven released a deep sigh. The problem she was having was the fact that she *was* remembering, which was something she didn't want to do. Ever since the plant had arrived she'd had memories of her and Linc's picnic on the beach one afternoon.

During the day the beach had been crowded, but in the late afternoon you could usually find a secluded spot. They had found the perfect place under a cluster of palm trees. She remembered Linc spreading a blanket out on the sand. He'd then pulled her down on the blanket next to him. Opening the picnic basket the hotel had prepared for them, he had withdrawn grilled chicken sandwiches, chips, grapes, a bottle of wine, and two wineglasses. After filling both glasses, he had handed one to her and then raised his own. "Here's to graduation in a few months, but more important, here's to what has been a beautiful and special week," he had murmured hoarsely.

"To graduation and to a beautiful and special week," she had repeated, touching her glass to his, then sipping the wine.

Raven shook her head, bringing her thoughts back to the present, not at all happy that she'd had them in the past yet again. Thoughts and memories were intruding into her work time, and she couldn't allow that to continue. No man had ever competed with her attention to her work assignments. And she was determined that Lincoln Corbain wouldn't be the first.

She didn't want to think about their nights together, the warmth and hard feel of his body as it lay atop hers, or the sounds she'd heard in the pitch-black of their hotel room: sounds of their heavy breathing, their moans, groans and passionate cries. And she refused to think about their mornings and waking up to the brightness of his eyes that still glowed with wanting and inner fire.

Raven picked up her glass to take another sip of her wine. The tingling warmth of the liquid that flowed down her throat matched the tingling warmth that flowed through her limbs and pooled at her core whenever she remembered Linc making love to her.

For the first time in four years she suddenly felt unbearably hungry, but it wasn't food that her body craved.

Sitting across the room at the crowded bar, Linc watched as Raven took another sip of her wine. His steady gaze observed as she lifted the glass to her lips, slightly tipped her head back, and arched her neck. Never before had observing a woman sipping her drink been sensuous enough to send involuntary tremors of arousal through him.

"Do you want a refill?" the bartender asked, intruding on Linc's thoughts. Linc noticed the man wasn't Flint and remembered that Flint only moonlighted a couple of nights of the week and Friday wasn't one of them.

"No, thanks, this is it for me tonight."

"You're planning on sticking around, aren't you?" the bartender asked.

Linc glanced over at the table where Raven was sitting alone. "Possibly. Why?"

"It's Sixties and Seventies Night. There's bound to be a lot of dancing going on."

Linc nodded. A delicious thought drifted through his mind. It was one of him holding Raven in his arms while he danced with her to a very slow tune, with the heat of his body pressing against hers long enough for him to savor the contact.

"In that case I'll definitely be sticking around."

An upbeat selection of sixties and seventies music filled the club as one singing group after another took center stage. First it had been the Commodores, then the Delfonics, and now the Dells. A large number of people crowded the dance floor. Most of them were couples, and others were in groups. There were even a few bold singles dancing anything and everything from swing to the bump, to the "whatever-you-want-to-call-it" current style of dancing.

Raven smiled as her gaze took in the entire scene. People were really enjoying themselves, as was evident in the laughter and rousing conversations surrounding her. She looked across the room and her gaze came into contact with Linc's. She had seen him earlier sitting at the bar, but other than lifting his glass in a silent greeting to her, he had kept his distance. In a way she was glad, but another part of her felt the least he could do was come over and say hello. Then she could thank him for the gifts he had sent and in a nice way ask him not to send her anything else.

She turned to the stage when the Dells came to the mike and the announcer said they were about to do one of their slow numbers. The dance floor crowd suddenly began thinning out when the groups and singles gave way to the couples.

"I want every man who has a special lady here tonight to use this opportunity to take her into your arms on the dance floor," the announcer said, smiling. Raven watched as more couples began heading forward.

"Raven?"

At the sound of her name, Raven turned and saw Linc standing next to her table. Stunned, she looked at him and watched as he reached his hand out to her. "May I have this dance?"

She tilted her head up, considering his request, knowing she should say no and reinforce her stand that there could not be anything between them. But instead she nodded, placed her hand in his, and stood. He led her to the dance floor.

Raven knew she was a goner the moment he took her into his arms. When he placed his arms around her, she inhaled sharply as their bodies began swaying in time to the music.

"You look good tonight, Raven," he whispered softly in her ear, tightening his hold on her.

"Thank you," she replied in a voice so low she knew he

probably had to strain to hear it. "And thanks for the gifts, Linc."

"You're welcome."

"But you're going to have to stop sending things for the sole purpose of recapturing memories of our time in Daytona."

"No, I don't," he said.

He heard her release a long sigh before saying, "You weren't this way before."

He leaned back and met her gaze. "What way?"

"Aggressive."

He smiled. "Thank you."

She frowned. "It wasn't meant to be a compliment, Linc."

His smile turned into a chuckle. "Yeah, I know."

Deciding to drop the subject for now, Raven pressed her cheek against his hard chest as they continued to dance to the slow music. She drew in a deep breath when he pulled her closer to his body and wrapped his arms around her more securely. Her body, so close to his, made her feel every hard part of him. Their movements were slow, charged, stimulating. By the time the last lyric had been sung and the last note played, a moan of pure wanting had arisen in her throat. She forced herself to swallow it.

"I have to go," she said when he escorted her back to her table. Her voice was trembling.

"I'll follow in my car to make sure you get in OK."

"That's not necessary. I've been going in after dark by myself for quite a while," she said sharply.

Slowly he smiled. "I'm sure you have, but I prefer doing it anyway."

Raven frowned. "Fine. Do whatever you want."

Linc's arm closed around her shoulder as they walked out of Leo's. He wished he could take her up on her offer to do whatever he wanted because his body was aching and, more than anything, he wanted to make non-stop love to her tonight.

* * *

"Lincoln Corbain is going to be the death of me," Raven said to herself in a low, deep growl of anguish as she looked in her rearview mirror to see the lights of the car following close behind her.

"The bottom line is," she raged on to herself, "the man is *not* going to get next to me. I refuse to let him do that. I got plans and dreams that don't include him. The sooner he realizes that, the better."

Her fingers tightened around the steering wheel. "If the reason he's following me is because he thinks he's going to get another kiss off me like he did a few nights ago, well, he has another thought coming."

Her heart pounded when she pulled into the driveway of her apartment complex. "I won't let him kiss me; I won't," she chanted to herself as she parked her car and got out with her door key in her hand. She wasn't surprised when he parked next to her and got out. But she was surprised when he said, "I'll wait right here until you get in. Flip the light switch twice to let me know you're inside and things are OK."

Raven frowned. *He wasn't going to try to talk his way inside her apartment? He wasn't going to try to kiss her good night? Well, that was just fine with her. That's what she wanted anyway, wasn't it?*

"Raven?"

She looked over at him. He was leaning against his car staring at her. "What?"

"Pleasant dreams." His words came with that megawatt smile that could always cause extreme sensual heat to settle in the lower part of her body, like it was doing now.

She fumed as she walked to her door. Pleasant dreams? In order to dream, one had to sleep, and there was no way she was going to get any sleep tonight.

Glaring at him one last time, she unlocked her door and went inside. And as he had asked her to do, she flipped the light switch twice.

*   *   *

Raven had undressed, showered, and gotten settled in bed when the phone rang. She looked at the digital clock on the nightstand, then back at the phone, wondering if it was Linc. She then thought there was no way it could be him because, as far as she knew, he didn't have her number. She picked up the phone.

"Hello."

"Took you long enough."

Raven smiled at her sister's impatient voice. "I was wondering who would be calling me this late. How are things going, Falcon?"

"They're going. You OK?"

Raven shifted her position in the bed to find a more comfortable spot. "Yeah, I'm OK. What about you?"

"Yeah, I'm fine. Have you heard from Robin lately?"

Raven frowned. Actually, she hadn't, at least not this week, and that was unusual. Robin was the one who made it her business to keep in touch on a rather frequent basis. "No, I haven't. You?"

"She called and left a message on my answering machine a few nights ago saying she's doing OK and to tell you she's been busy but will call you this coming week. I guess she wants to get with us to finalize the details for her birthday party."

Raven smiled, shaking her head. Of the three of them, Robin was the one into birthday celebrations big-time. "Yes, I suppose."

"How are things at work?"

"They're fine, and before you ask, he's doing OK, Falcon."

"I have no idea who you're talking about."

"Don't play dumb, Falcon. You're too smart. Besides, being coy doesn't become you."

There was a long pause. "I miss him, Raven. It's been a year tonight."

Raven sighed upon hearing the pain and loneliness in her sister's voice. She also had heard the occasional sniffing that indicated Falcon had been crying. "Yeah, I know. I thought about it this morning. It was the week before Robin's birthday last year that John asked you to marry him." She decided not to tell Falcon that John had not come into the office at all today. Chances were he had remembered, too, and the day had been just as miserable for him as it had been for Falcon.

"And I turned him down," Falcon finished. "But I did the right thing. I know I did."

"If you really believe that, then everything will eventually be all right, Falcon," Raven said softly, not knowing what else to say.

"Of course it will be. I think I'll have enough money saved in another year to get things started with the company I plan on opening."

"Oh, Falcon, that's wonderful."

"I can't wait." There was another pause. "That's what it's all about, isn't it, Raven? It's about working hard and fulfilling our dreams. Everything else can wait. Nothing else is important."

Raven sucked in a deep breath as she heard her sister's words. She let it back out slowly. Leave it to Falcon to always remind her of what came first with them. "You're right, Falcon," she said softly. "Nothing else is important."

8

Raven had just finished tying her shoelaces when there was a knock on her door. She frowned. It was just a little past six in the morning. She wondered who her early-morning visitor could be. She doubted it was Erica, although she had an open invitation to go running with Raven whenever she wanted. Some people weren't morning people, and Erica fell within that category.

Upon reaching the door Raven took a quick glance out the peephole.

Linc!

She immediately opened the door. Given the fact that she didn't get any sleep last night and she blamed him for it, Lincoln Corbain was the last person she wanted to see. "Wh-what are you doing here?"

Raven almost stammered on her words as she looked at the man standing in her doorway. A new kind of awareness pumped furiously through her veins. Oh, she had awakened in a bed with Linc before so she knew all about his sexy-as-sin early-in-the-morning look. And during their week together he had mostly worn tank tops and shorts, so she was well aware of the fact that he had a gorgeous body. But he must have gotten into some bodybuilding program since she'd seen him. The man looked absolutely stunning in his well-fitted "see-how-fine-the-brother-really-is" running suit. Just looking at how he looked in the outfit made a burning sensation sizzle from the tips of her breasts down to her middle. There it stopped. His body was so taut, so firm, so tight, so unbelievably built. There was not a flabby place anywhere on him. Her gaze automatically went to his mid-section. She sucked in a deep breath. Lincoln Corbain was also so well endowed. As she continued staring, she began remembering one particular morning while they were in bed together, sliding her fingers beneath the waistband of his shorts to feel just how well endowed he was.

Raven swallowed. That same moan that had threatened to erupt from her throat last night when she'd been in his arms while dancing was threatening now. She returned her gaze to his face and saw that he had been watching her ogle him. She cleared her throat. "I asked what you're doing here, Linc?"

His eyes bored into her in a way that seemed to touch every feature on her face. "I thought I'd go running with you."

Raven frowned as she searched her mind in response to what he'd just said. Fairly certain she had never mentioned her early-morning weekend activities to him, she asked, "How did you know I go running on Saturday mornings?"

"Erica mentioned it to Ben, and since Ben knew I also go

running early on Saturday mornings he mentioned it to me."

She narrowed her gaze on him. "So you just assumed it would be OK to join me?"

"Yes," he said, giving her a seductive smile. "That's about the shape and size of it."

Instinctively when he said those words her gaze immediately went back to his midsection, remembering another time he'd used those same words when he'd been discussing something else with her. She inhaled sharply as she tried to get her mind back on track. She looked back up at him. "I think you assume too much, Linc."

He studied her for a moment. "And what else is it that you think I assume?"

"That you can pick up where we left off four years ago in Daytona."

He cocked his head as if considering her words. He then said, "The only thing that I'm assuming and what I know for a fact, Raven, is that you prefer I left you alone. But I can't do that."

"And why not?"

Linc smiled. "I'll tell you some other time. You ready to go running? I promise to be good company."

You'll be more company than I need, she thought to herself. "If you want to tag along you can. Just as long as you keep up."

Linc let out a smooth chuckle. "I was going to give you the same advice."

"How about something to drink?" she offered after they returned to her apartment from their jog a couple of hours later.

"Water will do fine, thanks."

Linc followed her into the kitchen and sat down on one of the stools at her breakfast bar. "Nice place."

"Thanks." Raven went to the refrigerator to get him a thirty-two-ounce bottle that she always kept on hand full of drinking water. As much as she didn't want to admit it, she had enjoyed Linc's company while running. He had kept up with her pace, and they'd engaged in steady conversation most of the time without losing a beat.

He had told her that he had gotten into a fitness program right after law school and still went to the gym at least twice a week. He enjoyed keeping his body in shape by working out. She'd been tempted to tell him that in her opinion he was doing a super-nice job of it.

She walked back over to the kitchen counter and handed him the bottled water. She watched, fascinated as well as magnetized, as he uncapped the bottle and, tilting his head back, took a huge swallow of the clear liquid.

Raven's gaze was drawn to the muscular expanse of his neck, and she watched as the water flowed down his throat, making his Adam's apple move. Her body ached to go over to him and take her tongue and lap up the water that was missing his mouth and running freely down his neck. She stood there and watched as he consumed all thirty-two ounces of the water without stopping to take a breath. Amazing.

When he finished he licked his lips and smiled at her. "I guess I was thirsty. It's like that with me sometimes. When I get ahold to something I want bad, I almost become addicted to it."

She nodded as her heart thumped erratically in her throat. She thought of the many times that they had made love in Daytona. Had he become addicted to her that week? If so, what had been her excuse? Had she been addicted to him as well?

"What are your plans for the rest of the day?" Linc's question broke into her meanderings.

"I'm going to edit an article I'm working on about Leo's."

Linc's brow rose. "You're doing an article on Leo's?"

"Yes. It's an article about the revived popularity of supper clubs. I chose Leo's as my subject since I know the Hardcastles personally."

Linc nodded. "How about dinner and a movie later?"

Raven had known that sooner or later he would get around to asking her out. And just as she'd been prepared for the question, she should have been prepared to give him an answer of "no." But for some reason she held back. She told herself that it would just be a movie and dinner. No big deal. She hadn't been out to a movie in ages, and besides, she would have to eat sometime. As long as she remained in control of the situation there could be no harm in it. She had learned by Falcon's mistakes. The harm came in falling in love, and she had no intentions of doing that.

"Dinner and a movie sounds nice as long you understand that there's nothing between us other than friendship, Linc."

He stared at her quietly. "You want us to go from being former lovers to just being friends? Is that what you really want, Raven?"

"Yes. I won't go out with you otherwise. It's a friendship thing or nothing. No more sending me stuff to remind me of our time together in Daytona. What we shared then is in the past and I want to keep it that way."

After a brief moment he nodded slowly. "If that's the way you want it, then that's the way it will be. Will seven o'clock tonight be OK?" he asked as he stood to leave.

"Yes."

He leaned down and instead of giving her the heated kiss she had come to expect, he tenderly brushed his lips against her cheek. "I'll see you later, friend."

She nodded and drew in a deep breath, knowing she was getting just what she'd asked for, a platonic relationship with him.

Somehow she regretted it already.

9

Raven sat in her office at Augustan Publishers and pounded away at the keyboard of her computer. Never before in her life had she felt so frustrated, and she had only herself to blame.

It was a day short of being a week since Linc had agreed

to her stipulation that they be just friends, and ever since then she'd been a basket case. Not that he ever got out of line, mind you. He was playing the role of a friend to the hilt. Just like she had asked him to do, he was treating her like a friend and not a former lover. But she found that although he may not be treating her like a former lover, she felt like one just the same.

And that was the crux of her problem.

As much as she tried, she just couldn't see him in a whole new light. She kept seeing him in the old one, where his sensuous beam had once rendered her blind. Each and every time she saw him brought forth emotions from within her that she couldn't explain no matter how many times her mind evoked objective reasoning.

With a frustrated sigh she stopped typing to think about all that had happened during the past week. After dinner Saturday night he had taken her to a movie. It was a romantic comedy that she totally enjoyed. Then he had taken her home, and after walking her to the door and giving her a chaste kiss to her lips he had left. She had lain awake in bed that night hungering for his touch, reliving their last heated kiss, and wondering if she had ruined her chances of ever getting another one.

Linc had evidently reached the conclusion that although she wanted a platonic relationship, he would not be out of sight nor out of mind. He had shown up unexpectedly on Sunday after she had come from early-morning church service, inviting her to brunch at Leo's. After leaving the club they had gone for a walk in the park; then he had returned her home, saying he would call the next day.

On Monday he had called her at work inviting her to dinner at his place. After showing her around his neatly furnished apartment he had fed her a delicious meal that he had cooked himself. After dinner they had sat around talking about how their day had gone and about current events.

On Tuesday they had met for lunch at a sandwich shop not far from her office, and then on Wednesday he had taken her to Open Mike Night at Leo's.

Thursday he had come to her house straight from work bringing Chinese food. After they had eaten, he had sat at her breakfast bar silently reviewing a case he was working on, while she sat at her kitchen table editing her article on Leo's. Although she hated admitting it, she had liked the idea of him being there and hadn't felt threatened by his presence. She couldn't remember the last time since college that any one man had dominated so much of her time. Usually when it came to dates, she rarely went for seconds. Going out once with the same person was enough. But she had seen Linc each and every night without any thought of feeling crowded or having her style cramped. She didn't want to dwell on the fact that two people who were trying to have nothing more than a platonic relationship wouldn't be spending as much time together as they were.

The week she had just finished spending with him was totally different from the week they had spent together in Daytona. Then they had been lovers who hadn't been able to keep their hands off each other. Now it appeared that she was the only one suffering from the strong physical attraction she still felt for him, although she was pretending not to be.

And she didn't like playing the role of a pretender.

She didn't like pretending that she didn't notice the way he filled out a pair of jeans like nobody's business or that when dressed in a suit he looked like the prime candidate for a magazine cover. She didn't like pretending that his smile didn't make her thighs clench, her heart rate increase, or her breath catch. Nor did she like pretending that that morning they had gone running together the scent of his hot sweat and the pure masculinity that clung to him didn't completely arouse her. And she sure as heck didn't like pretending that she preferred sitting across from him on a sofa chatting about world news to sitting in his lap while kissing him senseless. Or better yet, him kissing her senseless.

Raven released a frustrated sigh. Her week had gone from bad to worse, and the prospects of it improving weren't looking too hot. "Something gotta give," she muttered to herself as she closed down her computer to bring her workweek to an end. It was Friday and she and Linc had another date tonight. And she was going to make sure that when the evening was over he was just as miserable as she.

Linc paced the confines of Raven's apartment waiting for her to finish dressing. He had arrived a little earlier than planned, and she had come to the door with a towel wrapped around her all-too-seductive body. His tongue would have fallen out of his mouth had it not been attached.

"You're early," she'd said breathlessly after rushing to open the door for him. "I just got out of the shower. You're going to have to wait a few minutes."

Somehow he'd found his voice to say, "Uh, no problem."

When she turned around to go back into the bathroom he couldn't help noticing that the towel barely covered anything.

Linc stopped pacing and lowered himself onto the sofa, wondering how much more torture he could take. Surely Raven could see that their being just friends wasn't working. The physical attraction they had for each other was too strong.

"I'm ready."

Linc glanced up. His breath immediately got lodged in his throat. A ripple of pure male appreciation ran up his spine. Dressed in a short, curvy black dress, Raven looked fabulous. She had both the body and the legs for the outfit she had chosen to wear. He forced himself to stand, hoping he didn't embarrass himself when he did. "You look great, Raven."

She smiled at him. "Thank you. You look good yourself." That definitely wasn't a lie, she thought. He looked handsome in a white dinner jacket and black pants. They were attending a dinner party that his law firm was giving, and she had wanted to look nice.

A moment of silence stretched out between them before Raven cleared her throat. "Ready?" she asked.

"As ready as I'll ever be." Taking her arm, Linc led her out of the apartment.

*   *   *

"It was a nice party," Raven said to Linc as he walked her to her apartment door.

Linc thought his eyes would pop out of their sockets at seeing the way Raven's dress clung to her body in all the right places with every step she took. He had forgotten just how small her waist was and how curvy her rear end was until tonight. He coughed to clear his throat. "Yeah, it was, wasn't it? And I think you were the most gorgeous woman there."

"Thanks."

"When will your sisters get in tomorrow?"

Raven opened her purse to pull out her door key. "I'm expecting them in the morning."

When she leaned down to look into her purse for the key, he caught a glimpse of a hefty amount of cleavage. The one thing he had not forgotten was how sexy her bare breasts were. He coughed to clear his throat for a second time. "Well, I hope everything with the birthday party goes as planned."

"Me, too." She took a deep breath. "Good night, Linc."

"Good night."

He waited for her to open the door and go in, but Raven hesitated. "Your throat sounds dry. Would you like to come in for something to drink?"

He stared at her for a long, thoughtful minute before saying, "Sure." He followed her inside and to the kitchen, sitting down at the breakfast bar.

"What would you like? I have water, tea, and soda."

"A glass of water will do."

Raven nodded as she opened the cabinet to take down a glass. She then began filling it with water from the pitcher in her refrigerator. After handing him the ice-cold glass of water, she leaned against the counter to watch him take a few sips.

"How's the article you're doing on Leo's coming along?"

"It's almost finished." As though drawn by a sudden thought, she asked, "Would you like to read what I've put together so far?"

"Sure."

"OK. I'll be right back." Like a kid who was eager to show her parent a paper that had been graded with a perfect score, Raven raced out of the kitchen. She didn't want to think about why it was so important to show Linc what she had written. It just was. Maybe it was because a part of her wanted to prove to him that she was not like the other reporters he had come to detest. That had to be the reason, she inwardly told herself, because she had never shared her work with anyone, especially while it was in the pre-publication stages.

Raven returned in no time and handed him the papers. He accepted them and sat back down at her breakfast bar and began reading. She tried not to make out his expression while he was reading, but she couldn't help but wonder what she thought of what she had written. It seemed it took forever before he had finished.

His eyes met hers. "This is an outstanding piece, Raven. You have a gift with words. You're a woman with a very special talent."

"Thank you." His opinion meant a lot. She didn't want to question the why of it just yet.

Nor did she want to question why she felt the need to kiss him, especially when he was staring at her with those deep, dark eyes of his. His gaze was seductive and magnetic, drawing her in closer. She suddenly leaned toward him, and bracing her hands on his thigh, she touched her lips to his and accepted that a platonic relationship between them had been doomed from the start. The passion that was always there surrounding them had the ability to consume completely, thoroughly, and burn hot.

Her senses immediately began spinning before she realized that he was not going to help her out with the kiss. *Fine, he can just sit there and be a stone, but I plan on getting my fill,* she thought as she closed her eyes and deepened the kiss. She'd been dying to taste him again. She let her tongue explore the recesses of his mouth as she ravaged it with a hunger that belied her outward calm.

And still he held back his tongue from her.

So she continued to assault his mouth, feeling the shivers racing through him with every stroke of her tongue, giving herself freely to the wantonness she felt and the fiery intimacy she was sharing with him as she feasted on his mouth.

She felt his arms tighten around her. She heard his breathing get heavy, then heavier. And then she felt him easing to his feet, without breaking her hold on his mouth. He pulled her closer to him, and her body felt every hard inch of him. She increased her assault as a sense of urgency drove her on.

She broke off the kiss for mere seconds, just to pull air in, then covered his mouth with hers once more. This time he joined in her attack.

Her senses reeled as if short-circuited when his tongue captured hers, taking over with demanding mastery and savage intensity. Nobody could kiss like Lincoln Corbain, she decided, giving her mouth up to his fiery possession. He took it, sending pleasure radiating through every part of her body.

As he further roused her passion she knew that his own had to be growing just as strong. Her emotions whirled and skidded as to how far she wanted him to go. And then she knew the answer. She wanted him to go all the way. She wanted him to make love to her.

So she relayed that message to him in her kiss.

He got it.

Pulling back, he sucked in a long gulp of air and looked down at her.

She nodded, meeting his unwavering gaze.

His mouth came down on hers at the exact moment he swept her off her feet and into his arms. Carrying her into the bedroom, he gently placed her on the bed. For the hundredth time that night, he thought she looked sexier than any woman had a right to be with the dress she had on. And he knew he hadn't been the only man at the party who had thought so.

Kneeling on the bed, he reached out for her and brought her close to him. Leaning down, he captured her parted lips.

Tonight they would create new memories. That thought overwhelmed him. He had never felt such uncontrollable desire before. The other times they had come together, he had claimed her body. Tonight he wanted her heart and soul.

He pulled away long enough to undress her. When that was done he stood back and looked down at her as a growl of need erupted from deep within his throat. He quickly began removing his own clothing. Fumbling with his wallet, he took out a foil packet and ripped it open. Moments later, he went back to her. Driven by want and need, he ran his hands over her body, reacquainting them with her soft flesh.

Raven whimpered under his touch. It had been four years since she had been touched this way. It seemed all the heat and passion of her body had lain dormant until Linc had returned into her life. She felt him sliding his hand up and down her stomach, then back up again to her breasts to give them special attention.

Need suddenly tore into her like the rush of a mighty wind when she felt the warmth of his tongue replace his hands on her breasts. Moans escaped her lips as he lavished attention from one tip to another. Her breath came out in short puffs and her fingers gripped his shoulders as he continued his assault.

"Linc . . ."

He heard the passionate plea in her voice. He wanted to delay everything and drag it out until the end but knew that would not be possible. Their desire, passion, and need for each other were too strong and too hot. But still he refused to be rushed. Slowly and completely, he continued his assault over every inch of her body, remembering the areas he could touch that would drive her nearly out of her mind.

Finally, when his need became just as great as hers, he placed his body over hers. "Raven." He groaned out her name like a dying man who was about to take his last breath.

Wanting what was about to come, Raven parted her lips and eagerly accepted the invasion of his tongue at the same time the hardness of him entered her. When he found her body tight, too tight, he tore his mouth away from hers and looked down into her eyes. The look in his gaze was questioning, confused.

She was torn between her desire to have him get on with it and finish what he had started and his need for her to explain why her body felt just as tight as it had the first time they'd made love. When she saw he was dead set on not moving . . . not even another delicious inch, she met his gaze and, drawing in a slow breath, said, "I haven't done this since that time in Daytona with you, Linc."

His gaze was intense as he stared deep into her eyes. He remained still as the meaning of her words sank in. Suddenly a deep sense of pride and elation swept over him. "Raven." Cupping her face in his hands, he whispered her name with deep emotion in his voice as he crushed her to his throbbing body, going deeper inside her. The magnitude of that connection made them both groan out loud as their mouths joined once again.

With tender care, he began moving inside her, savoring each stroke and letting his tongue move inside her mouth in the same slow rhythm. When the tempo of his rhythm increased, so did his lovemaking to her mouth. Their mouths mated just as wildly as their bodies.

He grasped her hips tightly as if to keep her in one place as he pushed deeper within her. He groaned tightly when he felt the first sign of tremors race through her body to his. His mouth swallowed each and every moan she made as red-hot passion splintered them both. It was exquisite. It was torture.

It was everything he remembered and had dreamed of having again.

Finally tearing his mouth from hers, Linc gave out a loud growl of male pleasure when he felt himself emptying within her in an explosion that rocked their bodies endlessly. He pulled her closer to him, ignoring the pain of her fingernails as they dug deep into his shoulders.

Recovering after the last tremor left him, he slowly forced his body off Raven so his weight wouldn't hurt her. Sliding to her side, he pulled her against him, closing his arms around her.

"Linc?"

He rose slightly until he could look at her. Her face was flushed, her eyes were glazed, and her lips were swollen from the intensity of his kisses.

"Yes?"

She smiled and whispered, "You're incredible."

"No, sweetheart, you are." He pulled her back into his arms and began kissing her again as passion blazed to life between them once again.

He took her through another round of passionate love-making. It was as if he couldn't get enough of her and she, in turn, couldn't get enough of him. The four years that had separated them had dissolved and everything they had meant to each other that week in Daytona had returned tenfold. When there was no way they could survive another bout of lovemaking, he was contented to rain kisses all over her face and neck, knowing that he neither could nor would let her out of his life again.

"I love you," he whispered, saying aloud what he had felt in his heart since seeing her again.

Raven's body stiffened, as she was certain she had heard him wrong. Her mind began to spin. Love? He couldn't love her. She didn't want him to love her. She didn't have time for love in her life.

She pulled away from him and took deep intakes of breaths to get her heart rate and breathing back in sync. She looked up at him and the eyes returning her gaze were as soft as a caress.

"What is it, Raven? What's wrong?"

"You just said you loved me."

"Yes, I do love you."

Raven shook her head, not wanting to believe it although he sounded as if he meant every word. "But you just saw me again two weeks ago."

"I fell in love with you in Daytona. I tried telling myself that there was no way I could have fallen in love with you in such a small amount of time, but I knew after returning to Louisiana that I had. That's the reason I went to Talla-hassee looking for you."

She stared at him, surprised by what he had said. "You went to Tallahassee looking for me?"

"Yes, the day after I graduated from law school. But the school officials said you had graduated a few days earlier and had already left. They wouldn't give me information about your whereabouts." He took a deep breath before con-tinuing. "I went home to Tennessee and began working with my family. But I thought about you often. The only thing I had left was the memories of our time together. After a while I gave up hope of ever seeing you again. When I ran into you at Leo's last week I knew I was being given a second chance."

Raven lowered her gaze. When she raised it moments later she blinked away the moisture that had begun gathering there. "You're mistaken, Linc. You haven't been given a second chance. I don't want any part of a relationship with you or anyone. My work is the most important thing to me. It's all I need."

"What about love?" he asked, frowning.

"Love only complicates things. That's what happened with Falcon and John. They started out being lovers; then they fell in love and after that everything went wrong."

"Only because you and your sisters think that falling in love is wrong," he said curtly. "It's the most natural thing in the world for a man to want a future with the woman he loves."

"Not if that woman doesn't want to have a future with him." She had to pull her gaze away from his face when she saw the hurt her words put there. "My work is my life and I don't want anything else in it, especially love." She paused and took a deep breath, hoping he had gotten her message loud and clear.

From the look on his face she knew he had. Raven looked at him, struck by the anger she saw there. She wondered if this was how John had handled Falcon's decision not to marry him.

Linc slowly got out of the bed and began getting dressed. Not one time did he look at her. It was only after he had all of his clothes back on that he turned to her. He stood there next to the bed, quiet, his eyes dark, his jaws clenched. Finally, gathering his composure, he said softly, "I admire any person, man or woman, who wants to make their mark by being successful in their chosen field. But there will come a time when your work won't be all you need, Raven. There will come a time when it won't give you everything you want. Without the one you love, life is meaningless, no matter how many goals you achieve. I love you."

"No," she said softly, lowering her head.

"Look at me," he whispered urgently. Leaning down, he took her chin in his hand and lifted it so their eyes could meet. "Can you honestly look me in the eye and say that I mean absolutely nothing to you? That what we shared tonight meant nothing?"

Raven swallowed, knowing that she couldn't, but she refused to admit it to him or anyone. "I want to be successful."

"And you will be. I've no doubt of that. I'll never ask you to give up anything for me."

Raven didn't answer for a brief moment. Then she spoke. "You can't say that for certain, and I can't take the chance that one day you might. Robin, Falcon, and I are a lot like our mother. She was a woman who loved her man with everything she had. She knew her daughters would probably do the same. If I were to love you, I'd gladly give up everything for you. I'd love you just that much. My mother loved my father so much that she gave him the world. In the end he gave her his behind to kiss. I can't and I won't let myself love anyone that much, Linc. I'm sorry."

He looked at her for a long moment before turning and walking out the door.

At the sound of the door closing Raven pressed her face to the pillow, letting her tears flow, knowing that she had done the very thing she had not wanted to do.

She had fallen in love with Lincoln Corbain.

Sweat of anger popped out across Linc's upper lip as he drove away from Raven's apartment. Although he admired her stubborn determination to succeed and not let anything or anyone stand in her way, he felt she was going about obtaining her dreams all wrong.

His hands on the steering wheel tightened. None of this made any sense. From what he'd been told, his own mother had once been a very vocal advocate for women's rights. She still was. She was also a very successful attorney. When she and his father had married they had formed a partnership. Neither one came first. They were both equal partners in their relationship. Why was it so hard for Raven to believe that that sort of relationship between two people who loved each other could exist?

Linc wasn't in the mood to go home just yet and found himself pulling into the parking lot of Leo's. It was an hour before closing, and he needed something a little stronger to drink than coffee.

Entering the establishment, he noted only one other individual sitting at the bar. Sliding onto the stool next to the man who was leaning down over his drink as if in deep thought, Linc waited for the bartender to take his order. "Scotch on the rocks."

Suddenly feeling like he was under someone's microscope, he turned to the man sitting next to him and found him staring. Linc frowned. "You got a problem?" he asked the man in a voice tinged with all the anger he felt.

The man's chuckle surprised him. "No, but it sounds like you do. Let me guess. One of the Anderson sisters has struck again."

Linc lifted his brow as he studied the man. Then it dawned on him as to who he was. John Augustan. Linc hadn't recognized him dressed in casual clothing.

Linc drew in a deep breath. He took a swallow of the drink the bartender had placed in front of him. If anyone understood how he felt it would be John Augustan. "Yeah, one of the Anderson sisters has struck again."

John met Linc's gaze as he lifted his drink and said somberly with a wry smile on his lips, "No pun intended but welcome . . . to the club."

10

Robin Anderson glanced around the decorated room that had balloons hanging from the ceiling and banners covering the walls before returning her gaze to her two sisters. They were waiting for her to make a birthday wish and blow out the twenty-eight candles on her birthday cake. Both Falcon and Raven had red puffy eyes that neither had managed to effectively hide behind carefully applied makeup.

Robin closed her eyes to make her wish, knowing what she was really about to do was say a birthday prayer instead. She needed to send up a prayer more than she needed to make a wish. She loved her sisters dearly, but knowing them, she realized they would not be open-minded and accept what she was about to tell them. Drawing in a deep breath, she let it back out over the cake. Hearing her sisters' cheers, she knew she had hit her mark. Opening her eyes, she saw that all twenty-eight candles had been blown out under one mighty breath.

It was only later while the three of them were sitting on Raven's living room floor Indian-style that Robin decided to drop the bomb: "I'm in love."

Falcon and Raven stopped eating their cake and drinking their wine and stared at her. By the look of horror on their faces she knew they had taken her news badly. There was no way she could soften the blow because there was more news to come. "I met him in Paris not long after I got there. His name is Franco and he's asked me to marry him and I've accepted." That last statement she knew was the finishing blow. It didn't take long for them to react.

"Whoa, wait just a minute here," Falcon was saying at the top of her voice. "You can't get married yet. You aren't even close to opening that cooking school you want in New York. You're at least three to four years away from doing that, Rob'. How can you even think of love and marriage?"

"Falcon's right," Raven chimed in. "How can you?"

A flash of defiance appeared in Robin's eyes. "Haven't either of you heard what I just said? I love him. That's how I can do it. And now after seeing you two today I know more than ever that I'm making the right decision."

Both Raven and Falcon set their plates and wineglasses down. "What do you mean by that?" Raven asked, pulling her eyebrows together in a frown.

"Just look at you two. Falcon's been in a state of funk ever since she turned down John's marriage proposal. I found myself not wanting to call her anymore because each time I did she would start crying, and it's been over a year."

Robin then turned her full attention to Raven. "And I don't know who your lover boy is, but by the looks of you, it seems you've also given him the boot, and you're suffering because of—"

"It's Linc," Raven muttered in exasperation, getting to her feet.

Robin lifted her gaze to Raven. "Ooh, you mean to say you've run into Lincoln Corbain again, after all these years?"

Raven thrust her hands into the pockets of her jeans, frowning. "Yes."

Falcon stood and glared at her. "And you didn't tell us? Why?"

Raven sighed. Her sisters knew all about that week she had spent with Linc in Daytona four years ago. And they had known that he must have meant a lot to her for her to have gone to bed with him. She had always sworn that the first guy she slept with would be someone she loved. "I was hoping he'd go away."

"And he didn't?" Robin asked.

"No." The word got caught in Raven's throat for a moment. She swallowed to let it down before continuing. "Not until last night. I sent him away."

Robin nodded. "So that's why you've been crying."

"She's been crying?" Falcon asked in alarm, walking over to Raven to study her face.

Robin smiled, amused by the question Falcon had asked. "You've been crying so much yourself this past year, Falcon, that it's not obvious to you when someone else has red puffy eyes. To you it's a normal look."

Falcon glared at Robin. "That's not funny."

Robin's smile widened. "You're right; it's not funny. It's pathetic. And that's the reason I have all intentions of marrying Franco. I refuse to go through life miserable and crying like the two of you have decided to do."

"What about your dreams? Your plans?" Raven asked in desperation.

"What about what Mama drilled into us?" Falcon added.

Robin shook her head. Sometimes she thought she should have been the oldest of the three. Falcon could take the smallest piece of information and run with it—usually in the wrong direction. "First of all, I still have every intention of pursing my dreams. Franco is also a master chef, who wants to share my dream. It's our desire to open a school together." She shifted her position to stretch out her legs as she gazed at her two sisters standing over her. "And furthermore, Mama's drilling was not about men in general. It was about the three of us, as individuals, as women who have choices and dreams. She wanted us to fulfill our dreams and not let anyone stop us from doing so. She died believing that she had given us every means in her power for us to be successful. And she did. I'm not giving up my dream to marry Franco. I'm expanding it to include him."

"I don't believe this," Falcon said, her tone tinged with anger. "Just like that, you think you have all the answers. Don't you think that I did a lot of soul-searching before I turned down John's marriage proposal? Don't you think if there was any way I could have made it work I would have?"

Falcon's dark eyes reflected her pain, and Robin knew she had to tread lightly. "I'm sure you did, Falcon. But your situation was a little bit more complicated than mine. John wanted you to move here to D.C. with him, which meant your losing the clientele you had worked so hard to build. With Franco, I don't have that problem. We both want to live in New York. But . . ."

Falcon frowned. "But what?"

"But regardless of the reason, I think if I had loved John as much as I know for certain that you do, I would have figured out a way to make it work."

Falcon's eyes flared from the sting of her sister's remark. "I couldn't do it."

Robin nodded. "Then why are you still crying over spilt milk? Why haven't you gotten over it and moved on?"

Robin knew those questions were stabbing at her sister's heart. She then turned her attention to Raven. "And what about you, Raven? You either want to be with Linc or not. You either love him or you don't. I suggest that you be happy and love him and still be successful, or you can take the advice you *think* Mama gave you and not love him and be miserable but successful."

After a lengthy silence and a sip of her wine, Robin said, "We all saw the movie *Mahogany*. Didn't either of you get anything from it other than a good drool over Billy Dee Williams? The whole moral of the movie was that success is nothing unless you have the person you love to share it with."

Standing up, Robin said, "So, sisters dear, on my twenty-eighth birthday I'm willing to be the first Anderson sister to walk out in faith and love. Our father was heartless. He was a jerk. He was a dog. But I don't believe all men are like him. I'm blessed to have met and fallen in love with one who's not. I believe if Mama was alive, after meeting Franco she would agree. And I also believe that she would have been happy for me."

She walked over to her sisters and took their hands in hers. "I don't need your blessings, nor do I need your permission. But I do want the two of you to be happy for me and accept that I love this man and that I'm putting our future plans in God's hands. And whatever the future holds, thanks to Mama I'll be prepared either way."

She kissed both of her sisters on the cheeks. Smiling softly, she said, "I'll see you guys later."

"Hey, where do you think you're going?" Falcon asked as she watched her sister head for the door, pausing long enough to grab her purse off the couch.

"To the hotel. Franco should have arrived by now and checked in."

"He's here?" Raven asked, amazed at the turn of events. Granted Robin had always been the most rebellious of the three, but all of them had agreed at one time or another that men and success didn't mix. Looks like Willow Anderson's middle child was now singing a different tune.

"Of course he's here. It's my birthday and I want him to meet my two closest friends—my sisters. But first, he and I have to celebrate my birthday in style, so don't wait up. You can both meet him in the morning. I'm inviting him to breakfast." With that said, Robin left, closing the door behind her.

"Well, what do you think of that?" Raven asked Falcon with utter amazement in her voice.

"I hate to admit it, but what I think is that Robin may have the right idea," Falcon said, shaking her head. "Hell, she has a man. We're the ones who don't."

The corners of Raven's lips lifted in a soft smile. "Are you insinuating that she's a lot smarter than we are?"

"I wouldn't go that far. Robin is just more daring. She's a risk-taker." Falcon couldn't help but laugh. "Always has been, and turning one year older hasn't changed her."

"I still can't believe she actually left her own birthday party," Raven was saying as she and Falcon took down the last banner.

"I can't believe she left the two of us here to clean up this mess," Falcon grumbled. "OK, what's next? And don't you dare suggest that we go to one of those video stores and get a copy of *Mahogany* and watch it again."

Raven grinned as she looked at her sister. "Don't worry; that's the furthest thing from my mind."

With no hesitation Falcon added, "Same here. But I have been thinking about what Robin said."

Raven released a deep sigh. "Me, too. You still love John, don't you?"

"Yes, terribly. Robin was right. I've been miserable this past year. But I think it's too late. He probably hates me. For all I know he may have someone else in his life now."

Raven knew she could at least get her sister out of her misery for one day. "He doesn't. He's turned into a workaholic. Just like you."

Falcon folded up the birthday tablecloth. "What about you and Linc, Raven? Is there any hope there?"

Raven tilted her head, her expression somber. "No. I said some pretty harsh words to him about not wanting a relationship with him. I told him in no uncertain terms that I didn't want him to be a part of my life and that my plans for the future came before anything, including him."

"Do you regret what you said?"

"Yeah, now I do. Robin's got me to thinking, too. I love him so much, Falcon."

At that moment the phone rang and Raven reached out and picked it up. "Hello."

"OK, you guys, here's the deal," Robin said, coming in over the phone line. "I just left Leo's. I thought I'd drop by and say hello to the Hardcastle twins since I had to pass by there to get to the hotel. I saw John and he was dining with another guy, a good-looking brother. When I asked Tyrell who the brother was, he said the guy was your friend Linc, Raven. I left Leo's before either of them saw me."

Raven raised a brow. "You saw John and Linc together at Leo's?"

"What about John?" Falcon asked, rushing over to where Raven stood with the phone glued to her ear. "Who are you talking to?"

"It's Robin," Raven whispered, taking the time to inform

her sister. "She stopped by Leo's and claims to have seen John and Linc eating dinner together."

Falcon frowned. "They know each other?"

"I introduced them a couple of weeks ago, but as far as I know they haven't come into contact since then," Raven said. She then turned her attention back to the phone. "Are you sure you saw John and Linc?"

"I'd know John Augustan anywhere, and as for your Linc, I can only go by what Tyrell told me. According to him, John and Linc were at Leo's together late last night. They were the last two customers who left the bar before closing."

Raven nodded. Evidently Linc had left her place and gone straight to Leo's and had run into John there.

"What is she saying?" Falcon wanted to know, so Raven told her.

"So why is she calling us?" Falcon asked.

Raven shrugged. "Why are you calling and telling us about it?" she asked Robin the same question Falcon had asked her.

"Because if either of you are having second thoughts about your future and the men you want to share it with, I suggest you two get your butts in gear and hightail it to Leo's and do whatever you have to do to get your men back before some other sistahs scoop them up." After that blunt suggestion Robin hung up.

Raven placed the receiver back on the hook. "What did she say?" Falcon asked.

Raven relayed her sister's message to Falcon.

Falcon gave her a level stare. "Just who does Robin think she is, suggesting that we do something outrageous like that?" she asked vehemently.

Raven shook her head, grinning. "She's the one who doesn't have the red puffy eyes." Grabbing her sister by the arm, she pulled her toward the bedroom. "Come on; let's get dressed and go to Leo's. And maybe, just maybe, if we're lucky, we'll be able to win the hearts of our men back."

*   *   *

Raven and Falcon entered Leo's. The place was crowded, which was no surprise. It was Saturday night and Earth, Wind & Fire was providing the live entertainment, jamming out their classic hit "Let's Groove."

"I think we should split up," Falcon said, glancing around the room.

Raven gave her a skeptical look. "You think that's a good idea?"

Falcon looked at her sister and nodded slowly and smiled. "Yes. I don't want you around if I have to resort to begging."

Raven chuckled as she laced Falcon's fingers with hers, tightening her hold on them before letting them go. "Good luck, Sis."

"Same to you."

"What if neither of us are successful in meeting our goals here tonight?" Raven asked as she pulled in a deep breath for courage.

"We *will* be successful. If not on the first try, then maybe the second, or the third, or the fiftieth. And the reason is that the Anderson sisters will always be successful in their endeavors. Willow Anderson willed it to be so. Now scat."

Raven sure hoped Falcon was right. Turning, she walked off alone toward the area where Earth, Wind & Fire had begun performing another of their classic hits, "Saturday Night."

Linc saw Raven the minute she walked in. The deep feeling of love and desire he still felt for her even after what she'd said to him last didn't stun him. It was the words she hadn't said that had meant a hell of a lot more. She had not been able to look in his eyes and say that she cared nothing for him. That still gave him hope.

Sighing deeply, he turned to the man sharing his table. "Raven just walked in," he said to John. "She came in with another woman who I believe is her sister. Is that the birthday girl or *your* woman?" Linc asked, nodding his head in the direction where the other woman had gone, choosing a table on the other side of the room from Raven.

John's gaze followed Linc's and his eyes lit on Falcon. Pain clutched at his heart. "That's Falcon. And she's *not* my woman." He frowned. "I wonder why they're sitting at separate tables."

Linc shrugged. "A sisters' spat perhaps?"

"Not hardly," John said, taking a sip of his wine. "They might disagree sometime, but never to the point of anything separating them. They stick together like glue."

Linc nodded. "I wonder where the third one is. The birthday girl."

"Who knows about those sisters and frankly, who cares?"

Linc shook his head, deciding not to remind John that *he* cared. They both did. If they didn't care, the two of them would not have stayed at Leo's until the place closed last night, nursing their pain with drinks. "Well, don't look now, but the one you claim is not *your* woman has seen you and is headed this way."

Linc chuckled at the curse he heard flow from John's lips. A few moments later a very attractive woman with features closely resembling Raven's stood before their table.

"Hi, John. It's good seeing you again."

Something about the way she said the words made John look up from studying his wine. His gut twisted. Falcon Anderson was more beautiful than ever. Then he remembered that this was the woman he had loved but who had chosen a career over his love. "Falcon, I would say, 'Likewise,' but it wouldn't be true. It's not good seeing you again. What the hell are you doing here?"

Deciding that this should be a private conversation, Linc stood. "Hello, I'm Linc Corbain." He offered Falcon his hand in a warm handshake. "I was just about to leave, so you can have my seat."

Linc's statement gave Falcon pause. He couldn't leave before Raven got a chance to talk to him.

"Hold up, Corbain; I think I'll call it a night myself. There's no reason for me to stick around," John said coldly, staring at Falcon.

Falcon's eyes reflected pain from John's remark. But then

the look in his eyes made her heart ache. She had hurt him and he was retaliating in the only way he knew how, by trying to hurt her in return.

"John, can we talk?" she asked quietly.

"Talk? Why do you want to talk to me?" John asked gruffly, almost growling the words. "I think you said all that you needed to say a year ago."

"I thought I had to."

Something in Falcon's voice made John uneasy, cautious, and curious. "OK, Falcon, you talk and maybe, depending on what you have to say, I might listen."

Linc decided that now was time to leave the two people alone and headed for the door.

Raven's heart sank as she watched Linc leave the club. She knew he had seen her when for the briefest of moments their eyes met across the room before he walked out the door.

"Would you like to order dinner?"

The waiter's question interrupted her thoughts. She looked at the door Linc had walked out of a minute ago. "No, I've changed my mind. I'm leaving."

She glanced across the room and saw Falcon sitting at the table with John. Feeling certain that she was not leaving her sister stranded, Raven didn't waste any time as she grabbed her purse and walked out of the club.

On instinct Raven drove to Linc's apartment, hoping that's where he had gone. She released a breath of relief when she pulled into his apartment complex and saw his car parked in the space he usually used.

"You can do this, Raven," she told herself as she parked her car alongside his and got out. "He's worth it and more."

Taking another deep breath, she knocked on his door.

Linc looked startled when he opened the door to find her there. "Raven, what are you doing here?"

Raven breathed in slowly. He had removed his shirt and stood in the doorway. Her gaze dropped from his bare chest and moved lower to his flat, hard stomach, then lower still to the unsnapped top of his pants. She sucked in a deep breath and forced her gaze back to his face. "I need to talk to you."

Linc studied her with an odd expression on his face before moving aside to let her enter, closing the door behind her. "What is it you want to talk to me about?"

She met his gaze. "It's about last night and—"

"Linc, sweety, where are your towels?" a woman asked, coming into the room. "Oh, sorry, I didn't know someone was here," she said, studying Raven with as much interest as Raven was studying her.

Raven's gaze took in everything about the very beautiful woman, even the fact that she was only wearing a bra and a slip. Raven's anger flared at the thought that the reason Linc had rushed from the club was that he'd had a woman waiting here for him.

"No, I'm the one who's sorry," Raven said before rushing out of the apartment without looking back. She went straight to her car and got in. She tried ignoring Linc's hard knock on her car window as she tried putting her car in reverse. She didn't want him to see her cry.

When another car that was coming into the apartment complex blocked her from backing up, she had no choice but to roll her window down. Her pride dictated that she do so.

"What do you want, Linc?"

He pulled a shirt over his head before stooping down beside the car's open window. "Why did you run out like that?"

Raven was speechless. She would think it would have been pretty obvious to him why she'd left the way she did. Evidently it wasn't, so she decided to tell him. "You had company."

"I don't consider Sydney company, especially when she pops up unexpectedly. But I'd like for you to meet her."

Raven couldn't believe his nerve. "You want me to meet *her!*"

Linc frowned as he stood. "Is there any reason you don't want to meet my sister?"

Raven's mouth dropped open. "Your sister?"

Linc's frown deepened as he studied her. "Yeah, my sister. She arrived this evening from Memphis." He crossed his arms over his chest. "Who did you think she was?"

Raven didn't want to tell him what she had thought. But she didn't have to. The deep coloring tint of embarrassment on her face gave her away.

Linc leaned over and rested both his hands on the opening in her door. "You actually think I'd leave your bed last night and find another woman to put into mine tonight, Raven? I told you last night that I loved you, and when a man loves one woman he doesn't sleep around with another one."

Elation spread through Raven as a rush of air entered her lungs, reminding her to breathe. "You still love me?"

Her question surprised him. "Of course I still love you. When you really love someone you don't fall out of love with them like that," he said, snapping his fingers for effect. "Besides, I have no intentions of giving up on you that easily, Raven. I made a promise to myself to not let you walk out of my life a second time, although I was about ready to do just that until I ran into John last night. Talking to him made me realize his mistakes in dealing with your sister."

"Which were?"

Linc stooped back down to be on eye level with her. "Giving up on Falcon too quickly and too easily. I decided not to make the same mistakes with you. I figured that sooner or later I'd succeed by wearing your resistance down."

Raven smiled softly, believing that eventually he would have. "It took Robin's announcement that she's getting married to make me and Falcon see the mistakes we were making. I love you, Linc. I first fell in love with you in Daytona and then fell in love with you all over again that night I saw you in Leo's." She leaned over out the car window and tasted his lips. "I love you and I *will* be successful because I'll have everything I've ever wanted or dreamed of having and more."

Linc stood up and opened her car door. "Slide over, baby," he said huskily, easing into the car as she scooted over into the passenger seat. "Do you know a place where we can go to be alone?"

Raven gave him a sensuous smile. "My place. I doubt either of my sisters will be returning there tonight. What about your sister?"

Linc grinned. "She's a big girl who can take care of herself." He paused before starting the car and turned to her. "Come here and tell me again."

Raven scooted over closer to him, glad that her car had bench seats. "I love you and I want it all—you, my dreams, your babies, the works."

Linc pulled her into his arms. "And I'm going to make sure you get it all. Starting tonight."

EPILOGUE

SIX MONTHS LATER

Sunlight poured into the room through the curtains. Raven yawned and stretched, still feeling tired and still not wanting to open her eyes just yet. Yesterday had been such a busy day. A beautiful triple wedding had made it understandably so. But she, Falcon, and Robin had survived and were gloriously contented with sharing the rest of their lives with the men they loved.

After an elaborate wedding followed by a just as elaborate reception in one of the large rooms set aside for parties at Leo's, Robin and Franco had flown to Europe to honeymoon on the Riviera. French and African-American, Franco Marcus Renoir was a very handsome man, and Raven knew he would make her sister happy.

Raven smiled thinking about Falcon and John, who had left the wedding reception heading for California. After a week of honeymooning there, they were flying to Hawaii for an additional week. Lines of happiness had replaced Falcon's red puffy eyes.

Raven then thought about her and Linc. They had flown into Daytona Beach to spend a few days here before driving to Port Canaveral to catch their cruise ship for a week's cruise on the Caribbean for their honeymoon.

The past six months had been wonderful for them. She had flown to Tennessee with him over the Thanksgiving holiday to meet his family, a family who had welcomed her with open arms. She had also convinced Linc to rethink his decision not to enter politics. She knew his fairness and honesty were assets he could offer the people he would represent. Besides, like she'd told him, she could easily add being a politician's wife to her agenda.

Raven barely caught her breath when she felt the sheet covering her naked body slowly being brushed aside. She didn't want to open her eyes just yet. She preferred just lying there and feeling the sensations she knew her husband could make her feel whenever he touched her.

Her heart began pounding furiously in her chest when she felt Linc's strong, firm hands slide over her, beginning with the calves of her feet and working their way upward, to her breasts, letting his lips follow the path of his fingers.

She wondered how much longer she could pretend sleep. Undoubtedly she was about to find out when his wet, hot tongue latched onto a nipple and feasted hungrily before moving to the other one.

The assault he was making on her body was one she could not bear any longer. She knew she was a goner when he moved from her breasts and attacked her mouth, making love to it in his own special way. She automatically wound her arms tightly around his neck as she mated her tongue with his.

"Open your eyes and look at me, Raven," he whispered as he pulled back from their kiss and moved his body over hers.

Raven opened her eyes and met his gaze the exact moment he entered her, hard and fast, lifting her hips to receive all of him, joining their bodies as one.

The look of wanting, desire, and love in his eyes inflamed

her, making her wrap her legs around him to enjoy the moment of being a part of the man she loved—her husband.

"I love you," she whispered to him as waves of heat consumed her with every thrust he made into her body.

"And I love you," he said huskily before throwing his head back and releasing a deep, guttural sound from his throat as he emptied his seed deep into her womb, glorying in the feel of having unprotected sex with his wife. They tumbled over into the throes of ecstasy together, savoring every moment until at last his mouth moved back over hers, absorbing her whimpers of pleasure.

When it felt like everything had been drained from him, Linc collapsed against the pillows, taking her with him and shifting their positions so his weight would not hurt her. Pulling her closer into his arms, he cradled her to him and kissed the top of her head. "This is where it all began, isn't it, Mrs. Corbain?"

Raven smiled against his chest, liking the sound of her new name. She rose slightly to look down at him, the man who had come to mean everything to her. "Yes, right here in this very room." They had managed to get the same room at the hotel where they had spent one hell of a passionate week four years ago.

"And there's a very good possibility this is even the same bed," she added, grinning. "At least it feels like it. The one thing I remember about the bed is that it had very good springs."

Linc laughed as he reached up and touched her cheek. His eyes then became dark and passionate. "We're making new memories to keep for always."

"Yes, for always. And I have a new main agenda," she said softly.

"Oh, yeah, what is it?"

"Loving you," Raven said, leaning down toward his lips. "My main agenda is loving you, Lincoln Corbain."

Sweet Temptation

=

Francis Ray

1

Time had run out for Chase M. Braxton. He knew it the instant he saw the neatly printed return address on the oblong box wrapped in plain brown paper stamped FRAGILE. An incongruent mixture of dread and anticipation swept through him. *Typical Monday,* he thought. The sigh that came from his wide chest was long and deep.

Shifting the unfamiliar weight of his briefcase to his left hand, Chase pulled the parcel from the black granite-topped front desk of Hotel George in the heart of Capitol Hill's business district. His thoughts unsettled, he strode through the two-story glass-and-stainless-steel lobby to the elevator and jabbed 8.

Less than a minute later the doors smoothly slid open on the top floor. Long, powerful strides quickly carried Chase to his door. Carefully shifting the bundle beneath his left arm, he pulled his plastic room key card from his shirt pocket and activated the lock. As soon as the light flashed green, he entered the room.

Decorated in cool beige and cream, the suite possessed a spacious sitting room with built-in wet bar, adjoining powder room, and custom-designed cherry wood furnishings. As a man topping six-foot-five, Chase welcomed the ability to move freely without bumping into furniture. That important aspect when he'd checked into the hotel eight extremely long days ago mattered little now compared with his current problem.

Skirting the lounge chair, he stopped on the other side of the coffee table positioned in front of a small couch. Tossing his briefcase on one of the cushions, he bent and edged over the twelve-inch-high, rickety stack of policy and procedure law enforcement manuals on the coffee table. He set the package down and straightened.

Hands on his narrow waist, he stared broodingly at the telephone a few feet away on the end table, then brought his troubled gaze back to the parcel.

He had definitely run out of time.

The phone call to Julia Anne Ferrington couldn't be put off any longer. Still, he hesitated at following through with action.

Indecisiveness was not a characteristic people who knew Chase would have associated with him. Few in law enforcement could come close to matching his outstanding reputation as a commissioned officer of the elite Texas Rangers. The wall behind his desk in Austin was covered with awards from civic organizations for his work with youth and with commendations for bravery in the line of duty.

Chase took special pride in the awards given for trying to make a difference in the lives of young people. As for the commendations, the way he saw it, he simply did the job he had sworn to do. In his line of work a moment's hesitation could cost lives. In the thirteen years that he'd spent working his way up from Trooper One with the Texas Department of Public Safety to Lieutenant in charge of his own Ranger unit in Austin, he'd always acted quickly and decisively.

He'd never choked . . . until now.

His large, callused hand ran over his clean-shaven face as indecision held him still. He didn't like the feeling. But neither was he thrilled at the prospect of calling a strange woman and making small talk. However, the neatly wrapped box with the Waco, Texas, postmark was a gentle reminder that he had to do just that. His procrastination for the past week since he had been in D.C. was about to come to an end.

Midnight black eyes narrowed as Chase stared longingly at the parcel. Mabel Johnson, the wife of his captain, Oscar Johnson, in Waco, had baited her trap well. She knew a gentle reminder worked better than a shove. Temptation worked even better..

Chase picked up the box and gently hefted its weight. He almost groaned in anticipation. Mabel made the best tea cakes his taste buds ever had the pleasure of meeting. He was probably holding at least three dozen of the delicious cookies the size of his palm. And unlike back in Austin when Mabel brought them to the station for all the Rangers to share, these were all his.

But first he had to make the phone call.

Pulling his billfold from the back pocket of his jeans, he plucked out Julia Ferrington's phone number. If Mabel had been the kind of lady to try to set him up, he'd have tossed the number despite the cookie bribe. But she wasn't. She simply was doing what she had always done, helping her husband take care of his men.

Chase had made no secret of the fact that he didn't want to leave his heavy caseload and come to D.C. for six weeks to teach a criminal law symposium at Howard University. Captain Johnson and his superiors hadn't given Chase a choice. They were honored that out of all the law enforcement agencies in the country the Texas Rangers had been chosen, and just as they had always done for the past 176 years, they sent their best, most qualified man to do the job. In their opinion, that was Lt. Chase Braxton.

Mabel, in her usual motherly way, had tried to ensure that Chase, who didn't know anyone in the city, not be lonely during his six-week stay. Mabel needn't have worried. Washington, D.C., like most metropolitan cities, had more women than men. Chase could have had a date, if he wanted one, even before the plane landed at Washington National Airport.

The pretty stewardess in first class had made him acutely aware she'd be more than happy to make his first night in D.C. a memorable one. Chase, still annoyed at his captain, had spent that night and the ones following alone ... by choice. He wasn't interested in sex for sex's sake. He'd learned more sense than that by the time he graduated from high school.

He wasn't a monk by any stretch of the imagination, just selective and careful in more ways than one. He planned to be the fifth African-American in the history of the Texas Rangers to make captain, and that meant no women. Women had sidetracked the career of more than one man in law enforcement. They didn't like the crazy hours or the dangers their men faced. The excitement of dating a man in uniform, a man with so much authority, soon wore off and reality set in. Chase had seen it happen time and time again. In his opinion it took a very special woman to put up with being married to a man in law enforcement. The chances of finding such a woman were slim to none. His father and brother had tried and failed. Thirty-four-year-old Chase wasn't trying.

His focus for the next few years had to be the job, not trying to keep some woman happy. The pain and heartache that followed wasn't worth it.

Mabel understood his plan and applauded him for his determination. She also understood he hadn't wanted to go to D.C., and in her own thoughtful way she wanted to see that his stay in D.C. was as pleasant as possible. Since a lady, in Mabel's old-fashioned opinion, never called a gentleman first, she had asked Chase to initiate the call. The cookies were both a reminder and an enticement if he had not.

His blunt-tipped forefinger traced the clear plastic tape. Mabel was well aware his conscience wouldn't allow him to rip into the box and satisfy his notorious sweet tooth if he hadn't done as he promised: called Julia Ferrington before he left D.C.

Sighing, Chase picked up the receiver and punched in Julia Ferrington's number. He should have known Mabel would realize he hadn't been specific in his promise. He had planned on calling the day before he left.

He wasn't much on small talk, and frankly, after hearing Mabel chatter about Julia Ferrington and her family's deep political and financial connections and clout, Chase didn't think he, a Ranger and a rancher, and Julia, a Washington socialite, would have much in common. The way he figured, he was saving them both a painful ten minutes, tops, of each trying to be polite and pretend interest in what the other was saying.

As the answering machine clicked on, a grinning Chase quickly stashed the phone between his ear and shoulder, then shoved his hand in the front pocket for his knife. By the time the electronic voice had asked him to please leave a message, the sharp blade had sliced through the wrapping paper and he had a golden brown tea cake in his hand.

"Ms. Ferrington, this is Chase Braxton. Mabel Johnson asked me to call and say hello. I'm at the Hotel George on Capitol Hill. You have a good day. Bye."

His duty done, he took a sizable bite out of the cookie, closed his eyes, and savored the taste. By the third cookie he was thirsty. Picking up the phone, he ordered milk from room service. Some decisions weren't that difficult. Propping his booted feet atop the table, Chase reached for another cookie.

Later that evening in her high-rise condo near the wharf, six miles from Hotel George, Julia Ferrington listened to the messages on her answering machine with her notebook in her hand and her black-and-gold Mont Blanc pen that had been a college graduation present from her oldest sister, Suzanne, poised. There had been five messages thus far.

Her handwriting was a reflection of Julia, elegant, neat, and precise. She had worked hard to change the insecure, awkward teenager into someone she and her family could be proud of. At age twenty-seven, her poise and self-assurance were as much a part of her as her sunny, caring nature.

The deep baritone of Chase Braxton's drawling voice brought her head up. She recognized the authority behind the rumbling sound, the confidence. She had grown up with and been around people just like him all her life. It was with a small bit of pride that she could now count herself in that number.

She recognized something else in his voice: impatience. Obviously the phone call to her had been made under duress. It appeared Mabel Johnson had been completely mistaken in her assumption that Chase would be lonely and homesick during his stay in D.C.

Mabel Johnson had called several weeks ago and asked Julia's permission to give Chase her phone number. Julia had been hesitant at first, until Mabel had said Chase didn't know anyone in the city. Julia had friends now, good friends, but she still remembered times when she did not. No one should be lonely with so many people in the world. It still saddened her that people were lonely.

She'd like to think she made a small positive difference in the lives of the residents in a nearby nursing home by visiting and reading to them twice a month. Her practical-minded family of bankers and politicians thought her time would be better spent crusading to raise volunteer awareness. Julia didn't. Her family might take pleasure from the spotlight and a calendar full of social events, but she enjoyed a quiet, simple life. More importantly, the people in the home would be left with no one if she weren't there.

"End of messages."

Clicking off the machine, Julia leaned back in her antique Queen Anne chair and stared out the window at the distant lights of Virginia. People visiting D.C. for the first time, usually were surprised that Virginia and Maryland were so close. Just as her family was surprised that she chose to live in D.C. instead of Virginia as they did.

The crowded city of D.C. was a government town with literally thousands of office workers. Yet because of the high cost of living and poor parking facilities, many people elected to live in one of the surrounding suburbs or cities, with their leisurely lifestyle, quaint shops, and deep historical presence.

No one expected the shy baby sister to leave the shelter and security of her family. But her parents and her two older sisters had made their mark. Julia had just begun to make hers with Sweet Temptation, her gourmet chocolate-and-candy shop. A small chain of Sweet Temptation stores was her dream, just as a house in the suburbs and a family were a dream to some. She was on her way. Her first store was a resounding success.

After triple-digit profits for the past four years, she now

felt comfortable enough to start scouting for a second location in Virginia. That way she could keep a close eye on both businesses and maintain her residence. If some people said she had used her family's far-reaching connections to become so successful so quickly, that was all right. This was Washington, where who you knew weighed just as important as what you knew. But she had little doubt her business had thrived because of the care she gave to the smallest detail and the excellent service. She took pride in knowing that when you purchased from Sweet Temptation you got much more than a delicious box of the finest candy money could buy.

The antique grandfather clock in the entryway chimed the half hour. Eight-thirty. She might as well get her own obligatory phone call over with. From the sound of his voice, he didn't want or need her help in becoming acclimated to the city or in fighting loneliness.

Flipping back through her telephone message book, she found the number of the Hotel George. In the past she'd had clients who stayed there, and she had worked with several conventions hosted there. Chase Braxton certainly hadn't given her the number, and judging by the high regard Mabel Johnson had of him as a Texas Ranger, he wasn't a man who forgot details that were important to him.

After the fourth ring, the message center activated. Emulating the same manner in which Chase had spoken, she said, "Good evening, Mr. Braxton. This is Julia Ferrington. Welcome to D.C. I'm sorry I missed your call. Good night and enjoy your stay in our fabulous city."

Hanging up, Julia stretched and walked into her bedroom, her retreat. She spent long hours away from home, and when she returned she enjoyed indulging herself with things that delighted the eyes as well as the other senses.

The elegantly romantic soft peach room held a mixture of Louis XVI and Empire furniture. On a glass-topped table were fresh flowers. French chairs flanked the cozy nook. Silk brocade ran the length of her picture windows and pooled on the thick cream carpeted floor. The fine old drawings and

art by African-Americans hanging on the soft white walls
had taken months to locate but were well worth the effort
and expense.

The focal point was a huge four-poster canopy bed draped
in peach silk. On the hand-made imported duvet were restored antique throw pillows. If romance was not in her immediate future, she could still enjoy the trappings by having
beautiful, sensuous surroundings.

Stepping out of her high-heel Italian pumps, she placed
them in a specially designed shoe box, unbuttoned her plum-
colored double-breasted jacket, then her knee-length matching skirt. Hanging the clothes on a padded hanger, she felt
a twinge of guilt about the call to Chase, then pushed it away.
Although she had sounded like an overworked representative
of the Visitors Bureau, the call had served its purpose. She
had other things to worry about.

Like trying to come up with a unique concept to add Leo's
to her growing lists of clients. If she could acquire the "in"
supper club in D.C., it would be quite a coup.

Noah Hardcastle, manager and one of the four owners of
Leo's, demanded only the best for his restaurant. Since his
and Julia's business philosophy was the same, they got along
fabulously. Her name and their friendship might get her an
appointment, but she had to deliver the goods.

Finished undressing, she slipped on a white terry cloth
robe with peach piping and headed for the bathroom, ideas
running through her head. As water gushed from the mouth
of a gold swan into the oversize marble tub, there wasn't a
doubt in Julia's mind that when she and Noah met on Thursday she'd have an idea that would meet with his approval.

It was after ten that night when Chase returned from his jog
and saw the red message light on the telephone in the sitting
room. Although the hotel had an exercise and steam room,
he preferred the unrestricted outdoors and fresh air. Pulling
his perspiration-dampened gray sweatshirt over his head, he
mopped the trickles of moisture gliding down his face and

chest. Leaning over, he hit the speaker button and dialed for his messages.

Black eyes narrowed as he listened to Julia Ferrington's cool, cultured voice. *Iceberg* was his initial impression. He tossed in *snooty* and *stuck-up* by the time she said good-bye. Deleting the message, he went to the wet bar and chugged a glass of mineral water. After turning the TV to the evening news, he headed to the bathroom. A soak in the Jacuzzi had become as much a part of his nightly ritual as his jog, and just as pleasurable.

As the water filled the oversize tub, Chase promised himself again that as soon as he returned to his ranch he was going to install a Jacuzzi in his bathroom. His modest home was large enough to give him room and small enough for him to be able to keep fairly clean by himself.

His extra money went to pay a ranch hand to take care of his growing herd of Herefords and horses. By most Texas ranch standards, a ten-acre spread wasn't much of a ranch, but to Chase it was a small piece of heaven on earth. He had another fifteen years of a twenty-year mortgage and it would be his.

Stripping off his pants, he climbed into the swirling water, stretched out his long legs, and leaned his head against the rim. Through the wall speaker in the bathroom the reporter's voice came through loud and clear, but the one Chase heard was Julia's. Cool, polite, distant.

Closing his eyes, he tried to come up with a face to match Julia's voice. Within seconds he visualized a thin nose, pinched features, an unsmiling mouth. Rich laughter filled the room. Thank goodness he had missed her call and hadn't had to talk to her. He certainly wasn't going to call her again and try to meet her. He'd kept his word to Mabel and now he could enjoy his tea cakes and put Julia Ferrington out of his mind.

Chase had a good day at Howard and planned a better evening. Not even the tailgating and lane-switching of fellow motorists trying to beat the inevitable bumper-to-bumper rush-hour traffic could dampen his mood. He and his students were finally on the same page. They'd gone from being faintly suspicious of his qualifications and vocally wanting to know why the law symposium class wasn't being taught by a person from the FBI or CIA to respectful and genuinely interested in what he had to say.

Chase stopped for the traffic light. Tires screeched. Horns honked. People yelled out of open windows. The cars on the other side of him went through the yellow caution light. Cars illegally followed on the red. Glancing across the street, he saw Howard University Hospital. At least they wouldn't have far to go for medical attention.

The light changed and Chase pulled off. This afternoon several students had followed him into the hall after the lecture and then to his car, their mood angry over the accounts he had given them of injustices to minorities. He'd told them to channel their anger into becoming involved in the political arena and the justice system and changing laws. A few promised they would. He believed them.

To celebrate his breakthrough and the distinct possibility that his superiors had been right about the necessity of his teaching the class, he was going to indulge himself with a meal from room service, watch some football on TV, and, if he were lucky, find someone who wanted to check out the hotel's billiard room.

Chase was smiling in anticipation as he pulled up in front of the hotel. Saying hello to the jovial valet on duty, he tossed him the keys and quickly crossed the sidewalk. He pictured the blood-red, two-inch-thick porterhouse he planned to order, the mound of French fries with catsup piled on top.

"Mr. Braxton."

Chase stopped on the steps and looked over his shoulder. Henri held his briefcase in his hand. "Sir, you forgot again." Light amusement trickled through in the valet's heavily accented French Creole voice.

With a shake of his Stetson-covered head, Chase bounded back down the steps. He never took paperwork home from the Ranger office, so he had problems remembering he had to do so now. Teaching meant notes and lesson plans.

For the first time, Chase didn't shudder at the words. Smiling, he reached for the briefcase. "Thanks for catching me. This time someone won't have to be bothered with bringing it to my room."

"No problem," assured the valet as he turned to get into the Jeep Cherokee. By the time he'd pulled away from the curb, Chase was walking through the automatic glass doors and whistling softly. Another thing the department had been right about was choosing the "boutique" hotel over a large chain. The staff was small and friendly. He knew everyone by the end of the first week there.

"Mr. Braxton," called the desk clerk. "Could I see you a moment, please?"

Chase paused, trying to figure out why Simone had called him, then figured the quicker he took care of the matter, the quicker he could get to his steak. He switched direction and went to the desk. "Yes, Simone."

"You have another package, sir."

Black brows bunched. "Another one?"

"Yes, sir. I'll get it for you."

Chase placed his briefcase on the desk and wondered who might have sent this one. He was close to his father and brother who lived in Austin, but all three preferred using the telephone to keep in touch. They did enough paperwork on the job to abhor writing letters. Sending a package to him would be out of the question.

The department had shipped all the material, too much in Chase's opinion, that they thought he'd need to teach his six-week seminar. There was no woman in his life who might want to make him think he'd be much better off with her in his life permanently. He was genuinely puzzled.

His thoughts came back to the present and his frown deepened as Simone returned with a large brown wicker basket wrapped in clear plastic and tied with a big red, white, and blue bow. There was a white star on the blue, just like the Texas flag. Although the clerk's slim arms were stretched to capacity, they were unable to encompass the basket.

"You're sure this is for me?"

White teeth flashed in Simone's ebony-hued face. "Positive." Her red nail tapped the envelope. " 'Chase Braxton. Hotel George.' "

His puzzlement growing, Chase opened the envelope. He stared at his name and the neat handwritten note welcoming him to D.C. Below in small, discreet gold print were the words: "Created by Julia A. Ferrington."

"Why would she send me this?" he mumbled.

"Since I don't know who 'she' is, I can't very well say, Mr. Braxton," Simone answered with open amusement. Her black eyes dancing with lingering humor, she glanced around the lobby, then leaned over and whispered, "But if you don't want it, I'd be delighted to take it off your hands. I'm a chocoholic and Sweet Temptation is renowned for their gourmet chocolate goodies."

Replacing the card, Chase picked up the basket and briefcase and flashed her a grin. "I'll be sure and keep that in mind."

"Please do that," Simone said, moving away to help another guest.

In his suite, Chase's gaze immediately zeroed in on the telephone, as if that would give him the answers he wanted. Seeing the red message light on, he quickly crossed the room and retrieved his message.

"Chase, this is Mabel. You sweet man. You must have made quite an impression on Julia. She called this morning to ask if you had any food allergies and if you liked candy. I told her no to the allergies, yes to the candy. If I don't miss my guess, you should be very happy by now. Enjoy and don't eat it all at one time."

Chase stared at the basket he still held in his hands. There were five sections, each filled with a different kind of candy. He recognized three: pralines, chocolate-covered peanuts, and divinity. The question remained, Why would she send him a gift basket? He knew enough to know that it hadn't been cheap, and although Julia Ferrington came from money, why would she want to spend it on a stranger?

Placing the basket on the coffee table, he removed the heavy card again. Seeing a telephone number on the back, he picked up the phone and dialed.

He needed answers. He prided himself on reading people correctly. In his profession it was almost second nature. It didn't set well that Julia Ferrington had somehow managed to prove him wrong.

"Sweet Temptation," answered a cheerful-sounding woman.

"Is this some kind of a candy shop?" Somehow he couldn't reconcile himself to the cool woman on the phone last night designing gift baskets.

"Sweet Temptation is more than just candy. As the name implies, it's a fabulous treasure trove of delicious and decadent goodies guaranteed to tempt the untemptable," she explained.

Her answer told him nothing. "Can I speak with Julia Ferrington, please?"

"I'm sorry, sir, she's not here."

"She works there, doesn't she?"

"Yes, sir. Is there a message?"

Leave it up to a woman to leave a man hanging. "Please have her call Chase Braxton at Hotel George. She has the number."

Hanging up the phone, he poked at the cellophane. The rich, tempting aroma of chocolate and other candies drifted out. The fat pralines, loaded with big pecan chunks, glistened like spun honey. He could see similar pecan chunks in the divinity. If he didn't miss his guess, macadamia nuts were in one of the other chocolate candies.

He loved nuts. People liked to joke about policemen eating doughnuts, but he preferred nuts any way he could get them.

What the heck. Ripping open the cellophane, he plucked out a praline and bit. His taste buds exploded in sheer ecstasy. The woman who'd answered the phone hadn't exaggerated. The sugary candy was as good as any he had ever tasted.

He still didn't understand why Julia Ferrington had sent the candy, but he had intended to find out. Unanswered questions annoyed him.

Speaking with Julia Ferrington wasn't as easy as he'd imagined. Over the next two days he called Sweet Temptation four times and each time she was out. They either got tired of him calling or took pity on him, because the fifth time he was informed she was out of town.

Hanging up the phone, he decided that, come what may, he was seeing Julia Ferrington before he left Washington. And he was getting some answers. She might be cool, but she was also exasperating, even though he had yet to meet her. But he would. That he promised, and Chase never broke a promise.

2

"You've made a wonderful choice, Mrs. Howard. Your mother will enjoy the Bavarian chocolate cream mints, and each time she reuses the crystal dish she'll think of you." Handing the young woman the white shopping bag with **Sweet Temptation** in bold red script, Julia held the shop's glass front door open for her.

"Thank you, Julia, for gift-wrapping it for me." The model-thin woman laughed and adjusted the strap of her Fendi bag on her shoulder. "She'll take forever trying to unwrap the lilac paper without tearing it. Then she'll store it and the lavender ribbon and silk orchid in her closet saying she'll use it, but she never will."

Julia smiled warmly. "I believe I've made the same prediction myself a time or two."

"So have I," the shopper agreed. "Thanks again."

Closing the door, Julia glanced around the shop to see if anyone needed help. When she was assisting a customer she always gave them her full attention. Nothing annoyed her more than a salesperson's impatience or curt dismissal if they saw the potential for a bigger sale.

An older couple browsed contentedly in Aladdin's Cove, a corner of the store that was devoted entirely to interesting and unique containers for the store's confections. A little boy of about four stared thoughtfully through the glass case, trying to choose which candy he wanted. At the register a well-dressed gentleman was checking out with a two-pound box of assorted chocolate creams. Since all the customers appeared content and taken care of, Julia decided she could go to her office for a few minutes.

Discreetly signaling Georgette, her assistant manager, who was patiently waiting for the little boy to walk down the twenty-foot glass candy case, Julia went to the back. She took special pride in everything in her shop and always saw that it came first. It had taken her a long time to finally decide in which direction she wanted her life to go, so she didn't treat her business lightly.

Two years after college, most of her friends had already started to make their mark in the world while she'd wandered aimlessly from job to job. It hadn't helped that her older sisters never seemed to have any doubts about their career choice. Suzanne was a lobbyist, and Amanda worked for the State Department.

The idea for Sweet Temptation had sprung from filling in for a sick friend for two weeks as a volunteer in the gift shop of a hospital. Julia had always been fond of people and soon learned she had an eye for detail and the unusual. Nine months and a small business loan later, she had opened Sweet Temptation. Her parents had been upset that she hadn't wanted them to help financially, but she had wanted to do it on her own. And she had.

She truly enjoyed being around people and helping them pick out just the right gift, whether the reasons were personal or business. Because she strongly believed it was equally important to please the eye as well as tantalize the taste buds, she was always looking for unique ways in which to package her goods. Thus the occasional buying trips.

Her wrapping paper changed with the season and never repeated itself; her baskets and containers, from paper to brass to crystal, came in an array of colors and shapes and prices. For those who became confused when offered so many choices, Julia, Georgette, or one of her assistants was there to gently guide them. This afternoon, however, Julia was the one in need of guidance.

Sitting behind the neat desk in her office, Julia stared at the five messages from Chase. She was more than a little puzzled. There had been five on her answering machine when she arrived home from her business trip last night as well. Of course, there were other messages from friends and family, but for some unexplained reason she felt the pull of Chase Braxton's messages more.

A manicured pale pink nail tapped the notes lying on the antique Chippendale desk. Never in her wildest imagination had she expected the distant, impatient man of three nights ago to try so hard to contact her. He certainly wasn't turning out to be what she had initially thought.

Leaning back in her chair, she bit her lower lip and felt somewhat guilty for putting him through so much trouble in trying to locate her. Since she lived alone, she never wanted the general public to have knowledge of when she was out of town. Her gated condo had security guards on-duty at all times, but it never hurt to be careful.

She had sent Chase the basket to make up for her less than cordial behavior when she returned his phone call. The bottom line was that regardless of her initial unflattering impression of his brash impatience, he was a friend of a friend. More important, just because his behavior was suspect, there was no reason for her to follow suit.

Besides, she'd learned long ago that first impressions could often be influenced by variables the other person wasn't aware of. Mabel Johnson was as kind as they came, but she wouldn't put up with a rude, arrogant man, nor would she subject Julia to one. The logical answer, she had concluded after a good night's sleep, was that there was another reason for Chase's abruptness.

Looking at the messages spread out on her desk, Julia was glad she had sent him the basket. Not many men would be that persistent in trying to contact a strange woman. It seemed Chase wasn't a man who gave up.

A smile lifted the corners of her mouth. With a name like Chase she should have guessed. Leaning forward, she flipped through her Rolodex until she found the phone number for Chase's hotel. She listened incredulously as the hotel's message center clicked on. *Figures,* she thought and blew out an exasperated breath.

This was ridiculous. She wasn't playing phone tag another day.

"Mr. Braxton, if you're as tired of talking to machines as I am, I'd like to offer a solution, if your schedule permits. I have a late appointment at Leo's, a supper club here in the city. I should be finished by nine, and then you and I could have drinks. I'll wait for you until nine-thirty. If you're able to come, just ask Erin, the hostess at Leo's, to direct you to my table. Good-bye."

Julia hung up the phone and sat back in her chair. She didn't make dates with men, certainly not with men she had never spoken with, but someone had to take action and since he had tried to contact her so many times, she felt it was her responsibility.

Leo's was perfect. The elegant supper club was a fabulous place to wine, dine, and unwind. Movers and shakers, working-class and corporate types frequented the restaurant. Maybe, just maybe, she'd finally get to put a face with a voice.

Chase wasn't coming.

Julia took another sip of the white wine she had been nursing for the past thirty minutes. She glanced again at the tiny eighteen-karat gold watch inlaid with diamonds on her wrist. Nine-forty-five. She had given him plenty of time if he planned to show up.

Her meeting with Noah Hardcastle had gone extremely well. He liked the idea of Sweet Temptation supplying him with special desserts during the holidays, starting with a chocolate cranberry upside-down cake topped with cognac whipped cream for Christmas. In the meantime they would partner on a gift basket. She would supply the basket and giant chocolate-covered strawberries, Leo's the vintage wine, crystal glasses, and signature linen napkins. Leo's would be the exclusive outlet.

The popular supper club was already known as the happening place to meet, relax, and have fun, so why shouldn't it, Julia reasoned, also be known as the place where romance begins? Glancing around the room bathed in soft light, the smooth sound of jazz flowing over the intercom, couples snuggled next to each other, their rapt expressions illuminated by the Tiffany lights on the round tables, or dancing on the intricately patterned parquet floor, she didn't doubt for a moment the success of the baskets.

People fall in love every day. And one day, when my business is solidly successful, I might let myself fall in love, too. But for now, Sweet Temptation is my only *temptation,* she mused. Smiling at her little play on words, Julia ran her finger around the rim of her wine glass. Across the room, the double mahogany front doors opened. She straightened, then sat back in the chair. An elderly gentleman crossed to the elongated rosewood bar and slid onto one of the tall, padded stools.

Groans emanated from the four women at the table directly behind Julia.

"It's certainly slim pickings tonight."

"He's old enough to be our grandfather."

"There's a football game on tonight."

"It was drizzling when I came in."

Julia listened to the four women and tucked her lower lip between her teeth. Was that where Chase was, watching a football game? Married and single female friends had told her, "Never try to compete with a football game. Even if you win, you lose." Perhaps she should have scheduled their meeting later in the week.

The front door opened again and she glanced up sharply,

unaware of the hope shining in her brown eyes. A tall, broad-shouldered man stood poised in the doorway. His black Stetson-covered head moved in a slow arc as he searched the room. His gaze paused briefly on her, then moved on. A sudden gust of wind pressed the long black rain slicker to his athletic body, then away. Julia got an immediate impression of strength and leashed power. A little shiver raced up her spine.

Jeans lovingly encased muscular thighs and long legs. His skin was the color of burnished teak. The white shirt emphasized his wide chest.

"Mercy, look what the rain drove in."

"Now there's a man who looks like a man."

"If any of you are wondering what to give me for my birthday, you can stop."

"Since I'm your friend, why don't I make sure he's in good working condition first?"

Laughter drifted from the table behind her. They were unabashedly man-watching but until now Julia hadn't paid much attention to their rating scale. This time she did and wholeheartedly agreed with them.

This man was spectacular, and for some reason, she thought, dangerous. Perhaps it was the way his gaze encompassed the room in a single all-consuming glance. She could almost feel the intensity from across the room.

Finally, he let the doors swing shut and came farther into the restaurant. Erin stepped forward to greet him, then moments later turned and looked in Julia's direction. Julia felt her breath catch. Tipping his Stetson to Erin, he started toward Julia.

"Oh, goodness, he's heading in this direction."

"If he passes us, I may grab his leg."

"If you grab one, I'll grab the other one."

"Just make sure that's all you grab."

The women erupted into bawdy laughter. Julia briefly wondered why their laughter sounded muted, as if from a long distance away. She didn't seem capable of anything except watching the man's slow, purposeful stride toward her. The brim of his hat shaded the upper half of his clean-shaven face, but she easily distinguished the strong jaw, broad nose, mobile lips. His eyes were hidden from her, but for some odd reason, she felt their pull.

Another tiny shiver raced up Julia's spine. Instinctively she wrapped her arms around her. The long-sleeved red suit jacket did little to help. Moistening her lips, she reminded herself it was always on the cool side in Leo's and continued to watch the stranger who was creating such disquiet within her.

With each step that brought him closer, she hoped the man heading straight for her wasn't Chase Braxton. She had asked to be seated near the back of the restaurant because she hadn't wanted to appear conspicuous while she waited for Chase. There were three other tables behind her besides the one where the four women were seated. Maybe he was going to one of them.

Her hope died when he stopped directly in front of her and removed his hat. She almost groaned. The women behind her did.

No man should be that handsome. His lush black eyelashes were longer and thicker than hers. His eyes were black and entirely too intense. His mouth was full and sensuously inviting. Worst of all, he had a charming and irresistible dimple in his stubborn chin.

How could Mabel have done this to her?

"Julia Ferrington?"

Her throat went dry. This man was nothing like she had expected and everything that could make a woman act very, very foolish. "Chase Braxton?"

He nodded, his handsome face unsmiling. "You're not what I expected."

"Neither are you."

3

Studying the flawless oval face of Julia Ferrington, Chase tried to reconcile what he was seeing to what he had imagined. He couldn't. She was . . . lovely. It was not a word he used often, but he could think of no other way to describe the woman in front of him. Her smooth skin was the warm, inviting color of cinnamon. The eyes watching him warily were a deeper shade of brown. So was the lustrous curly hair that brushed her tense shoulders. He had never thought of bangs as being flirtatious. Hers were. The red suit was another surprise.

He'd thought she'd be buttoned-down, hidden from the prying and unwanted eyes of men. Again he had guessed wrong. She was dressed completely in red. Here was a woman with enough confidence to draw attention to herself with an eye-stopping combination of sexy style and classy elegance.

"May I sit down?" He thought that best since his legs weren't all that steady.

"Of course," she said, her voice smooth and oddly breathless.

Pulling out a chair, Chase sat down across from Julia and studied the becoming flush on her face. Another surprise.

"We meet at last," she said.

Chase grunted in the affirmative. There was nothing cool about her voice now. The tone was soft, shy, and enticing.

Julia twisted uneasily in her seat, trying to understand whatever it was about Chase that made her decidedly . . . restless and scattered. Then she decided it was his eyes . . . dark, hot, and mysterious.

To combat the feeling, she took a sip of wine and quickly discovered her mistake when his gaze shifted to her mouth. The scorching intensity had her gripping the stem. "I—I didn't think you were coming," she said, hoping to avert his attention from her lips.

Slowly his gaze widened to encompass her face once again. "I was out with some friends from the university and didn't get your message until about thirty minutes ago."

Julia's eyes widened. The hotel was a good thirty minutes away in the best of travel conditions, and with the rain . . . "You must have rushed over here."

Chase shrugged, then leaned forward in his seat and braced his arms on the table, telling himself he was just getting comfortable and not moving to get closer. "Why did you send the basket?"

She fiddled with her wineglass, then looked straight at Chase. She had always demanded honesty of herself and others, even when it was difficult to face. "I had been less than cordial and rather austere when I returned your phone call, and I wanted to make amends."

Chase never took his eyes from Julia. Cordial, austere, amends. More words he didn't hear or use. But he admired her honesty. She didn't shift blame, just took responsibility for her actions. Since he admired those qualities and tried to emulate them, he had to admit he shared in the blame. His phone call to her had been impatient at best. "Then I should have been the one to send the basket. I was less than cordial and rather austere first."

A slow smile curved her magenta-colored lips. "Now that you mention it."

Did she know her mouth was enough to make a man weep? Somehow he didn't think so.

"No wonder she was waiting so long."

"Some women have all the luck."

"Maybe she'll throw him back."

"Would you?"

Julia's eyes widened in embarrassment. Her gaze skirted to Chase, then away. She had forgotten about the women. Heat pooled in her cheeks. "Chase, I'm sorry."

"Why? You're gonna throw me back?" he asked, enjoying the husky sound of his name on her lips.

She blinked.

"Forget it," he said, annoyed with himself because for one crazy moment he had toyed with the idea and wanted her to disagree with him.

"I'm not much of a fisherman, but even a novice knows you have to catch something before you can throw it back," she countered, trying not to be affected by the sensuous mouth, the dimpled chin, the drawling voice that stroked the skin and the senses. Most of all by the little voice in her head wondering what it would be like to "catch" a man like Chase Braxton.

His gaze strayed to her lips again. What was the matter with him? He went for the fun-loving, no-strings type. Somehow that wasn't stopping him from fantasizing about how Julia Ferrington's mouth would feel beneath his. He barely kept the scowl from his face.

What was the matter with her? Julia wondered. This man was a stranger. An annoyed-looking one at that. Perhaps she shouldn't have had the wine on an empty stomach. All she'd had to eat today was a bagel and a cup of tea. Her first day back after a trip was always hectic. Noah had offered her dinner, but she'd declined. She had been afraid dinner might run over the time she expected Chase.

"Would you like another glass of wine?"

Opening her mouth to say, "No," she yawned instead. "I'm sorry," she murmured, covering her mouth with both hands in abject embarrassment and apology. "I caught the red-eye last night so I wouldn't miss another day in the shop. I've only had a couple of hours' sleep."

"Surely your boss would let you off another day."

Julia smiled. "I *am* the boss."

Chase straightened. Black eyes widened. "You own Sweet Temptation?"

"Yes," she answered proudly. "We celebrated our fourth anniversary two months ago."

Chase floundered. "I thought you just did the baskets."

"I do it all, including sweep floors and wash the windows," Julia said without shame. "If I don't take pride in the store I can't expect my employees to."

Chase stared at the well-dressed, elegant woman in front of him. "But Mabel didn't mention you owned a business."

"It's no secret," Julia said, but she wondered why herself. Mabel had always seemed so proud of Julia.

"I guess," he said, then watched Julia fight back another yawn. She had to be exhausted, yet she had waited past the time she had stated to meet a stranger. Certainly not the action of an iceberg, but he had already discovered his mistake in judging her.

Julia Ferrington was turning out to be a complex, fascinating woman. Too bad he didn't have time to explore the possibility of getting to know her better and learning if her mouth was as sweet as it looked.

Standing, Chase closed his hand around the back of her chair. "Come on. I'll walk you to your car."

Oddly reluctant, but aware that her body wanted to sleep, Julia picked up her briefcase from the corner of the table. "Thank you. I apologize."

Strong fingers closed around her elbow. "No need. I'm just sorry I kept you waiting."

"I didn't mind," she said, looking up at him. "I wanted to meet you."

The genuine sincerity and warmth in her voice caused Chase's fingers to tighten briefly on her arm. He felt the fine bones beneath his callused fingers, the silk of the tailored suit, and loosened his hold. Wrong woman. Wrong time.

Outside they stopped beneath the restaurant's awning and watched the steady downpour. Julia turned to Chase. "Good night. I'll have to make a dash for it."

Chase didn't release her arm. "Where's your car?"

"In the back I'm afraid."

He pulled off his rain slicker and placed it over her shoulders in one easy motion. "It's a little big, but it will keep you dry."

Julia felt enveloped by his compelling, clean male scent, the lingering warmth from his body. It was almost like being in his arms. She flushed at the thought. "I couldn't take your coat."

"I'm wearing a hat, Julia," he told her. "Besides, my clothes can take a little rain; that suit you're wearing can't."

The dry cleaner could probably handle getting the Dior back in shape. What she couldn't handle was Chase's unnerving nearness or the way her pulse sped up when he said her name. Shaking her head, Julia reached up to take the slicker off.

"The coat stays." With surprising gentleness, his hand closed over hers. Again Julia felt the tiny shiver.

The door behind them opened. Automatically they moved in tandem to one side, the motion bringing them closer. The nearness of the man was intoxicating. But his stubbornness was annoying. "I will not take your coat."

"Then we'll share it." Before Julia could answer, he lifted the coat from her shoulders, stepped beside her, and raised it over their heads. "Now we both stay dry."

His muscled thigh brushed against hers, sending more little tingles of awareness up and down her spine. The coat over and around them became a seductive cocoon. She had the ridiculous notion to step closer, press her lips to the dimple in his chin, then to his lips.

The door opened again. A young couple came out, nodded in greeting to Julia and Chase, then ran hand in hand laughing into the hard-driving rain. They were soaked within seconds. Carefree laughter drifted back to Chase and Julia. Clearly neither cared about being wet if they were together. Unexpectedly Julia felt a pang of envy, then pushed it away.

"Unless you want to follow their example and get drenched, we better get moving."

"If you insist." Julia turned briskly away from Chase, the cause of her strange and unwanted mood, and headed down the sidewalk to the parking lot just off the street. Chase's long, easy strides easily matched hers.

Approaching her white unmarked minivan, she removed the key from the pocket of her suit jacket and disengaged the lock. Chase reached the door handle before she did, inadvertently pressing his long muscular frame against her. The intense heat and hardness was impossible to ignore.

Quickly she climbed in, as much to escape Chase's disturbing presence as to let him get out of the rain. She was well aware that he had shielded her from the rain at his own expense.

Starting the vehicle, she let the window down. "Good night, Chase, and thanks for seeing me to my car."

"I'm in a black Jeep Cherokee a couple of rows up front. Wait for me on the street. I'll follow you home."

"Ha—" He was already turning away. Julia let the window up and pulled out of the parking space. She could ignore his command couched as a request, but why bother? As it happened, she didn't have a chance even if she wanted to. As soon as she hit the street, the Cherokee pulled out behind her.

Ten minutes later she pulled up to her condo building. Letting down her window, she waved good night to Chase and drove through the black iron security gates. It hadn't escaped her attention that Chase had not asked to see her again, which was just as well. She was honest enough with herself to admit she was attracted to him. And practical enough to see that any relationship was impossible. According to the information Mabel had given her, he had only a little over four weeks in D.C. remaining.

Too bad, she thought as she parked the van and got out. Chase had a kind of sexy magnetism that she found absolutely fascinating, if a bit overpowering. Or perhaps that was what attracted her to him.

She wouldn't have minded getting to know him better if the situation were different. The intriguing thought stayed with her all through getting ready for bed and followed her into a restless sleep.

For four days Chase tried reason, and when that failed he tried exercise, which also failed. He couldn't get Julia Ferrington out of his mind. She was nothing like he'd expected. Her warm, caring nature invited a man to get closer. Then there was the vulnerability he'd glimpsed in her dark brown eyes, eyes that could quickly change into fire if she was crossed.

She was a woman of contrasts.

Hands stuffed in the pockets of his jeans, Chase stood outside Sweet Temptation on Monday afternoon. The day was beautiful. Blue skies stretched forever.

Unlike the sweltering heat in Texas in September, the temperature in D.C. was in the upper sixties. Best of all, after the past few days of showers no rain was in the forecast. Judging by the heavy crowds passing by, people fully intended to take advantage of the good weather.

Watching people enter and leave the shop, most of the time with a handled shopping bag with the Sweet Temptation logo, he debated his options. He was a man of action, a Texas Ranger whose courage was well documented. He didn't have to be nervous about seeing a woman. Besides, if he stood beneath the pin oak tree much longer, the birds might decide to try to roost on top of his Stetson.

He had to get a grip, and fast.

He'd been the same way, indecisive and unsure of himself, when he went to the flower shop to order her flowers the morning after he met her. In the past he'd faced a crazed, knife-wielding junkie high on crack with less concern. But then he had known to expect the unexpected.

In selecting the flowers he'd had nothing to go on. There was just the driving need from somewhere that the flowers be just right. He instinctively knew she had put a great deal of thought into his basket, and he wanted to do the same with the flowers. It was impossible to do less. By the time he'd left the florist, the poor woman working there had practically pushed him out the door.

Julia Ferrington was changing him, and it wasn't for the better. What was it about her that tugged at him? Had him thinking about her throughout the day? Maybe it was because she didn't act or look as he'd expected and that had captured his attention and interest.

He was a seasoned law enforcement officer. He knew how

to step back and analyze a situation. This was no different. He just needed to see her again to figure out what was happening to him; then he could get on with his life.

Without further hesitation, Chase crossed the busy sidewalk and strode into the shop, sure he would find the answer he sought . . . until her saw her. And seeing her, he wanted to touch, to taste.

She wore a lemon yellow dress that reminded him of the daffodils that shot up yearly around the perimeter of his ranch house. Although he didn't particularly pay attention to flowers, at least until three days ago, he'd always admired the way the daffodils foreshadowed spring, their delicate beauty, their tenacity for life.

Across the room, Julia gracefully bent from the knees to pick up a crystal bowl from the lowest shelf of a six-foot glass-and-brass étagère. The silky material flowed down the gentle curve of her back to lovingly cup her hips. Standing, she traced her delicate fingers over the fragile curved glass, her touch reverent and loving.

Grace. Beauty. Strength. She was all that and more.

Would she touch a man the same way or with greedy anticipation? Chase rammed his hands deeper into his pockets because he couldn't fool himself any longer as to why he had come.

He wanted Julia Ferrington. Wanted her badly. There wasn't a thing he could do about it. The fact that she was out of his class and that he had less than four weeks left in D.C. didn't seem to matter.

Julia felt him. She didn't understand how; she simply knew Chase Braxton was in the shop watching her. Her hands trembled. Carefully she set the crystal bowl on a nearby table.

Forgetting one of her ironclad rules, she shifted her attention from a client. Chase stood ten feet away, watching her. The impact of seeing him again, this time in the bold revealing light of day, stole her breath and scattered all thoughts, but one. He affected her as no other man ever had.

He was impossibly handsome. Once again he was in jeans

that appeared to have been sculpted to his muscled legs and a white long-sleeved shirt. The cuffs were rolled back to reveal a gold watch on one powerful wrist and a thick gold link bracelet on the other. If *GQ* or *Code* could get him to pose, he'd certainly set the style and have the magazines flying off the shelf.

He slowly crossed to her and paused a few feet away. "Hello, Julia."

"Hello, Chase," she answered, trying to calm her racing pulse and booming heart. "Welcome to Sweet Temptation."

Midnight black eyes glanced around the crowded upscale shop that gleamed in the bright sun like a mullet-prism jewel. "You have quite a place here."

"Thank you."

He shifted from one eel-skinned boot to the other. "I'd like to talk with you, if you have time."

"Certainly." Did he ever smile? "Just as soon as I finish with my customer."

"Sure. I'll just look around."

"All right." Julia followed him with her eyes as he moved away, much in the same way she had seen so many children in the shop stare with such intense longing at the wide array of candy behind the glass casing, wanting to taste everything but resigned that it was not to be.

With an annoying shake of her head, Julia went back to helping the customer, making sure her attention didn't wander. Admiring a good-looking man was acceptable; letting it interfere with business was not. Certainly not a man who wouldn't be around long. Five minutes later, she rang up the sale.

Satisfied she had whatever crazy musing she had about Chase under control, she turned to seek him out. One glimpse and her heart thumped sharply against her breastbone. So much for control. He made her restless. He made her contemplate throwing caution to the wind.

Brushing her damp palms on the sides of her dress, she went to Chase. He was in Toyland watching a working replica of a chocolate Ferris wheel. Thankfully, no children or adults were nearby. She had a feeling the conversation might get heavy. "I hope I didn't keep you too long."

Hands still firmly in his pockets, his gaze shifted to her. "No."

"Thanks again for the flowers, Chase. They're lovely."

"They reminded me of you," he said, then frowned as if annoyed with himself.

For the first time since he had walked in, Julia relaxed. She could because Chase was nervous enough for both of them.

For a man who had single-handedly captured three bank robbers and rescued their hostage, according to a proud Mabel, a nervous Chase seemed incongruent. He was also annoyed. Somehow it made her erratic emotions easier to deal with. Neither one of them was entirely comfortable with what was happening between them.

Her eyes had foolishly teared up on seeing the dozen white roses. She'd taken half of them home so she could enjoy them there as well while she watched the tight, perfect buds blossom into an aromatic profusion of white. She'd been touched by his thoughtfulness and unspoken apology. She also understood perfectly his dilemma because it mirrored her own.

"You didn't want to come here, did you?"

His gaze sharpened. "No."

"Then why did you?"

"Because I wanted to more than I wanted to stay away."

Her heart sighed. "Chase, that's the most beautiful thing anyone ever said to me."

His scowl deepened.

She laughed.

"This isn't funny."

"Believe me, I know."

"I'm leaving in a less than a month." He tossed the words almost as if they were a challenge.

"Yes, I know."

"I don't want to get involved."

"Neither do I."

He nodded as if that settled everything. "Would you like to meet for a drink or something after work?" he asked, then rushed on. "You understand it wouldn't be a date or anything."

"Of course." Whatever this was, they were going to pretend it wasn't there. She decided to show him she understood the unspoken rules. "Why don't we meet at Leo's around seven?"

"I could pick you up."

"I can get there myself. It's not a date or anything," she said, giving his words back to him.

"All right. See you at seven."

"Fine."

Still he didn't move, simply frowned at her as if she were an annoying puzzle he had yet to figure out. The front door opened and three shoppers came in. "I better get back to work," she told him.

"Yeah." Tipping his Stetson, he spun on his booted heels and left the shop. The interested gaze of the three women followed. Julia didn't blame them.

Now *that*, Julia thought as she watched Chase through the glass storefront, was another kind of sweet temptation.

4

Chase was waiting for Julia when she arrived at Leo's. Seeing her walk through the double mahogany doors smiling and looking beautiful somehow calmed the doubts that had plagued him all day. It was natural for a man to be attracted to a friendly, attractive woman. Feeling more confident, Chase leaned back in his chair and studied the woman who was seldom far from his thoughts since he had met her.

She wore a long-sleeved jacket in jewel tones over the yellow dress. She had a way with colors that drew the eyes and made a man think of what lay beneath. Desire, fierce and hard, hit Chase low and fast. Grimacing, he rocked forward. His logic of moments ago went out the window. The deep intensity of his attraction was unreasonable, undeniable, and, worse, uncontrollable.

Her progress across the room was slow. First one man, then another stopped her. Her warm, open smile never faltered despite the continued apologetic glances she kept throwing in Chase's direction. It didn't help his mood that all the men she stopped to speak with were young, well dressed, and good-looking.

Finally, she made it to the table. "Hello, Chase."

Standing, his mood decidedly testy, he held out her chair. "Do you know everybody in this place?"

Her black eyebrows lifted regally at his brusque tone. "Three of the men I was speaking with are co-owners of Leo's. We were discussing business. The other is an old friend. Any other questions?" Her tone was civil but tinged with frost.

Her message came through loud and clear: *Back off.*

She was absolutely right. It shouldn't matter to him if she talked to a thousand men. She had waited much longer for him and greeted him with a smile instead of accusation. If it had been another woman, he wouldn't have been bothered by the length of time it took to reach their table or the number of men she spoke to on the way.

But it wasn't another woman. It was Julia, and therein lay his problem. A problem he was determined to rectify. He just had to figure out how.

"Sorry," he muttered.

She smiled, sending his heart thumping in his chest, and placed her small yellow handbag on the corner of the table. "Long day."

"Yeah." Long because he had wanted to see her, kiss her. *Concentrate, Chase, concentrate.* "What do you want to drink?"

"White wine. I took the precaution of eating a quick sandwich around four, so I shouldn't fall asleep on you."

"You work too hard," he told her, then signaled a waitress to take their drink orders.

"True, but I enjoy what I do." She leaned forward, wondering if she'd ever get used to the little leap in her heart when she saw him. "So do you, I heard."

"Mabel?"

"Mabel," she confirmed, accepting her wine. "She says you have quite a reputation as a Texas Ranger."

"I have a good unit. We work together as a team to get the job done." Chase sipped his mineral water. He never drank while on duty, and in his opinion the six-week assignment in D.C. was duty. "There's only the four of us, myself and three sergeants, assigned to the Austin area. We investigate major felony crimes and other related incidents. You already know I report to Captain Johnson in Waco. I fought the assignment of coming here. They sent a replacement for me, but since there are only six field captains and seven lieutenants out of one hundred and seven commissioned members in the entire Ranger force, someone's job had to go lacking to do mine."

"You'd rather do the job yourself, wouldn't you?"

He frowned into his glass. "My temporary replacement is a good man."

"But he's not you."

"Yeah. Captain Johnson says I should learn to delegate more," Chase told her, not sure why he was telling her this except she listened well.

"Chase, you don't appear the type of man to take your responsibility lightly. You'd want to make sure every detail is taken care of."

He arched a brow. "How did you know?"

She sipped her wine and sat back. "I used to be the same way. I've just learned to let my assistant manager do what I had hired her for. I found out the hard way I couldn't do it all and do it all well. This time away from your unit should convince you that it won't fall apart without you there."

Black eyes narrowed. "You're saying I'm not needed."

"I'm saying I can't imagine you having people working under you who didn't know what they were doing or who don't have the intelligence to act independently."

Studying her closely, he leaned back in his chair. "Every time I think I have you figured out, you say or do something that baffles me."

"Is it so important to figure me out?"

"Yes."

Julia was afraid she knew why. He hated the attraction between them, and with his analytical mind he was probably trying to figure out the how and the why to put an end to it. She wasn't waiting around until he did. She'd had enough rejection in her life.

She picked up her purse. "Let me know if you come up with an answer."

He frowned. "You're leaving already?"

"Yes."

"You just got here."

"I have a feeling things won't be any different an hour from now," she said sadly and stood.

Slowly coming to his feet, Chase signaled the waitress. What had he said or done to make Julia leave so abruptly? "I'll see you to your car."

"No need. I promised Noah I'd stop by his office on the way out." She extended her hand. "Good night, Chase."

Her hand was soft, smooth, her grip surprisingly strong. He didn't want to let go. He had a sinking feeling that she was saying good-bye, not just good night. But he didn't know the words to stop her or if he should.

"Good night, Julia."

Pulling her hand free, she headed for Noah's office in the back of the restaurant. *Keep walking,* she told herself. *Keep walking away from temptation and heartache.*

Chase got as far as the parking lot. The area was well lit, but lighting in itself wasn't enough of a deterrent to a determined criminal. Retracing his steps, he positioned himself in the deep shadow of the building beside the restaurant and waited for Julia. She might not want to talk with him and they may not have had a date, but he was going to make sure she got home safely.

Ten minutes later, she came out. One of the men she had spoken with earlier was with her. Chase gritted his teeth in annoyance when Julia held up her keys and firmly refused the man's offer to see her to her minivan. Lord save him from stubborn, independent women.

Brisk steps quickly carried Julia to her minivan. By the time she reached the first signal light, Chase was a car length behind. She drove fast but competently. When she pulled into her complex, Chase lagged back and watched her speak briefly to a security guard, then proceed through the black iron gates into the underground garage.

Chase felt a strange something in his chest as the taillights of her vehicle disappeared. Probably the chili dog he had for lunch. Putting the Jeep into gear, he drove to his hotel and went to bed.

Two hours later a wide-awake Chase stared at the ceiling and finally gave in to the inevitable. Whether he liked it or not, it wasn't over between him and Julia.

The next morning Chase was standing in front of Sweet Temptation when Julia unlocked the door. "May I come in?"

She debated only a second. "Of course." She stepped aside, noticing that he didn't look as if he had slept any better than she had.

He glanced at the other young black woman in the shop, then faced Julia. "Is there a place where we can speak privately?"

"Georgette, I'll be in my office if you need me." Julia went to the back, past the gift-wrap area, to her small office. She didn't offer him a seat. "We don't have long, Chase."

"Tell me something I don't know."

"Chase, you're not making sense."

"Right again." His hands closed around her upper forearms with surprising gentleness and undeniable strength. "Wanting you is not making sense, but I can't seem to help it. I go to bed thinking of you. Wake up thinking about you, wondering about how you'd taste. I'm tired of wondering."

His determined mouth came down on hers, demanding a

response. Julia didn't hesitate. Her tongue greeted his with greedy anticipation and bold acceptance. Fierce pleasure swept through her.

With a ragged groan, his arms tightened around her waist, anchoring her to the hard length of his muscular body. On tiptoes, she strained to get closer, her arms locked around his neck.

The kiss was fire and heaven, bliss and hunger.

Chase finally lifted his head, but as if he couldn't bear to be away from her, his hands palmed her face as he pressed soft kisses to her mouth. "I'm not sure what I would have done if you had slapped my face."

"Too Victorian. Kneeing is the modern method for unwanted advances."

"Ouch. Then I'm doubly glad." He kissed her again. "This is crazy. I'll be gone in a few weeks."

"I've told myself the same thing, but I don't think I'm listening."

Black eyes stared down into brown ones. "Maybe it'll wear off."

"Maybe," Julia answered, her hands now on his wrists. She turned her head to brush a kiss against the top of his hand, the dimple in his chin, his soft mouth.

He shuddered, then captured her lower lip and suckled. "I want to see you tonight."

"W-what?"

"Tonight. What time?"

"Six," she murmured, seeking his lips again.

He barely lifted his mouth from hers. "I'm picking you up at your place and taking you home."

"So this is a date?" she asked breathlessly.

"You better believe it, and just so there'll be no misunderstanding . . ." His mouth came back down on hers.

By four-thirty that afternoon Julia knew she'd never leave the shop by five and be ready for Chase by six. As sometimes happened, they'd had a rush. Men who had forgotten birthdays or anniversaries. Women who had forgotten the same thing. Or customers who simply wanted the best chocolate on the East Coast.

Smiling at her own boastfulness, Julia gave a final pat to the pink ribbon bow on the basket she had just finished, then carried it out to the waiting hands of a young man. "Happy first anniversary. I wish you many more."

"Thanks," he said and moved to get in the growing line at the register.

Julia glanced around the shop to see who needed help next. They were four deep. She barely refrained from glancing at her watch. She needed to call Chase and tell him she'd be late, but the customers always came first. Why since Chase had come into her life did she have to keep reminding herself of that fact?

The little tingles of awareness that swept through her at the mere thought of him were her answer. She'd just have to learn how to deal with whatever was between them. She definitely wasn't going to turn her back on it.

Moving to help an elderly couple in Toyland, she saw her older sister with her cell phone glued to her ear as usual, a briefcase in the other hand. Suzanne capably juggled the four two-pound gold foil boxes of truffles under her arm just as she did her hectic life as a lobbyist.

With a sigh of resignation, Julia scanned the store. Still full, and Georgette was on the phone by the register. She didn't have time to go to her office. She switched direction.

"Hi, Suzanne." Careful not to disturb the delicate balance of her sister's packages, Julia gave her a hug. Taller by two inches, Suzanne was stylishly dressed in a black Prada pantsuit and shoes by the same designer.

"Can I ask you a favor?" Julia preferred not to involve her overprotective sister in her personal life, but at the moment she had no other choice.

"Hold on, Harold," Suzanne said. "What's up?"

"Please call Chase Braxton at the Hotel George and leave a message that I'm running late and I'll call."

Suzanne lifted one naturally arched black brow in a face that had been known to stop traffic on the busy D.C. streets and said into the receiver, "Harold, let me call you back." She disconnected the call. "Is he a client?"

"No." Julia moved away before Suzanne could ask questions but knew they would come later. She hadn't had a meaningful date in over five years. Since she had opened Sweet Temptation, the store had always been her top priority. Dating took a back seat. Socialization was work- or family-related.

Ten minutes later when she was in the gift-wrap room in the back, someone tapped her on the shoulder. She glanced around.

"Chase said to tell you he'd wait for as long as it took."

"You actually talked to him?" Julia asked, surprised and impossibly touched by his words.

"Yes." Suzanne's intelligent brown eyes narrowed. "He seemed surprised by the fact also. He says he's a Texas Ranger."

Julia was well aware that Chase had not volunteered the information. He wasn't the talkative type. Suzanne wouldn't have let that stop her. She made her living ferreting out secrets and obtaining information. "He's a lieutenant in charge of his own unit," Julia told her. Unabashed pride rang in her voice.

"So this is a date?"

"Yes," Julia answered, sure of what was coming next. She was not disappointed.

"How long have you known him?"

Julia rolled her eyes and tore off a two-foot length of wrapping paper with footballs scattered on a white background, then set a specially constructed box with a hollow chocolate replica of a Washington Redskin football inside on top of the paper. "Suzanne, I love you dearly, but I'm busy."

"Two years ago, I could have probably gotten the answer," Suzanne said with a hint of annoyance.

Julia sealed the wrapping paper around the box with invisible tape and spoke without turning. "Yes, you could have."

"Even before you opened this shop, you never went out much. You need experience in the trenches, so to speak, to be able to tell if a guy is on the level. Experience you don't have. Sweet Temptation is a testament to your being a savvy businesswoman, but when it comes to people, you're too trusting and naive," Suzanne said, obviously worried. "There are some real dogs out there. They get sneakier and more underhanded each year."

"Chase isn't one of them," Julia defended him, turning at last to face her sister.

"You sound serious about this guy." The words came out as an accusation.

Julia returned to wrapping her package. "Suzanne, I really am busy."

"Do you know how difficult it is to have a good relationship with a man when you're in the same city? Long-distance romances are doomed. You're setting yourself up for heartache if you let yourself become involved. I've seen it happen over and over again."

"Do you think the white or the brown ribbon? Brown, I think." Quickly Julia made the bow and attached a referee whistle. "Their six-year-old grandson will love the whistle, but his parents may want to strangle me."

"I can certainly empathize with them," Suzanne said, glaring at Julia. "I'm calling in the morning."

Accepting the thinly veiled threat and the love behind it, Julia reached for a Sweet Temptation sticker. "I love you, too."

Chase's black eyes narrowed as Julia's vehicle came barreling around the corner of her condo building at ten miles over the speed limit. In a town crowded with expensive imported cars and SUVs of the same makes, her white Caravan minivan stood out. He applauded her sense at not putting her store's name on the side, since she obviously drove the vehicle all the time. Too many thieves would view a woman driving as an easy mark.

Julia pulled to one side and braked across from the white guardhouse where he and Percival, the security guard on duty, had been talking.

"Hi, Percival. Hi, Chase. Sorry I'm late."

"Evening, Miss Ferrington," the guard greeted her.

Chase took his time answering. She looked beautiful, delectable, and harried. He wanted to kiss the frown from her face, watch her fall asleep in his arms. Each time he saw her, she surprised him by causing some new emotion to churn within him.

Slowly, when he wanted to run, he went to her van. "You were speeding." She had been speeding last night when he had secretly followed her home as well.

She had the audacity to grin. "Unless you park in a restricted area the police here are very liberal."

"I noticed on my drive in from the airport and every day since. People jaywalk and disobey traffic laws at will." He shook his head in disgust and placed his hand on the roof of the vehicle. "Driving in this city is a real challenge. My brother and father in the Austin Police Department would have a field day issuing citations."

"They'd have to catch us first."

"They would."

Julia easily heard the assurance in his voice. "Any other siblings?"

"It's just the two of us."

"There are three of us. All girls. My father always joked that he could open a clothing store if he ever left banking. Suzanne is the oldest."

He chuckled. "The interrogator."

Julia put her head on the steering wheel, then glanced up. "I knew I was taking a chance when I asked her to call."

"No problem. It showed she cares."

"Thanks for understanding. As the oldest, she grew up watching out for me. Unfortunately, at times she forgets I'm a grown woman. I hope you'll be equally understanding if you meet Amanda, who can be just as bad as Suzanne. Amanda is two years older than I am and works in the State Department."

"You're the baby."

She wrinkled her nose. "Guilty."

"So am I, and in their eyes we never grow up."

"True."

"We'll have to show them differently." He studied her closely. "I have a feeling you already have with your shop."

"You're right. At first they thought I had lost my mind," she said.

"I remember something similar when I decided to go into the Department of Public Safety instead of the Austin Police Department."

"You broke tradition."

"The same for you?" he questioned.

She nodded. "Politics and high finance. Those were the choices. My mother actually has records dating back to 1886 where my great-great-great-uncle loaned money."

"My brother is a third-generation city police officer."

"But you're still in law enforcement."

"Not the same branch. Each of us takes pride in his area of enforcement and thinks he can do better than the other."

"But I bet you both can't stand the FBI."

"True."

They stared, grinning, at each other. "My family still can't believe I'm not in some form of politics like my sisters." Her brown eyes twinkled. "If they only knew how diplomatic I have to be sometimes with customers trying to decide on a gift."

"From what I saw today, you're very good at your job."

Pleasure shone on her face. "Thanks. I try. Hopefully they'll realize we want to make a difference in a different way, but that difference is still important."

"You have a nice way of putting things."

"Practice," she said with feeling.

Chase had noticed something else very nice. Julia's mouth. He felt its inexplicable pull. He wanted his mouth on hers again. Instead of acting on his desire, he glanced around at the approaching darkness. "I thought we might do a little sightseeing since I changed our dinner reservation to eight, but it's too late now."

She shook her head. "D.C. by night is even more beautiful and powerful. I'll be ready to go in fifteen minutes."

He stepped back from the vehicle instead of leaning closer and sampling her mouth. "Take your time, I've enjoyed talking with Percival."

She smiled at the gray-haired man in the booth. He was lazily flipping through several sheets of paper on a clipboard. "He's a hoot and a good man."

"He thinks highly of you as well. Says he's known you since you were in diapers," Chase told her.

Julia wrinkled her nose. "He knows the whole family. He was one of the security guards at my father's bank until five years ago when the board decided to replace all the guards with off-duty policemen."

"I think he likes it here better so he can keep an eye on you."

Her smile returned. "We keep an eye on each other."

"So I'm finding out." Chase had also found out from the outspoken Percival that Julia seldom dated. "Get going. We might as well put off the sightseeing until after dinner. You probably were too busy to eat."

"I was," she said, delighted that he had thought of her.

"Then go on and we'll see if we can get seated early."

"Yes, sir." Putting the car in gear, she backed up, then drove past the black iron gate, down the slight incline, and abruptly stopped. Expecting that she had forgotten to tell him something, Chase started toward her.

Her door opened, and out she came at a fast clip with a small Sweet Temptation bag in her hand. Without a glance in his direction she went straight to the booth. After a brief conversation with a grinning Percival, she gave him the bag and planted a kiss on his heavily lined cheek. Waving to a watchful Chase, she ran back to her car.

His gaze followed. He openly admired her ability to run in three-inch heels, the graceful way she moved, the sway of her hips. He watched until she got in her van, then turned and started for his Jeep.

"Chase."

He spun back around. This time she was running straight for him. Seeing the anxiety in her face, he quickly sprinted to her. Automatically his hands closed over her shoulders. "What's the matter?"

"I forgot to tell you where to park."

He barely managed to keep from laughing aloud. "Percival told me."

"Oh. Of course. Then I'll just run along. I'll leave the door open."

Chase's hands tightened, his expression changed. "No, you won't. Percival says there's a seating area by the elevator. I'll wait there."

"You can't wait in the hall," she protested, outrage in her lovely face.

"I can and will." He pointed her toward her car. The driver's door was still open. "Now get going and don't worry."

"I'll hurry."

This time Chase watched until she rounded the corner in the parking garage. Still shaking his head, he started for his Jeep. He'd just seen another side of Julia: flustered. The idea pleased him immensely, especially since he had felt the same way that morning before entering her shop.

Percival waved Chase down as he walked past. "I get off at ten. You make sure Miss Ferrington gets home safely."

"I will." She also had people who cared about her. Her sister had politely asked where they planned to go, then inquired if possibly she had met him. Chase had gotten the distinct impression that if his answers hadn't satisfied her, the pleasantries would have abruptly ended. "You don't have to worry."

"Miss Ferrington is a fine young woman," Percival said. "She cares about people."

Chase rubbed his stomach with remembered pleasure. "I found that out before we met when she sent me one of her special baskets."

"Sounds just like her. She saved my life," Percival said quietly, then continued, "The stress and tension of my job at the bank had me hitting the bottle pretty hard. I blamed everyone but myself. Then came the layoff and I started reaching for the bottle more and more. Miss Ferrington came by my place one day to visit me and saw what a mess I'd made of my life. She didn't preach or turn away in disgust, just fixed me a decent meal and kept coming back, kept encouraging me to go to AA and get help. Finally I listened."

Percival held up his bag. "My reward for sticking with the twelve-step program. I haven't had a drink in almost four years." He inclined his head toward the eight-story building behind them. "After my first AA meeting she got me the job here."

Chase's expression saddened. "I've had friends and associates who couldn't or wouldn't turn away from the alcohol and drugs and ended up losing their family, their jobs, their self-respect, and, as you said, their lives." His sigh was long and telling. "Being in law enforcement isn't easy, but it's a job that has to be done."

"I agree." Percival's eyes narrowed. "There are a lot of mean, unscrupulous people in the world who won't hesitate to take advantage of others."

Chase lifted a heavy brow. Had Percival's comment been a veiled insinuation? "I'm not one of them."

"Never said you were, but just so you know, I keep a close eye on Miss Ferrington." Percival leaned closer, his gaze direct. "Don't you go forgetting she's a lady."

"That's one thing neither of us have to worry about. Good night, Percival." Chase continued to his Jeep and got in, his face thoughtful.

The lady and the lawman were an impossible mix, but he was finding that with Julia the impossible became possible. That was another thing he didn't understand. He wanted to lay her down and make love to her in every way known to man, but he also wanted to protect her, cherish her. He had a sinking feeling that he could do one but never both.

True to her word, Julia was ready in fifteen minutes. Slowly Chase rose from the settee in front of the elevator and watched her walk gracefully toward him. She literally took his breath away.

Her knee-length, long-sleeved black knit dress bared smooth brown shoulders. The clinging material flowed irreverently over her body. His mouth watered. A man could spend a lot of time debating what was under the dress and how fast he could get it off.

She stopped inches from him. As if the dress weren't enough, her perfume reached out and punched him in the gut. "I hope I didn't keep you waiting."

"You made it worth the wait."

"Thanks," she said, hoping her voice didn't sound as giddy as she felt.

His gaze wandered down her shapely legs to the high-heeled sandals on her feet. "If we decide to check out some sites after dinner and walk, will you be comfortable in those?"

"My other shoes are in here."

Chase glanced at the small bag in her hand. "In there?"

She pulled out a pair of soft-soled black ballerina shoes. Carrying a canvas bag would have ruined what she hoped was the impact of the dress. Usually she wasn't so vain, but she was honest enough to admit her attraction to Chase wasn't the usual.

"Next time, bring sturdier shoes."

Next time. Julia's heart soared. "I will."

The food, the ambience, the soft jazz music in the background at Leo's were absolutely perfect. Julia cherished every moment and eagerly looked forward to being in Chase's arms again, to having his lips on hers again. Apparently so did he, because he took her straight home after they left the restaurant, and as soon as she opened her door he pulled her into his arms.

Standing on tiptoes, Julia clung to Chase, her senses alive and her body humming. When he asked her to go out with him the following night, she eagerly accepted.

In the days that followed they spent every possible moment together. The place didn't seem to matter. They had just as much fun playing billiards at Chase's hotel as they did at a Howard University faculty get-together, helping with a birthday party at the nursing home, and wandering the many museums and national monuments D.C. had to offer.

An unexpected pleasure for Chase was going with her to see *Swan Lake* at the Kennedy Center. Ballet wasn't his thing. He had little doubt his eyes would cross with boredom and he'd embarrass Julia by falling asleep before the end of the first act. However, instead of watching the dancers, he'd watched the play of emotions on Julia's expressive face. He'd never seen anything more beautiful or more heart-wrenching. His pleasure came from seeing her happy. His hand closed over hers. Inexplicably he felt content and rest-less as the same time when she laid her head on his shoulder at the swan's metamorphosis into a beautiful woman. Caring for Julia was ridiculously easy and undeniably foolish.

He had never wanted to love a woman or to be loved by one. He had always thought the risks for both of them far outweighed the brief span of happiness they might share. His family and friends in law enforcement had taught him that. However, when he touched Julia, held her, looked into her eyes it was difficult to remember he never wanted that heavy-duty responsibility. He had to.

His life was in Texas, just as hers was in D.C.

The next afternoon, when he went with her to Virginia to scout out a possible location for her second store, he felt more at ease with their situation. They were just enjoying each other's company. Neither one of them could afford to forget that their futures lay in different directions.

After dating Chase for almost two weeks, Julia now well understood why couples sat across from each other instead of next to each other. You wanted to see the person's face, catch, learn, then study all the little nuances that made them who they were.

You also just liked looking, liked getting that little quiv-ering sensation in the pit of your stomach when they looked back, like the way your senses were heightened yet somehow strangely muted and focused on that special someone across from you.

They were dining at what was becoming their favorite table at their favorite restaurant, Leo's. Wearing a charcoal gray sports jacket that fit his broad shoulders perfectly, Chase looked dangerously handsome. She'd certainly been right about the place being conducive to romance.

Blissfully happy she sipped her white wine and accepted the growing sexual awareness between them, the pull that she realized would only become stronger if she continued to see him. She searched her mind for a reason to pull back besides the obvious one.

"Would you like to dance?" Chase asked. He laughed at the flash of surprise that crossed her face. "In high school, dancing was a sure way to get the girls into your arms," he confessed with a roguish grin.

"I'd say it still works." Setting her glass down, she placed her hand in his and allowed him to lead her to the crowded dance floor.

Slowly he pulled her into his arms. She fit perfectly with her head resting over his heart. They moved as one, as if they had always danced together, as if they always would.

The live music curled around them like the arms of a jealous lover. Raw, possessive, driven. The slow, mournful wail of the sax warned them of a lost love, of a love gone bad, of the pain and heartache that replaced the joy of falling in love.

Julia lifted her head from Chase's jacket and stared into midnight black eyes. Yes, she could understand the pain and heartache, but she could also see that sometimes your heart made a decision without consulting you.

"What are you thinking?" he asked, his thumb lazily stroking her back.

"Different things," she answered evasively, then laid her head back on his chest, following his steps with her thoughts elsewhere. Could it be possible that her heart had decided already?

Lips, warm, gentle, and fleeting, brushed across her temple. Shock waves of pleasure and surprise had her lifting her head.

"That's what I was thinking," Chase murmured.

She studied the passion burning in his coal black eyes. Sometimes your heart and mind made a decision they both could agree on. "How fast can you get us back to my place?"

He grabbed her hand and started from the dance floor. "Not fast enough."

"Then maybe you should let me drive."

5

She was having second thoughts.

Her increased nervousness as they neared her condo, her silence on the ride up the elevator, made that fact abundantly clear. Her reaction helped to explain and solidify what he had suspected even without Percival's comment or Suzanne's interrogation: Julia's experience with men was minimal.

She stood several feet inside her condo, her bottom lip caught between her teeth, her hands gripping her purse. The sight tore at him. He wanted to give, not take, and only then if she wanted. He went to her and traced a long, lean brown finger down her cheek. She trembled beneath his touch and he breathed easier. Her unease hadn't destroyed her desire.

"We can always leave."

"You must think I'm silly."

His fingers followed the curve of her jaw and pressed against her lips. "I think you're a beautiful, desirable woman who might be having second thoughts."

She wasn't. At least not about kissing Chase. It was where the kisses might lead that had her a bit nervous. "Do you want—"

"Yes." Slowly Chase pulled her into his arms, his lips lowering toward her, giving her time to retreat if she wished. She didn't. Closing her eyes, she sighed and leaned into him.

Her lips were sweet, soft, yielding. Chase took his time

tasting and learning her mouth, getting reacquainted with their taste and texture, savoring each new discovery, nibbling as a child miserly bites his favorite candy.

Something dropped to the floor. Chase realized it was Julia's purse when her hands pressed flat against his chest. He rewarded her by suckling her lower lip. She rewarded him by sinking more heavily against him.

One arm locked securely around her waist, he gave his full attention to her mouth and took her on a slow glide into passion, building the heat, degree by incredible degree. Slowly he backed her toward the sofa.

Julia felt the yielding softness of the silk sofa at her back and Chase's hardness above her. A moment of unease swept through her; then he deepened the kiss, his hand running boldly over her body, and thinking ceased to be important.

She whimpered. Her fingers clutched his lapel, telling him of her need.

Boldly his tongue swept into her mouth. His hands moved down to cup her hips, molding her to his rigid hardness. When he moved against her in the same slow rhythm as his tongue inside her mouth, she shuddered.

One hand closed over her breast, his thumb flicking over the turgid point of her nipple, again and again.

She was on fire. She needed. She wanted.

Julia wanted the dress gone. She wanted his hands on her body, hers on his. She whimpered in growing frustration.

"The dress stays!"

Her eyes flew open and she stared into Chase's equally wide ones. His outburst was a direct contradiction to what she'd been thinking, what she wanted.

Groaning, he buried his face between the crook of her neck and her shoulder. "Sorry. I don't usually argue with myself." His mouth brushed tantalizingly against her neck.

"I don't understand?" she stammered.

"If the dress comes off, only an act of God will keep me from making love to you."

Julia was caught between being indignant that he thought she was that easy and trying to come to grips with the possibility that she just might be when he continued speaking: "Percival was on duty when we came back."

Her puzzlement increased. "Percival? What has he to do with this?"

Chase lifted his head, stared down into her open face, felt the softness of her body beneath his, and knew it was the wrong way to have a conversation. Sitting up, he pulled her into his lap. "Besides being a Saturday night, it's the first time we've come back from a date before he got off duty." There was no way he would embarrass her by telling her of Percival's initial warning. "Then there is the interrogator."

"I can handle Suzanne," Julia said with confidence. "She asked about you after the first time we went out. I didn't tell her anything."

"Because there was nothing to tell," he told her, accepting that there would be nothing to tell about tonight, either. "You're not very good at hiding your feelings and I don't think you'd like people knowing we had been intimate."

Julia bit her lip. He was right. She laid her head back on his chest, her fingers idly toying with a white button on his shirt. "Not very modern, is it?"

"No." Chase brushed a kiss across the top of her head to soften his pronouncement. "But in your case, I approve."

"You're not angry?" she asked, softly angling her head up to see his face.

"A woman should always be able to say no."

Julia heard what he said, but she was sitting on very hard proof that his body was saying something vastly different. He wanted her. She wanted him. But she needed more.

Men tended to think with their eyes, women with their hearts. At the moment, hers was telling her she was falling in love.

"What do you want from me, Chase? Beside the obvious?" she asked, making herself maintain eye contact with him.

His large hands cupped her face. "I stopped having sex for sex's sake in high school. If I didn't care about you, I wouldn't be here. As for what else I want, I don't know. All

I know is that I can't wait to see you, and when I'm not with you I want to be."

"Oh, Chase." Her voice trembled. "What are we going to do?"

"Steal each moment we can to be with each other," he told her.

"Then what?" she asked, dreading the answer but voicing it anyway.

For the first time that night, his gaze wavered. "For as long as I can remember I've wanted to be a Texas Ranger. It's not just a job; it's what I believe, what I'm good at. Just like you are with your customers at Sweet Temptation. I watched you and them. They're not just there because of the candy; they're there because of you. You plan to open a second store soon. Your life is here."

He was right. "You have your family and job in Texas and I have mine here in D.C.," she said, her voice unsteady.

"Yes."

There it was. When it was over, it was over.

Julia stared into Chase's set features and took a deep breath. He was leaving her with no false illusions about their relationship. Could she continue seeing him and risk her heart, as Suzanne had warned against?

"I know it's selfish," Chase said, interrupting her thoughts as he pulled her back into his arms. "But is it wrong to want to see you, hold you, kiss you, make love to you?"

The rapid pounding of his heart that matched her own answered her question and his. Sometimes the greatest risks yielded the greatest gain. It wasn't wrong. She wanted to be with Chase, felt alive as never before in his arms. She was mature enough to give him part of what he wanted, what *she* wanted.

"Excuse me." As gracefully as possible, she got off his lap.

Chase came to his feet, surprise, frustration, and disbelief in his eyes. "You're throwing me back."

The desolate words stopped Julia two feet away. She came back to him, her gaze locked with his every inch of the way.

"Like the woman said, only a fool would do that."

He frowned. "Then where were you going?"

She grinned. "To the kitchen to set the timer. Percival gets off at ten, and until then I intend for you to be too busy paying attention to me to care about the time."

He flashed her a roguish smile. "Julia Ferrington, you never cease to amaze me."

"After I set the timer, you can show me how much you appreciate that fact."

He wasn't going to make it.

Jumping into the Cherokee, Chase started the engine, then shoved the vehicle into reverse. He threw a glance at the digital clock on the dashboard before straightening and shifting into second: 10:06.

He had followed Julia into the kitchen to cut off the timer; then she had kissed him. They'd immediately become more interested in each other than the passage of time. Regaining some control, he'd gone to the door, turned to say good night, and looked at her lips glistening and pouty from his kisses, her eyes dark with passion, and hauled her into his arms.

His jaw set, he drove out of the garage wishing he were holding Julia instead of a steering wheel. He fully intended to bypass Percival. If not for his interference, Chase would still have Julia in his arms, seeing how close he could take them both to the edge and not go over.

The elderly security guard apparently had other ideas. Stepping out of the booth with the other guard, Percival directed Chase to pull over to one side. With ill-concealed annoyance, he did as directed.

Percival stared at Chase's profile long and hard; then the older man's dark, leathery face split into a wide grin. He slapped Chase on the shoulder with surprising strength. "I knew I could trust you."

Chase cut him a look.

"Now don't be angry." The older man looked back at the new guard on duty, then leaned closer and opened his gray metal lunch pail. "Have some of my candy. Luther's got hands like a linebacker. If he saw, I'd lose half. I figure you deserve a reward, too."

Chase looked at the candy, which the older man no doubt greatly enjoyed, hoarded, and looked forward to but was willing to share to show his appreciation. Chase's annoyance changed to gratitude. Percival would always watch out for Julia. Chase reached for a chocolate and popped the cream-filled candy in his mouth.

Percival nodded. "You'll do."

"Thanks," Chase said, acknowledging the older man for more than just the candy.

"My pleasure." Percival straightened. "Miss Ferrington backed me, believed in me. There isn't anything I wouldn't do for her to keep her safe and happy. So if I seem nosy, I am."

Chase grinned. "The thought had crossed my mind."

"I'll just bet it did." Humming, Percival walked off.

The phone was ringing when Chase entered his room. He rushed to the end table in the sitting room and jerked up the receiver. "Hello."

"So you're finally home."

"Oh, it's you." Disappointed, Chase plopped down on the arm of the sofa.

A deep chuckle came through the receiver clearly. "Don't tell me you've been out of my sight four weeks and you let some woman get her hooks into you."

"Don't start, Colt."

"Dad, Chase is having women problems!" Colt yelled. "No wonder he didn't come home this weekend or last."

"I thought you two were always telling me to stay here." Chase plucked a chocolate peanut cluster from the basket and eased onto the couch.

"That was before we knew about her. So give."

In between bites, Chase briefly told Colt about Julia, intentionally leaving out the last hour of heavy petting. He and his big brother were extremely close and shared a lot, but neither of them discussed the intimate details about the women they dated.

"Watch it, Bro," Colt warned once Chase finished. "The candy was just to soften you up."

"You are too suspicious." Chase polished off the candy and considered another piece. "You sound like her sister, who, by the way, could beat you at interrogation."

"Sounds like a busybody," Colt said. "Stay away from that family."

Chase knew it was useless arguing with his brother. Ever since he'd caught his ex-wife in an affair, he'd been distrustful of women. With a start, Chase realized some of Colt's resentment had rubbed off on him—until he met Julia. "From experience, I'd say this is one family I wouldn't judge until I met them in person."

"Maybe Dad and I should come up there to make sure you aren't getting in over your head."

"Big brother, I can handle it."

"See that you do. Marriage and lawmen don't mix." Bitterness tinged Colt's words.

Chase straightened, all thought of the candy forgotten. "Who said anything about marriage?"

"You're the noble, romantic type. All those mystical, heroic stories about the Texas Rangers are what attracted you in the first place," Colt told him. "I'm surprised you've stayed single this long."

"You're just mad because you have to wear a uniform and I don't."

"But I'm cuter."

"So is a baby elephant to its mother."

Both men laughed and settled down to talk. From time to time Chase's father, Charles, got on the phone. An hour later Chase hung up the phone and pushed to his feet. Restless, he opened the cabinet doors of the entertainment center and turned on the TV. He channel-surfed for several seconds, then shut it off. The remote control still in his hand, he stared at the telephone.

He knew why he was edgy, what would take the edge off,

and just as certainly knew it wouldn't happen tonight. If ever. Crossing the room, he picked up the phone and dialed. With Julia he was finding he wanted much more than her body. However, by the eighth ring he vacillated between anger and concern.

"Hello. Hello," she finally answered breathlessly.

"Where were you?" Chase asked, his voice sharp and accusatory.

"In the shower. I tried to hurry."

If she had wanted to pay him back, she couldn't have chosen a better method. He didn't have to close his eyes to imagine droplets of water rolling down her sleek body or imagine his tongue lapping them from her skin. He groaned.

"Chase. Chase, are you all right?"

"I hope you grabbed a towel."

"I, er, actually—"

"If you're trying to put the screws to me, you're succeeding," he told her, then plopped on the edge of the sofa. "Go get a towel." He tortured himself further by visualizing her running naked to the bathroom.

"I'm back," she said, her voice as breathless as the first time. "I'm sorry it took me so long to answer. I couldn't hear over the shower."

"Julia, let's not talk about the shower, if you don't mind."

"Sorry." Securing the oversize bath towel between her breasts, she pushed aside the antique throw pillows, then drew back the duvet and sat on the bed. Chase sounded grouchy, and she fully realized why. She wasn't at her best, either. She was beginning to fully understand the term *sexual frustration.*

"Not as sorry as I am," Chase said. "You have any plans for tomorrow afternoon?"

"No."

"You want to go to a movie or take a drive?"

"Why don't I prepare a picnic basket for lunch? It will give me a chance to try out a new enterprise I have with Leo's. Is twelve all right?"

"Fine. What should I bring?"

"A huge appetite."

He chuckled. "That shouldn't be a problem. See you at twelve."

"Good night, Chase. I had a wonderful time before and after."

"So did I. Good night, Julia." Letting the phone drop into the cradle, Chase went into the bedroom, gazed at the king-size bed's wide expanse of emptiness, and went to the closet for his sweat suit.

He was going jogging. Maybe if he got tired enough his brain and body would shut down and he'd stop craving what he couldn't have: Julia, hot, naked, and needy beneath him.

The flat of his hand slammed the closet door closed. It was going to be another restless night.

"Will you leave so I can get dressed?" Julia requested for what seemed to be the fifth time since her sisters had followed her home from church.

Neither Suzanne nor Amanda moved from their side chairs in Julia's bedroom. Both were strikingly attractive, with flawless skin, intense brown no-nonsense eyes.

"It isn't like we haven't seen you before, Julia," Suzanne said, sipping her favorite Earl Grey.

"She's right," Amanda agreed, critically assessing the two outfits in her sister's hands. "Wear the magenta."

"Thanks." Ignoring her sister's unsolicited advice, Julia hung up the magenta pantsuit and laid the flowing tangerine dress on the bed. The wide belt would accent her waist, and the drop shoulders would certainly keep Chase's attention. Her matching flats would allow her to keep pace with him without having to wear her unflattering walking shoes.

Suzanne set her porcelain cup on the table. The sisters traded worried glances. In the past, Julia had always followed their advice on clothes and men. It seemed both might be changing. "You *really* like him."

"Yes." Julia unbuttoned her skirt and went to the closet to hang it up. Her jacket followed.

"I downloaded a picture of his unit from the Internet last

night and I can see why," Amanda commented. "Even in the grainy black-and-white picture he looked handsome, strong, and tough."

"He *sounded* the same way," Suzanne said.

There was no sense reprimanding her middle sister for what some might see as snooping. With her connections she could have gone much deeper into Chase's file, if she had wanted. Going to the high chest, Julia pulled out fresh undergarments and turned. "Amanda, aren't you supposed to be flying to Camp David this afternoon?"

"The plane isn't scheduled to leave until late," she stated. "I have plenty of time."

Julia's annoyed gaze fastened on Suzanne. "Don't you have someone's arm to twist about their vote on a bill or something?"

"We aren't leaving until we meet him. You've been evasive about him and out every night. It's time we checked this brother out. You know Mother and Father always told us to watch out for each other." Suzanne crossed long, well-shaped legs. Her slim black skirt inched up higher. On her feet were four-inch heels. "Stop fussing and go get dressed. You don't want us to meet him without you, do you?"

The threat worked. Grabbing the dress, Julia rushed into the bathroom to change. "Don't you dare embarrass me in front of Chase!" she yelled, pulling off her slip and flinging it carelessly in the direction of the marble countertop. Her hands were unfastening her bra when she heard the doorbell.

"Don't worry!" Amanda called sweetly. "We'll get it!"

"No!" Grabbing the dress, Julia pulled it over her head and raced out of the bedroom, zipping as she went. Bra or no, she wasn't about to let Chase meet her sisters without her being there.

6

Chase's gaze lingered on Julia's flushed face, then moved to the two beautiful women behind her who were staring daggers at him. Interrogation time again. Looked like Suzanne had brought reinforcements. He'd learned long ago to start as he intended to finish.

"Hi, Julia." Leaning over, he brushed his lips across her cheek, then straightened. Two pair of assessing brown eyes openly sized him up. He didn't mind. He was doing the same.

The one in black would be the lobbyist; the other one in pale gray would work for the State Department. Classy and elegant, both women would draw a man's attention and have enough spunk to cut him to the quick if necessary.

"Hello, Suzanne, Amanda." He extended his hand. "I'm Chase Braxton."

Their handshakes, as he had imagined they would be, were firm. "Chase," they greeted in unison.

Her stomach still doing little flip-flops from Chase's unexpected kiss in front of her sisters, Julia opened the door wider, hoping they would take the hint. "I'll talk to you later. Bye."

Neither took her gaze from Chase. Amanda spoke first, "I pulled your photo up on the Internet."

"That's what it's there for." Chase's gaze went to Julia. "Where's the picnic basket?"

Julia frowned at her stubborn sisters. "In the kitchen."

"Why don't you get it, and your sisters and I can become better acquainted?" he said easily.

Indecision held Julia still. Because she had been shy, awkward, and insecure growing up, her family, especially her sisters, had always been protective of her. Now that she had grown up, they still thought she needed them to watch out for her.

Chase reached behind him and closed the door. "The Rangers have a motto: 'One Ranger. One Riot.' I'll be fine."

Julia looked at Chase, jaw-dropping handsome in a chambray shirt, jeans, and blue jeans jacket, and noticed none of the nervousness her pitiful few dates had suffered when confronted with Suzanne and Amanda while Julia was in high school and college. Chase could hold his own. The kiss should have told her.

She relaxed. "Excuse me; I won't be but a minute."

Chase, Suzanne, and Amanda waited for all of ten seconds. Chase got the first volley off. "Julia is a unique young woman who knows her own mind and doesn't need you or anyone else telling her what to do or looking over her shoulder."

"Wait a minute, buster," Suzanne said, stepping forward.

"No, you wait a minute," Chase replied. "How do you think she feels knowing you're here to check out her date, as if she is still in high school? She knows what she wants."

"And I suppose that's you."

Chase cut his gaze to Amanda. "Whether it is or not, she has to make the decision. And all you can do is be there for her. Sometimes you have to let go."

"She's our baby sister and much too softhearted and trusting."

"She's also a grown, intelligent woman, in case you hadn't noticed."

"I hate to interrupt, but here is the basket," Julia said sweetly, handing it to Chase.

He hefted the weight and grinned. "I see you've packed enough."

"I hope you like it."

"I will. You better get something to sit on. While you're at it, grab a pair of walking shoes."

Julia stopped and turned; the long skirt of the dress swirled around her shapely legs. "These shoes are fine."

"Not if you decide you want to traipse through monuments again."

"Chase, I'll be fine."

"Indulge me and grab the shoes, and don't forget your keys."

She made a face, muttering as she went, clearly not pleased.

He looked at Suzanne and Amanda. "See. She's no push-over. For that you probably should take some of the credit, but it's time to back off and let her make her own mistakes, if it comes to that. But I don't think she will."

"I was prepared not to like you," Suzanne said with a sigh. "I'm just realizing that about her myself."

"Me, too," Amanda agreed.

"Why did you see it and we didn't?"

"Because, as you said, you still see her as your baby sister and not the woman she has become."

"She grew up on us." Thoughtfully Amanda folded her arms.

"That she did," Chase said with frank male appreciation. "Does this mean we call a truce?"

"For now," Amanda said, a slow smile curving her lips.

"Good. I didn't want to argue with my brother *and* you."

"What's your brother got to do with this?" Suzanne asked, a frown on her beautiful face.

"Absolutely nothing, but he's as opinionated as they come." Chase shook his head. "After I told him about our conversation, he thought you were a busybody."

Suzanne's brown eyes flashed. "Opinionated and annoying."

Chase chuckled. "At times. However, in Colt's defense, he was only trying to look out for my best interest, just as you and Amanda were doing for Julia. All of your intentions were good, but unnecessary and unwanted." Looking over their heads, he saw Julia. He suppressed a smile when he saw the canvas bag in her hand. He took the things from her. "You'll thank me tomorrow."

"I suppose," she admitted.

He took her hand in his, pleased by the slight tremble he felt. "Ladies, would you like to join us?"

Julia shook her head and mouthed, *No.*

"We can tell when we're not wanted, can't we, Amanda?" Suzanne went to the sofa and picked up her oversize black purse and slung the twin straps over her shoulder. "Have fun, you two."

Amanda's gray purse was a fourth of the size and bulk of Suzanne's. She stuck the bag under her arm. "I have a plane to catch. Nice meeting you, Chase."

Chase's arm lifted to circle Julia's shoulders, his eyes direct and sincere. "I'll do my best to make sure you always feel that way."

"We believe you." The door closed softly behind them.

Julia gazed up at him in amazement. "How did you do that?"

"First things first." His lips settled on hers, his tongue slipping inside her mouth to gently mate with hers. Long seconds later, he lifted his head. "You taste sweeter each time I kiss you."

"So do you," Julia breathed, curling her arms and her body closer to his. "You could make me a kissaholic."

"That . . ."—he nipped her lower lip—"works both ways." Stepping back, he opened the door. "Come on. Let's get out of here while I still have some willpower left."

The morning was sun-kissed and magical. Julia freely admitted it was because she was with Chase. She selected a sunny spot on the lush grass of the Mall, the popular corridor between the Capitol and the Lincoln Monument, for their picnic. People strolled its length, played baseball, soccer, jogged.

Chase placed the basket on top of the plaid blanket, then helped Julia sit. She came down on her knees and immediately began dragging food from the hamper. "I hope you like chicken salad."

Propped on his side, Chase watched her economical, graceful movements. "I love food, period."

Laughing, she looked up at him, felt the familiar pull, and ducked her head. If she wanted him to wait, she had to stop staring at him as if she could eat him with a spoon.

Chase's hand settled over hers, causing her to jump. "It's all right to want me. Lord knows I want you."

Some small part of her wanted to tuck her head and shy away from the words. Another part of her wanted to embrace his words as she wanted to embrace him.

She had overheard Chase talking to her sisters. He saw the woman that she so desperately wanted to be, the woman she hoped she was. Not for anything would she give him cause to think he had been wrong. "I don't know what to say."

"You don't have to say anything," he said, his eyes and his words tender. "I've heard the practiced words too many times in the past. I've forgotten them and the women who said them. Your honesty and, although it might annoy you, your vulnerability are much more appealing."

She made a face and reached into the basket for a Thermos of lemonade. "You make me sound pitifully childish."

"A childish woman wouldn't keep me awake at night, and I certainly wouldn't arrive thirty minutes early for a date."

"You did?" she questioned, delight and amazement in her animated voice and face. "You arrived at the door on time. Where were you?"

Seeing the joy shining in her brown eyes banished the mild annoyance he had felt with himself. "With Percival. He had a good laugh watching me try to decide if I should go up early or play it cool and wait."

"He likes to tease."

"So I found out," Chase said. "The important thing is that I'm where I want to be."

"So am I." That she was sure of. "And next time come on up."

"I will." He gave her hand a gentle squeeze before releasing it to rummage in the basket. He came out with the thermal cooler containing chocolate-covered strawberries. He held one up to her lips.

Her eyes locked with his. She bit. Juice ran down one corner of her mouth. Her tongue followed. So did Chase's hot gaze.

She began to tremble. Leaning toward her, he slowly traced the path her tongue had taken with his tongue, then sat back and bit into the strawberry, chewed, swallowed. He closed the container with hands that were not quite steady. "Why don't we save them until we get back to your apartment?"

It took a couple of moments for her speak. "I'd like that."

A soccer ball rolled onto the blanket, breaking the tension-filled moment. Coming to his feet, Chase expertly shot the ball back to the young man loping toward him.

Catching the ball, the ponytailed player began rolling the ball in his hand. "Wanna play?"

"No, thanks," Chase told him, then sat back down.

"I don't mind if you want to play." She poured the lemonade into a slender glass.

Chase popped an olive into his mouth and accepted the glass. "I would."

She paused in unwrapping the thick sandwich loaded with chunky chicken salad, lettuce, tomatoes. She had purposefully left out the sweet onions. "I don't understand?"

"To play, I'd have to be away from you."

Her insides went shivery. Her eyes misted. "Chase, you say the most beautiful things to me."

His knuckles tenderly grazed her cheek. "If you cry I'll have to kiss the tears away, and one thing might lead to another. It wouldn't look good on my record or on yours if we were arrested."

Julia brushed away the tears forming in her eyes. "No, it wouldn't. So why don't you tell me why you broke tradition to become a Texas Ranger?"

"I think it was probably after my hundredth or so rerun episode of *The Lone Ranger* when I was ten," he began, regaling her with stories as they ate their lunch. He told of playing the Lone Ranger and riding Silver, the kitchen broom, to capture the neighborhood kids playing outlaws. He'd cut holes in his father's best black socks to make a mask. Although his father had tanned his backside, he'd still gotten the holstered guns and hat set he'd asked for for Christmas.

"What did your mother have to say?" Julia asked, smiling.

His face and body tensed. "She left when I was nine and Colt was twelve. Daddy and his partner answered a domestic dispute that went sour. Daddy's partner was killed and he was wounded. Mama left as soon as he was released from the doctor. She said she couldn't take the possibility of Daddy not coming home one night."

"Chase, I'm sorry. I didn't mean to pry."

He shrugged broad shoulders and sat up. "It happens."

"But that doesn't make it any less painful," she said, placing her hand over his.

It always amazed him how intuitive and supportive she was. His hand turned, enclosing hers within his. "We did all right."

"I'd say you did more than all right," Julia said, wanting to take the shadows from his eyes. "I haven't met your father or Colt, but from the way you speak about them I know they must be wonderful men, and the three of you must be very close. That took hard work on your father's part to raise two responsible, honorable, hardworking men."

"He never missed a day telling or showing us how much he loved us," Chase said. "I've counseled too many kids not to know how it could have turned out. Policemen's kids or not."

"It must have been hard at times on all of you."

"For a long time, Daddy blamed himself."

"Did you?"

"Oddly enough, Mama helped me to understand. He wouldn't have been happy doing anything else, and if she had taken his children thousands of miles away it would have killed him. She loved us all enough to sacrifice. Not a week went by that she didn't call or write. Sometimes both. In the summer, off we'd go to Pittsburgh."

"It sounds as if she loved you very much."

"She did. Losing her when I was in high school to a ruptured appendix was hard on all of us." His gaze bore into

Julia. "She never remarried. She fell in love with the wrong man and paid the price the rest of her life."

Julia listened, her heart growing heavier with every word Chase spoke. He was warning her against falling in love, but it was already too late. "Was your father ever injured again in the line of duty?"

"No."

"Your mother chose her way to deal with her fear, but another woman might choose to stay and cherish each minute, each second," Julia said with feeling. "If given the opportunity, another woman might choose to fight to hold onto what she loved most."

He pulled his hand free. "Maybe. Let's repack the basket and you can drag me through another museum."

Sighing, Julia began putting things back in the basket. Chase wasn't going to give them an opportunity to find out if it was left up to him.

"Chase," she said softly, waiting until his dark gaze met hers. "What would you say if we skipped the museum and went back to my place and finished the rest of the strawberries?"

"I'd say pack faster."

His hot, hungry mouth was on hers the instant the door closed behind them. Holding nothing back, she met him with passion and greed, her slim body pressed eagerly against his. He felt the difference immediately. High, firm, unrestrained breasts pushed against his chest. He groaned and thanked the increasing temperature that had made him leave his jacket in the Jeep.

Nibbling her lower lip, he slid his hand from her waist to close possessively over the soft mound of her breast, felt the nipple harden instantly. The pleasure pulsating through him doubled as she pressed against him. Her eyelids drifted shut for all of five seconds before they flew upward. Eyes wide, she blushed and stumbled back.

"Julia, what is it?"

She shook her head and backed up a step.

Worried, Chase matched her step for step. "Honey, what's the matter?"

Somehow the endearment only made her predicament worse. Her mouth opened, then closed. Several seconds passed before she stammered, "I don't have on . . . I forgot . . . I mean I didn't have time." She swallowed. "Y-you were at the door and Suzanne and Amanda were going to answer it. I didn't have time."

A slow smile of understanding spread across Chase's handsome face. He reached out, his hands gently settling on her shoulders to keep her from backing up farther. "You weren't thinking of leaving your guest, were you?"

"I—"

His lips brushed across hers. She swayed closer, her mouth lifting to his. "Because I'd be very disappointed if you did."

"But—"

He kissed her again, scattering her thoughts and sending heat and desire racing through her bloodstream. "Do you trust me?"

"Yes. It's me I don't trust."

For some odd reason her words disturbed him. "Never say anything like that to any man."

"I wasn't saying them to any man."

His hands on her shoulders tightened a fraction. He stared into her wide eyes and felt the floor shift beneath his feet. "I told you when I leave, this is over."

"I know."

"Then stop looking at me as if you expect this to continue."

Biting her lower lip, she tucked her head. So much for good intentions and maturity, for believing she could enjoy what they had, then let him go. It wasn't what she wanted or what she could accept. "I'm sorry."

"You have nothing to be sorry for," he said, angry at the impossible situation. "I can't give you what you want."

"How do you know? You haven't tried," she told him tightly.

"And I won't," he shot back.

She recoiled from the harshness of his voice. "I see."

"No, you don't. I don't have time for anything but the job," he riled. "When I leave D.C. and go back to Austin I'll have to catch up on six weeks of work that was already behind six months. I'm on call twenty-four/seven. I can't remember the last time I had a full day off."

"I'm sure other single men in the Rangers find time to date."

A muscle leaped in Chase's jaw. Why was she being so stubborn? "The women they're dating aren't four hours away by plane, nor is there the likelihood that they run their own successful businesses. Both of us have too many obligations for this to continue."

"I don't mind the trip, and as you've seen, I make time for the things that are important to me," Julia told him, hoping it didn't sound as if she were begging and afraid it did.

Chase's mouth flattened into a narrow line. "What about when you open your second shop?"

Doubt that Julia was unable to hide flickered in her eyes. "I didn't say it would be easy."

Wearily he shook his head. One of the things he admired about Julia was her dogged determination. He just wished she wasn't now using it against him. "Both of us have too many responsibilities. It couldn't work."

She met his hard gaze with more courage than she had imagined. "How can you be so positive? You won't even try."

"No, I won't." His hands dropped to his sides. "When I leave in two weeks, I won't be back."

Her small hands clenched. She hadn't imagined the pain, the immense sense of loss, could be so intense. "I thought I could be very modern and adult about this, but I can't. Making love should mean something between a man and a woman, not just passing time."

"I never lied to you, Julia."

"No, you didn't. I lied to myself." She lifted her hand, extending it as though she expected nothing more from him than a perfunctory businesslike handshake. "Good-bye, Chase."

He stared at the delicate hand with narrow eyes; then his gaze lanced up to her. "So this is it?"

Her hand and voice wavered. "Yes."

With a curt nod, he turned to leave.

Pain and disbelief rushed through Julia as Chase opened the door. How could he just walk away without trying? She knew he cared.

"I thought Texas Rangers were fearless," she tossed out, then rushed on when he whirled back toward her, his eyes sharp and cutting. "You're not giving either of us enough credit. We both go after and fight for what we want. Make no mistake, you're what I want, but not for just a brief interlude. If you ever find you feel the same way, you know where to find me."

For a long moment, he simply stared. Hope leaped in Julia's heart; then he opened the door, walked through it, and closed it softly behind him.

"Oh, Chase!" Julia cried, finally letting the tears fall.

7

Chase was in a foul mood. The Saturday afternoon rush-hour traffic wasn't helping. There had been a full moon the night before, and the lingering effects seemed to have carried over into the full light of day. People were zipping in and out of lanes, tailgating, honking horns, and in general being nastier than usual.

His hands clenched and unclenched on the steering wheel. He wasn't at his best himself. He didn't like the restless, edgy feeling. It was as if he had overdosed on caffeine or was coming down from the aftermath of an adrenaline rush. But he was honest enough to admit it wasn't caffeine or adrenaline that had him uncomfortable in his own skin but a woman who wanted something from him he couldn't give.

He wasn't afraid of anything. He was just doing what was best for both of them. You knew fire would burn without sticking your hand in it!

Thirteen days! It had been thirteen miserable days and unbelievably long nights since Julia had politely kicked him out of her life and issued her impossible challenge. The thought still had the power to make his temper rise. How could she stick out her hand to him as if he were a stranger when they set each other on fire every time they kissed?!

He wanted that fire again. But in twenty-two hours he was taking a flight home. Why couldn't she accept and understand—

Suddenly a BMW coupe darted in front of him. Chase slammed on his brakes to keep from hitting the sports car and heard the squeal of brakes behind him. He jerked his gaze sharply to the rearview mirror, fully expecting to feel the Mercedes that had been on his bumper for the past ten minutes ram into him.

Instead the Mercedes took the sidewalk, giving the cab behind him enough time to safely stop. *Good reflexes,* Chase thought and waved out the open window.

Shifting the Cherokee into gear, Chase had started to pull off when he saw the car that had cut in front of him do the same thing to another driver in a Maxima. This time the BMW didn't make it.

The car clipped the Maxima's left fender, causing both cars to spin out of control and careen into cars in front and on the side of them. The impact pushed automobiles through the approaching stop sign into the oncoming right-of-way traffic. The sickening sound of metal crashing into metal filled the air.

Chase had his car phone in his hand, dialing 911, when everything within him went icy cold and still. A white Caravan minivan was heading straight for the pileup.

The phone slipped from his hand. *Please, no!*

In an instant he was out of the car and running. He had barely taken a step past his Cherokee when the minivan slammed headfirst into the other cars.

"Julia!"

* * *

Chase hated hospitals. He'd lost his mother in a hospital.

Hands deep in the pockets of his jeans, he stared out the window of the surgery waiting room and tried desperately to remember that his father's life had been saved in a hospital. He couldn't. His mind was too busy remembering the agonized screams of a woman in pain and his frantic attempts to pry open a door with his bare hands.

"Chase."

He spun around, his hand coming out of his pockets. His heart leaped before he could tell it to do otherwise. Julia stood ten feet away from him. Safe. Alive. Healthy. She wasn't in surgery fighting for her life. She could have been.

He felt stinging in his eyes and fought to keep the moisture at bay. There was nothing he could do about the trembling in his legs, the knot in his throat.

"Chase. Are you all right?"

Chase briefly shut his eyes and thanked God that he had heard his name on her lips one last time, because no matter what, nothing had changed between them.

"Thank you—"

He shook his head. He didn't want to hear the words of gratitude again because then he'd have to relive the fear. What he desperately wanted was to take Julia in his arms and keep her safe. To keep from doing just that he picked his hat up from the chair he had never bothered to sit in.

"Your friend is still in surgery. Her father finally talked her mother into going down to the cafeteria for a cup of coffee. I told them I'd stay in case any family members or friends came."

Julia's hungry gaze searched Chase's drawn face, the jagged tear in his shirt, the dirty jeans. He seemed so cold and distant. She clenched her hands to keep from touching him to reassure herself that he was all right and fought to remain calm.

She'd been in her office when she heard the radio broadcaster announce that a Texas Ranger, disregarding his own safety, had single-handedly rescued a young couple from a

burning van after a traffic pileup. He was also credited with
saving others with his swift action to get bystanders to help
accident victims to safety before the police and fire department arrived.

Until Georgette's mother called, Julia hadn't known the
couple was her assistant manager and her husband, Michael,
who had borrowed Julia's van to pick up a sofa they had
purchased. Julia had barely been able to understand what the
woman said because she was crying so hard. Georgette was
bleeding internally and had been rushed into surgery.

"How is Michael?"

"Broken leg. He'll survive."

"Because of you," she whispered softly.

Chase rolled his shoulders; his large hand crushed the
brim of his Stetson. "Any law enforcement officer would
have done as much."

Julia didn't think so. It took a special man to risk his life
again and again for strangers. "Perhaps."

Chase's gaze bounced off the wall, the door, the floor.
Anyplace except where he most wanted it to be. He slipped
the hat on his head, tugging down hard on the misshapen
brim. "Since you're here, I'll be going."

"Chase."

He stopped but didn't face her. "Yes?"

The door behind them opened. Millie Watkins, Georgette's mother, saw Julia and began to weep.

Instantly Julia went to the older woman and pulled her
into her arms. Reaching behind the older woman's back, Julia briefly squeezed Mr. Watkins's hand. His usually smiling
face was ravaged with fear. Georgette was their only child.
"Georgette is a fighter. She'll make it."

Julia felt Mrs. Watkins's nod of agreement against her
shoulder and pulled the frightened woman closer, comforting
both of them. Georgette was only thirty-six. She had two
adorable children and a husband who worshiped her. Her
whole life was ahead of her.

Looking up, Julia met Chase's impenetrable stare. A shudder went through her. His mother had had two children and a husband. Life offered no guarantees.

Trying to hide her own fear, Julia helped a distraught Mrs. Watkins to a seat, then sat beside her. Mr. Watkins remained standing, his gray head bowed. Instead of leaving as he had said, Chase walked over to the father and began quietly talking to him.

Julia was glad Chase had decided to stay. His presence comforted her. Obviously he didn't feel the same. He wouldn't even look at her.

Chase stoically accepted the torture of being near Julia. He thought he could leave. He couldn't. Not while she was bravely comforting Georgette's parents and obviously in need of reassurance herself. But he already knew Julia put those she loved before herself. A rare woman. If her friend didn't make it, he wanted to be there for her. He could give her that at least.

Two hours after Julia arrived, a woman in a scrub suit entered the waiting room. Mr. and Mrs. Watkins rushed to her.

"I'm Dr. Durant. We had to remove the spleen and tie off several bleeds, but none of the vital organs were involved. Your daughter is a very lucky woman. She'll be fine."

Julia closed her eyes in thanks. When she opened them Chase was gone.

Chase couldn't deal with the situation. More accurately, he didn't want to deal with it. Each second that ticked by made him more acutely aware of his own limits, of the fragility of life, and of the uncorrectable mistakes fools make.

Head bowed, he slowly went up the front steps of the hotel, feeling wearier than he ever had in his life.

"Mr. Braxton, there's someone here to see you."

Head still bowed, Chase kept walking. He didn't want to see anyone or talk anymore. What he wanted was blissful oblivion. His jog had done nothing to smooth the jagged edges since he had seen Julia's minivan pile into the carnage of mangled vehicles.

"Chase."

He pivoted. Julia. He read the weariness in her beautiful face, saw the puffiness in the eyes that searched his. She had been crying. He felt a pain in the region of his heart. "Yes?"

She flinched at the brusqueness of his voice. "I just wanted to make sure that you were all right."

"You saw that at the hospital."

"I . . ." She seemed to falter, tucking her lower lip between her teeth.

His hands slid into his pockets to keep from reaching out for her. How much misery could one man take and remain sane? "Go home. It's getting late."

She didn't move.

The automatic doors directly behind him whooshed open. Two men came barreling through. One of them held a camera. The other carried a microphone.

Chase let out an expletive and turned his head.

The bright light of the camera flared, centering on the other man who now held the microphone under the nose of the desk clerk. "Good evening. I'm Harold Kent, reporter with Channel Eight at WFRA. I understand Texas Ranger Chase Braxton is registered in this hotel. I'd like to interview him."

Not in this lifetime, Chase thought. He wasn't reliving that hell again just to be a sound bite on the nightly news. "Come on." Spinning on his heels, he headed for the elevator. Silently she followed. Neither spoke until they were in Chase's suite.

"Once the reporter finds he can't get any information on me from Simone, he'll try to find other guests or acquaintances to pump. I was afraid he might try to talk with us next."

"Chase, are you sure you're all right?"

His hands came up to keep her from touching him. He saw the pain in her eyes and turned away from it. "I'm sweaty. I'm going to take a shower. I'm sure I don't need to show you the way to the door."

Her chin lifted. "No, you don't."

Nodding briskly, he went through the sitting room and into the bathroom. Stripping off his clothes, he stepped into the shower stall and turned the blast on full force. Maybe, just maybe, it could wash her from his mind.

Julia stood in the living room listening to the shower, her stomach churning. She'd been that way since she heard the news of the accident.

Her hand clutching her stomach, Julia sank in the nearest chair. Several cars around the van had been badly charred, but thanks to Chase no one had lost their lives.

After he'd left them in the waiting room, she had called him several times and had always gotten the hotel's message center. Worried, she'd taken a cab to the hotel after leaving the hospital. She called him again from the lobby. Getting the message center again, she had decided to wait. She needed to touch him.

Seeing him at the hospital, disheveled and distant, had broken her heart. But he wanted nothing from her.

Her gaze strayed to the closed bathroom door. He had shut her out. The sensible thing, the proper thing, to do would be to leave as he requested. But love wasn't sensible, she was finding out.

Standing, she slipped off the long cranberry-colored jacket, heedlessly letting it fall to the floor, and walked into the bathroom. Steam fogged the frosted glass. Through it she could still distinguish the shape of Chase's powerfully built body.

She might have lost him today. The terrible thought still made her weak. Trembling fingers tugged the silk blouse from her skirt.

She had managed three buttons when the door swung open.

Water glistening on his skin, Chase stopped in mid-stride. His hand gripped the shower door. "What are you doing?"

"I don't want to live with regret. If this is all there is to be, then I'll take it."

"Julia—"

"I'm not asking for a commitment," she rushed on, cutting him off.

He brushed by her and snatched a towel from atop the marble countertop and wrapped it around his waist. "Put your clothes back on."

"No."

"Leave!" he shouted, his hands braced on the counter, his head bowed.

"Don't worry. You don't have to stop this time."

Shaking his head, he pressed his hands against the countertop. "Why are you being so stubborn about this?"

"Because I think I love you, and if something had happened to you this afternoon, I would have lived with regrets the rest of my life." The other buttons slipped free. The blouse fell to the floor. The skirt followed. "You'll have to help with this."

Chase heard the rustle of clothes. Despite his best effort, he was unable to keep from lifting his head. His breath snagged. She was all that he desired, all that he had tried to convince himself that he couldn't have.

He saw her reflection in the mirror. She wore a scandalous lacy black bra, bikini panties, and thigh-high stockings edged in lace. Need struck low, fast, and hard.

He wanted to tell her to go, but he wasn't capable of pushing the words through the tight knot in his throat. Then she tenderly placed her hand on his arm and he was lost.

Whirling, he pulled her into his arms, crushing her in his embrace. "I thought I'd lost you. I didn't know it wasn't you until I wrenched open the van's door."

Julia held him tighter, listening to the tortured words that echoed her own misery. She rubbed her chin against the dampness of his wide chest, felt the muscled warmth, and tried to get closer. "I was at the office when I heard. I could have shaken you, but I was so proud. I didn't know Georgette and Michael were involved until her mother called."

Setting her away, he stared down into her eyes. "They weren't sure when they wheeled her into surgery."

Her trembling hand palmed Chase's tense jaw. "You gave her another chance at life, Chase."

As Chase remembered Georgette's husband's gut-wrenching sobs in the Emergency Room, his arms tightened around Julia. "It could have gone the other way."

"I know," Julia said. "That's why it's important to live life to the fullest when you have the chance. I realize that now. Tomorrow isn't promised."

"No, it isn't." His gaze softened. "I don't know what tomorrow brings, but I know I don't want to go through another day without knowing you're going to be there for my tomorrows."

"Neither do I. Please take me to bed."

"I can do nothing less." His voice shook. "You're all that I desire." Sweeping her up in his arms, he carried her into the bedroom and placed her gently on the bed. With exquisite care and tender kisses he finished undressing her, then tugged the towel from his waist.

His mouth slowly settled on hers again, both aware that their time had finally come. There was no need to rush. Each kiss, each feverish touch, was simply a prelude to fuel the need, heat the blood, fire the passion until their hunger could only be satisfied in one way. Their eyes and hands locked, he brought them together.

The fit was perfect, the sensations exquisite. He took her on a ride that was at times slow and lazy, at times fast and frenzied, but always, always, deep and hot and immensely pleasurable for them both. Release came in a torrent that left both shaken and too weak to speak.

Rolling to one side, Chase pulled Julia into his arms. Trustingly she curled against him and drifted into sleep. His body relaxed, but his arms didn't. He found himself unwilling to let her go now or ever. There was only one way that was possible.

He accepted his fate and tightened his hold.

Julia woke up the next morning a little after eight with a smile on her face. Usually she never slept past seven. But she had never made love half the night, either.

Laughing, she hugged the feather pillow to her hot cheek. Her skin still felt sensitized, her senses heightened. Afraid that reporters might have hung around, Chase had insisted that they leave the hotel separately. He'd picked her up down the street from the hotel, then taken her home and to bed again.

Her heart beat wildly in her chest in remembrance of the things they had done, things she couldn't wait to do again.

Laughing again for the sheer pleasure it gave her, she rolled on her back and stared up at the silk canopy. Loving someone made you reckless and daring and needy. You desperately wanted to please, but in the pleasing, you also pleased yourself.

They were on two separate paths, had two separate career goals in cities miles apart. But when Chase looked at her, touched her, and gave her one of those toe-tingling, thought-scattering kisses, practicality was the last thing on her mind. All she could think about was getting closer, grabbing, and never letting go.

Now they'd have a chance to run laughing in the rain, to feast on chocolate-covered strawberries and each other. And it had all begun at Leo's. She'd always known there was something uniquely wonderful and romantic about the supper club.

The phone rang on the bedside table. *Chase.* He had gone to his hotel to pack. She eagerly reached for the phone. "I miss you already."

"Julia?"

Eyes wide, she sprang up in bed. "Mabel!"

"Yes," came the southern-accented voice. "Do you have any idea why Chase called this morning to talk about resigning?"

"What?" Throwing back the covers, Julia sat up on the side of the bed. "Chase's whole life is the Texas Rangers!"

"We all thought so, too," Mabel said, unhappiness in each word. "Oscar would roast me alive if he knew I listened to his conversation, then told someone else, but I know how proud of Chase he is, how proud the entire force is. For Chase to be planning to resign is unthinkable."

"Then he hasn't resigned yet?" Julia asked.

"No. From what I heard, Chase just wanted to prepare Oscar. He's going to formally resign when he returns to work tomorrow."

Julia breathed a sigh of relief. "Tell Oscar not to worry."

"Do you think there's a chance you can change his mind?"

"I'm certainly going to try my best, but we both know how stubborn Chase can be."

"Oh, dear."

"Good-bye, Mabel." Hanging up the phone, Julia headed for the shower undaunted by the worry in Mabel's voice. She didn't know the reason behind his sudden decision, but he *wasn't* quitting the Texas Rangers. Not if she had her way.

She was stepping into the glass enclosure of the shower when she head the doorbell. She started to ignore the summons, but judging by the repeated rings, the person wasn't leaving. Pulling on her robe, she stalked to the door, determined to get rid of whoever it was.

"Chase!"

Grinning, he came in. Taking the door from her, he closed it behind him and kissed her lips. "I see I'm in time to join you in the shower. These are for you."

Julia automatically took the bouquet of white roses.

Chase took the opportunity to untie the belt of her robe. His gaze narrowed with hungry appreciation at the expanse of smooth brown skin.

"I won't let you do it."

Lazy amusement danced in his black eyes. "Wanna bet?"

Julia realized they were talking about two different things. "I don't mean that. I mean resign from the Texas Rangers."

His hands settled heavily on her waist. "Mabel."

"You can't do it. The Rangers mean too much to you."

"Sweet Temptation means just as much to you."

"What has this to do with my shop?" she asked with a frown.

"I have no intention of trying to have a long-distance marriage."

Her eyes widened. "M-marriage?"

"Yes, I told you that last night."

"Chase, do you think I could sit down?" Without waiting, she went to the sofa.

Frowning, he stared down at her. "You all right?"

"A great deal happened last night, but I would have remembered you asking me to marry you."

He shifted uncomfortably. "I didn't exactly ask, but I thought you understood. We made love, didn't we?"

"Several times, as I remember," Julia said.

"Then there you are," Chase said triumphantly.

Julia stared up at Chase's long length, trying to understand his reasoning. "Chase, perhaps you should help me remember."

"Last night you told me you thought you loved me and I told you I wanted you to be there for all my tomorrows and you agreed."

"But I thought—"

"You accepted and you can't back out now after I finally stopped fighting it," he said fiercely, coming down in front of her.

"What did you stop fighting?"

"That I love you completely, irrevocably," he answered, his voice and gaze softening. "The accident opened my eyes. Life isn't promised, so you have to grab hold of the one you love and never let go. That's what I'm doing." Tenderly his hand closed over her free one. "I love you and you love me. If you didn't, you wouldn't have made love with me."

Everything fell perfectly into place. "No, I wouldn't. I love you more than I ever thought possible."

His hold tightened for a brief moment. "The accident showed me something else. I don't ever want to see you scared or worried about me again. I don't want you going through what my mother went through." Pausing, he took a deep breath. "With a master's in criminal law, I shouldn't have any difficulty getting a job here."

Love and tenderness and determination filled her. "You're not resigning. I can handle the dangers of your job. You're staying a Ranger."

His mouth took on a stubborn slant. "My ranch is isolated. Here you have people who watch out for you, a secure place to live."

Laughing, she kissed him. "You can't tell me your ranch doesn't have security, and I happen to know every year you have to qualify on the shooting range. I bet you're a crack shot, and you can teach me."

His lifted eyebrow told her he was. "Mabel tell you that?"

She grinned. "The Texas Ranger Internet site."

He glanced around her stylishly furnished condo. "My house is comfortable, but it's nothing like this."

"As long as you're there, I'll be happy. The only thing I definitely have to have is my bed." Her grin widened. "I have a lot of warm memories of being in it with you and I plan a lot more."

Passion blazed in his black eyes. "That's not fair."

"By whose standards?" she asked with a regal tilt of her chin.

Shaking his head, he said, "I still don't like the idea of leaving you alone so much."

"I have the perfect solution. People in Washington have been doing it for years and it will be a great tax deduction. I'll get a place in town for us, and if you have to work late, we'll spend the night in our second home," she told him, then continued as his gaze sharpened. "Don't tell me you're one of those men who cares if a woman pays her own way or earns more than he does?"

He looked abashed. "I did. I finally figured out that's probably why Mabel didn't tell me you owned Sweet Temptation. You'll keep *it* and open your second location as planned. I don't intend to start our lives with regret or recriminations."

"Neither do I," she said. "The accident taught me something as well: we don't always get a second chance."

His lips brushed across her hand clasped in his. "I'll always be thankful I got another chance to get it right."

"No more than I. Virginia's loss is Austin's gain. It will be a unique marketing concept. The flagship store in the national capital and the other in a state capital. I have family and friends with contacts everywhere," she told him, the excitement growing in her voice. "I wanted a chain of Sweet Temptations. Austin will be my second location."

"You'd do that for me?"

"Not for you. For us."

"You're sure?"

"Well, I may need some convincing." Smiling, she walked to the bedroom. The robe dropped at the door.

Grinning, Chase hurried after the sweetest temptation he'd ever known.

EPILOGUE

How deeply could a man love a woman?

Chase asked himself that question when he saw Julia coming down the aisle of the crowded church toward him wearing a moon white ball gown embellished with rose appliqué of lace around the scooped neck and scattered over the wide hem of English net. In the glow of the candlelight with the scent of vanilla candles in the air she appeared eternal and breathtakingly beautiful. In her gloved hand was a single long-stemmed white rose.

Like most brides she had kept her choice of gown a secret, but he did know that the diamond tiara in her chignon had been worn by her mother and her mother before her at their weddings. The long embroidered lace veil from France was a gift from her sisters. The double strand of pearls circling her throat was a wedding gift from him.

She'd cried when he'd given her the necklace last night after their wedding rehearsal. With the pad of his thumb he had brushed the tears from her cheeks and tried to keep any more from falling by teasing her that he hadn't cried when she'd surprised him with his wedding gift. Impish woman that she was, she'd seductively whispered that her motives were partly selfish, then sent his blood singing in his veins by telling him some of the things she planned for them in the Jacuzzi.

How deeply could a man love a woman?

As the minister asked, "Who gives this woman away?" and Julia's father answered, "I do," then stepped back, Chase pondered the question again. Love meant sharing as Julia's father shared his daughter with a man who loved her. Love meant leaving home, friends, family, as Julia was doing for him.

With Julia's hand in his, Chase slipped the wedding band on her finger next to the heart-shaped two-carat diamond he'd given her a week after he'd asked her to marry him. Whenever she looked at the ring, he wanted her to be reminded that his heart belonged to her. The heavy gold intricately carved wedding band she slid on his finger was perfect. So was the inscription inside: J.A.F. ALWAYS & FOREVER. C.M.B.

"You may kiss the bride."

He'd meant to keep it light, a brush of lips, but something happened when their lips met and she leaned eagerly into him. This woman was his; he was hers. The kiss deepened into a vow, a pledge of forever, of need that would never die.

"Uh, hm, there will be time enough for that later," the minister whispered.

Laughter boomed from beside him. Chase lifted his head and shot Colt a hard look. Nonplussed, he shrugged, still grinning.

Julia's squeezing of his hand and the recessional music had him turning away. With his arm around his wife's waist, they went back down the aisle. Outside, the June day in Virginia was perfect, with blue skies and a light breeze that ruffled Julia's veil as she and Chase ran laughing down the church steps to the waiting limousine that would take them to Leo's for their reception.

"How about we skip the reception and see if we can get the pilot to take off early?" Chase suggested, nibbling on Julia's lips.

Julia moaned. "Do you think we could?"

"No, but it's nice to know you'd go." A jet, courtesy of Julia's parents, was standing by to take them to Monterey. From the airport a car would take them to a resort on the beach. Her parents had wanted to pay for their accommodations as well. Chase had politely refused. The only reason he'd accepted the jet was because they'd have privacy while traveling and they didn't have to worry about the hassle of checking and claiming baggage or changing planes in Los Angeles.

Her eyes filled with love when she said, "I'd follow you anywhere."

He kissed her. He couldn't help himself. Nor did he want to. There was no longer a question in his mind whether she was sure or had any regrets; love had a way of overcoming problems and establishing trust. "One dance, one quick trip around the room to meet everyone, and we're out of there."

"You lead. I follow."

He'd tried, but too many people wanted to kiss the bride, congratulate the groom. Julia, as always, took time to greet each and every one of them. Percival had proudly told Julia's family that he'd known all along Chase and Julia would end up getting married. A fully recovered Georgette was there with her husband, Michael, and their two daughters, who had been flower girls.

Chase had hired a bus to bring the residents from the nursing home where Julia volunteered. They were having a ball. She hadn't rested until she had found another volunteer to take her place.

Violins serenaded the guests, waiters plied them with vintage champagne, chefs tempted them with delicacies in the room decorated with tall, gilded candelabras that were overgrown with flowers in muted antique tones. No one seemed inclined to leave, but if they did waiters were stationed at the door to present them with a specially prepared gold-foil

box of chocolate candy. The label read: SWEET BEGINNINGS,
CREATED BY CHASE & JULIA.

Two hours and countless handshakes and hugs later they
left for the airport in a shower of birdseed and soap bubbles.
Once aboard the plane Chase thought he showed admirable
strength when he undid the twenty-eight buttons on the back
of Julia's gown, then left her to change in private. The next
time he took her in his arms he didn't plan on letting her go
for a long, long time.

Instead he used the time to unpack the hastily gathered
dinner and set the small table in the main cabin. As usual
Julia had been too busy seeing to others to see to herself.
He'd have to see that she took better care of herself now that
she had two stores.

Sweet Temptation had been an instant success when it
opened in Austin a month ago. If things continued to go as
well, she planned on publishing a catalogue next year.

He glanced up the moment the door opened. Surprised
delight shone on her lovely face as her gaze touched the huge
slice of wedding cake, succulent slices of roast beef, smoked
salmon, rolls, and champagne. "You always think of me."

"And I always will."

Lush flowers in the deepest hues scented the salt-tinged night
air. A gentle wind rustled the palm trees. Standing on the
stone terrace leading to the private beach two hundred feet
away, Julia listened to the sounds of the waves crashing
against the shore. Overhead, a full moon shone.

The secluded cottage was perfect for a honeymoon, Julia
thought. As soon as they had arrived, she'd changed into her
nightgown. After sharing a glass of champagne they had
gone outside to enjoy the night. Happiness flooded her. No
woman could be happier.

Chase's strong arms slid around her waist from behind
and pulled her up against him. His cheek rested against hers.
"You want another glass of champagne?"

Snuggling closer, she felt the warmth and security and,
yes, the temptation of his hard muscular body through her

long sheer white robe and nightgown. Soon she could freely explore those temptations, but for now she was content. They had a lifetime ahead of them. She shook her head. "I have everything I want."

His hold gently tightened. "Same here."

"The wedding was beautiful."

He slowly turned her and stared down into her face. "*You're* beautiful."

"Oh, Chase. You make me feel so special."

"You are." He kissed her forehead, her nose, her lips. "Not many women could open a new store and find a town house in a strange city while coordinating a big wedding hundreds of miles away."

She grinned. "These past eight months have been busy, but my mother and sisters helped. I had a strong incentive to get everything done by May. Once we were married I didn't want to be away from you."

"Me neither. There's nothing in the world more important than us. I plan to spend the rest of my life loving you." His hands tenderly palmed her face. "Ever since you started down the aisle toward me, I've asked myself the question of how deeply could a man love a woman."

"D-did you find an answer?" she asked, her voice tremulous.

"Partially." Picking her up in his arms, he went into the bedroom, then placed her on the four-poster bed and came down beside her. "I finally figured out that discovering the answer will take a lifetime of loving you, watching our children grow inside you, growing old beside you, and it all begins now."

"It all begins now," she repeated, lifting her face to meet his kiss. Their journey was about to begin, a journey that had all started with a sweet temptation and would last a lifetime.

Turn the page for a look ahead to
The Turning Point by Francis Ray—
available soon from St. Martin's Paperbacks!

The Turning Point

Lilly was out of bed at first light the next morning. She never lingered. Before Mother Crawford's death it had been to check on her. Now it was to escape her husband. Easing out of their bedroom, she closed the door softly and went to take her bath. Walking down the narrow hall she wondered how she had let her life come to this. How could she have been so wrong about a man?

She had had such hopes and dreams when Myron first asked her out. That he was sixteen years older, a widower with two children aged fourteen and sixteen, had made her feel somehow special that he had chosen her.

In the town of twenty thousand, he had a good job as a short-haul truck-driver, a neat little house, and was a respected deacon in the church. In everyone's opinion he was a good catch, and for the first time in Lilly's life, women envied her.

She'd grown up being referred to as "that Dawson girl," and the reference had never been good. Marva Dawson, Lilly's mother, hadn't cared what others thought of her and certainly not what they thought of her daughter. To Marva's way of thinking, her life was her own to live as she pleased. It was her turn to have some fun after what she'd suffered. Her unwanted and unplanned pregnancy with Lilly had ruined Marva's life, just as her washout of a husband had.

Johnny Dawson was supposed to be the next great Jim Brown. Instead he had been cut in spring training from the New York Giants. Marva had banked heavily on Johnny being her ticket out of Little Elm.

If she hadn't been pregnant with Lilly, Marva could have stayed in New York and used her face and figure to be an actress or find a rich man. Instead she had had to come back

with a disgraced jobless husband who took off to parts unknown a year later.

Unemployed, Marva had used the face and figure she was
so vain about to get "her due" from other men. She had no
intention of standing in line for government cheese or have
some social worker look down her snooty nose at her. If one
man couldn't give her the things she thought she needed, she
found another.

Lilly had grown up with people talking about her mother's
lifestyle, and speculation on how long it would take for her
to turn out the same way. The girls of the good families
didn't speak to her, and the boys who asked her out were
mainly interested in how fast she'd take off her clothes. Even
the girls with a reputation for being fast wanted nothing to
do with her. Books became her friends.

At fourteen she lied about her age to get a job at the Dairy
Queen in a wasted effort to help her mother so she wouldn't
have to take money from men. Her mother had looked at the
fifty-six dollars Lilly had proudly handed her after two weeks
of work, and flatly told Lilly her perfume cost more than
that. Lilly hadn't offered again.

She'd met Minnie Crawford when she'd gone to J. C.
Penney to buy a hat for Women's Day at Little Elm Baptist
Church. Since Penney's was one of the few places to buy
ladies' hats in town, and elderly black women wouldn't think
of setting foot in church without their hats, Lilly had waited
on several women in her first three weeks of working in
ladies' accessories.

However, Minnie Crawford hadn't looked at Lilly's name
tag and stuck up her nose because some man in her family
had biblical knowledge of Lilly's mother. She hadn't taken
her merchandise to another salesperson to ring up, as a few
of the women had. She'd looked Lilly in the eyes and asked
her if she knew the Lord. Taken aback and sure she was
being condescending, Lilly had flippantly replied that He
wasn't on her Christmas mailing list.

She'd always remember Minnie Crawford's reply. "Doesn't

matter about your mailing list. I meant in your heart. Now, how much is this hat gonna cost me?"

Befuddled, Lilly had rung up the sale, thinking that was the last of it. It wasn't. Minnie Crawford kept stopping by, and before Lilly was sure how it had happened, they were having lunch at the deli in the mall, then supper at Minnie's home.

Lilly had gone to church with Mother Crawford, as she liked to be called, out of respect for her and their growing friendship. Lilly went back because of the peace she'd found there, and because of Myron.

The first time she'd seen him, handsome and tall, in his black suit, his Bible clasped to his wide chest, her heart had beat a mile a minute. She had been so nervous, she'd had trouble getting her words out. For the first time she had been conscious of people whispering about her, and she hadn't cared.

Myron had taken her home after Sunday dinner at Mother Crawford's, and after prayer meeting that following Wednesday night. They easily fell into a routine of him picking her up for church services and seeing her home. Always he was respectful and nice.

After a month of them being seen together, people no longer whispered or speculated if she was as free with her body as her mother. They nodded cordially. Lilly could look people in the eye, hold her head up. Each time she was with Myron, she fell in love a little more and dared to dream that he loved her in return.

Thirty-six-year-old Myron Crawford was everything her naive twenty-year-old heart had wished for. He represented all the things she had never had: love, respectability, a family, and security.

Stepping out of the tub, Lilly grabbed a towel and rubbed it briskly over her body. She'd been starved for affection enough to believe he loved her, believe he wanted to share his life with her, believe he'd give her the children that as a neglected child she'd always wanted.

Hanging up the towel, she stepped into her plain white

cotton underwear and hooked her bra. If Myron had felt any love for her it had disappeared fast. He'd wanted her as a caretaker for his children and a convenient bedmate. Pulling the slip over her head, she shot her arms through the shirt-waist dress. All her praying hadn't helped them to grow closer. Then Mother Crawford had suffered a stroke a year after their marriage and come to live with them.

That had been five years ago. Lilly had been trapped by her devotion and respect of the woman she had come to love dearly, a woman who had become her surrogate mother. Trapped by the two lost children who didn't understand why their mother had to die in a senseless automobile accident on her way to a meeting at the church. Trapped by her dream.

Making her way to the kitchen, she put on the coffee. Arms folded, she stared out the window at the red roses climbing the cyclone fence in the backyard. She and Rafe had worked an entire morning on the project as a birthday surprise for Mother Crawford. Rafe, intelligent, proud and determined to butt heads with his overbearing, tyrannical father at every turn. Rafe, the son that Myron now refused to acknowledge. The son he had tried to beat and cow into submission.

Rafe had stayed because Lilly begged him to finish high school, but he had never come back to the dinner she had prepared after his valedictory speech. His leaving had broken her heart. They were too close in age for her to think of him as her son, but he was the younger brother she never had. She wished she could have done more to shield him from Myron's anger.

She'd thought many times of leaving and taking him with her before Mother Crawford's stroke, but since Lilly wasn't his legal guardian, it would have been considered kidnapping. Mother Crawford might have helped, but she had a weak heart and the doctors had already warned them that too much excitement wasn't good for her.

The first light heart attack Mother Crawford ever had was caused when Rafe and Myron's arguing became physical shortly after he and Lilly married. Lilly had never seen that side of Myron, mean and hateful, spewing foul words meant to hurt as much as the belt in his hand. But Rafe had refused to bow down to his father's whipping because he hadn't mowed the lawn the way Myron liked. Mother Crawford's sudden illness had stopped that argument, but others followed.

Lilly did her best to protect Rafe and when she failed, it was as if her soul was being wrenched from her body. Before long Myron's meanness killed any love and respect she had for him. She couldn't leave Rafe, no more than she could have left Mother Crawford after Rafe left home.

She understood Rafe's leaving; she just missed his easy smile, his laughter in a house that had seen too much misery and hate. He'd been back several times in the four years since his graduation to see Mother Crawford, but he'd always called first to make sure Myron wasn't there.

Hearing the coffee dripping, Lilly opened the cabinet for a cup. She didn't know how to contact Rafe to tell him about his grandmother. Somehow she felt he knew. They'd had a way of silent communication that was as powerful as it was beautiful. Mother Crawford would say more than once, "Rafe's gonna call," and the words would barely be out of her mouth before the telephone would ring.

Their connection was something Lilly envied. She'd never been that close to her mother, a woman who was seldom home unless she was expecting one of her men friends. She'd never known the father who had walked out when she was six months old and never returned.

Sipping her coffee, Lilly stared back out the window, watched a bluebird light on the fence, then fly away. Wistfully, her gaze followed. Freedom. What a wonderful thing that must be.

Lilly was at the stove tending the bacon and sausages when Myron came into the kitchen. Immediately, she went to pour him a cup of coffee. " 'Morning."

He rubbed his large hand over his unshaven face, then sipped his coffee, syrupy with sugar and enriched with condensed canned milk. " 'Morning. Anyone else up?"

"David came in a few minutes earlier. Shayla's hungry," she told him. "They're staying over another couple more days." Slowly she shook her head. "I'm so tired from caring for Mother Crawford. I wish I could just rest." The words were out of her mouth before she realized it.

He was across the kitchen and on her before she knew it, his large frame looming over her. "This was Shayla's house before it was yours. If she's hungry, you better cook her breakfast or anything else she wants."

"Good morning, Mr. Crawford," David greeted from the kitchen door.

Myron swung around with a quickness that belied his six-feet-two height and two hundred pounds, his posture relaxing as he did so. " 'Morning, David," Myron greeted cordially. "I understand Shayla's hungry."

"Yes, sir," David said, worry in his voice and on his clean-shaven face. "She didn't eat much yesterday. I don't want her getting sick."

"Me neither. Tell her to stay in bed today and Lilly will bring all her meals today on a tray," Myron told him.

"Thank you, sir."

Myron didn't move until David left. He turned and stared at Lilly with dark narrowed eyes. "Don't make Shayla wait too long for her breakfast. You know what she likes. Cook it fresh. You know she don't like leftovers." Her orders given, he marched away.

Lilly was at the stove before he was out of sight. Removing the bacon and sausage, she placed them on paper towels to drain.

Rage almost choked her. Rage toward Myron, but also toward herself. She had been stupid and careless.

Rafe might have been his mother's and grandmother's favorite, but Shayla was her father's. Lilly had never understood why he felt that way unless it was because his daughter expertly played on Myron's need to feel important.

He never seemed to realize that when Shayla fussed over him the most, she always wanted a new dress, a new pair of shoes, or money. Unlike her self-sufficient and loving brother, Shayla was usually out for Shayla. If it didn't benefit her, she wasn't interested.

Shaking her head, Lilly took down the plates. She had to remember Myron doted on his youngest child and to be more careful. She had to be as smart as Rafe until she left. And as God was her witness, now that Mother Crawford was gone, Lilly was leaving Myron.

Read the novel by and about best friends
that has swept the country!

Tryin' To Sleep in the Bed You Made

VIRGINIA DEBERRY AND DONNA GRANT

*Gayle was the beauty who thought a man could
make her world complete. Climbing the corporate
ladder made Pat feel whole. And Marcus was the
man who linked both women together, through a
childhood tragedy that bonded them in secrecy
and forever changed their lives . . .*

"Driven by believable characters . . . this sisterhood-
is-powerful first novel seems a natural for
Oprah's Book Club. It eventually boils down to
one affirmative, 'You Go, Girl!'"

—*Kirkus*

**AVAILABLE WHEREVER BOOKS ARE SOLD
FROM ST. MARTIN'S PAPERBACKS**